CLASSICS
Illustrated ®

Deluxe

#2

TALES FROM THE
BROTHERS
GRIMM

Adapted by Mazan,
Cecile Chicault, and Philip Petit

PAPERCUTZ™
New York

Tales From The Brothers Grimm

Hansel And Gretel
Adapted by Philip Petit
Learning How To Shudder
Adapted by Mazan
The Devil And The Three Golden Hairs
Adapted by Cecile Chicault
The Valiant Little Tailor
Adapted by Mazan
Translation by Joe Johnson
Lettering by Ortho
Jim Salicrup
Editor-in-Chief

ISBN 13: 978-1-59707-100-0 paperback edition
ISBN 10: 1-59707-100-5 paperback edition
ISBN 13: 978-1-59707-101-7 hardcover edition
ISBN 10: 1-59707-101-3 hardcover edition

Printed in China.
Distributed by Macmillan.
10 9 8 7 6 5 4 3 2 1

CLASSICS Illustrated®

Deluxe

TALES FROM THE BROTHERS GRIMM

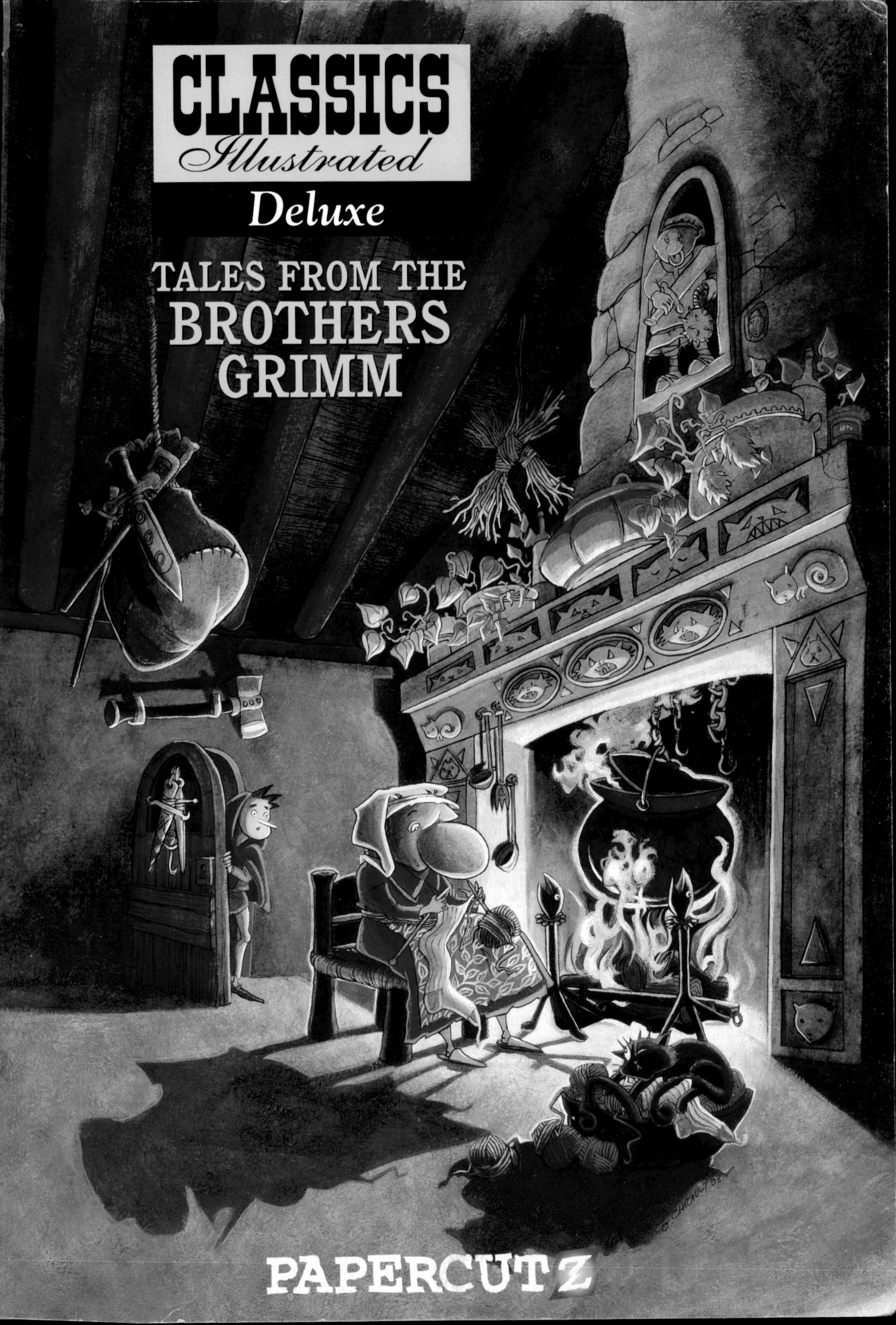

PAPERCUTZ

CLASSICS ILLUSTRATED GRAPHIC NOVELS AVAILABLE FROM PAPERCUTZ

CLASSICS ILLUSTRATED DELUXE:

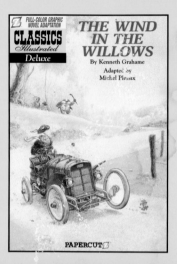

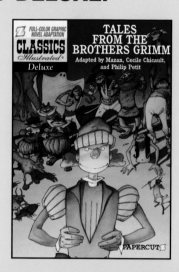

Graphic Novel #1
"The Wind In The Willows"

Graphic Novel #2
"Tales From The Brothers Grimm"

CLASSICS ILLUSTRATED:

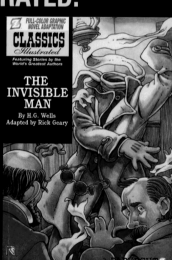

Graphic Novel #1
"Great Expectations"

Coming Soon:
Graphic Novel #2
"The Invisible Man"

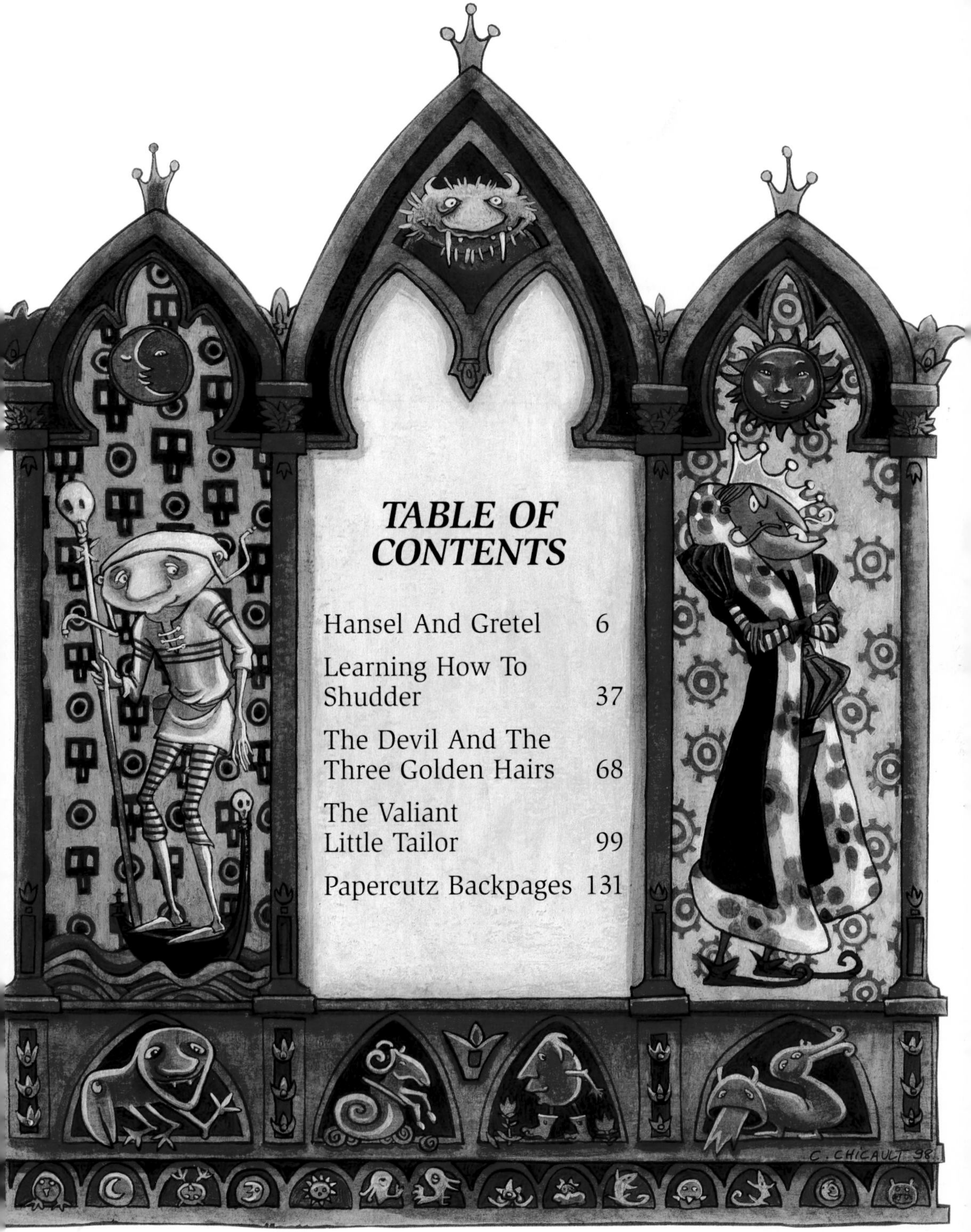
C. CHICAULT 98

TABLE OF CONTENTS

HANSEL
AND GRETEL

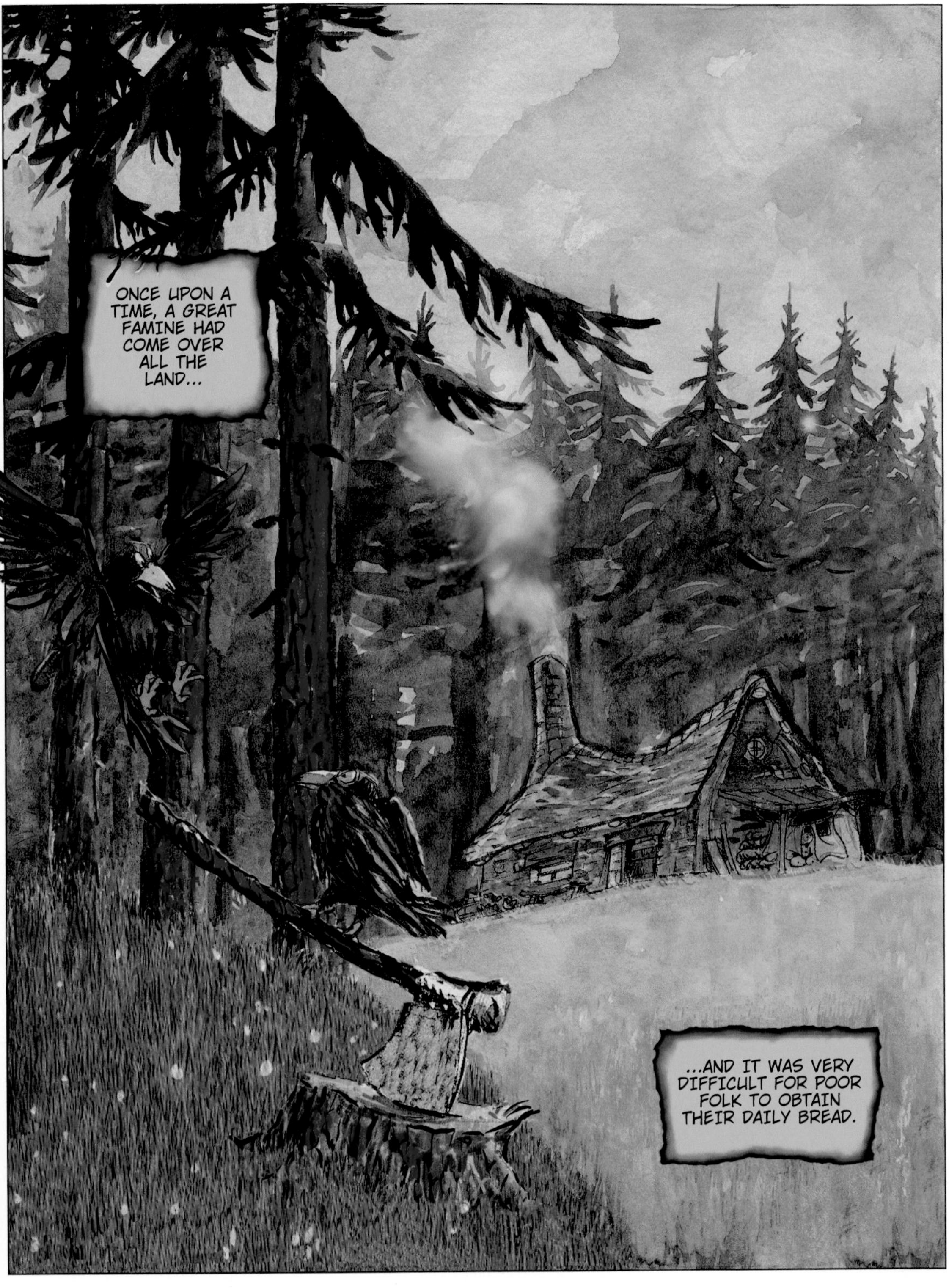
ONCE UPON A TIME, A GREAT FAMINE HAD COME OVER ALL THE LAND...
...AND IT WAS VERY DIFFICULT FOR POOR FOLK TO OBTAIN THEIR DAILY BREAD.

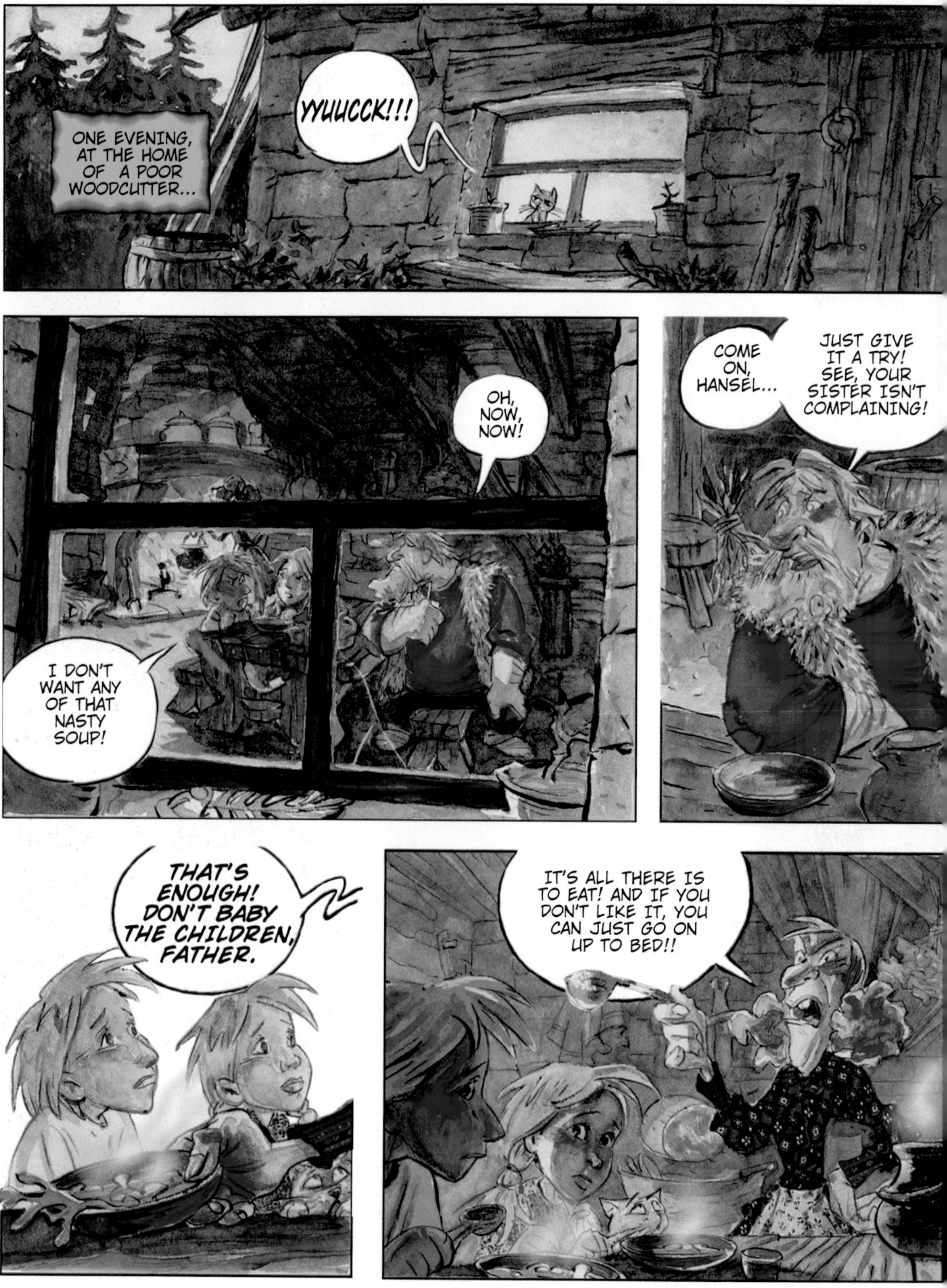
ONE EVENING, AT THE HOME OF A POOR WOODCUTTER...
YYUUCCK!!!
OH, NOW, NOW!
I DON'T WANT ANY OF THAT NASTY SOUP!
COME ON, HANSEL...
JUST GIVE IT A TRY! SEE, YOUR SISTER ISN'T COMPLAINING!
THAT'S ENOUGH! DON'T BABY THE CHILDREN, FATHER.
IT'S ALL THERE IS TO EAT! AND IF YOU DON'T LIKE IT, YOU CAN JUST GO ON UP TO BED!!

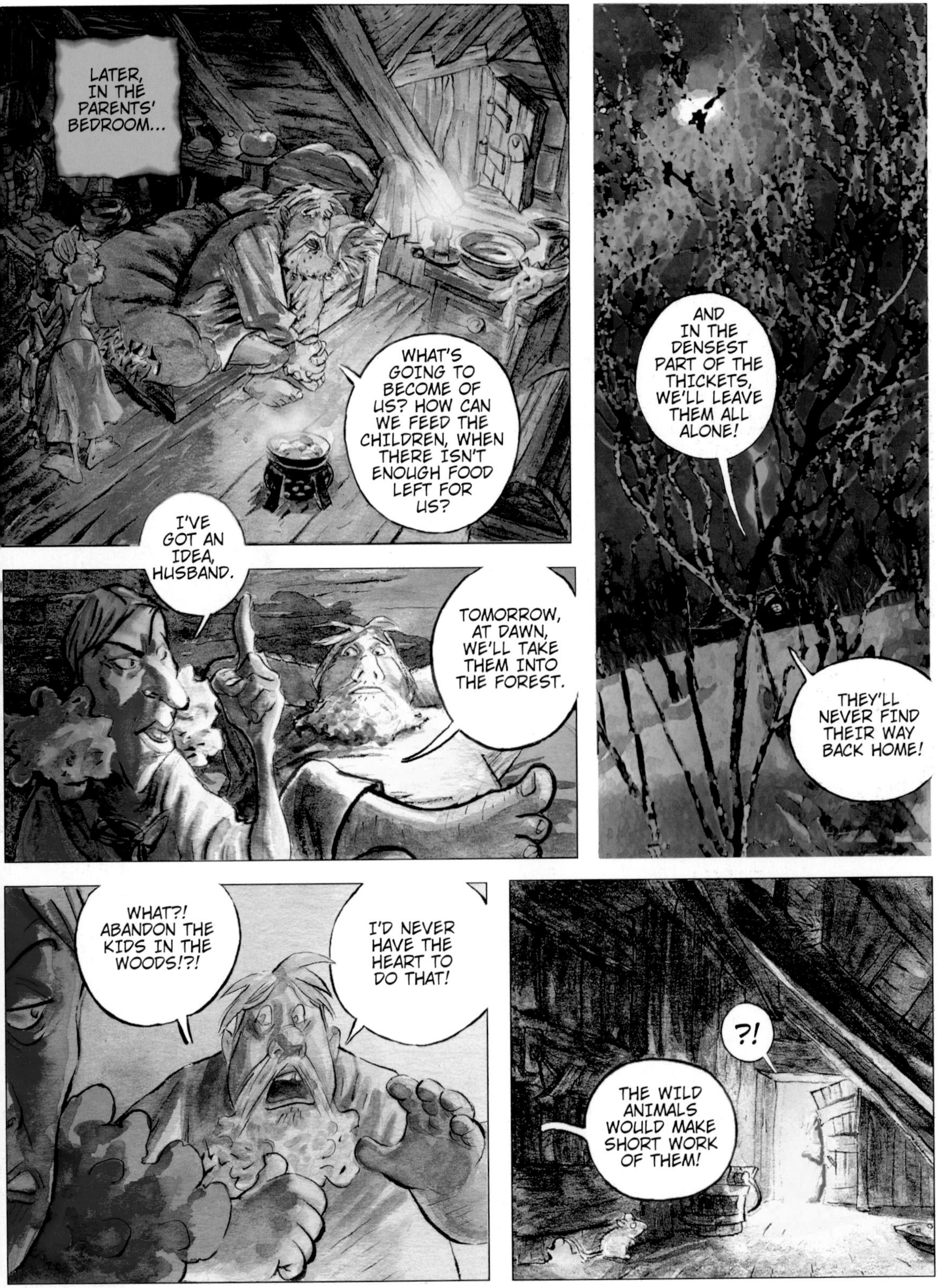
LATER, IN THE PARENTS' BEDROOM...
WHAT'S GOING TO BECOME OF US? HOW CAN WE FEED THE CHILDREN, WHEN THERE ISN'T ENOUGH FOOD LEFT FOR US?
I'VE GOT AN IDEA, HUSBAND.
TOMORROW, AT DAWN, WE'LL TAKE THEM INTO THE FOREST.
AND IN THE DENSEST PART OF THE THICKETS, WE'LL LEAVE THEM ALL ALONE!
THEY'LL NEVER FIND THEIR WAY BACK HOME!
WHAT?! ABANDON THE KIDS IN THE WOODS!?!
I'D NEVER HAVE THE HEART TO DO THAT!
?!
THE WILD ANIMALS WOULD MAKE SHORT WORK OF THEM!

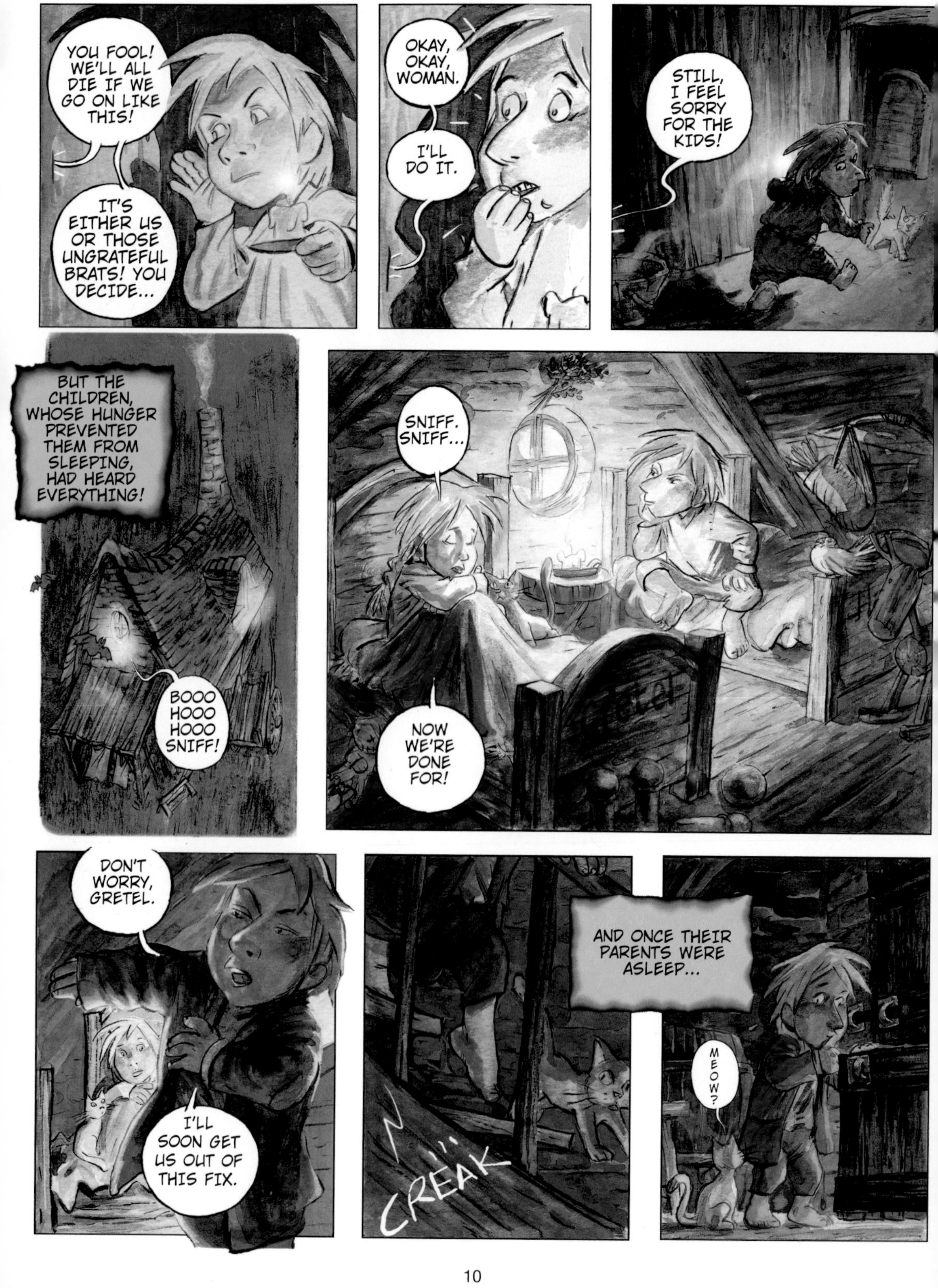
YOU FOOL! WE'LL ALL DIE IF WE GO ON LIKE THIS!
IT'S EITHER US OR THOSE UNGRATEFUL BRATS! YOU DECIDE...
OKAY, OKAY, WOMAN.
I'LL DO IT.
STILL, I FEEL SORRY FOR THE KIDS!
BUT THE CHILDREN, WHOSE HUNGER PREVENTED THEM FROM SLEEPING, HAD HEARD EVERYTHING!
BOOO HOOO HOOO SNIFF!
SNIFF. SNIFF...
NOW WE'RE DONE FOR!
DON'T WORRY, GRETEL.
I'LL SOON GET US OUT OF THIS FIX.
CREAK
AND ONCE THEIR PARENTS WERE ASLEEP...
MEOW?

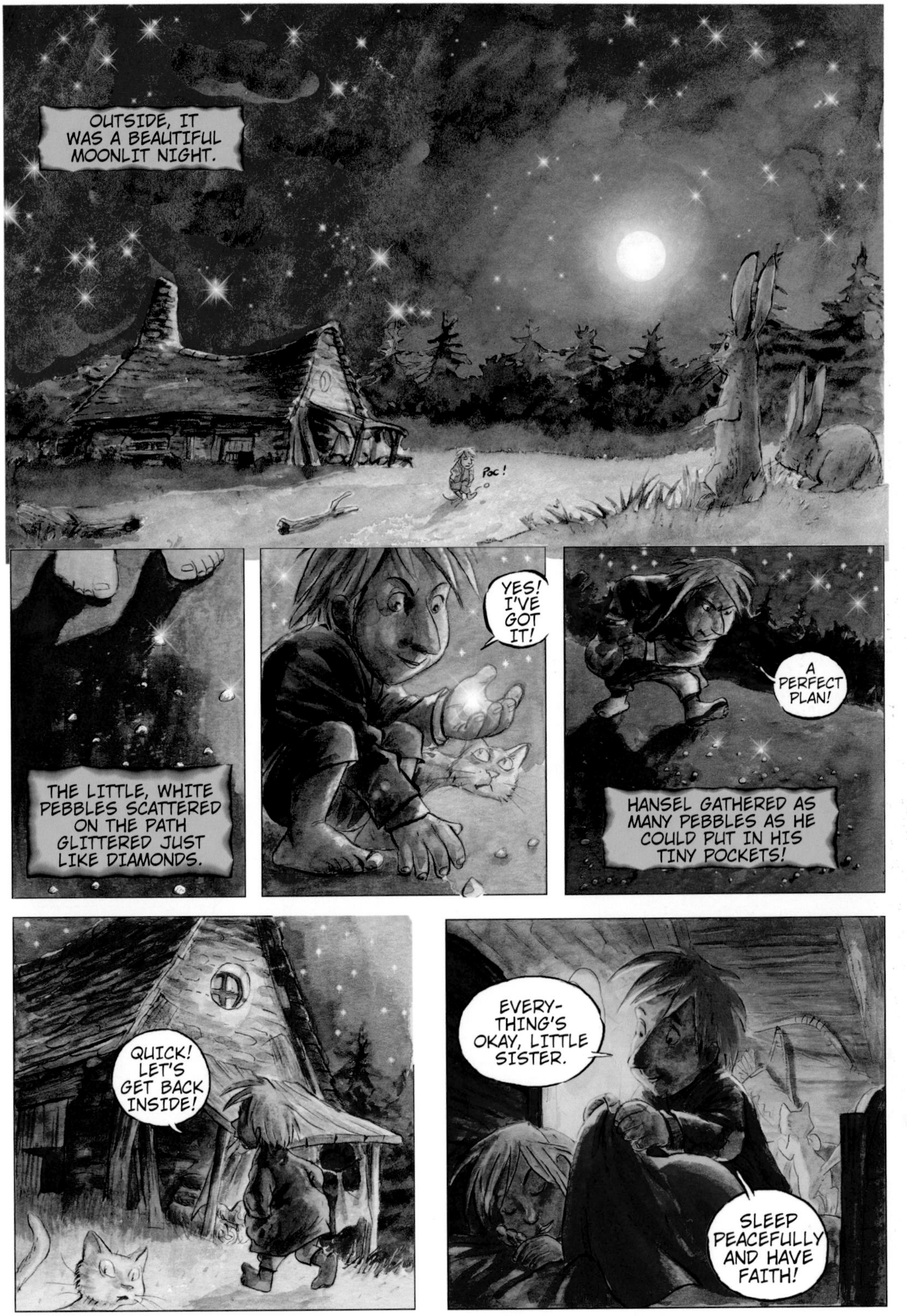
OUTSIDE, IT WAS A BEAUTIFUL MOONLIT NIGHT.
Poc!
THE LITTLE, WHITE PEBBLES SCATTERED ON THE PATH GLITTERED JUST LIKE DIAMONDS.
YES! I'VE GOT IT!
A PERFECT PLAN!
HANSEL GATHERED AS MANY PEBBLES AS HE COULD PUT IN HIS TINY POCKETS!
QUICK! LET'S GET BACK INSIDE!
EVERY-THING'S OKAY, LITTLE SISTER.
SLEEP PEACEFULLY AND HAVE FAITH!

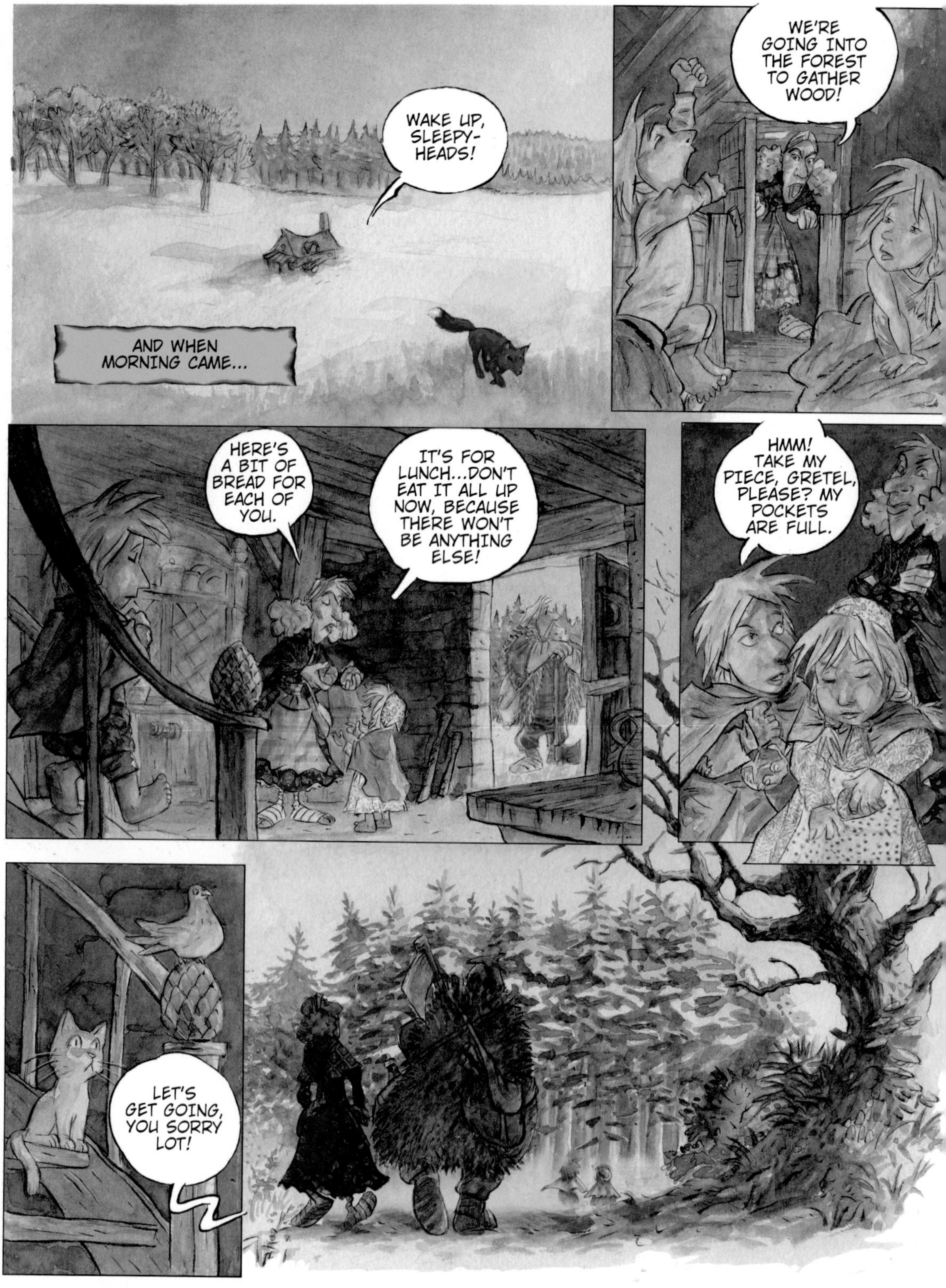
WAKE UP, SLEEPY-HEADS!
AND WHEN MORNING CAME...
WE'RE GOING INTO THE FOREST TO GATHER WOOD!
HERE'S A BIT OF BREAD FOR EACH OF YOU.
IT'S FOR LUNCH...DON'T EAT IT ALL UP NOW, BECAUSE THERE WON'T BE ANYTHING ELSE!
HMM! TAKE MY PIECE, GRETEL, PLEASE? MY POCKETS ARE FULL.
LET'S GET GOING, YOU SORRY LOT!

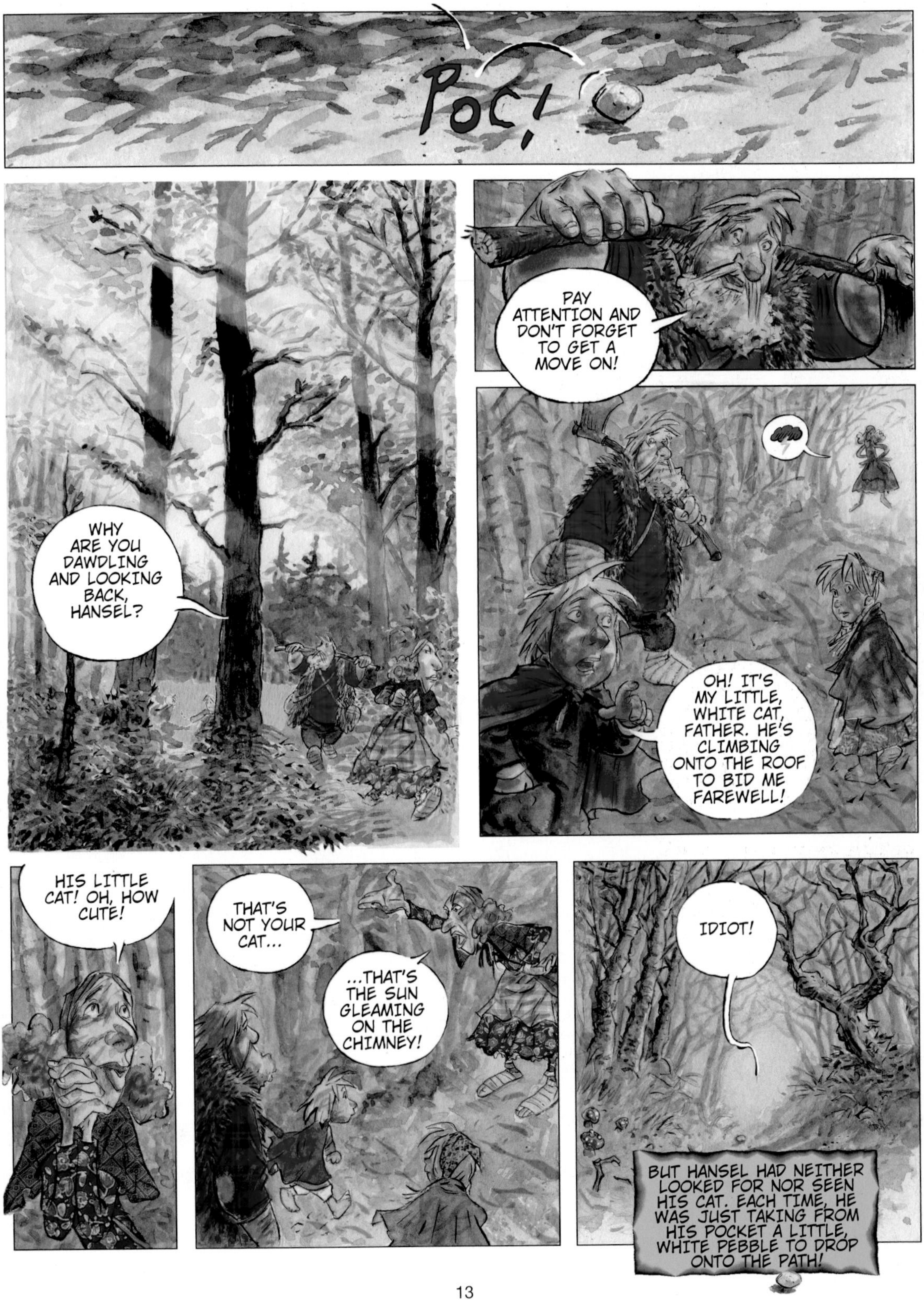
POC!
PAY ATTENTION AND DON'T FORGET TO GET A MOVE ON!
WHY ARE YOU DAWDLING AND LOOKING BACK, HANSEL?
OH! IT'S MY LITTLE, WHITE CAT, FATHER. HE'S CLIMBING ONTO THE ROOF TO BID ME FAREWELL!
HIS LITTLE CAT! OH, HOW CUTE!
THAT'S NOT YOUR CAT...
...THAT'S THE SUN GLEAMING ON THE CHIMNEY!
IDIOT!
BUT HANSEL HAD NEITHER LOOKED FOR NOR SEEN HIS CAT. EACH TIME, HE WAS JUST TAKING FROM HIS POCKET A LITTLE, WHITE PEBBLE TO DROP ONTO THE PATH!

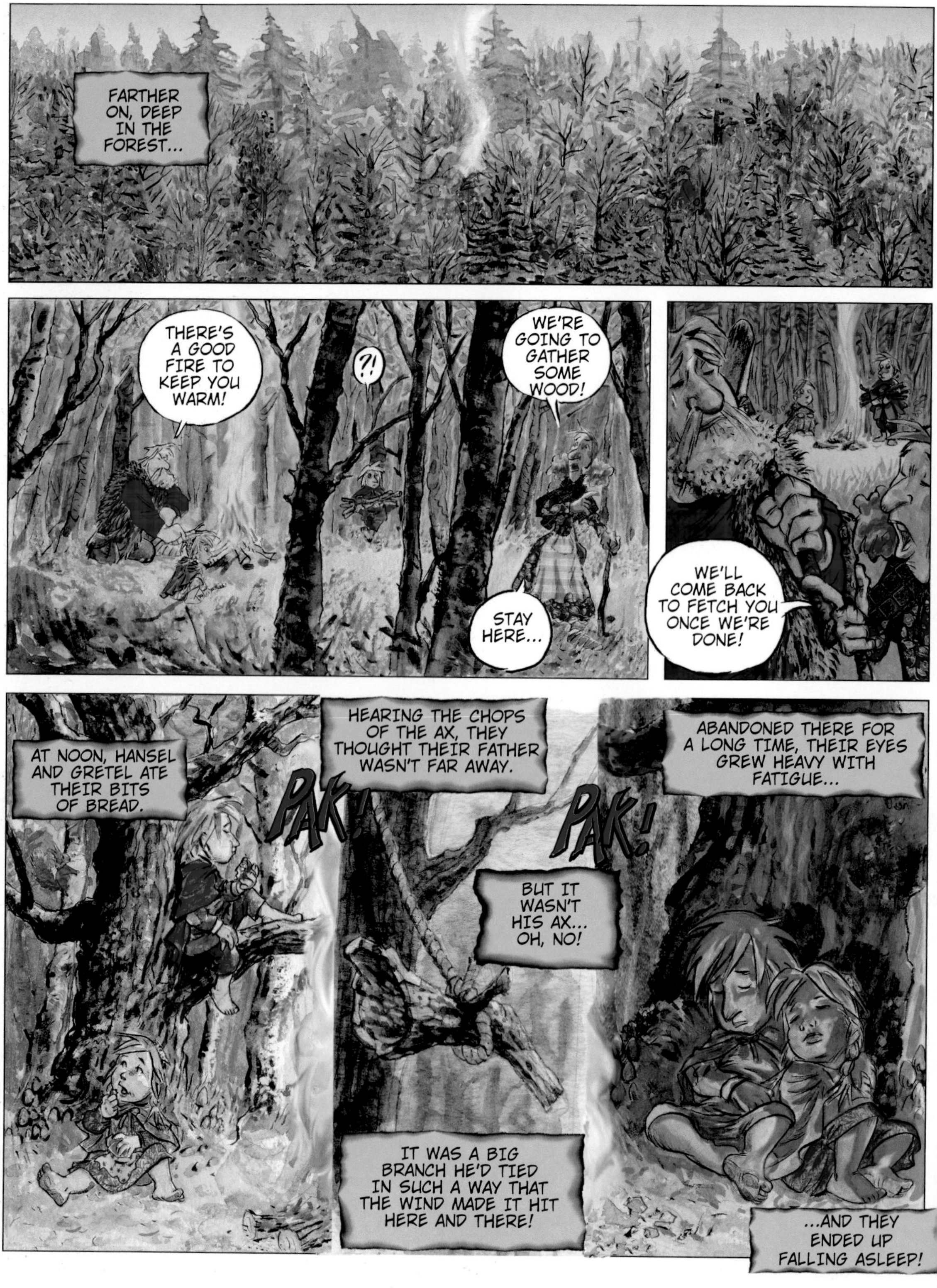
FARTHER ON, DEEP IN THE FOREST...
THERE'S A GOOD FIRE TO KEEP YOU WARM!
?!
WE'RE GOING TO GATHER SOME WOOD!
STAY HERE...
WE'LL COME BACK TO FETCH YOU ONCE WE'RE DONE!
AT NOON, HANSEL AND GRETEL ATE THEIR BITS OF BREAD.
PAK!
HEARING THE CHOPS OF THE AX, THEY THOUGHT THEIR FATHER WASN'T FAR AWAY.
PAK!
BUT IT WASN'T HIS AX... OH, NO!
IT WAS A BIG BRANCH HE'D TIED IN SUCH A WAY THAT THE WIND MADE IT HIT HERE AND THERE!
ABANDONED THERE FOR A LONG TIME, THEIR EYES GREW HEAVY WITH FATIGUE...
...AND THEY ENDED UP FALLING ASLEEP!

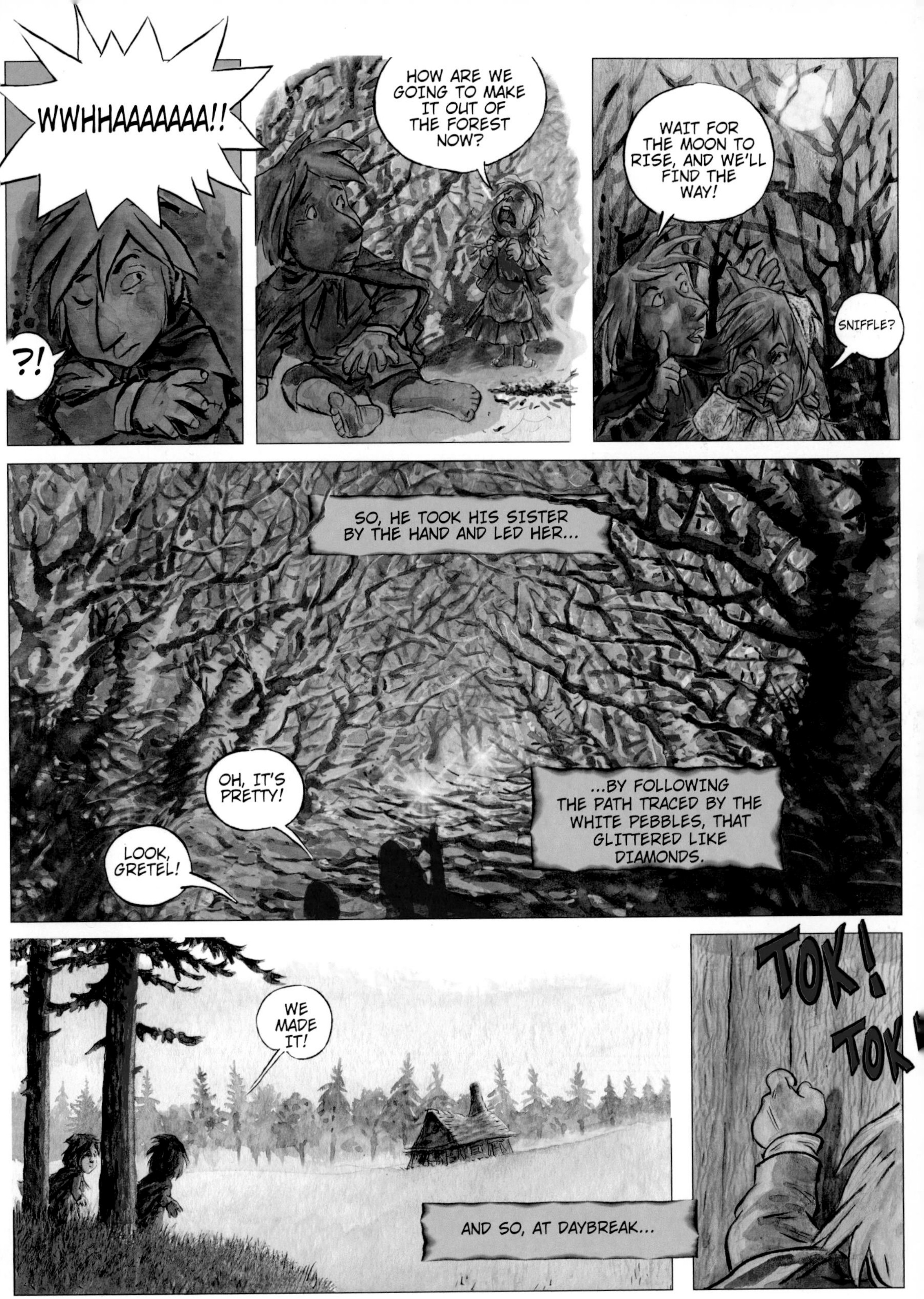
WWHHAAAAAAA!!
?!
HOW ARE WE GOING TO MAKE IT OUT OF THE FOREST NOW?
WAIT FOR THE MOON TO RISE, AND WE'LL FIND THE WAY!
SNIFFLE?
SO, HE TOOK HIS SISTER BY THE HAND AND LED HER...
LOOK, GRETEL!
OH, IT'S PRETTY!
...BY FOLLOWING THE PATH TRACED BY THE WHITE PEBBLES, THAT GLITTERED LIKE DIAMONDS.
WE MADE IT!
AND SO, AT DAYBREAK...
TOK!
TOK!

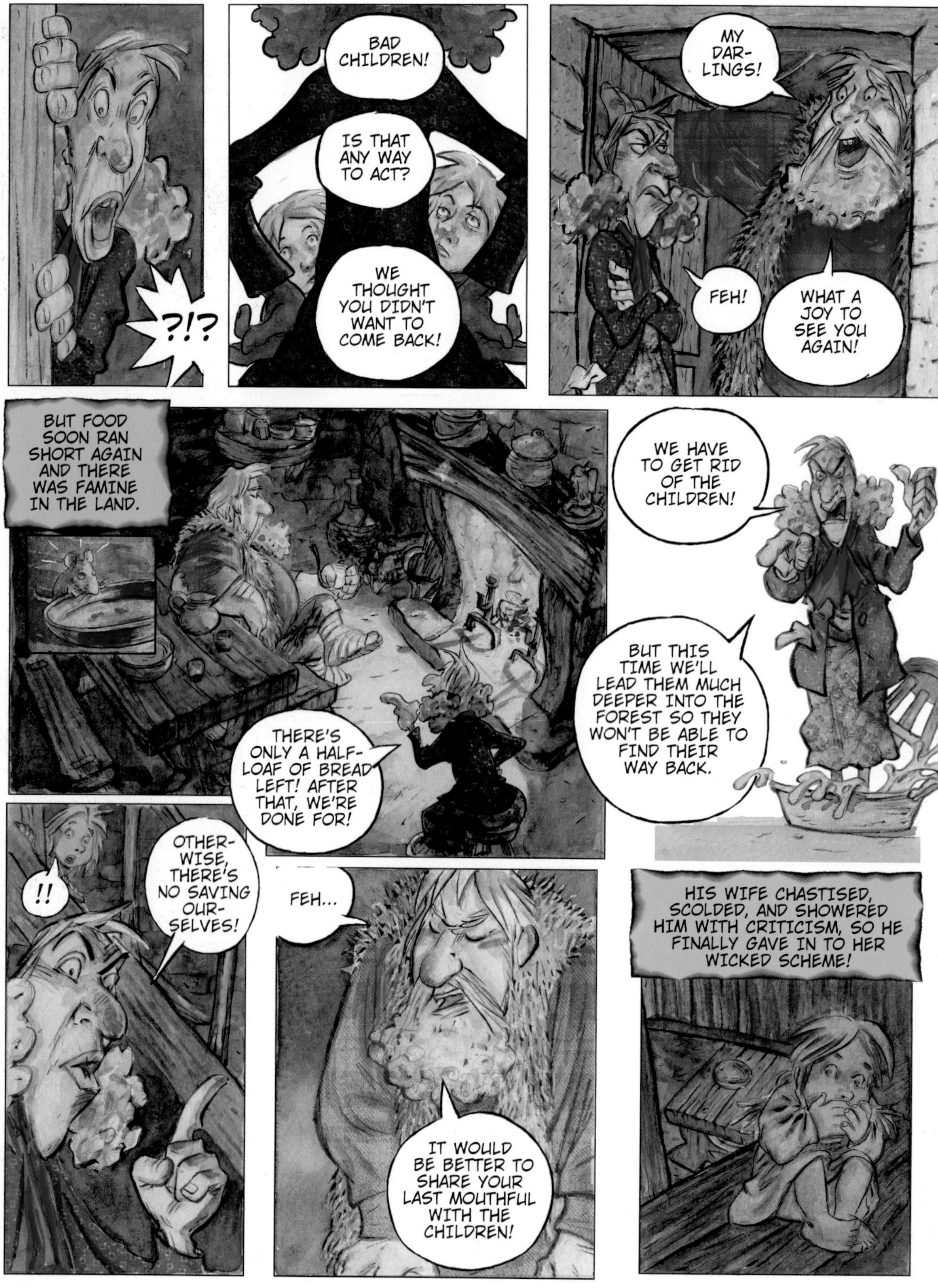
?!?
BAD CHILDREN!
IS THAT ANY WAY TO ACT?
WE THOUGHT YOU DIDN'T WANT TO COME BACK!
MY DAR-LINGS!
FEH!
WHAT A JOY TO SEE YOU AGAIN!
BUT FOOD SOON RAN SHORT AGAIN AND THERE WAS FAMINE IN THE LAND.
THERE'S ONLY A HALF-LOAF OF BREAD LEFT! AFTER THAT, WE'RE DONE FOR!
WE HAVE TO GET RID OF THE CHILDREN!
BUT THIS TIME WE'LL LEAD THEM MUCH DEEPER INTO THE FOREST SO THEY WON'T BE ABLE TO FIND THEIR WAY BACK.
!!
OTHER-WISE, THERE'S NO SAVING OUR-SELVES!
FEH...
IT WOULD BE BETTER TO SHARE YOUR LAST MOUTHFUL WITH THE CHILDREN!
HIS WIFE CHASTISED, SCOLDED, AND SHOWERED HIM WITH CRITICISM, SO HE FINALLY GAVE IN TO HER WICKED SCHEME!

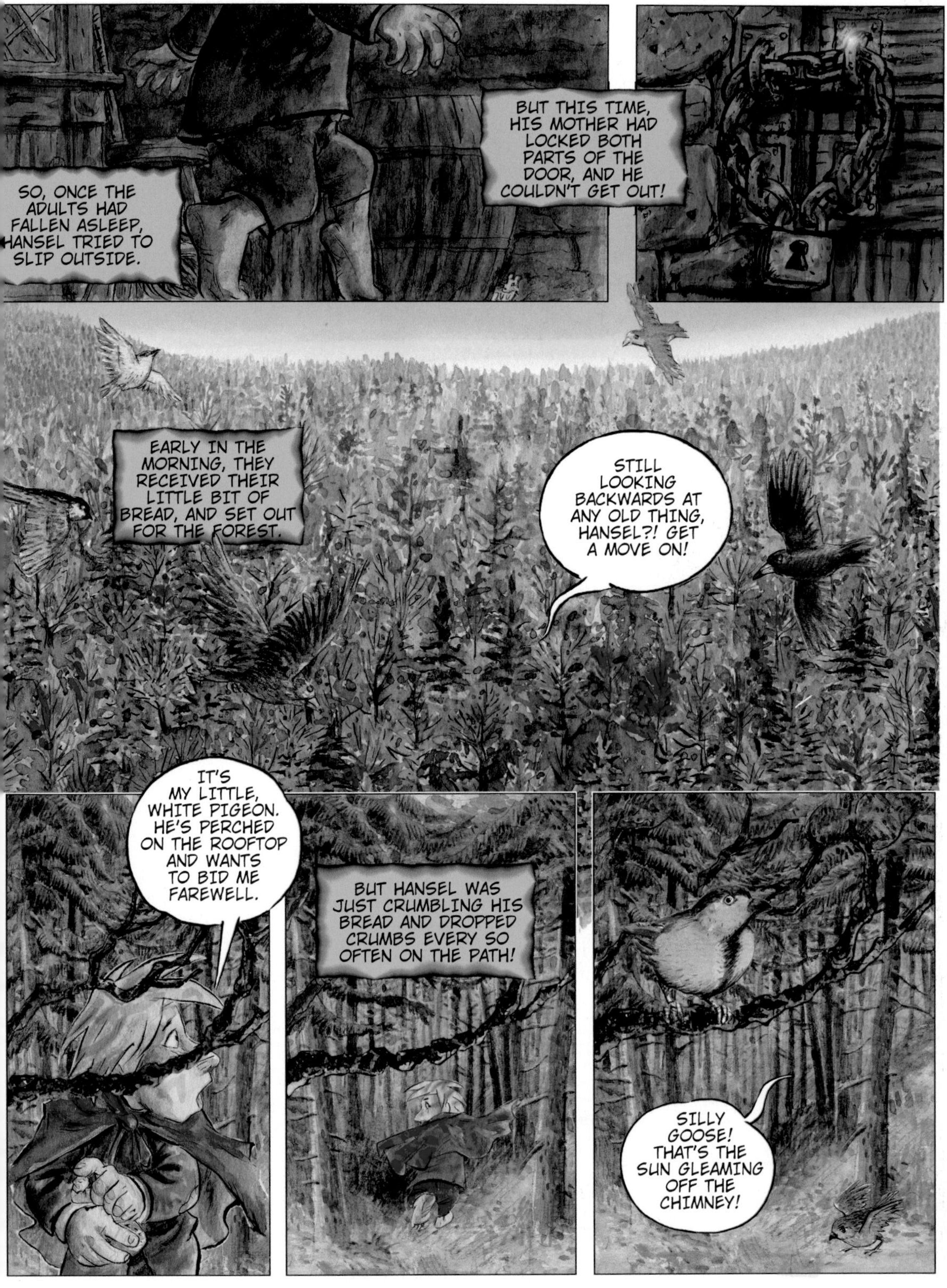

SO, ONCE THE ADULTS HAD FALLEN ASLEEP, HANSEL TRIED TO SLIP OUTSIDE.
BUT THIS TIME, HIS MOTHER HAD LOCKED BOTH PARTS OF THE DOOR, AND HE COULDN'T GET OUT!
EARLY IN THE MORNING, THEY RECEIVED THEIR LITTLE BIT OF BREAD, AND SET OUT FOR THE FOREST.
STILL LOOKING BACKWARDS AT ANY OLD THING, HANSEL?! GET A MOVE ON!
IT'S MY LITTLE, WHITE PIGEON. HE'S PERCHED ON THE ROOFTOP AND WANTS TO BID ME FAREWELL.
BUT HANSEL WAS JUST CRUMBLING HIS BREAD AND DROPPED CRUMBS EVERY SO OFTEN ON THE PATH!
SILLY GOOSE! THAT'S THE SUN GLEAMING OFF THE CHIMNEY!

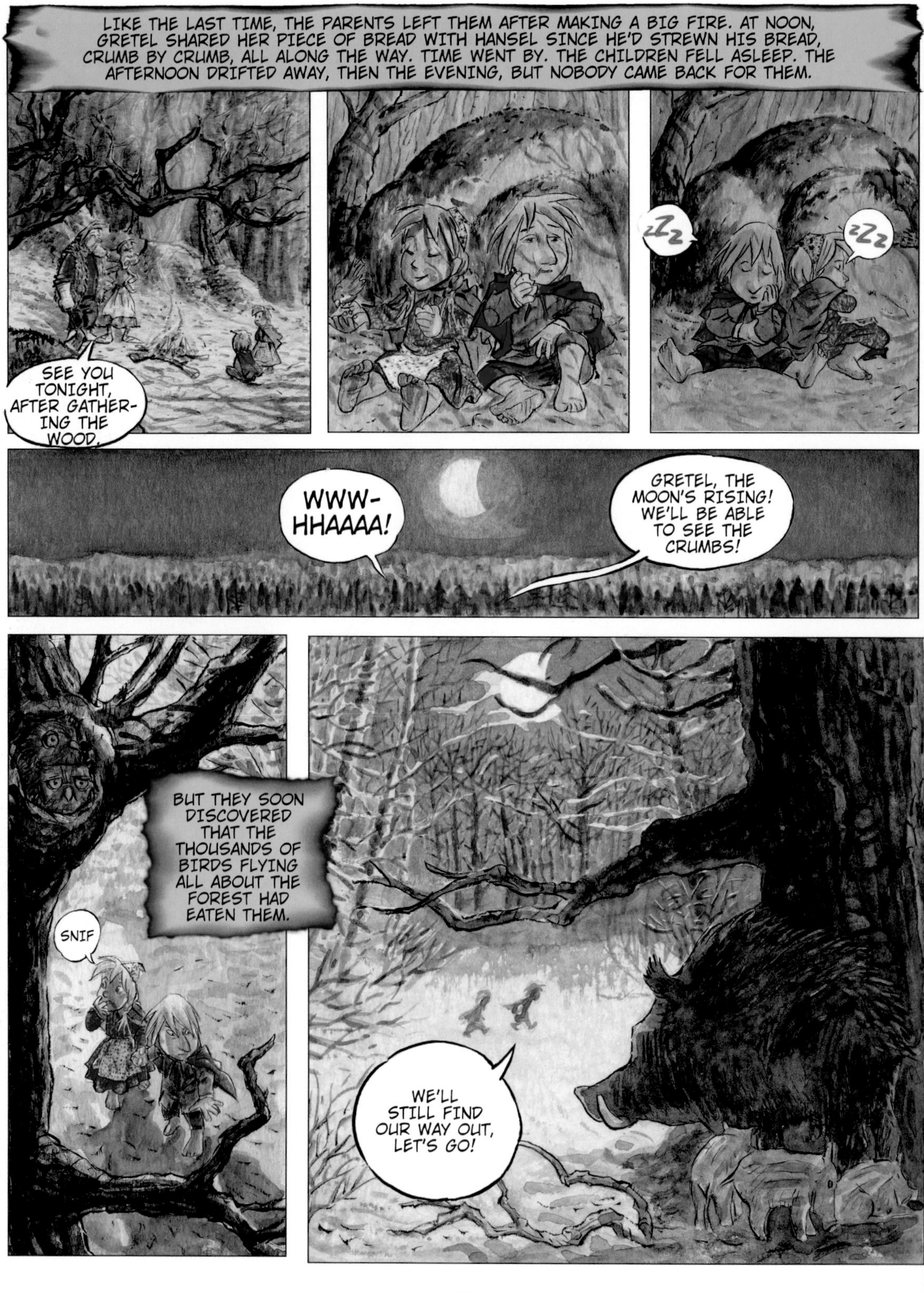
LIKE THE LAST TIME, THE PARENTS LEFT THEM AFTER MAKING A BIG FIRE. AT NOON, GRETEL SHARED HER PIECE OF BREAD WITH HANSEL SINCE HE'D STREWN HIS BREAD, CRUMB BY CRUMB, ALL ALONG THE WAY. TIME WENT BY. THE CHILDREN FELL ASLEEP. THE AFTERNOON DRIFTED AWAY, THEN THE EVENING, BUT NOBODY CAME BACK FOR THEM.
SEE YOU TONIGHT, AFTER GATHERING THE WOOD.
ZZZ
ZZZ
WWW-HHAAAA!
GRETEL, THE MOON'S RISING! WE'LL BE ABLE TO SEE THE CRUMBS!
BUT THEY SOON DISCOVERED THAT THE THOUSANDS OF BIRDS FLYING ALL ABOUT THE FOREST HAD EATEN THEM.
SNIF
WE'LL STILL FIND OUR WAY OUT, LET'S GO!

BUT THEY WALKED THE WHOLE NIGHT AND THE WHOLE NEXT DAY...

...WITHOUT FINDING ANY- THING...

GOING EVER DEEPER INTO THE FOREST...

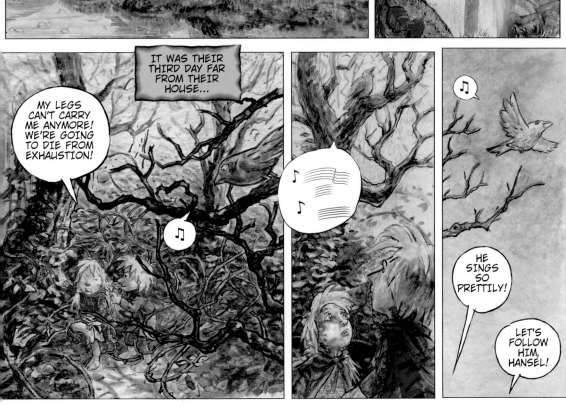

IT WAS THEIR THIRD DAY FAR FROM THEIR HOUSE...

MY LEGS CAN'T CARRY ME ANYMORE! WE'RE GOING TO DIE FROM EXHAUSTION!

HE SINGS SO PRETTILY!

LET'S FOLLOW HIM, HANSEL!

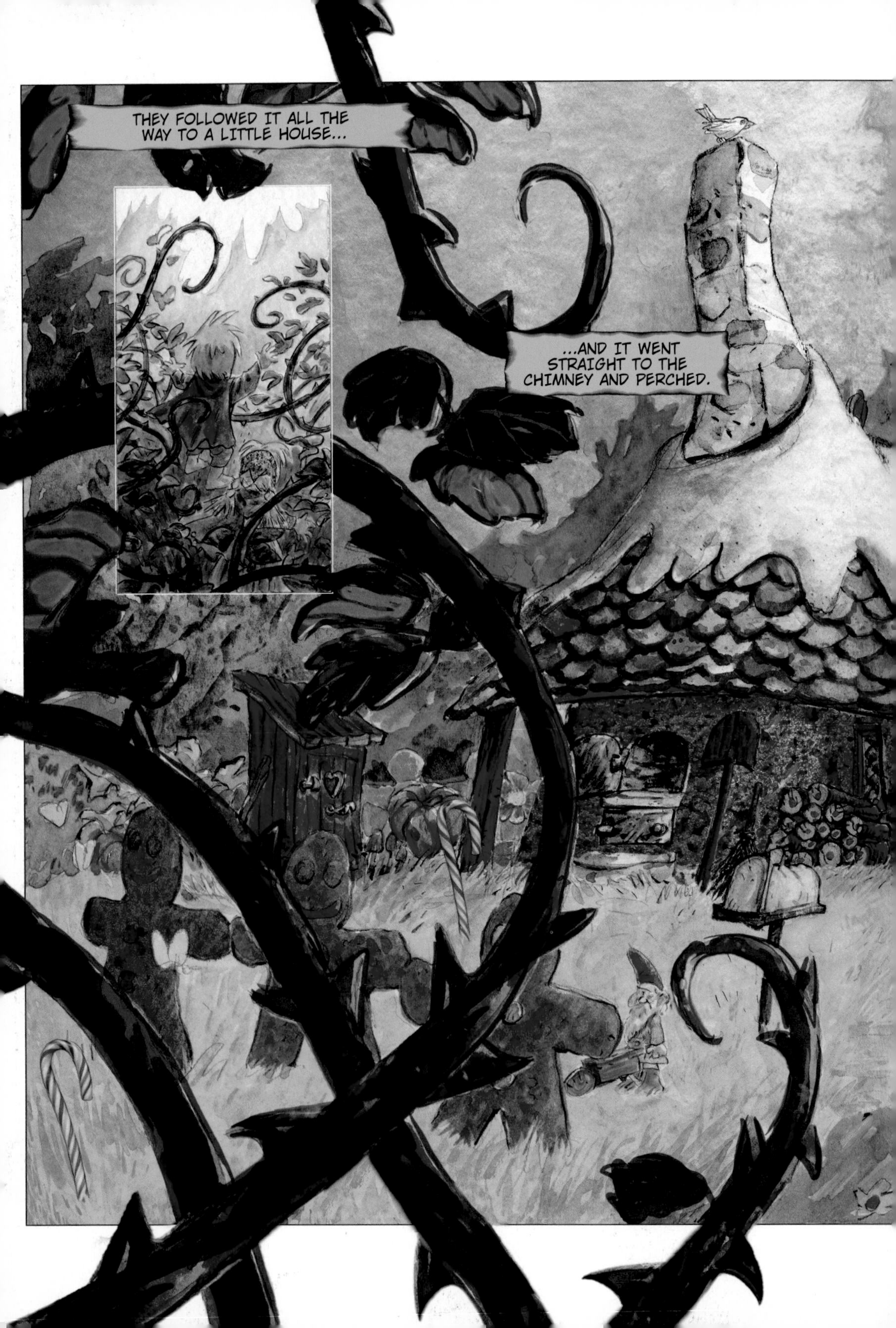
THEY FOLLOWED IT ALL THE WAY TO A LITTLE HOUSE...
...AND IT WENT STRAIGHT TO THE CHIMNEY AND PERCHED.

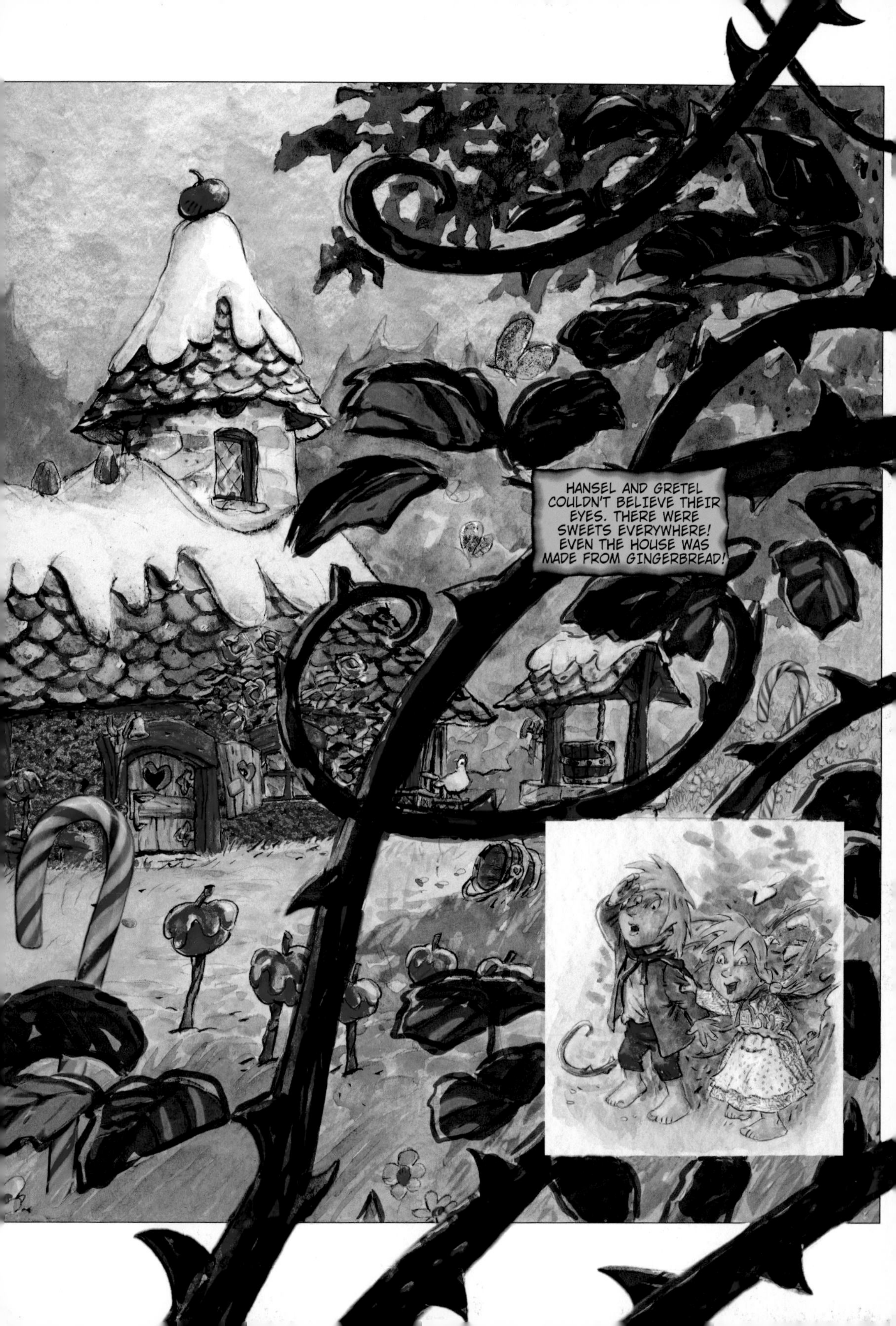
HANSEL AND GRETEL COULDN'T BELIEVE THEIR EYES. THERE WERE SWEETS EVERYWHERE! EVEN THE HOUSE WAS MADE FROM GINGERBREAD!

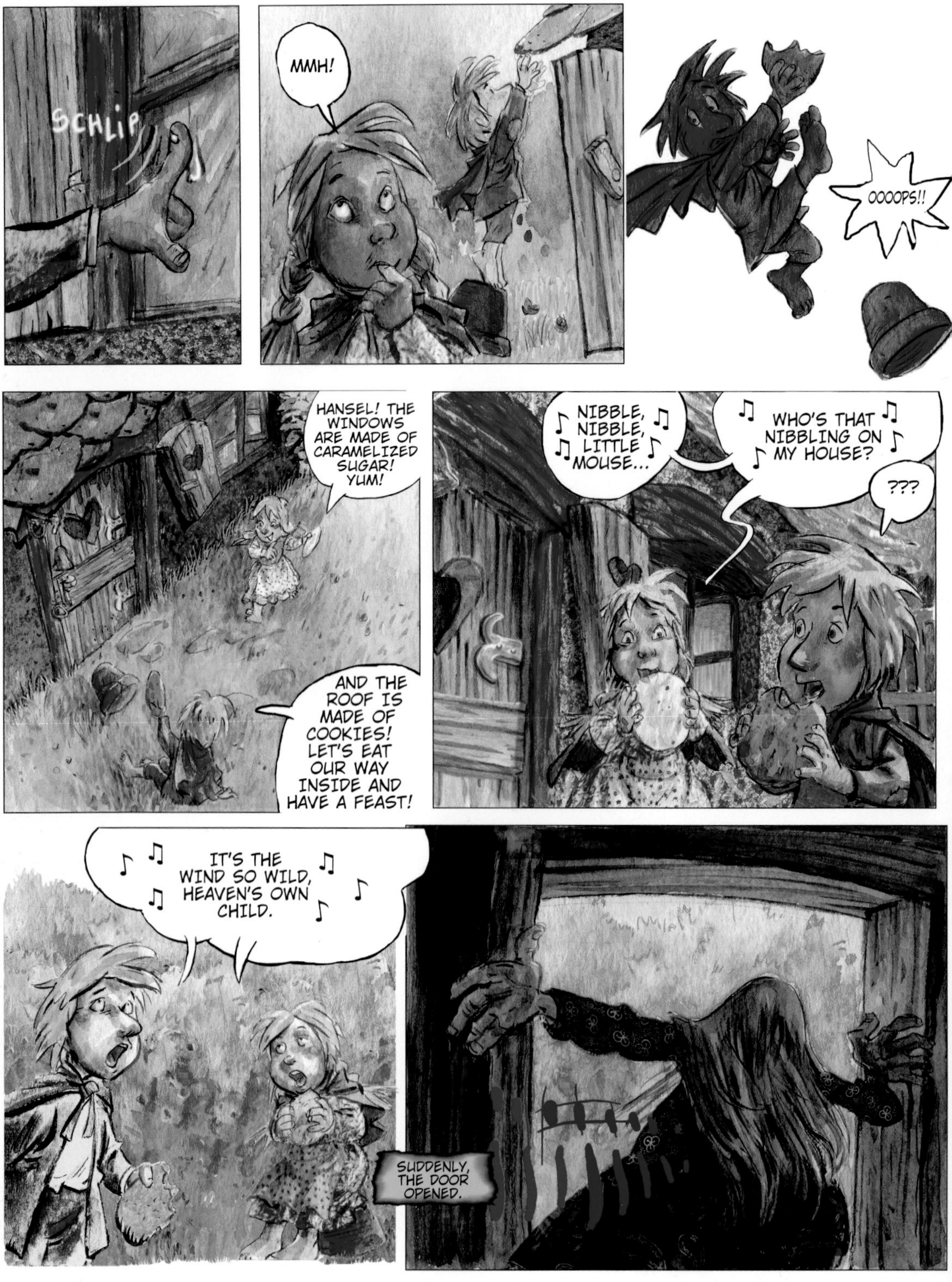
SCHLIP
MMH!
OOOOPS!!
HANSEL! THE WINDOWS ARE MADE OF CARAMELIZED SUGAR! YUM!
AND THE ROOF IS MADE OF COOKIES! LET'S EAT OUR WAY INSIDE AND HAVE A FEAST!
♪ NIBBLE, NIBBLE, LITTLE MOUSE... ♪
♪ WHO'S THAT NIBBLING ON MY HOUSE? ♪
???
♪ IT'S THE WIND SO WILD, HEAVEN'S OWN CHILD. ♪
SUDDENLY, THE DOOR OPENED.

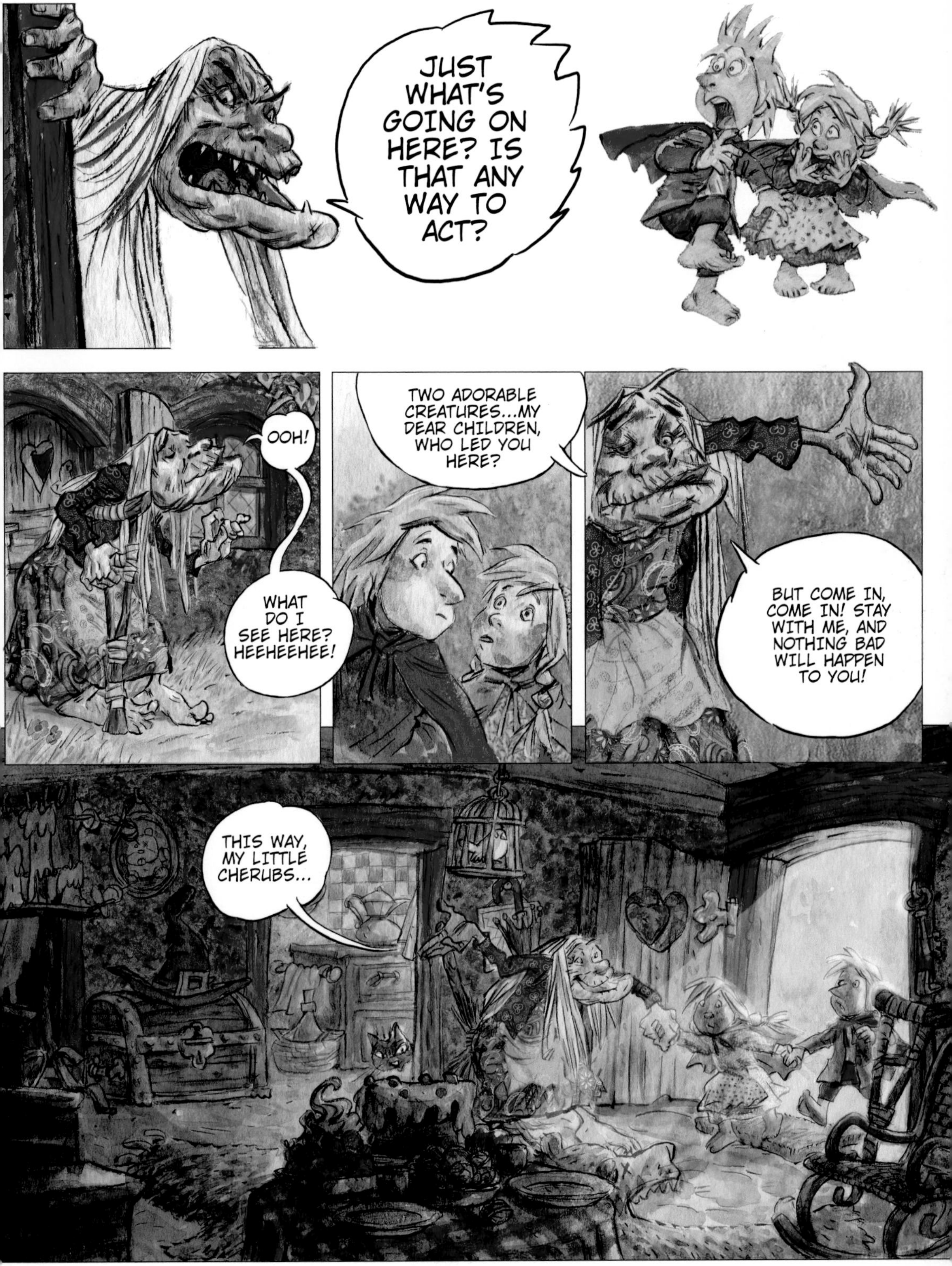
JUST WHAT'S GOING ON HERE? IS THAT ANY WAY TO ACT?
OOH!
WHAT DO I SEE HERE? HEEHEEHEE!
TWO ADORABLE CREATURES...MY DEAR CHILDREN, WHO LED YOU HERE?
BUT COME IN, COME IN! STAY WITH ME, AND NOTHING BAD WILL HAPPEN TO YOU!
THIS WAY, MY LITTLE CHERUBS...

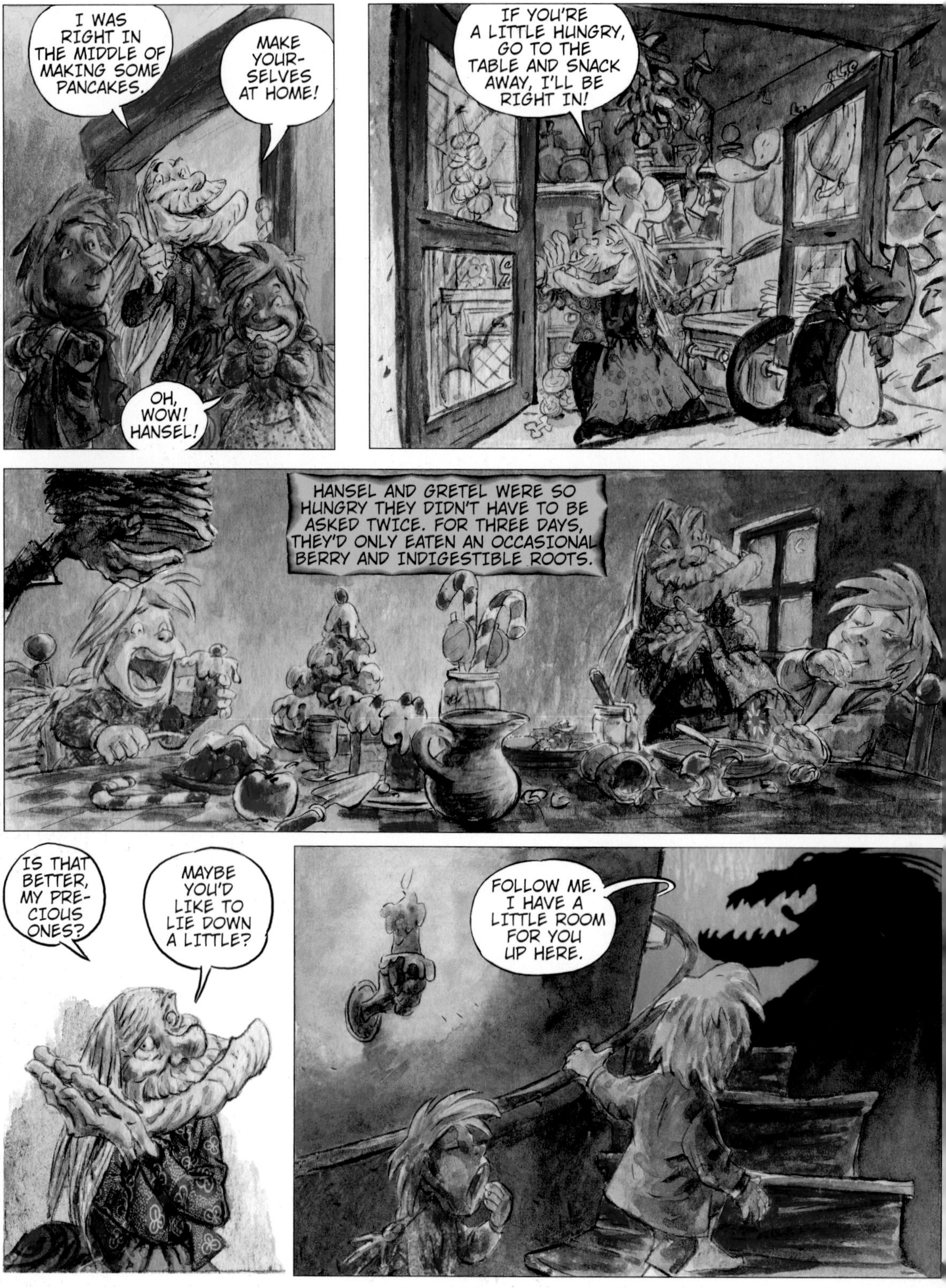
I WAS RIGHT IN THE MIDDLE OF MAKING SOME PANCAKES.
MAKE YOUR-SELVES AT HOME!
OH, WOW! HANSEL!
IF YOU'RE A LITTLE HUNGRY, GO TO THE TABLE AND SNACK AWAY, I'LL BE RIGHT IN!
HANSEL AND GRETEL WERE SO HUNGRY THEY DIDN'T HAVE TO BE ASKED TWICE. FOR THREE DAYS, THEY'D ONLY EATEN AN OCCASIONAL BERRY AND INDIGESTIBLE ROOTS.
IS THAT BETTER, MY PRE-CIOUS ONES?
MAYBE YOU'D LIKE TO LIE DOWN A LITTLE?
FOLLOW ME. I HAVE A LITTLE ROOM FOR YOU UP HERE.

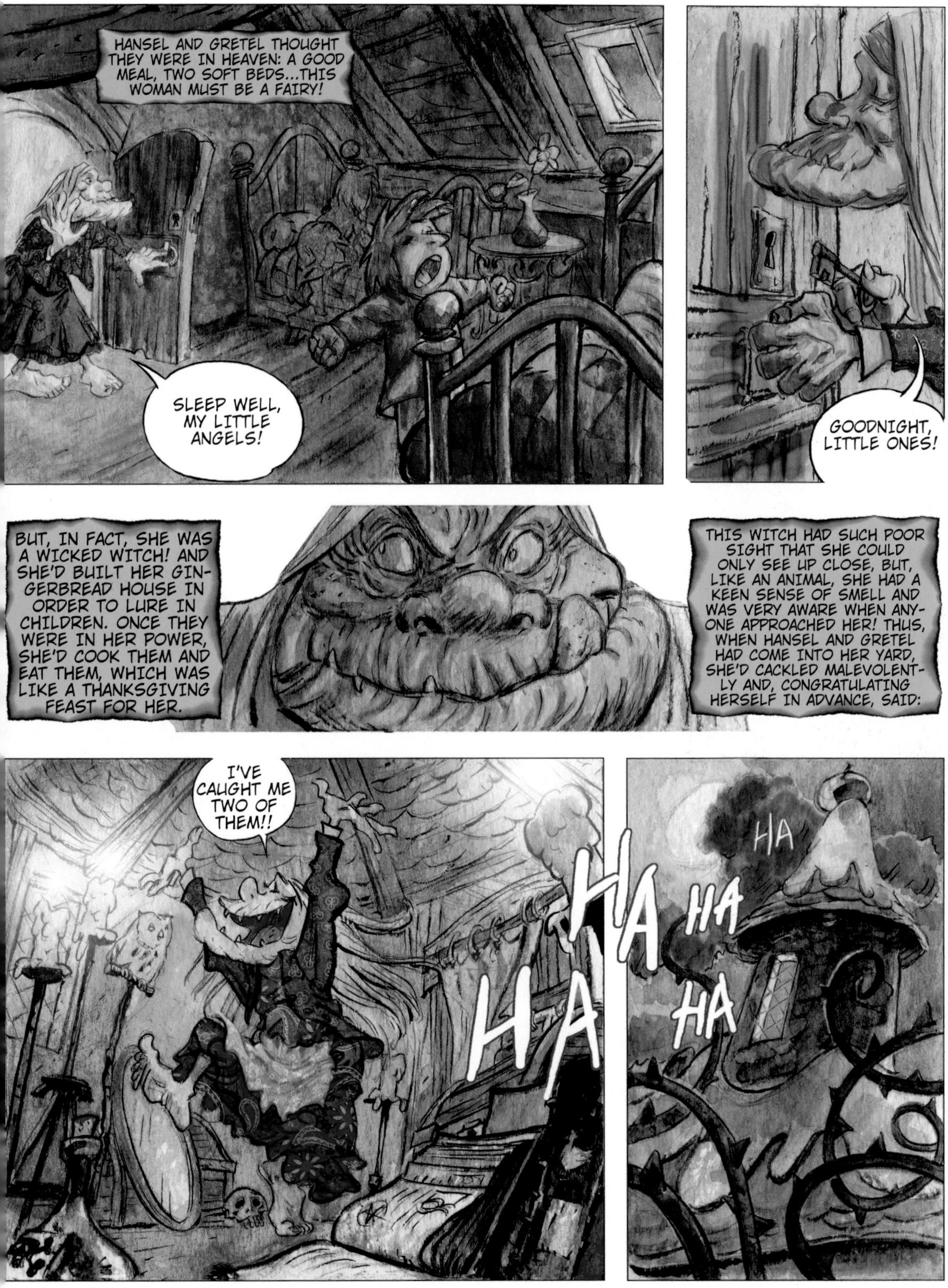
HANSEL AND GRETEL THOUGHT THEY WERE IN HEAVEN: A GOOD MEAL, TWO SOFT BEDS...THIS WOMAN MUST BE A FAIRY!
SLEEP WELL, MY LITTLE ANGELS!
GOODNIGHT, LITTLE ONES!
BUT, IN FACT, SHE WAS A WICKED WITCH! AND SHE'D BUILT HER GINGERBREAD HOUSE IN ORDER TO LURE IN CHILDREN. ONCE THEY WERE IN HER POWER, SHE'D COOK THEM AND EAT THEM, WHICH WAS LIKE A THANKSGIVING FEAST FOR HER.
THIS WITCH HAD SUCH POOR SIGHT THAT SHE COULD ONLY SEE UP CLOSE, BUT, LIKE AN ANIMAL, SHE HAD A KEEN SENSE OF SMELL AND WAS VERY AWARE WHEN ANYONE APPROACHED HER! THUS, WHEN HANSEL AND GRETEL HAD COME INTO HER YARD, SHE'D CACKLED MALEVOLENTLY AND, CONGRATULATING HERSELF IN ADVANCE, SAID:
I'VE CAUGHT ME TWO OF THEM!!
HA
HA
HA
HA
HA
HA

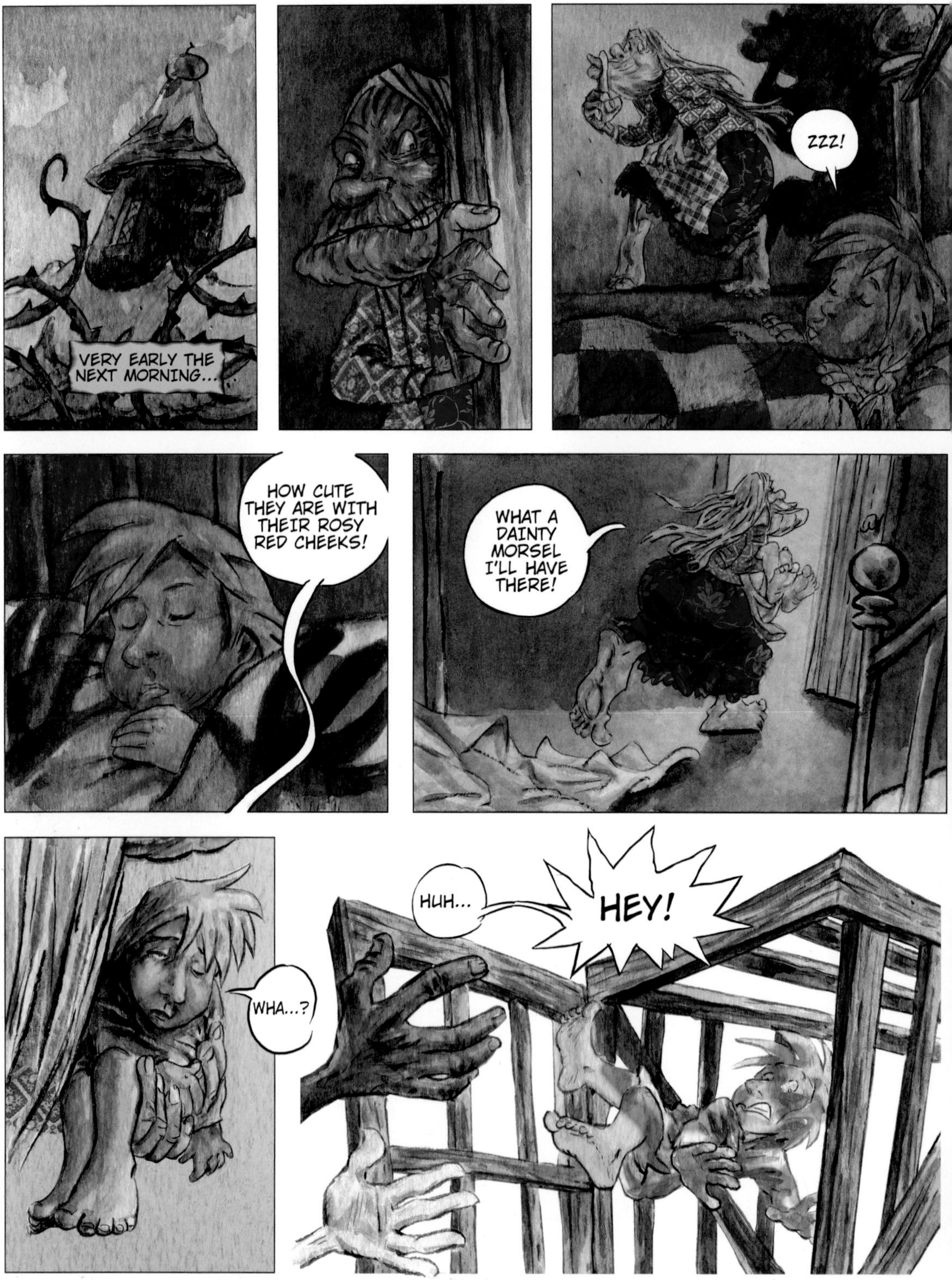
VERY EARLY THE NEXT MORNING...
ZZZ!
HOW CUTE THEY ARE WITH THEIR ROSY RED CHEEKS!
WHAT A DAINTY MORSEL I'LL HAVE THERE!
WHA...?
HUH...
HEY!

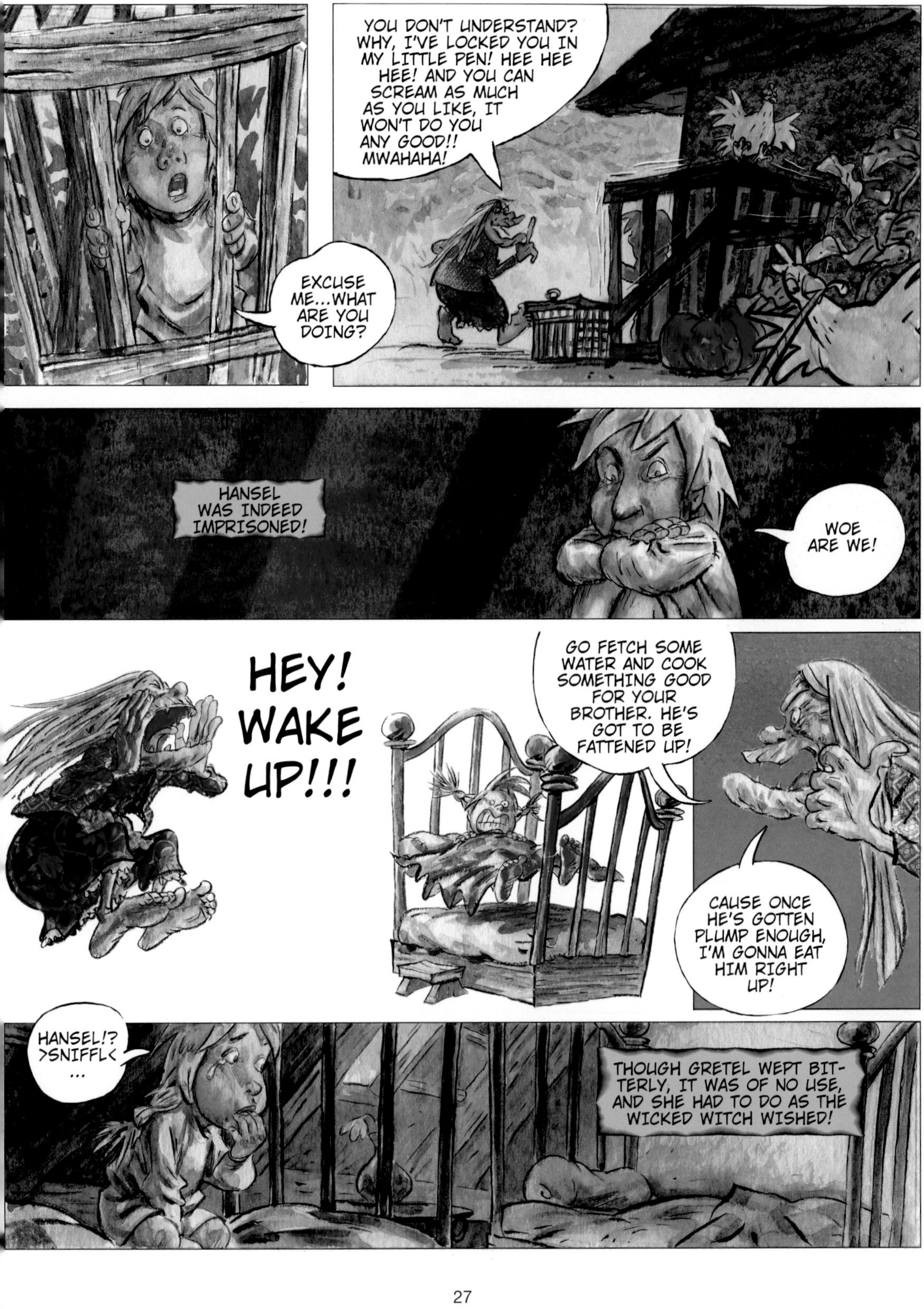
EXCUSE ME...WHAT ARE YOU DOING?
YOU DON'T UNDERSTAND? WHY, I'VE LOCKED YOU IN MY LITTLE PEN! HEE HEE HEE! AND YOU CAN SCREAM AS MUCH AS YOU LIKE, IT WON'T DO YOU ANY GOOD!! MWAHAHA!
HANSEL WAS INDEED IMPRISONED!
WOE ARE WE!
HEY! WAKE UP!!!
GO FETCH SOME WATER AND COOK SOMETHING GOOD FOR YOUR BROTHER. HE'S GOT TO BE FATTENED UP!
CAUSE ONCE HE'S GOTTEN PLUMP ENOUGH, I'M GONNA EAT HIM RIGHT UP!
HANSEL!? >SNIFFL< ...
THOUGH GRETEL WEPT BITTERLY, IT WAS OF NO USE, AND SHE HAD TO DO AS THE WICKED WITCH WISHED!

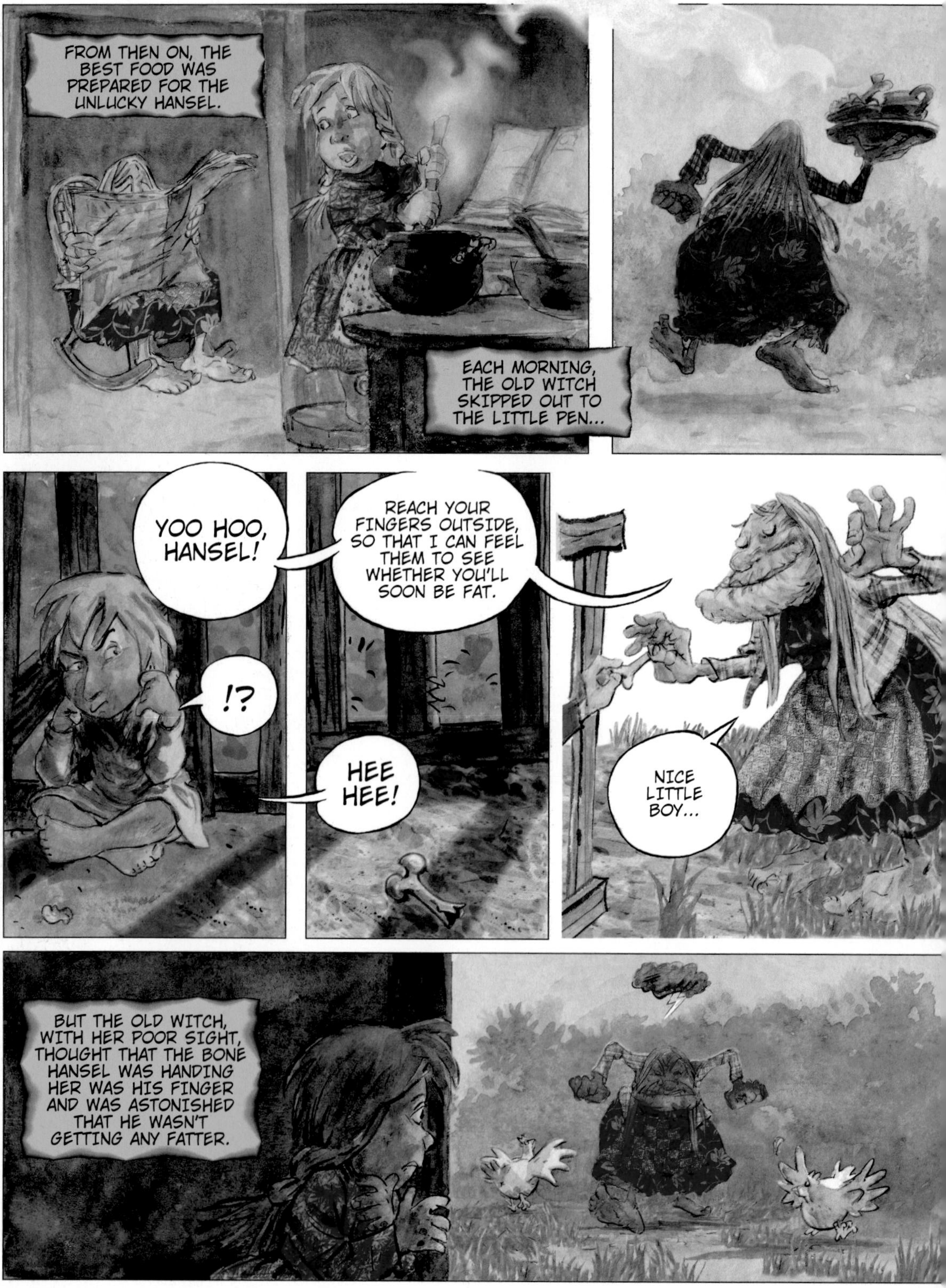
FROM THEN ON, THE BEST FOOD WAS PREPARED FOR THE UNLUCKY HANSEL.
EACH MORNING, THE OLD WITCH SKIPPED OUT TO THE LITTLE PEN...
YOO HOO, HANSEL!
REACH YOUR FINGERS OUTSIDE, SO THAT I CAN FEEL THEM TO SEE WHETHER YOU'LL SOON BE FAT.
!?
HEE HEE!
NICE LITTLE BOY...
BUT THE OLD WITCH, WITH HER POOR SIGHT, THOUGHT THAT THE BONE HANSEL WAS HANDING HER WAS HIS FINGER AND WAS ASTONISHED THAT HE WASN'T GETTING ANY FATTER.

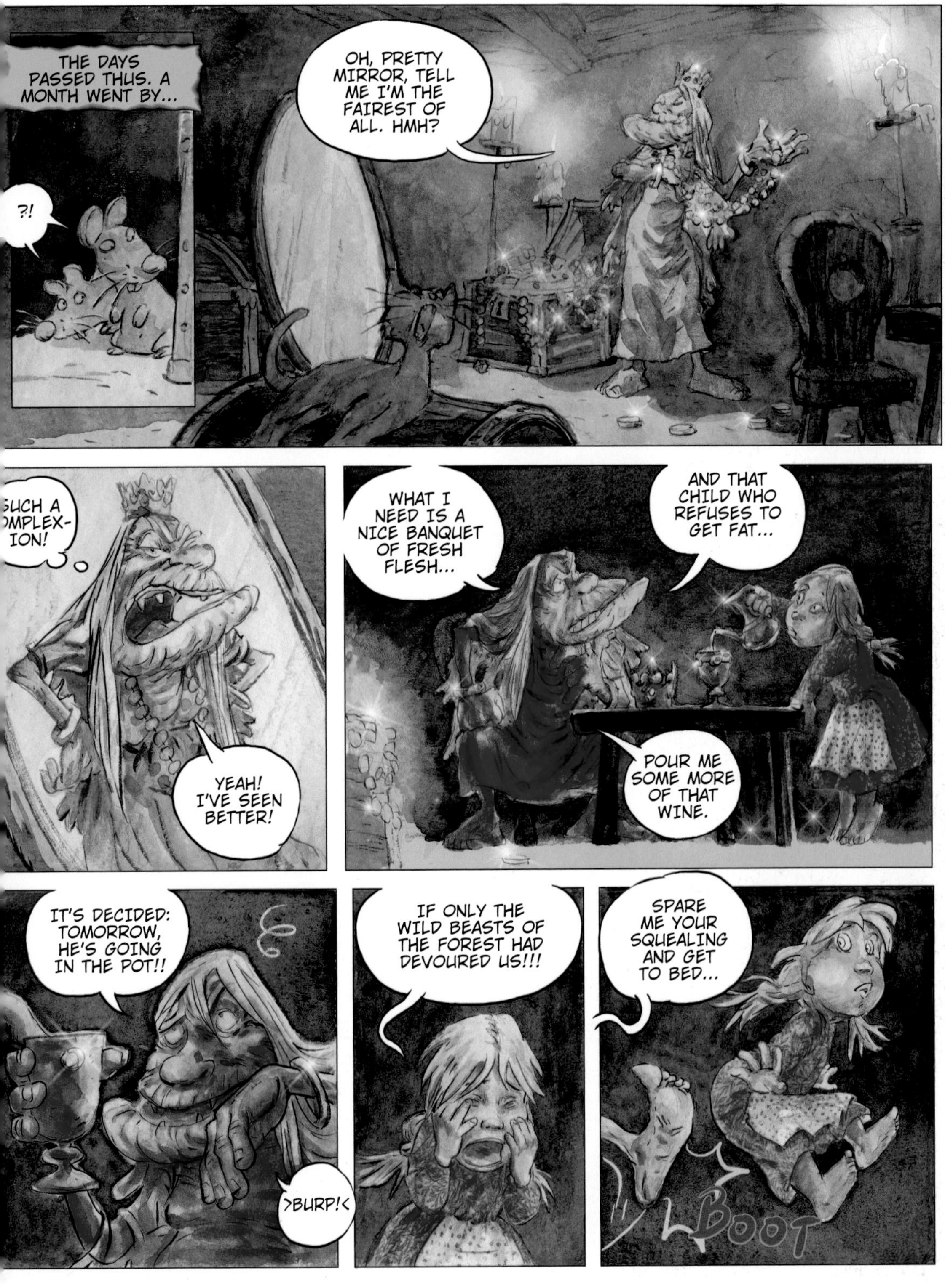
THE DAYS PASSED THUS. A MONTH WENT BY...
OH, PRETTY MIRROR, TELL ME I'M THE FAIREST OF ALL. HMH?
?!
SUCH A OMPLEX-ION!
YEAH! I'VE SEEN BETTER!
WHAT I NEED IS A NICE BANQUET OF FRESH FLESH...
AND THAT CHILD WHO REFUSES TO GET FAT...
POUR ME SOME MORE OF THAT WINE.
IT'S DECIDED: TOMORROW, HE'S GOING IN THE POT!!
>BURP!<
IF ONLY THE WILD BEASTS OF THE FOREST HAD DEVOURED US!!!
SPARE ME YOUR SQUEALING AND GET TO BED...
BOOT

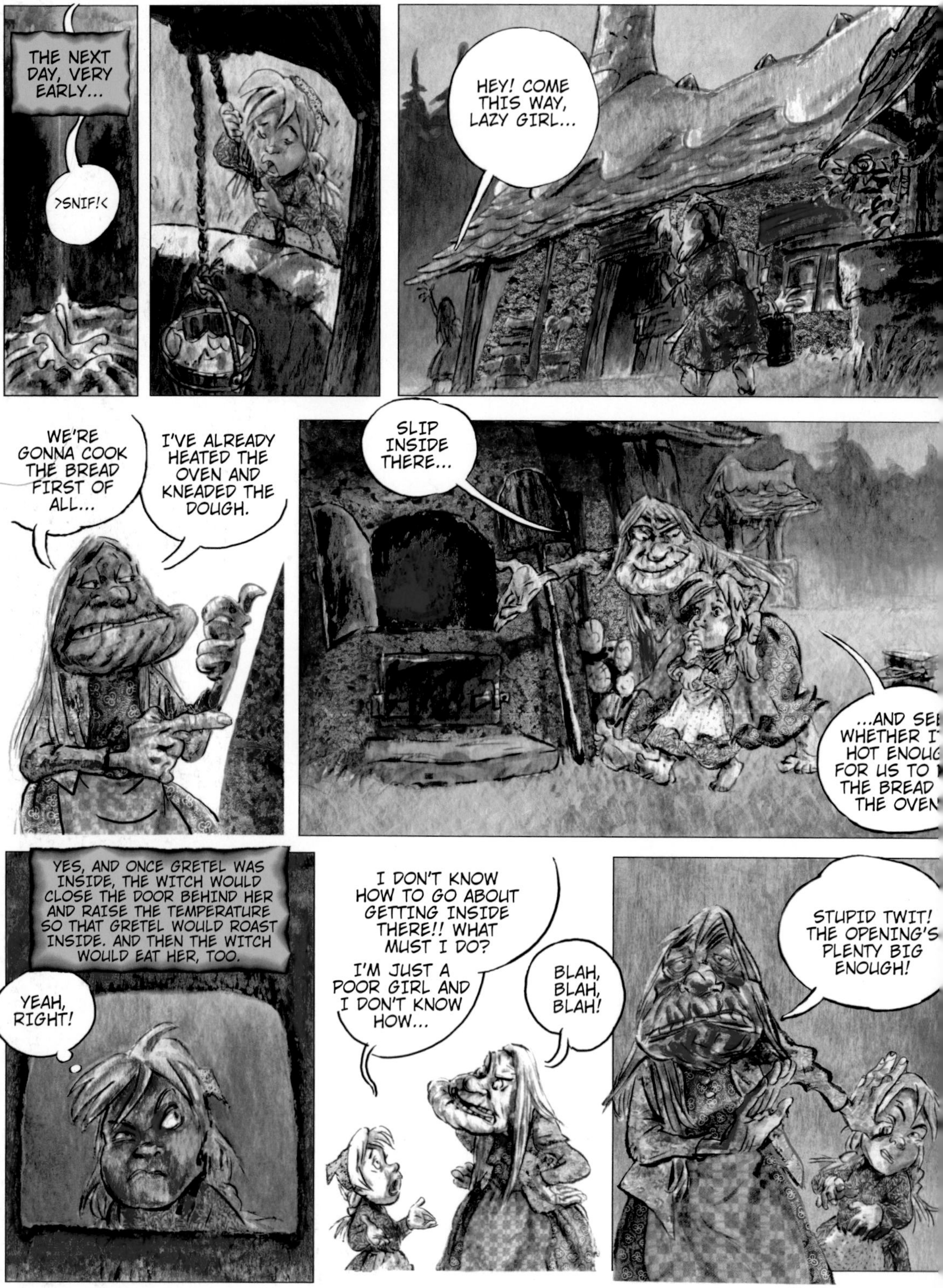

THE NEXT DAY, VERY EARLY...
>SNIF!<
HEY! COME THIS WAY, LAZY GIRL...
WE'RE GONNA COOK THE BREAD FIRST OF ALL...
I'VE ALREADY HEATED THE OVEN AND KNEADED THE DOUGH.
SLIP INSIDE THERE...
...AND SE WHETHER I HOT ENOUG FOR US TO THE BREAD THE OVEN
YES, AND ONCE GRETEL WAS INSIDE, THE WITCH WOULD CLOSE THE DOOR BEHIND HER AND RAISE THE TEMPERATURE SO THAT GRETEL WOULD ROAST INSIDE. AND THEN THE WITCH WOULD EAT HER, TOO.
YEAH, RIGHT!
I DON'T KNOW HOW TO GO ABOUT GETTING INSIDE THERE!! WHAT MUST I DO?
I'M JUST A POOR GIRL AND I DON'T KNOW HOW...
BLAH, BLAH, BLAH!
STUPID TWIT! THE OPENING'S PLENTY BIG ENOUGH!

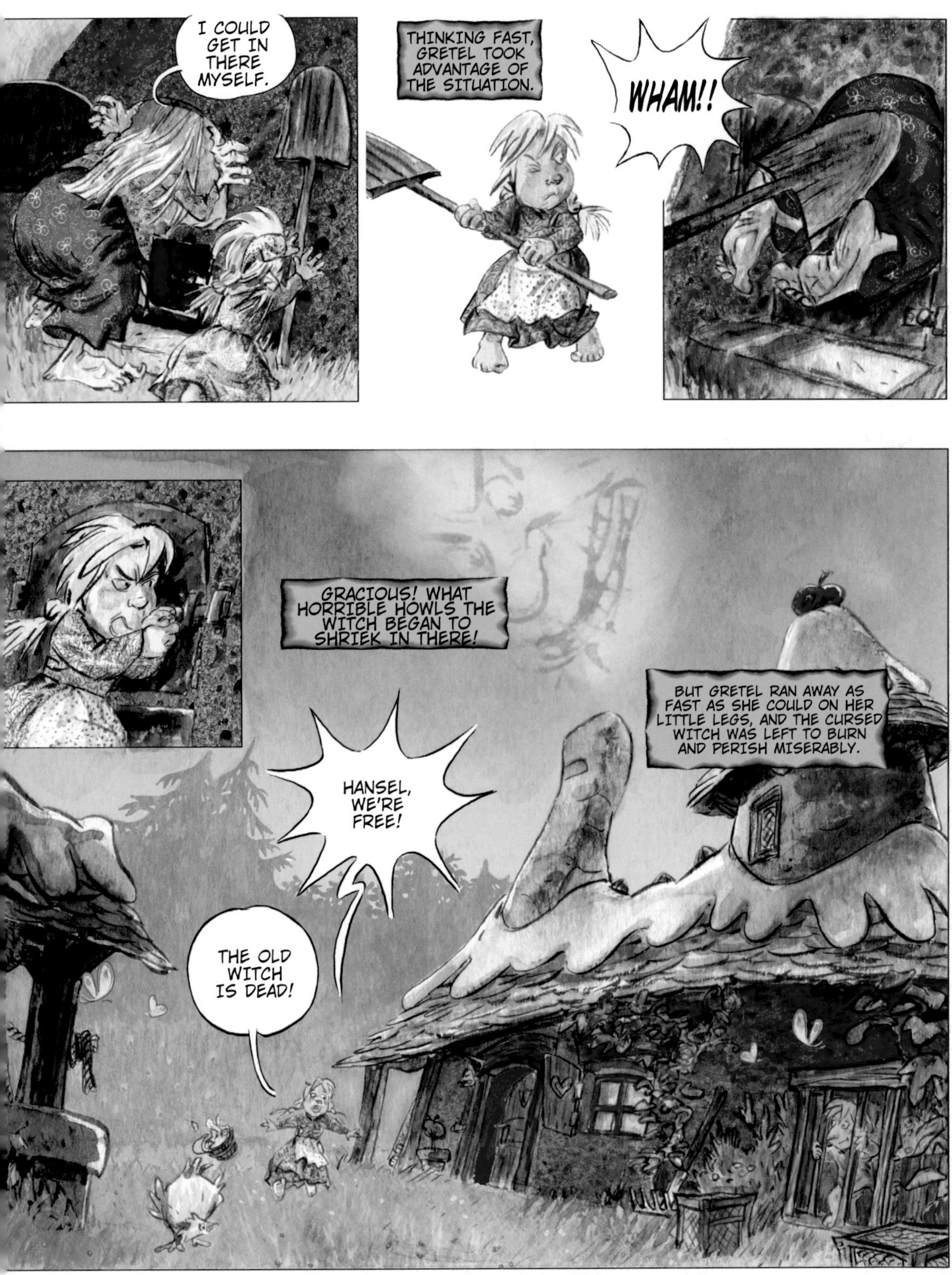
I COULD GET IN THERE MYSELF.
THINKING FAST, GRETEL TOOK ADVANTAGE OF THE SITUATION.
WHAM!!
GRACIOUS! WHAT HORRIBLE HOWLS THE WITCH BEGAN TO SHRIEK IN THERE!
BUT GRETEL RAN AWAY AS FAST AS SHE COULD ON HER LITTLE LEGS, AND THE CURSED WITCH WAS LEFT TO BURN AND PERISH MISERABLY.
HANSEL, WE'RE FREE!
THE OLD WITCH IS DEAD!

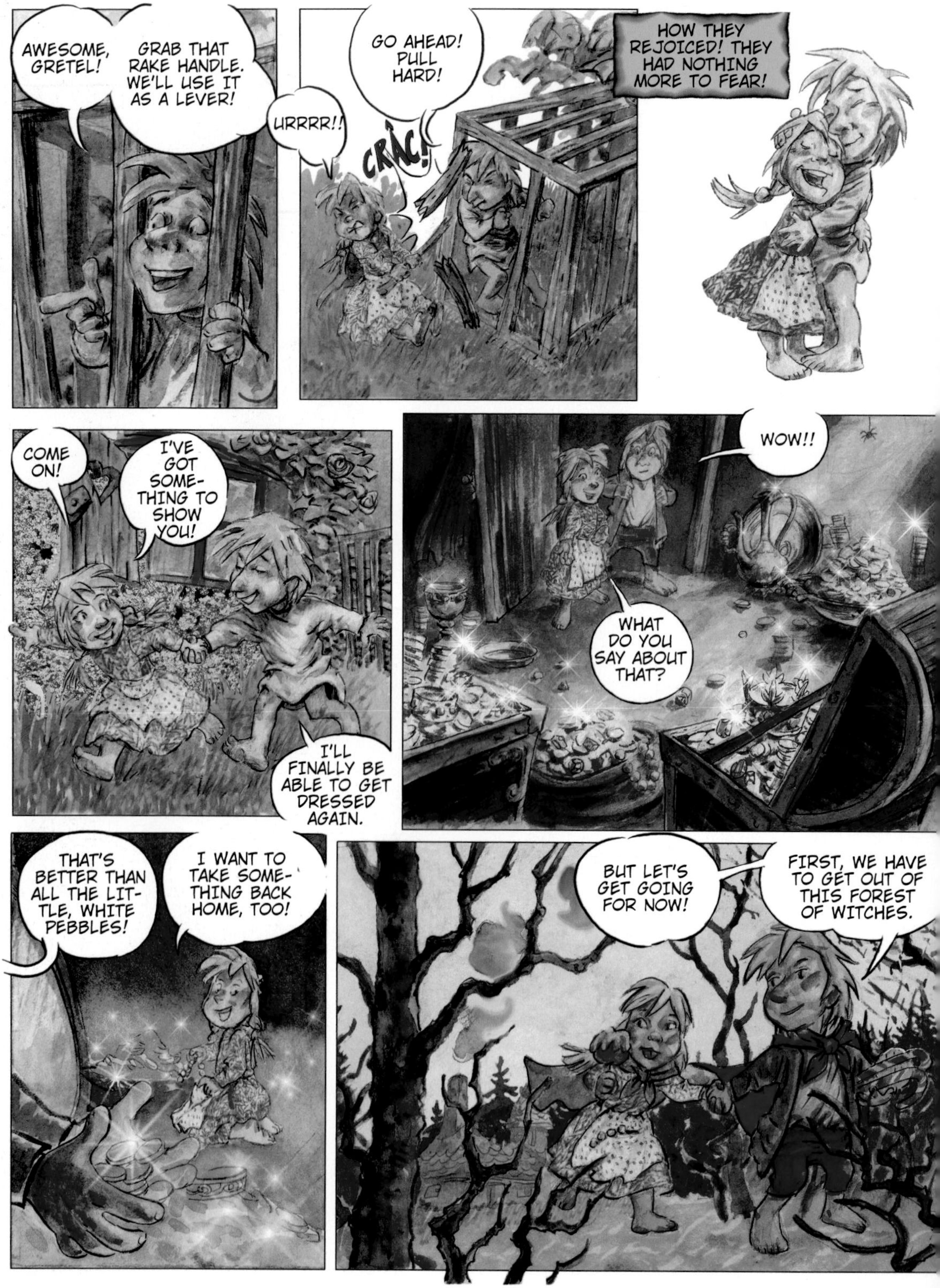
AWESOME, GRETEL!
GRAB THAT RAKE HANDLE. WE'LL USE IT AS A LEVER!
GO AHEAD! PULL HARD!
URRRR!!
CRAC!
HOW THEY REJOICED! THEY HAD NOTHING MORE TO FEAR!
COME ON!
I'VE GOT SOME-THING TO SHOW YOU!
I'LL FINALLY BE ABLE TO GET DRESSED AGAIN.
WOW!!
WHAT DO YOU SAY ABOUT THAT?
THAT'S BETTER THAN ALL THE LIT-TLE, WHITE PEBBLES!
I WANT TO TAKE SOME-THING BACK HOME, TOO!
BUT LET'S GET GOING FOR NOW!
FIRST, WE HAVE TO GET OUT OF THIS FOREST OF WITCHES.

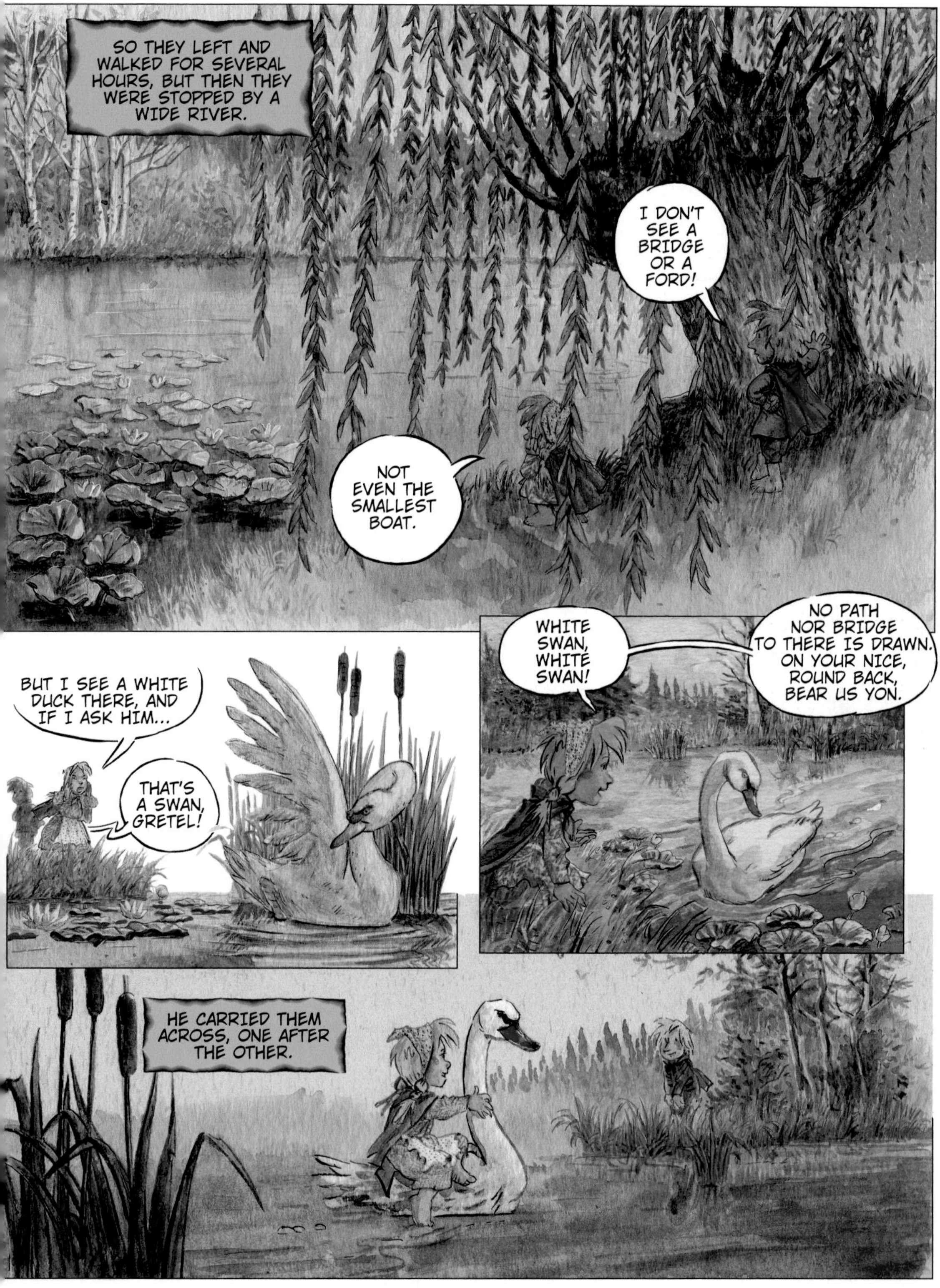
SO THEY LEFT AND WALKED FOR SEVERAL HOURS, BUT THEN THEY WERE STOPPED BY A WIDE RIVER.
I DON'T SEE A BRIDGE OR A FORD!
NOT EVEN THE SMALLEST BOAT.
BUT I SEE A WHITE DUCK THERE, AND IF I ASK HIM...
THAT'S A SWAN, GRETEL!
WHITE SWAN, WHITE SWAN!
NO PATH NOR BRIDGE TO THERE IS DRAWN. ON YOUR NICE, ROUND BACK, BEAR US YON.
HE CARRIED THEM ACROSS, ONE AFTER THE OTHER.

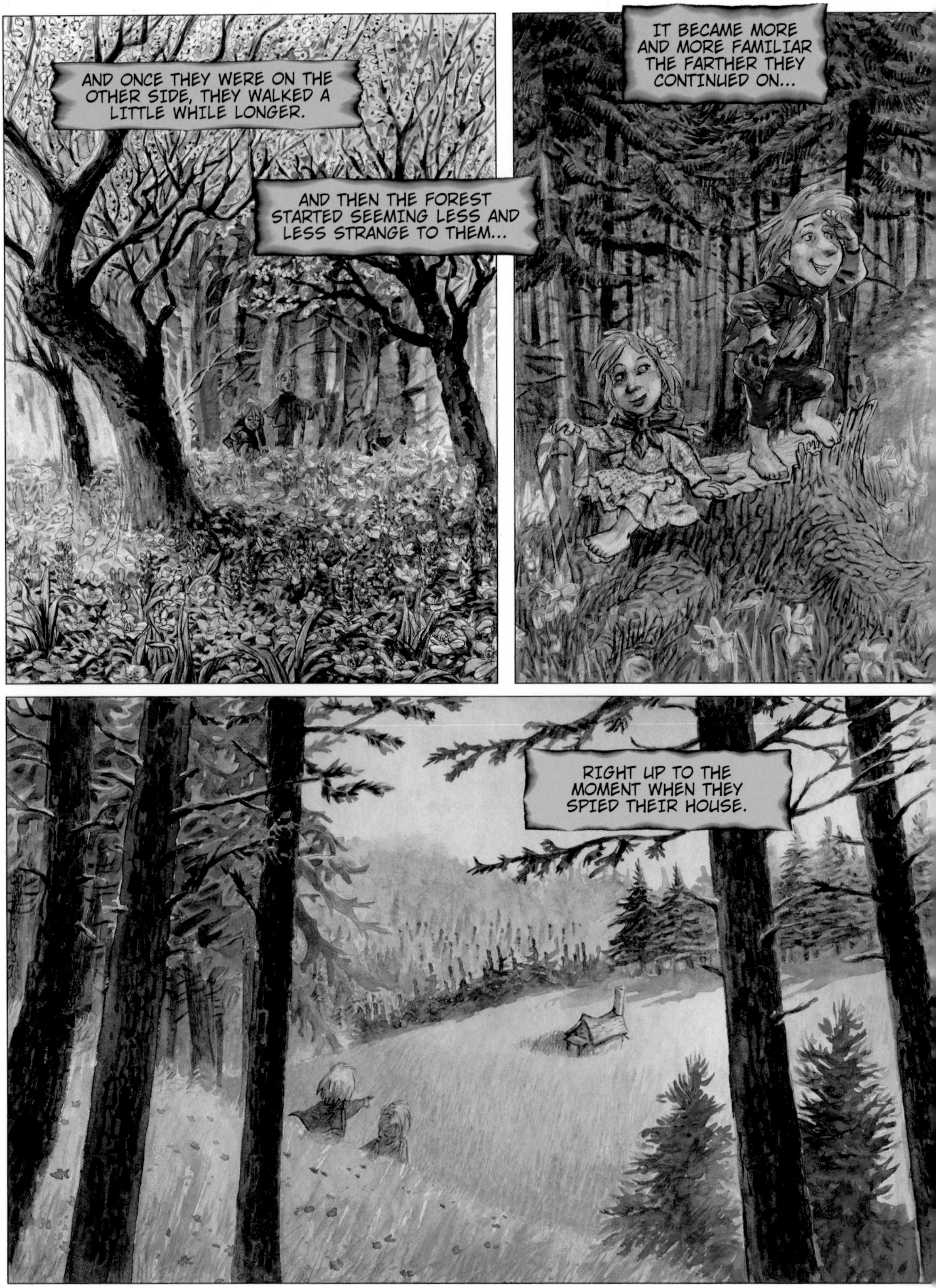
AND ONCE THEY WERE ON THE OTHER SIDE, THEY WALKED A LITTLE WHILE LONGER.
AND THEN THE FOREST STARTED SEEMING LESS AND LESS STRANGE TO THEM...
IT BECAME MORE AND MORE FAMILIAR THE FARTHER THEY CONTINUED ON...
RIGHT UP TO THE MOMENT WHEN THEY SPIED THEIR HOUSE.

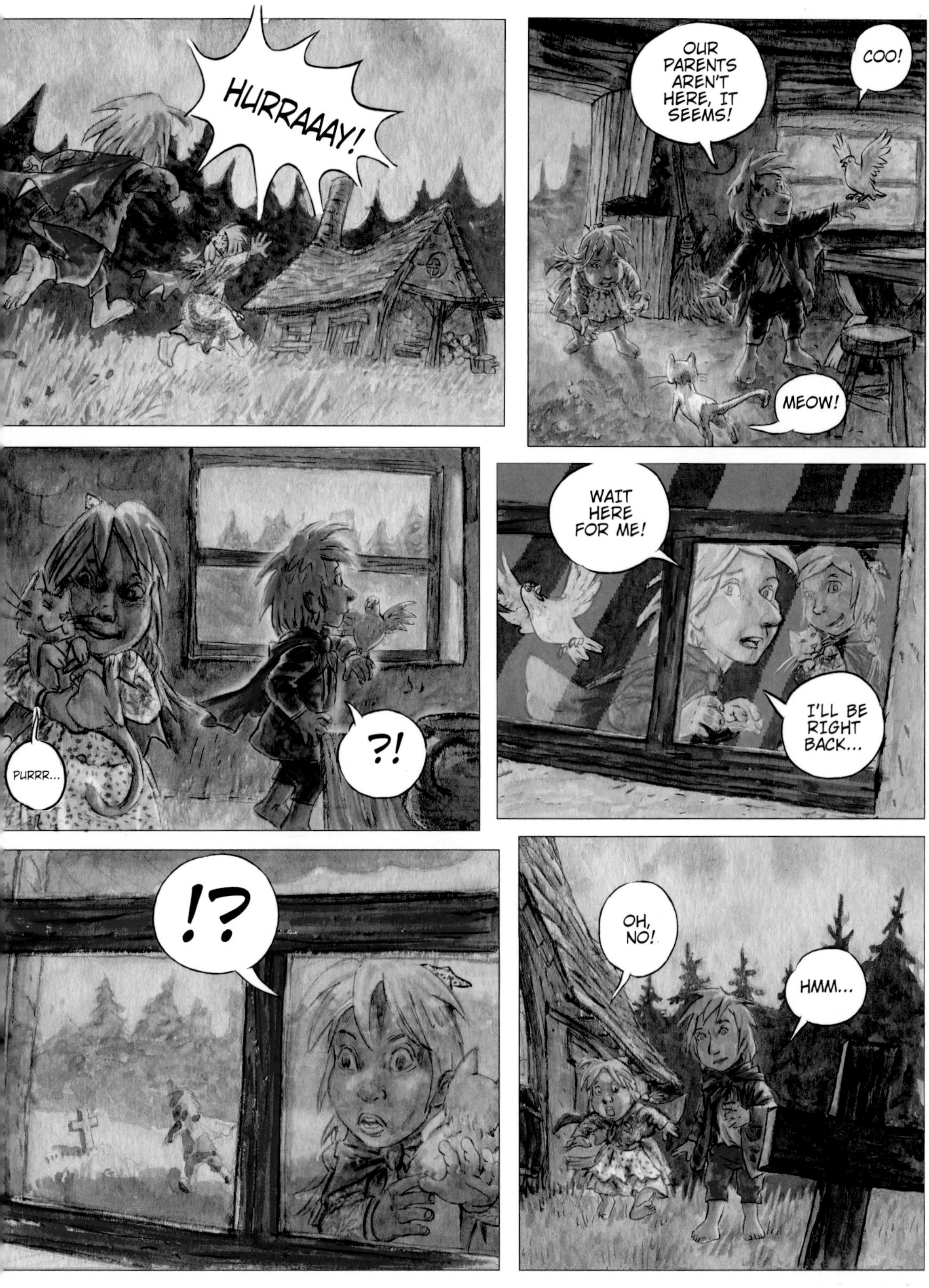
HURRAAAY!
OUR PARENTS AREN'T HERE, IT SEEMS!
COO!
MEOW!
PURRR...
?!
WAIT HERE FOR ME!
I'LL BE RIGHT BACK...
!?
OH, NO!
HMM...

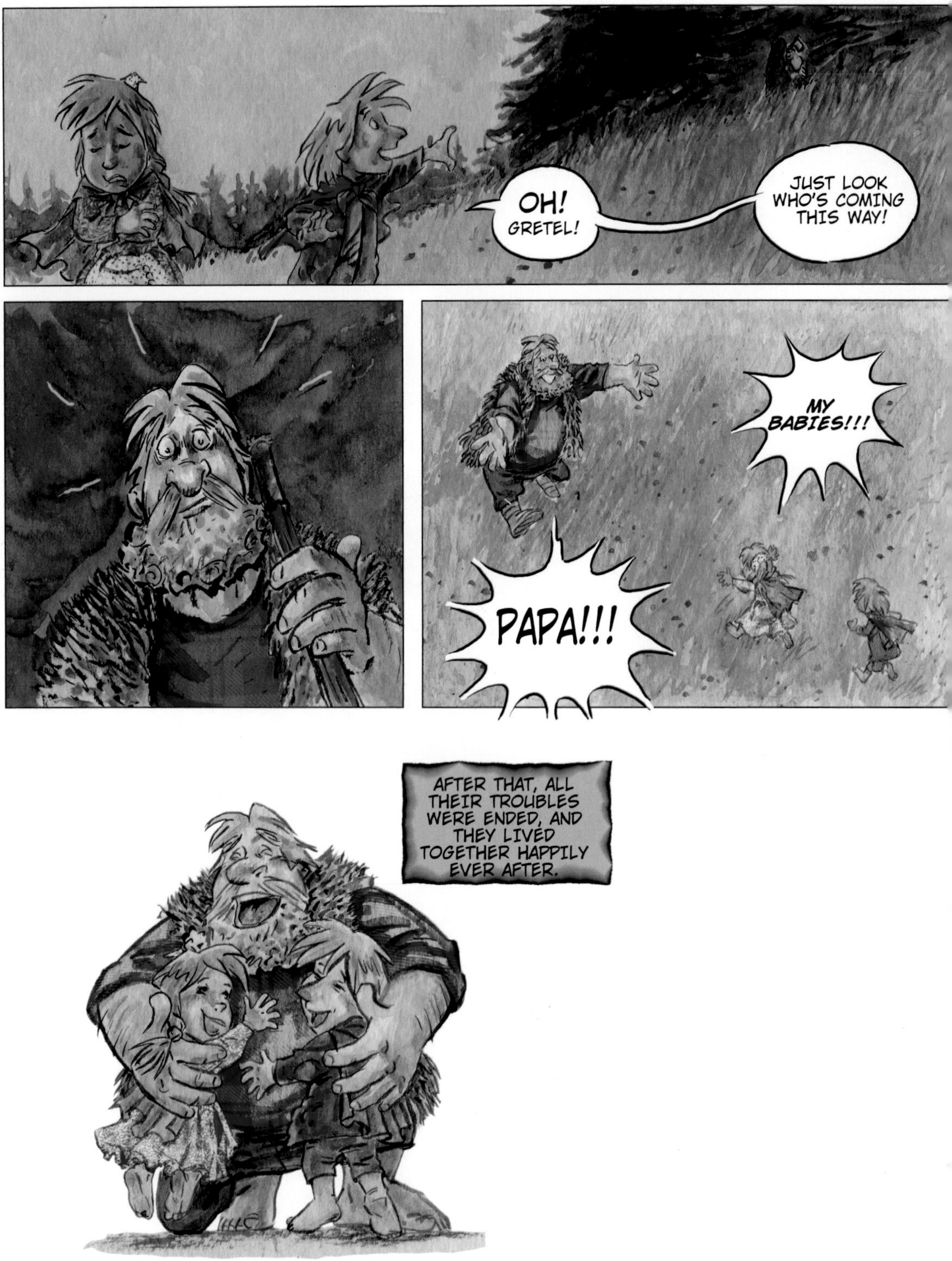
OH! GRETEL!
JUST LOOK WHO'S COMING THIS WAY!
MY BABIES!!!
PAPA!!!
AFTER THAT, ALL THEIR TROUBLES WERE ENDED, AND THEY LIVED TOGETHER HAPPILY EVER AFTER.

LEARNING HOW TO SHUDDER

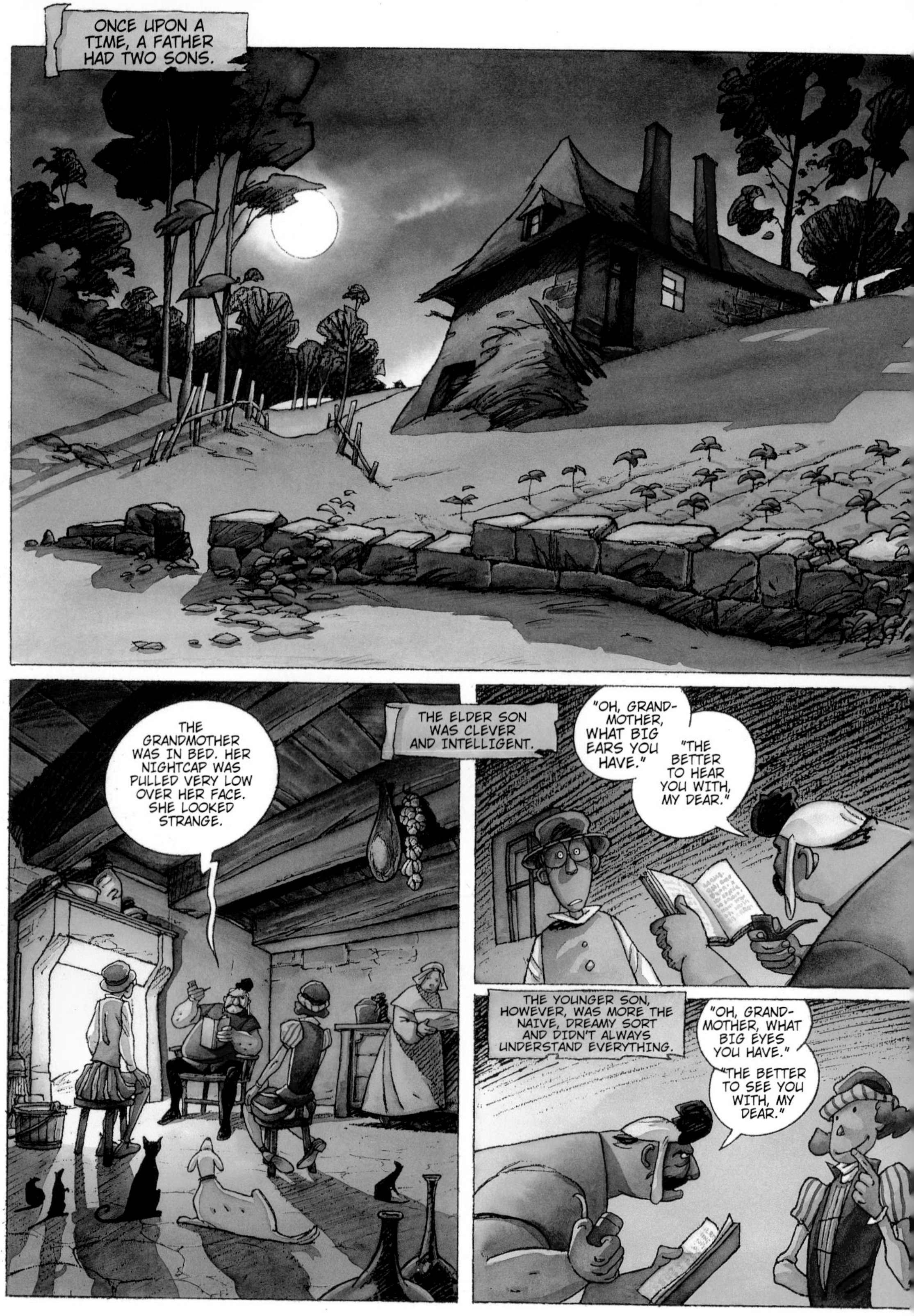

ONCE UPON A TIME, A FATHER HAD TWO SONS.
THE GRANDMOTHER WAS IN BED. HER NIGHTCAP WAS PULLED VERY LOW OVER HER FACE. SHE LOOKED STRANGE.
THE ELDER SON WAS CLEVER AND INTELLIGENT.
"OH, GRAND-MOTHER, WHAT BIG EARS YOU HAVE."
"THE BETTER TO HEAR YOU WITH, MY DEAR."
THE YOUNGER SON, HOWEVER, WAS MORE THE NAIVE, DREAMY SORT AND DIDN'T ALWAYS UNDERSTAND EVERYTHING.
"OH, GRAND-MOTHER, WHAT BIG EYES YOU HAVE."
"THE BETTER TO SEE YOU WITH, MY DEAR."

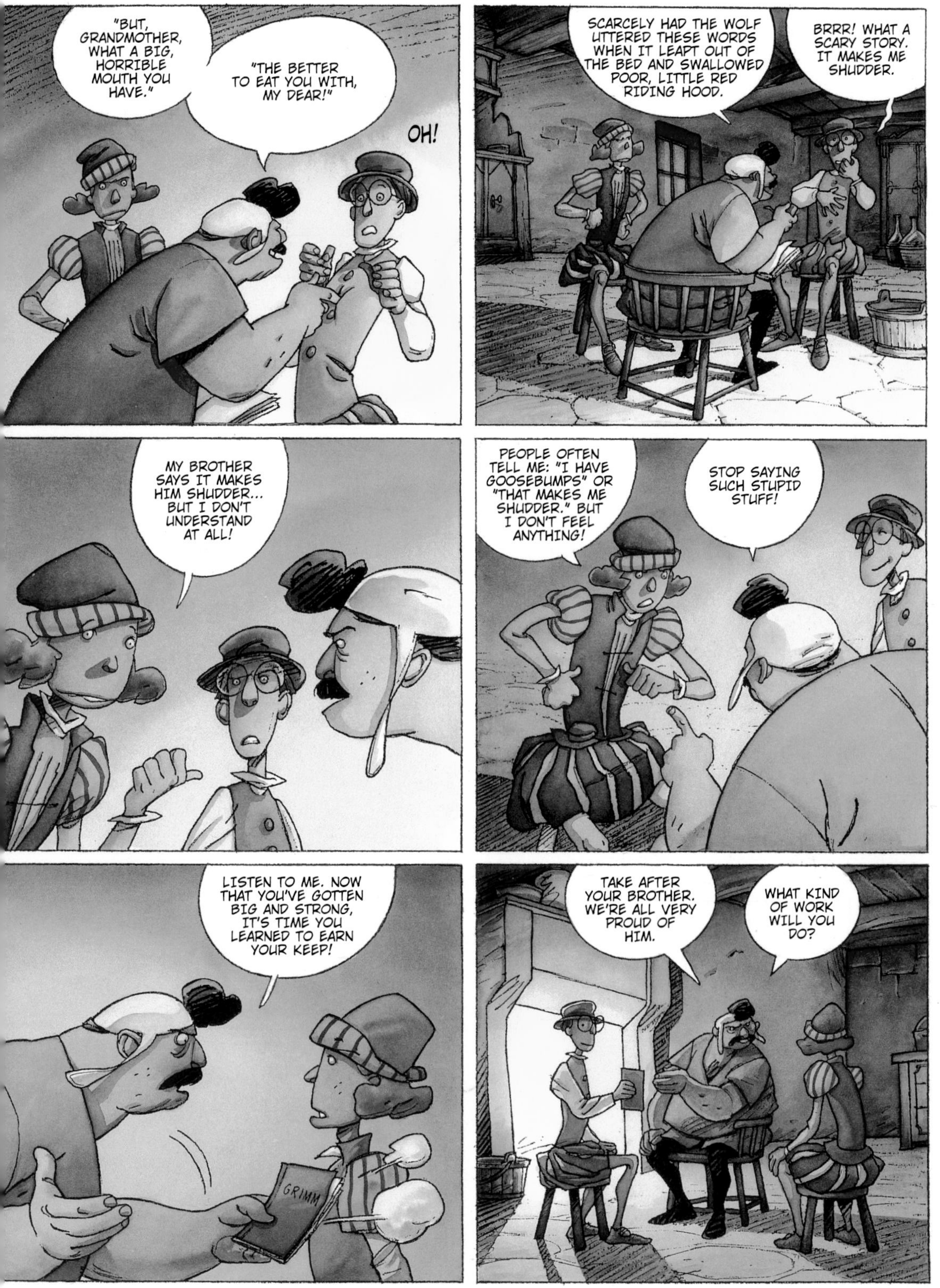
"BUT, GRANDMOTHER, WHAT A BIG, HORRIBLE MOUTH YOU HAVE."
"THE BETTER TO EAT YOU WITH, MY DEAR!"
OH!
SCARCELY HAD THE WOLF UTTERED THESE WORDS WHEN IT LEAPT OUT OF THE BED AND SWALLOWED POOR, LITTLE RED RIDING HOOD.
BRRR! WHAT A SCARY STORY. IT MAKES ME SHUDDER.
MY BROTHER SAYS IT MAKES HIM SHUDDER... BUT I DON'T UNDERSTAND AT ALL!
PEOPLE OFTEN TELL ME: "I HAVE GOOSEBUMPS" OR "THAT MAKES ME SHUDDER." BUT I DON'T FEEL ANYTHING!
STOP SAYING SUCH STUPID STUFF!
LISTEN TO ME. NOW THAT YOU'VE GOTTEN BIG AND STRONG, IT'S TIME YOU LEARNED TO EARN YOUR KEEP!
GRIMM
TAKE AFTER YOUR BROTHER. WE'RE ALL VERY PROUD OF HIM.
WHAT KIND OF WORK WILL YOU DO?

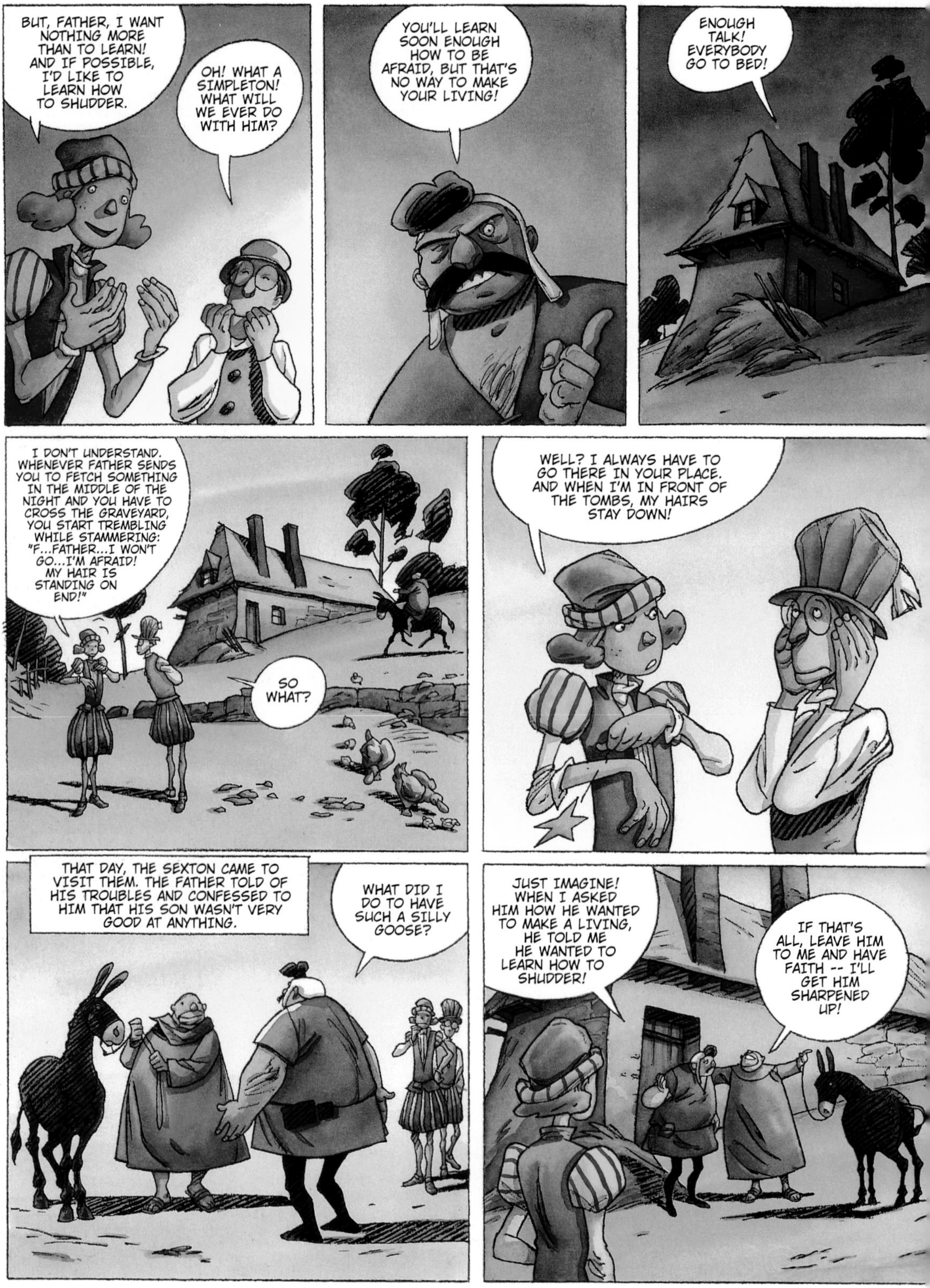
BUT, FATHER, I WANT NOTHING MORE THAN TO LEARN! AND IF POSSIBLE, I'D LIKE TO LEARN HOW TO SHUDDER.
OH! WHAT A SIMPLETON! WHAT WILL WE EVER DO WITH HIM?
YOU'LL LEARN SOON ENOUGH HOW TO BE AFRAID, BUT THAT'S NO WAY TO MAKE YOUR LIVING!
ENOUGH TALK! EVERYBODY GO TO BED!
I DON'T UNDERSTAND. WHENEVER FATHER SENDS YOU TO FETCH SOMETHING IN THE MIDDLE OF THE NIGHT AND YOU HAVE TO CROSS THE GRAVEYARD, YOU START TREMBLING WHILE STAMMERING: "F...FATHER...I WON'T GO...I'M AFRAID! MY HAIR IS STANDING ON END!"
SO WHAT?
WELL? I ALWAYS HAVE TO GO THERE IN YOUR PLACE. AND WHEN I'M IN FRONT OF THE TOMBS, MY HAIRS STAY DOWN!
THAT DAY, THE SEXTON CAME TO VISIT THEM. THE FATHER TOLD OF HIS TROUBLES AND CONFESSED TO HIM THAT HIS SON WASN'T VERY GOOD AT ANYTHING.
WHAT DID I DO TO HAVE SUCH A SILLY GOOSE?
JUST IMAGINE! WHEN I ASKED HIM HOW HE WANTED TO MAKE A LIVING, HE TOLD ME HE WANTED TO LEARN HOW TO SHUDDER!
IF THAT'S ALL, LEAVE HIM TO ME AND HAVE FAITH -- I'LL GET HIM SHARPENED UP!

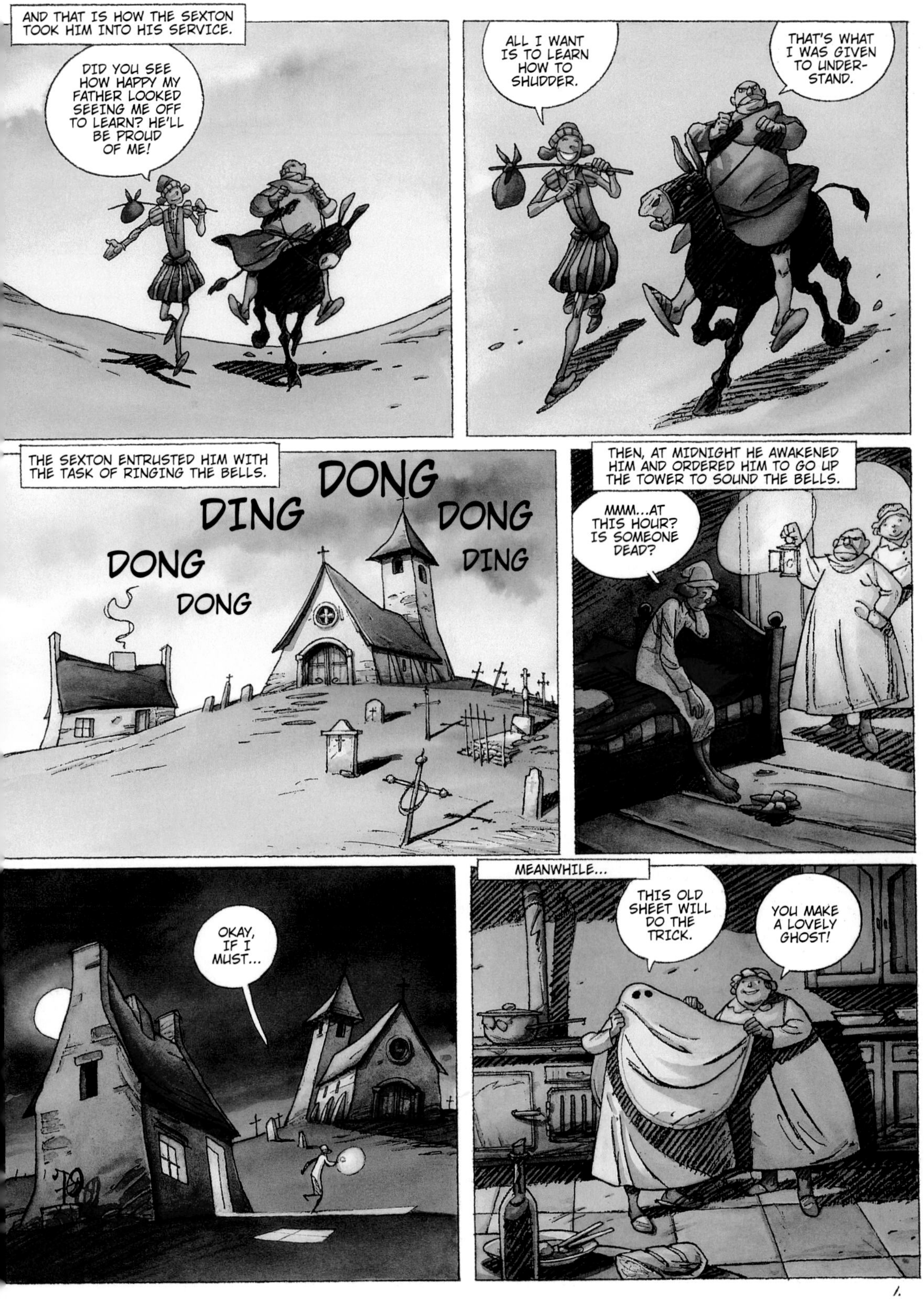
AND THAT IS HOW THE SEXTON TOOK HIM INTO HIS SERVICE.
DID YOU SEE HOW HAPPY MY FATHER LOOKED SEEING ME OFF TO LEARN? HE'LL BE PROUD OF ME!
ALL I WANT IS TO LEARN HOW TO SHUDDER.
THAT'S WHAT I WAS GIVEN TO UNDER-STAND.
THE SEXTON ENTRUSTED HIM WITH THE TASK OF RINGING THE BELLS.
DONG
DING
DONG
DONG
DING
DONG
THEN, AT MIDNIGHT HE AWAKENED HIM AND ORDERED HIM TO GO UP THE TOWER TO SOUND THE BELLS.
MMM...AT THIS HOUR? IS SOMEONE DEAD?
OKAY, IF I MUST...
MEANWHILE...
THIS OLD SHEET WILL DO THE TRICK.
YOU MAKE A LOVELY GHOST!

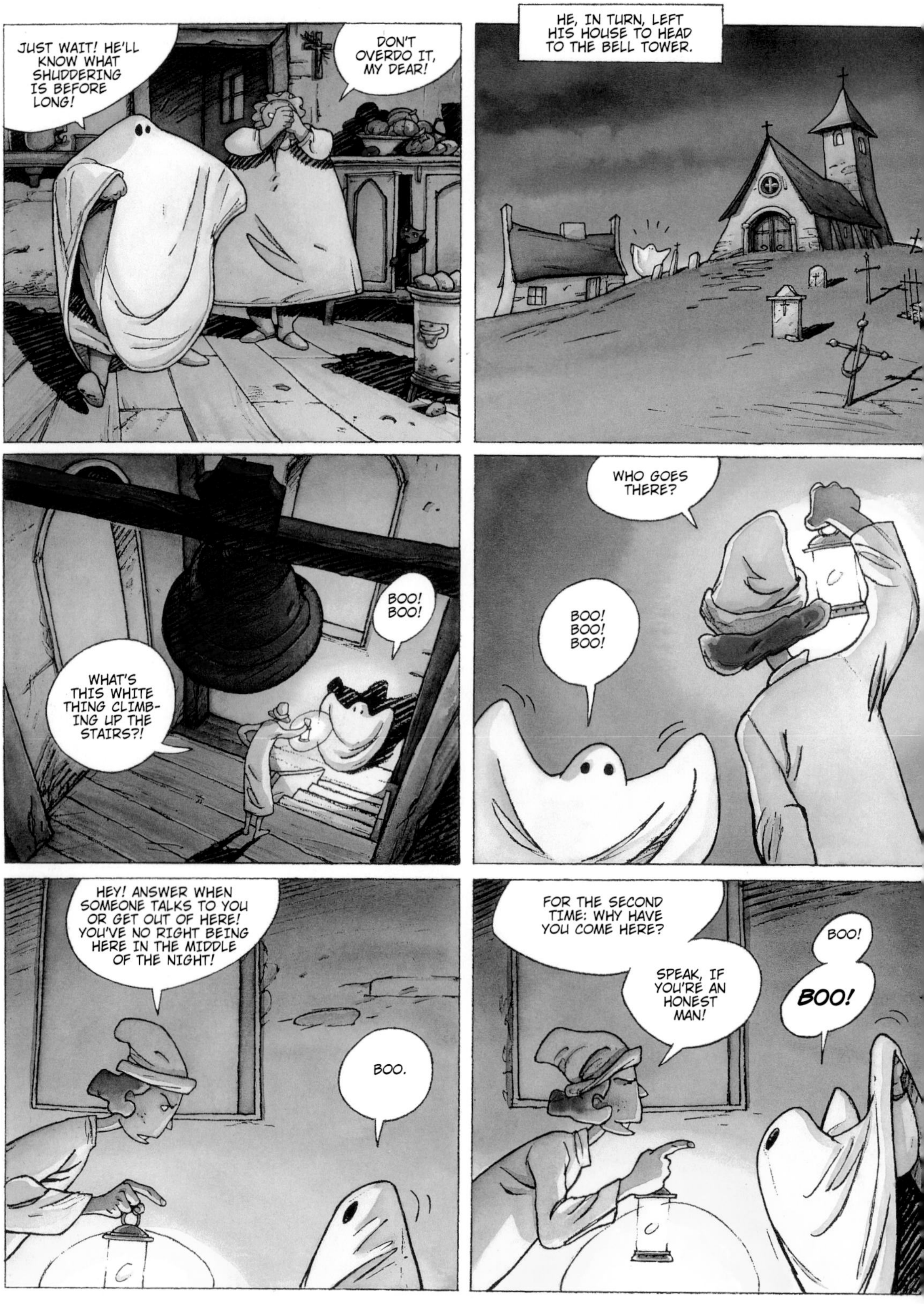
JUST WAIT! HE'LL KNOW WHAT SHUDDERING IS BEFORE LONG!
DON'T OVERDO IT, MY DEAR!
HE, IN TURN, LEFT HIS HOUSE TO HEAD TO THE BELL TOWER.
BOO! BOO!
WHAT'S THIS WHITE THING CLIMBING UP THE STAIRS?!
WHO GOES THERE?
BOO! BOO! BOO!
HEY! ANSWER WHEN SOMEONE TALKS TO YOU OR GET OUT OF HERE! YOU'VE NO RIGHT BEING HERE IN THE MIDDLE OF THE NIGHT!
BOO.
FOR THE SECOND TIME: WHY HAVE YOU COME HERE?
SPEAK, IF YOU'RE AN HONEST MAN!
BOO!
BOO!

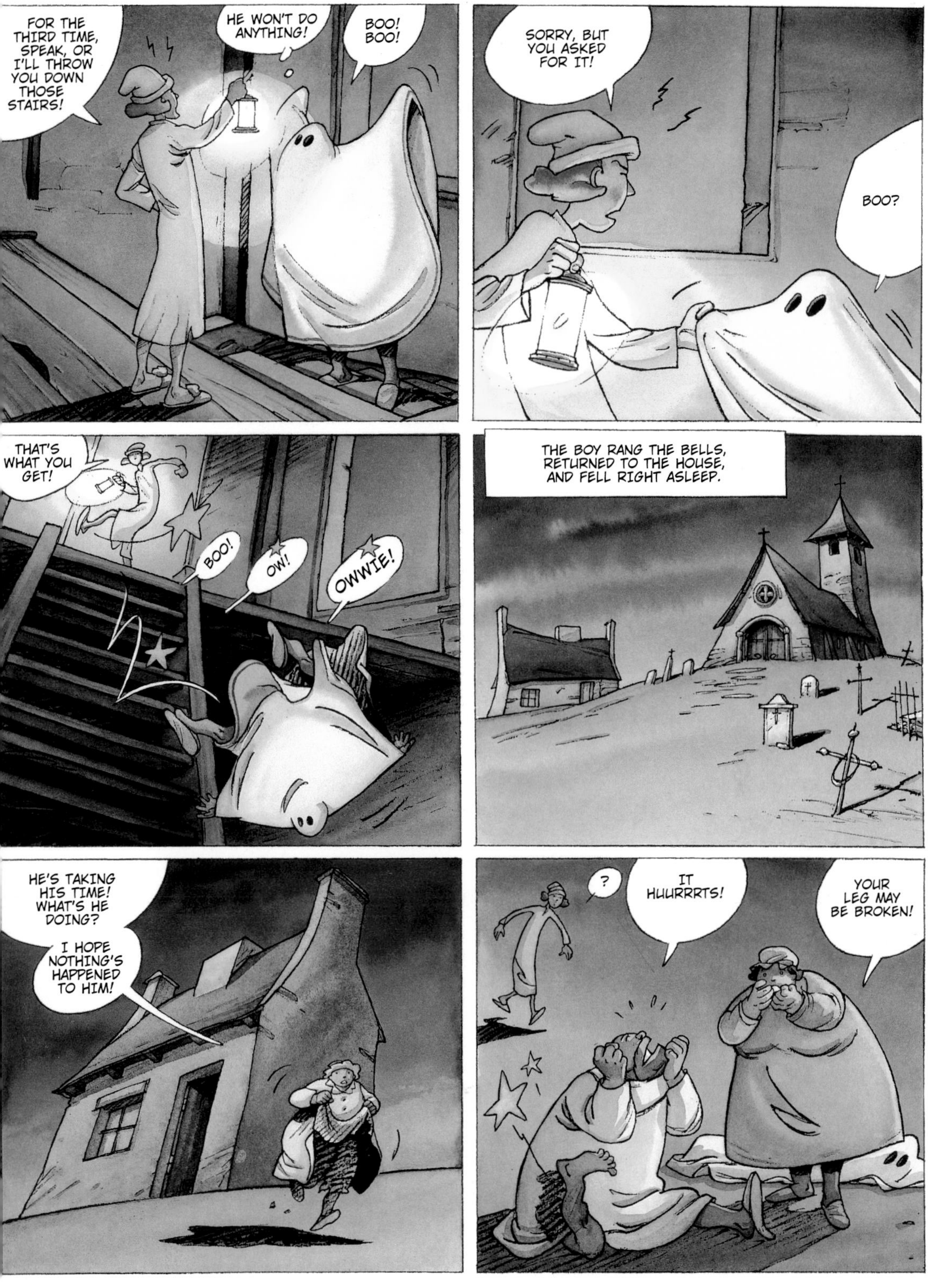

FOR THE THIRD TIME, SPEAK, OR I'LL THROW YOU DOWN THOSE STAIRS!
HE WON'T DO ANYTHING!
BOO! BOO!
SORRY, BUT YOU ASKED FOR IT!
BOO?
THAT'S WHAT YOU GET!
BOO!
OW!
OWWIE!
THE BOY RANG THE BELLS, RETURNED TO THE HOUSE, AND FELL RIGHT ASLEEP.
HE'S TAKING HIS TIME! WHAT'S HE DOING?
I HOPE NOTHING'S HAPPENED TO HIM!
?
IT HUURRRTS!
YOUR LEG MAY BE BROKEN!

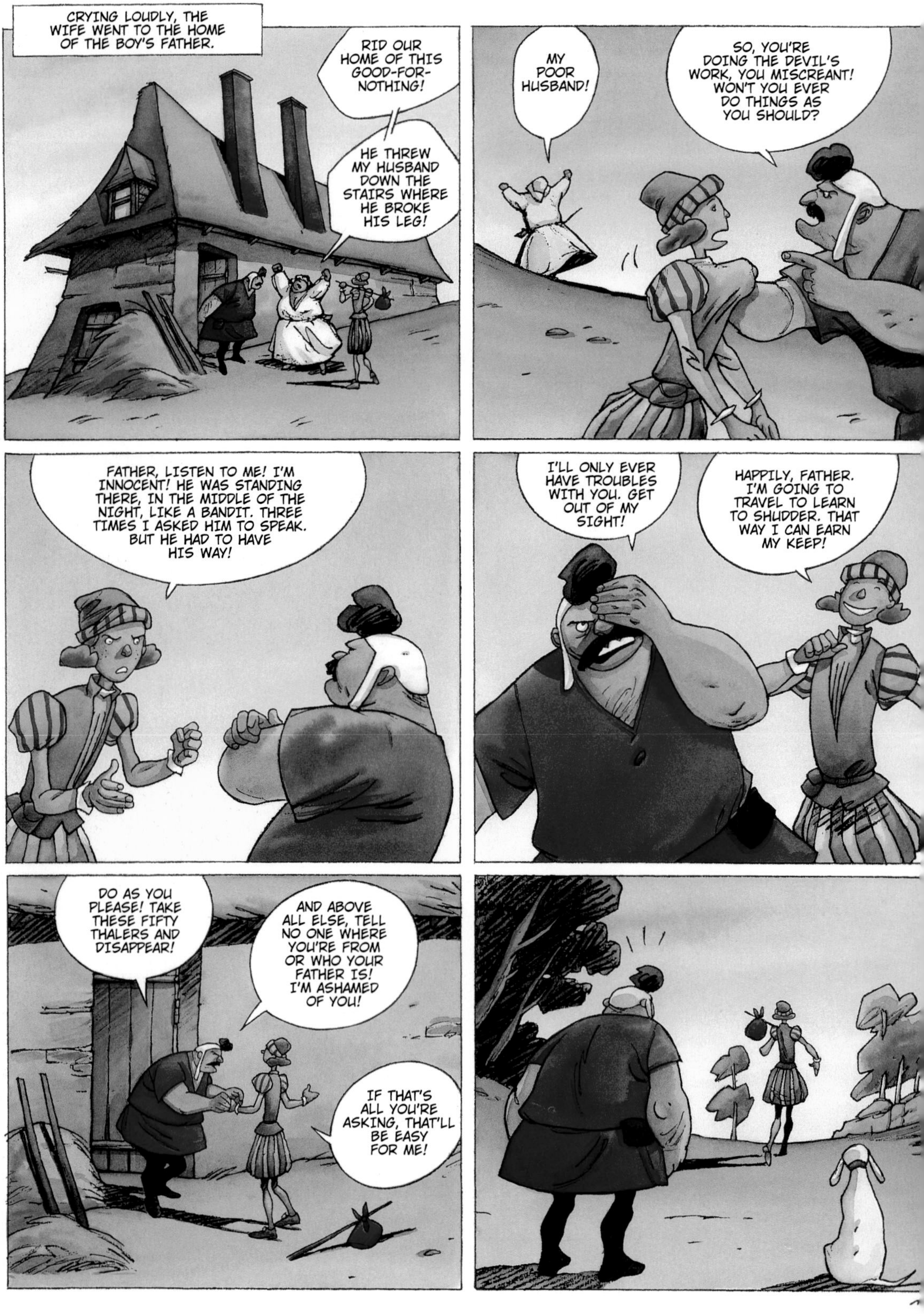
CRYING LOUDLY, THE WIFE WENT TO THE HOME OF THE BOY'S FATHER.
RID OUR HOME OF THIS GOOD-FOR-NOTHING!
HE THREW MY HUSBAND DOWN THE STAIRS WHERE HE BROKE HIS LEG!
MY POOR HUSBAND!
SO, YOU'RE DOING THE DEVIL'S WORK, YOU MISCREANT! WON'T YOU EVER DO THINGS AS YOU SHOULD?
FATHER, LISTEN TO ME! I'M INNOCENT! HE WAS STANDING THERE, IN THE MIDDLE OF THE NIGHT, LIKE A BANDIT. THREE TIMES I ASKED HIM TO SPEAK. BUT HE HAD TO HAVE HIS WAY!
I'LL ONLY EVER HAVE TROUBLES WITH YOU. GET OUT OF MY SIGHT!
HAPPILY, FATHER. I'M GOING TO TRAVEL TO LEARN TO SHUDDER. THAT WAY I CAN EARN MY KEEP!
DO AS YOU PLEASE! TAKE THESE FIFTY THALERS AND DISAPPEAR!
AND ABOVE ALL ELSE, TELL NO ONE WHERE YOU'RE FROM OR WHO YOUR FATHER IS! I'M ASHAMED OF YOU!
IF THAT'S ALL YOU'RE ASKING, THAT'LL BE EASY FOR ME!

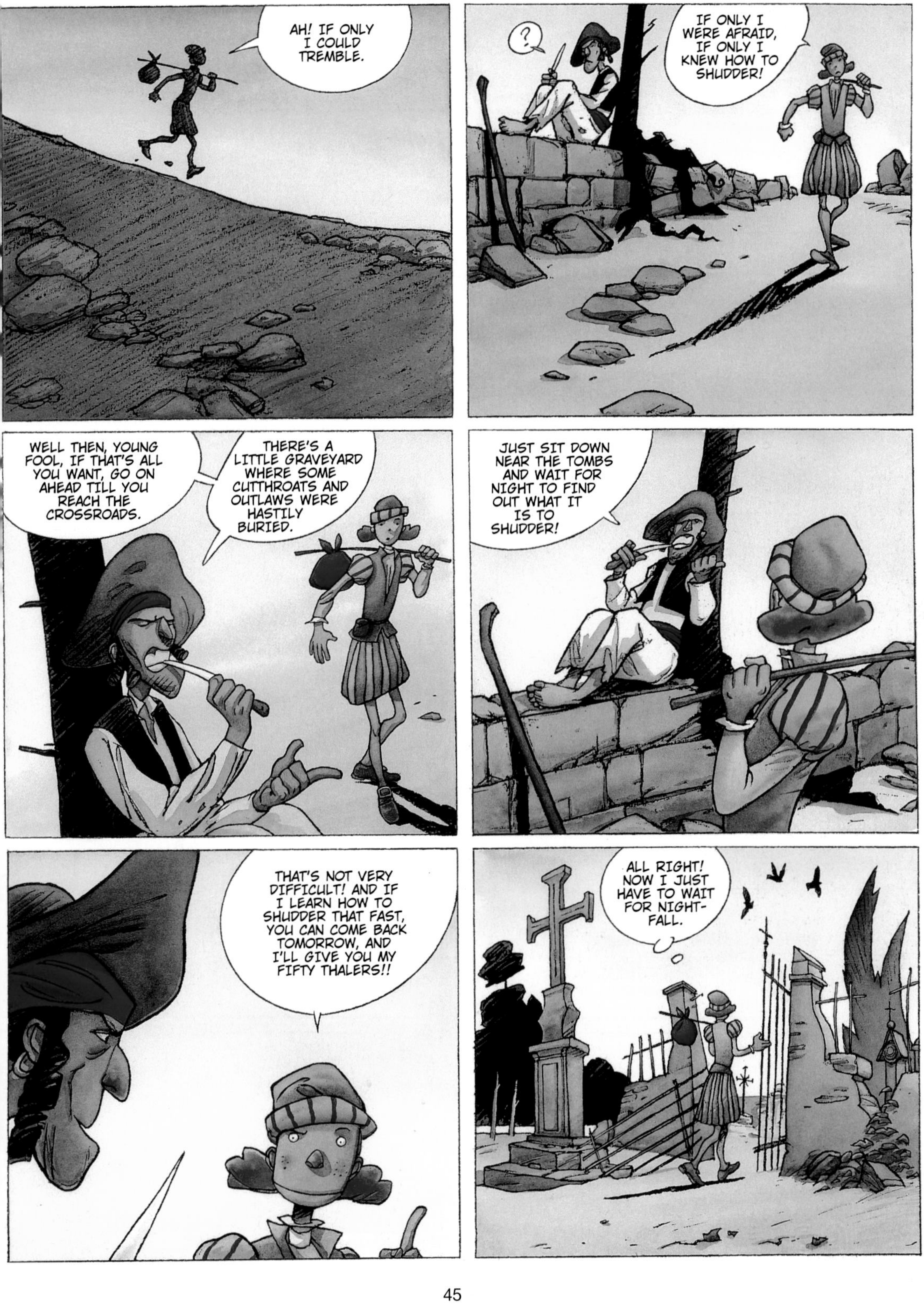
AH! IF ONLY I COULD TREMBLE.
?
IF ONLY I WERE AFRAID, IF ONLY I KNEW HOW TO SHUDDER!
WELL THEN, YOUNG FOOL, IF THAT'S ALL YOU WANT, GO ON AHEAD TILL YOU REACH THE CROSSROADS.
THERE'S A LITTLE GRAVEYARD WHERE SOME CUTTHROATS AND OUTLAWS WERE HASTILY BURIED.
JUST SIT DOWN NEAR THE TOMBS AND WAIT FOR NIGHT TO FIND OUT WHAT IT IS TO SHUDDER!
THAT'S NOT VERY DIFFICULT! AND IF I LEARN HOW TO SHUDDER THAT FAST, YOU CAN COME BACK TOMORROW, AND I'LL GIVE YOU MY FIFTY THALERS!!
ALL RIGHT! NOW I JUST HAVE TO WAIT FOR NIGHT-FALL.

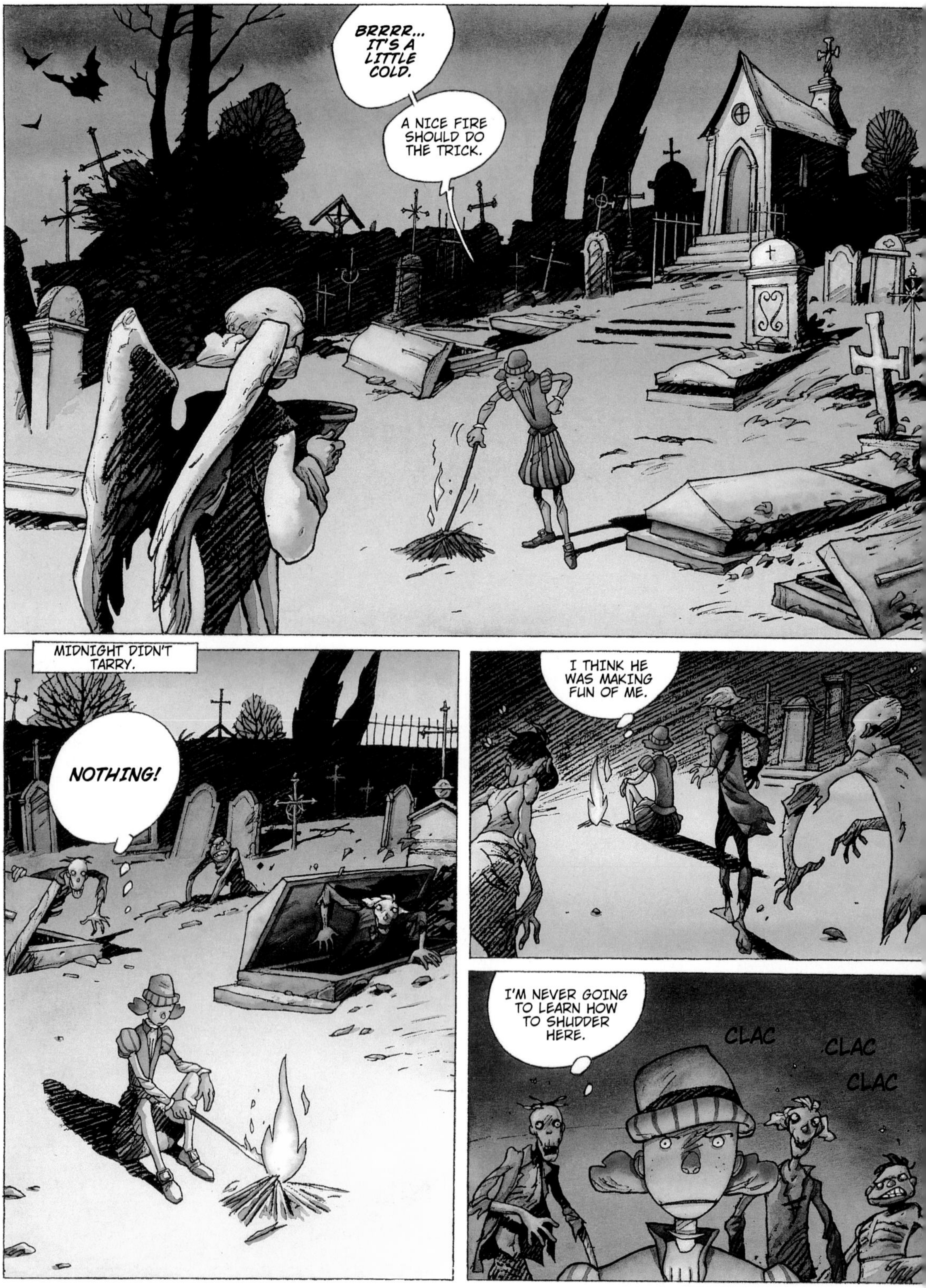
BRRRR... IT'S A LITTLE COLD.
A NICE FIRE SHOULD DO THE TRICK.
MIDNIGHT DIDN'T TARRY.
NOTHING!
I THINK HE WAS MAKING FUN OF ME.
I'M NEVER GOING TO LEARN HOW TO SHUDDER HERE.
CLAC
CLAC
CLAC

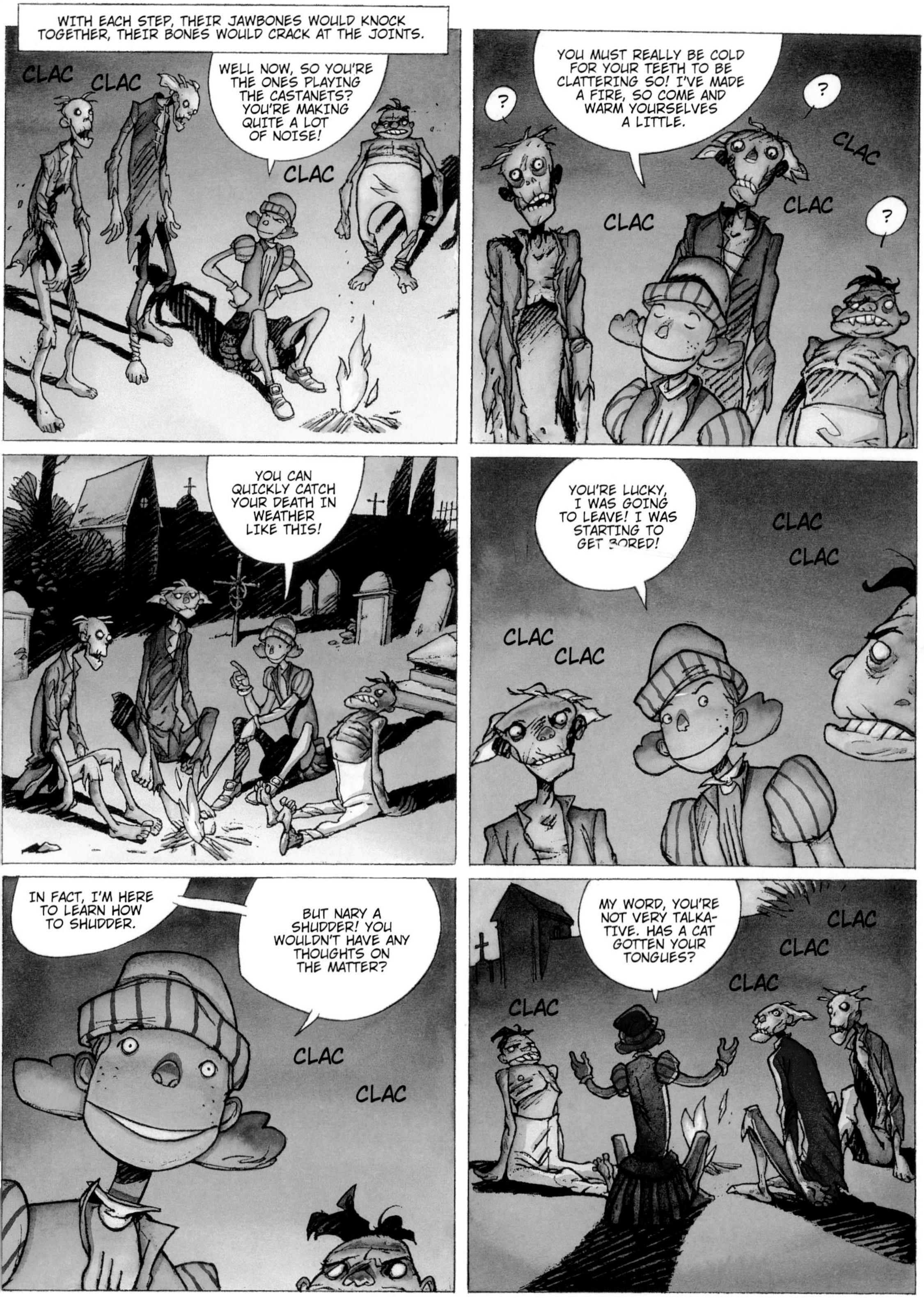
WITH EACH STEP, THEIR JAWBONES WOULD KNOCK TOGETHER, THEIR BONES WOULD CRACK AT THE JOINTS.
CLAC
CLAC
WELL NOW, SO YOU'RE THE ONES PLAYING THE CASTANETS? YOU'RE MAKING QUITE A LOT OF NOISE!
CLAC
YOU MUST REALLY BE COLD FOR YOUR TEETH TO BE CLATTERING SO! I'VE MADE A FIRE, SO COME AND WARM YOURSELVES A LITTLE.
?
?
CLAC
CLAC
CLAC
?
YOU CAN QUICKLY CATCH YOUR DEATH IN WEATHER LIKE THIS!
YOU'RE LUCKY, I WAS GOING TO LEAVE! I WAS STARTING TO GET BORED!
CLAC
CLAC
CLAC
CLAC
IN FACT, I'M HERE TO LEARN HOW TO SHUDDER.
BUT NARY A SHUDDER! YOU WOULDN'T HAVE ANY THOUGHTS ON THE MATTER?
CLAC
CLAC
MY WORD, YOU'RE NOT VERY TALKA-TIVE. HAS A CAT GOTTEN YOUR TONGUES?
CLAC
CLAC
CLAC
CLAC

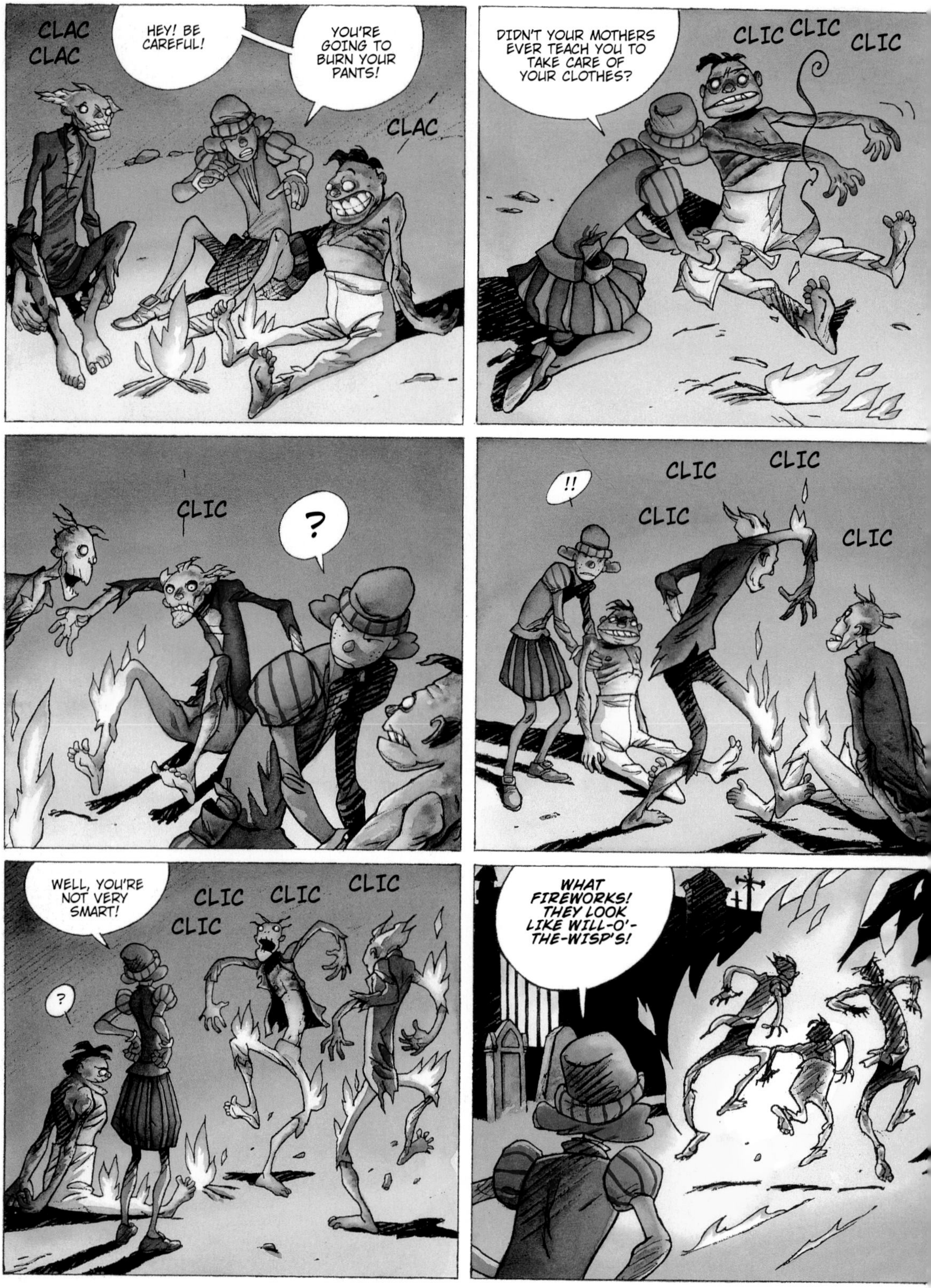
CLAC CLAC
HEY! BE CAREFUL!
YOU'RE GOING TO BURN YOUR PANTS!
CLAC
DIDN'T YOUR MOTHERS EVER TEACH YOU TO TAKE CARE OF YOUR CLOTHES?
CLIC CLIC CLIC
CLIC
?
!!
CLIC
CLIC
CLIC
CLIC
WELL, YOU'RE NOT VERY SMART!
CLIC
CLIC
CLIC
CLIC
?
WHAT FIREWORKS! THEY LOOK LIKE WILL-O'-THE-WISP'S!

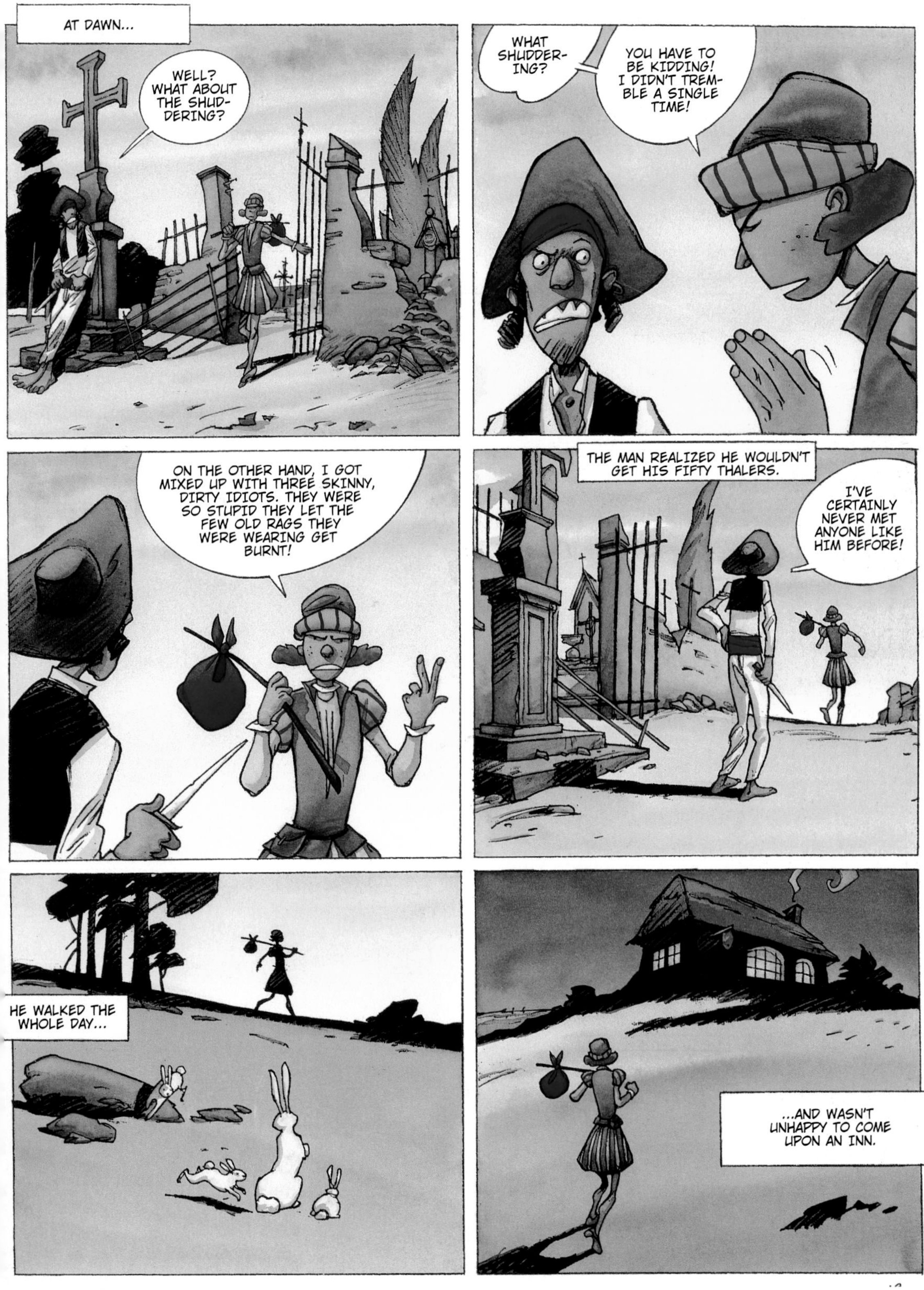
AT DAWN...
WELL? WHAT ABOUT THE SHUDDERING?
WHAT SHUDDERING?
YOU HAVE TO BE KIDDING! I DIDN'T TREMBLE A SINGLE TIME!
ON THE OTHER HAND, I GOT MIXED UP WITH THREE SKINNY, DIRTY IDIOTS. THEY WERE SO STUPID THEY LET THE FEW OLD RAGS THEY WERE WEARING GET BURNT!
THE MAN REALIZED HE WOULDN'T GET HIS FIFTY THALERS.
I'VE CERTAINLY NEVER MET ANYONE LIKE HIM BEFORE!
HE WALKED THE WHOLE DAY...
...AND WASN'T UNHAPPY TO COME UPON AN INN.

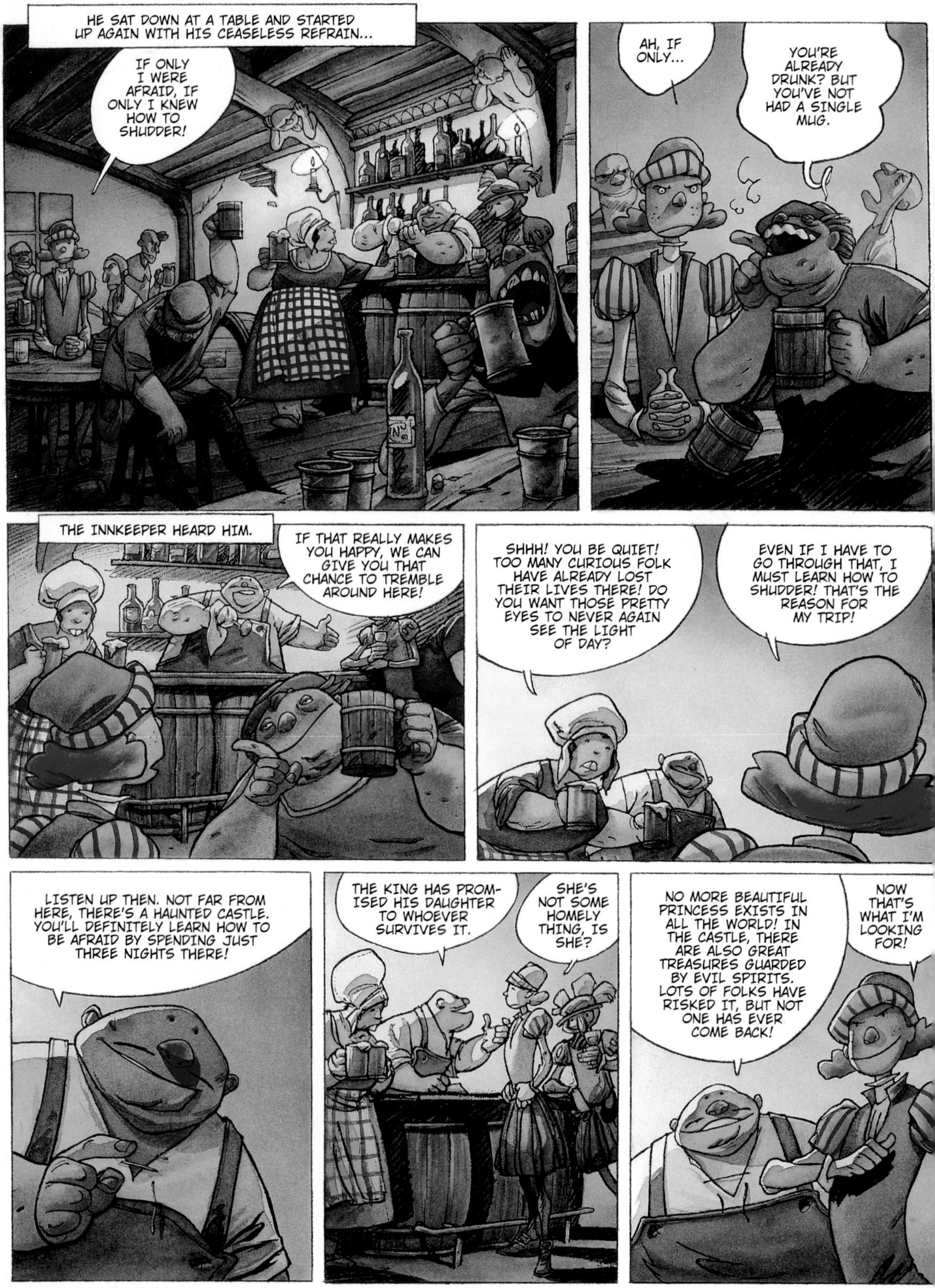
HE SAT DOWN AT A TABLE AND STARTED UP AGAIN WITH HIS CEASELESS REFRAIN...
IF ONLY I WERE AFRAID, IF ONLY I KNEW HOW TO SHUDDER!
AH, IF ONLY...
YOU'RE ALREADY DRUNK? BUT YOU'VE NOT HAD A SINGLE MUG.
THE INNKEEPER HEARD HIM.
IF THAT REALLY MAKES YOU HAPPY, WE CAN GIVE YOU THAT CHANCE TO TREMBLE AROUND HERE!
SHHH! YOU BE QUIET! TOO MANY CURIOUS FOLK HAVE ALREADY LOST THEIR LIVES THERE! DO YOU WANT THOSE PRETTY EYES TO NEVER AGAIN SEE THE LIGHT OF DAY?
EVEN IF I HAVE TO GO THROUGH THAT, I MUST LEARN HOW TO SHUDDER! THAT'S THE REASON FOR MY TRIP!
LISTEN UP THEN. NOT FAR FROM HERE, THERE'S A HAUNTED CASTLE. YOU'LL DEFINITELY LEARN HOW TO BE AFRAID BY SPENDING JUST THREE NIGHTS THERE!
THE KING HAS PROMISED HIS DAUGHTER TO WHOEVER SURVIVES IT.
SHE'S NOT SOME HOMELY THING, IS SHE?
NO MORE BEAUTIFUL PRINCESS EXISTS IN ALL THE WORLD! IN THE CASTLE, THERE ARE ALSO GREAT TREASURES GUARDED BY EVIL SPIRITS. LOTS OF FOLKS HAVE RISKED IT, BUT NOT ONE HAS EVER COME BACK!
NOW THAT'S WHAT I'M LOOKING FOR!

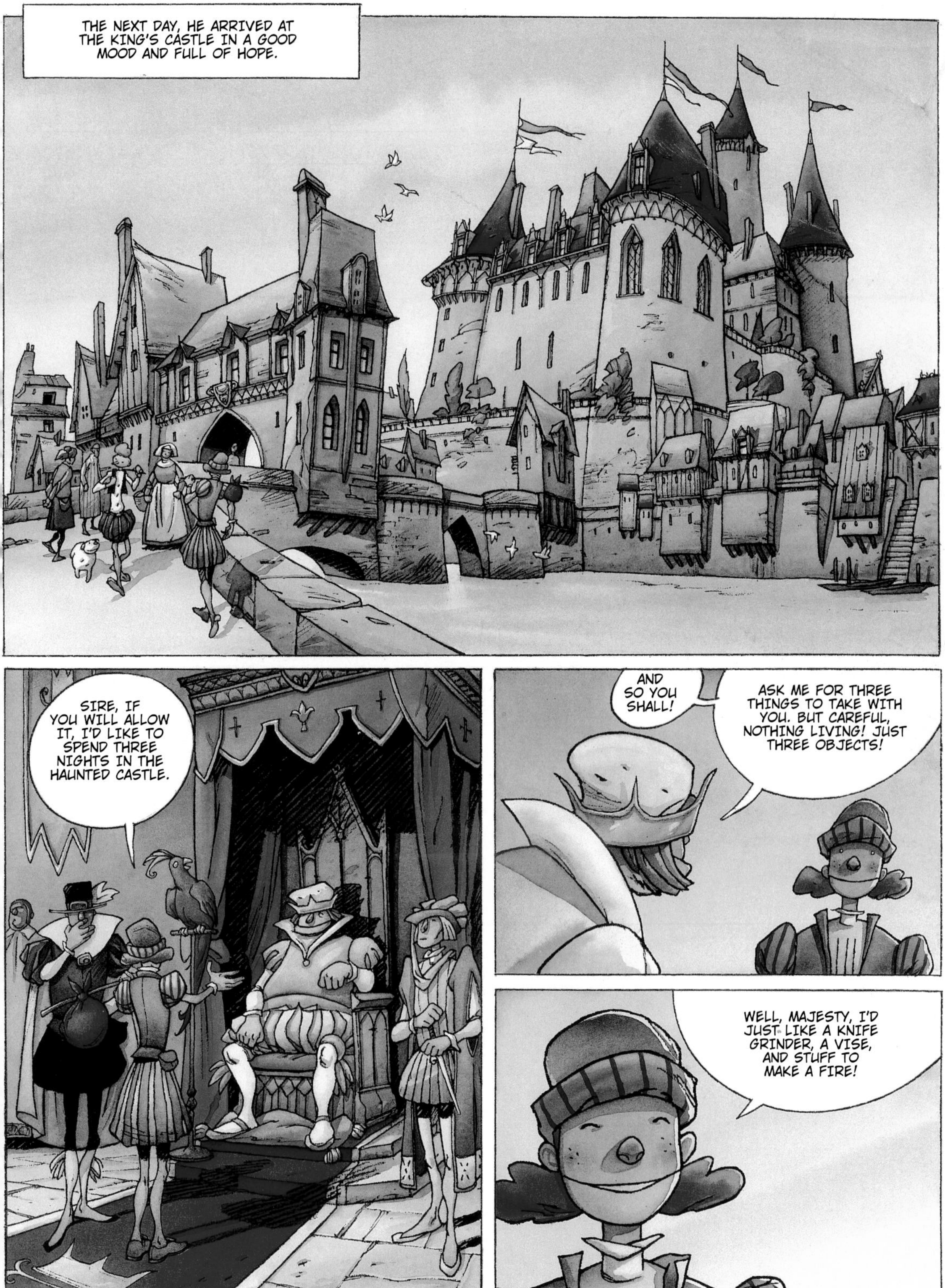
THE NEXT DAY, HE ARRIVED AT THE KING'S CASTLE IN A GOOD MOOD AND FULL OF HOPE.
SIRE, IF YOU WILL ALLOW IT, I'D LIKE TO SPEND THREE NIGHTS IN THE HAUNTED CASTLE.
AND SO YOU SHALL!
ASK ME FOR THREE THINGS TO TAKE WITH YOU. BUT CAREFUL, NOTHING LIVING! JUST THREE OBJECTS!
WELL, MAJESTY, I'D JUST LIKE A KNIFE GRINDER, A VISE, AND STUFF TO MAKE A FIRE!

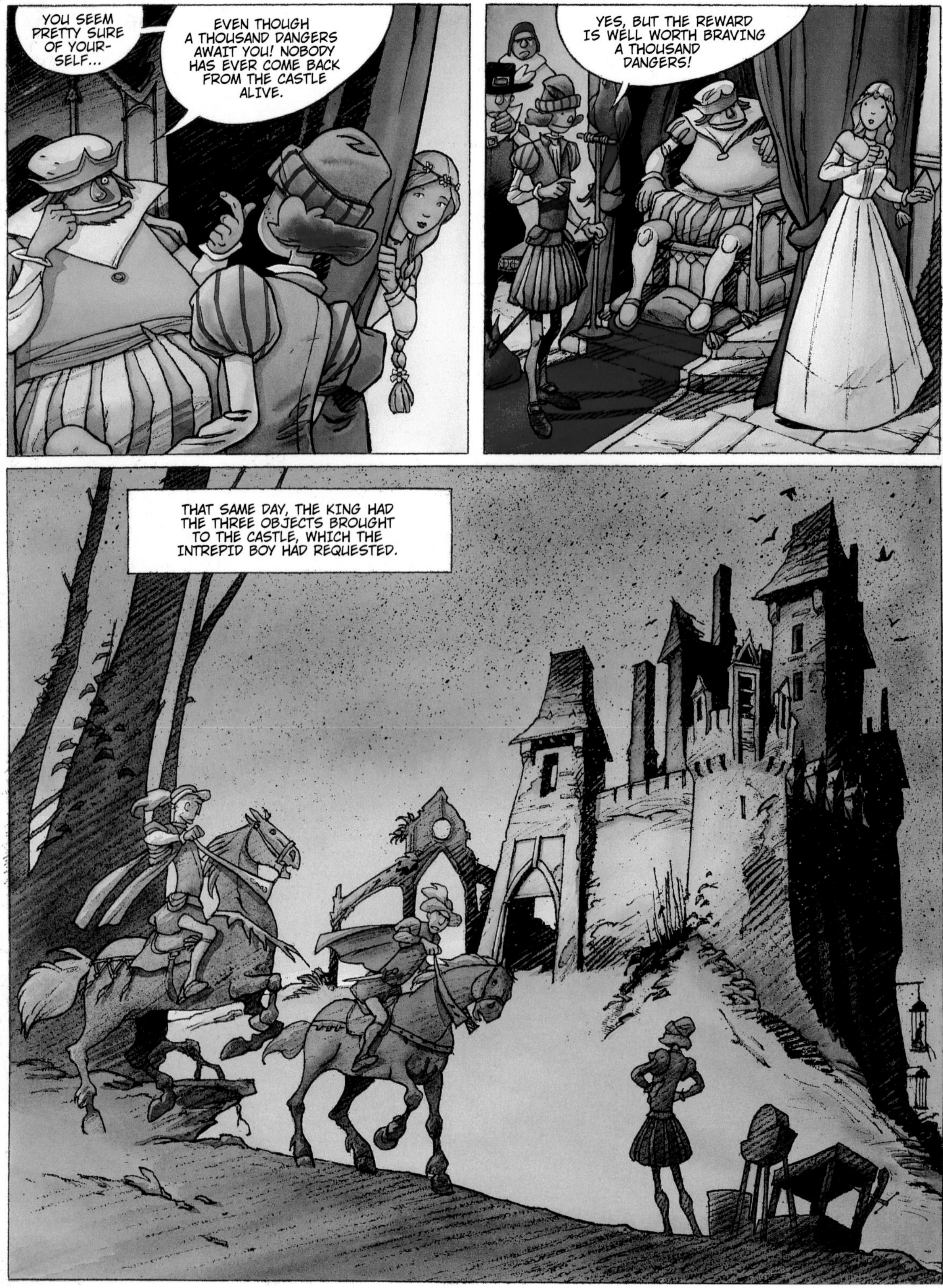
YOU SEEM PRETTY SURE OF YOUR-SELF...
EVEN THOUGH A THOUSAND DANGERS AWAIT YOU! NOBODY HAS EVER COME BACK FROM THE CASTLE ALIVE.
YES, BUT THE REWARD IS WELL WORTH BRAVING A THOUSAND DANGERS!
THAT SAME DAY, THE KING HAD THE THREE OBJECTS BROUGHT TO THE CASTLE, WHICH THE INTREPID BOY HAD REQUESTED.

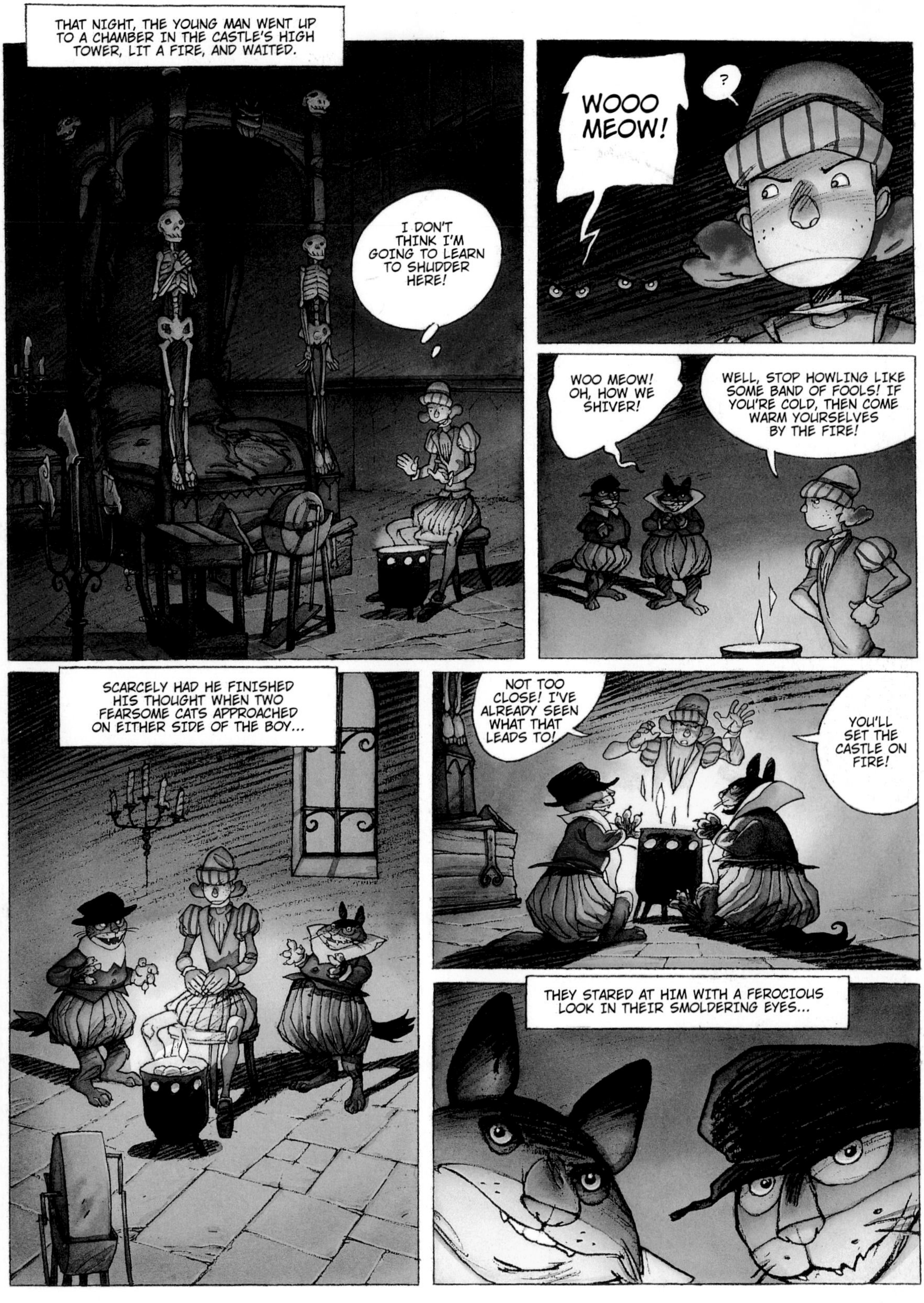
THAT NIGHT, THE YOUNG MAN WENT UP TO A CHAMBER IN THE CASTLE'S HIGH TOWER, LIT A FIRE, AND WAITED.
I DON'T THINK I'M GOING TO LEARN TO SHUDDER HERE!
WOOO MEOW!
?
WOO MEOW! OH, HOW WE SHIVER!
WELL, STOP HOWLING LIKE SOME BAND OF FOOLS! IF YOU'RE COLD, THEN COME WARM YOURSELVES BY THE FIRE!
SCARCELY HAD HE FINISHED HIS THOUGHT WHEN TWO FEARSOME CATS APPROACHED ON EITHER SIDE OF THE BOY...
NOT TOO CLOSE! I'VE ALREADY SEEN WHAT THAT LEADS TO!
YOU'LL SET THE CASTLE ON FIRE!
THEY STARED AT HIM WITH A FEROCIOUS LOOK IN THEIR SMOLDERING EYES...

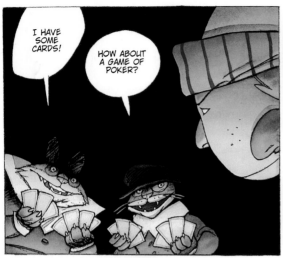

I HAVE SOME CARDS!

HOW ABOUT A GAME OF POKER?

SURE, WHY NOT?

IF WE WIN, THEN YOU'LL BECOME CAT FOOD!

HMM! HOW CLUMSY YOU ARE! YOU CAN'T HOLD YOUR CARDS IN YOUR PAWS!

YOUR CLAWS ARE SO LONG, IT'LL TAKE US ALL NIGHT JUST TO PLAY A SINGLE HAND!

HE GRABBED THEM BY THE SKIN OF THEIR NAPES, PLACED THEM ON THE VICE, AND WEDGED IN THEIR PAWS.

LET ME TAKE CARE OF IT.

HOWL! MEEEEEOOWW!

I'M GOING TO FILE YOUR CLAWS ON MY GRINDER!

LET US OUT OF HERE SO WE CAN GUT YOU!

WHAT'S THAT NOW?

54

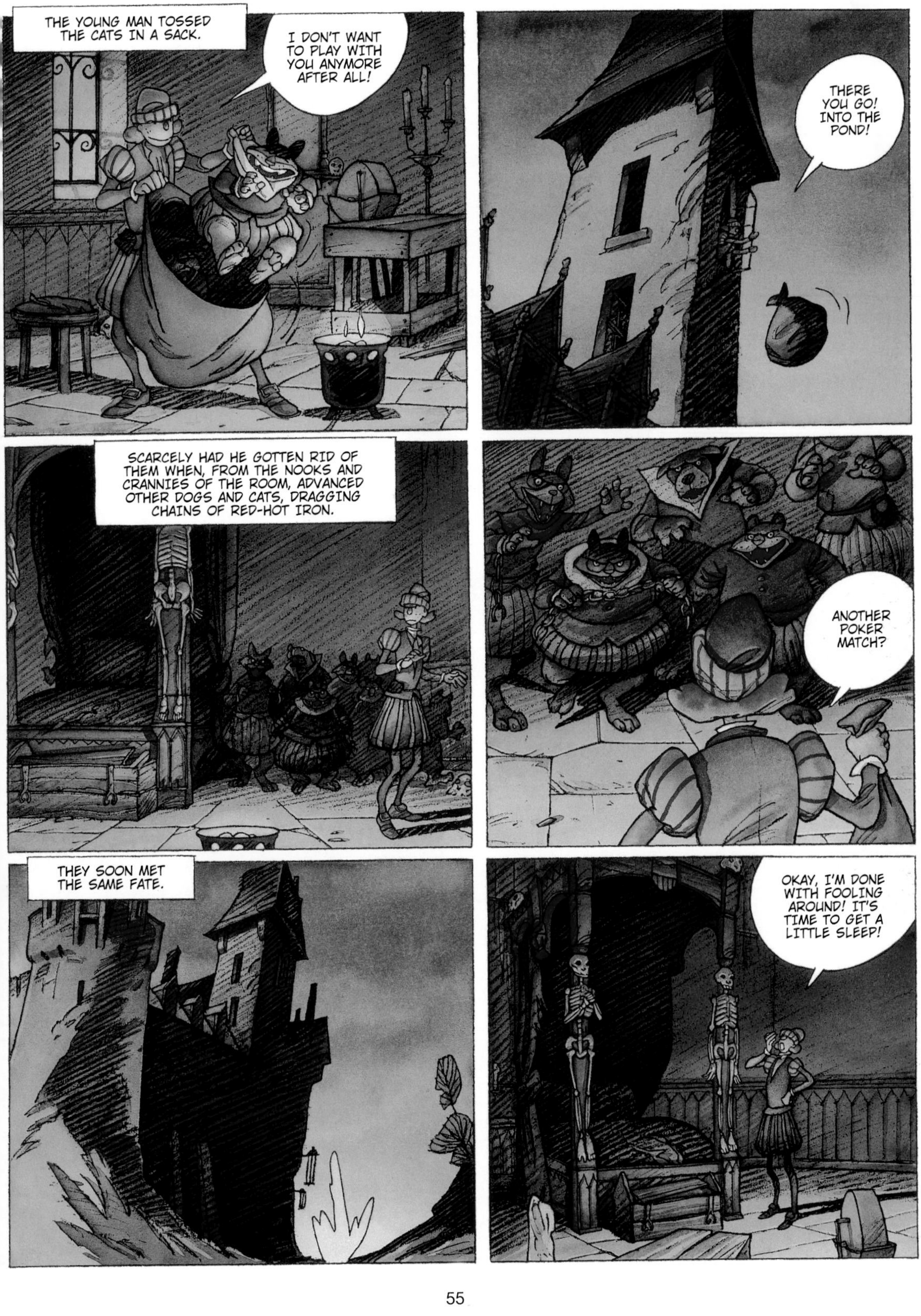
THE YOUNG MAN TOSSED THE CATS IN A SACK.
I DON'T WANT TO PLAY WITH YOU ANYMORE AFTER ALL!
THERE YOU GO! INTO THE POND!
SCARCELY HAD HE GOTTEN RID OF THEM WHEN, FROM THE NOOKS AND CRANNIES OF THE ROOM, ADVANCED OTHER DOGS AND CATS, DRAGGING CHAINS OF RED-HOT IRON.
ANOTHER POKER MATCH?
THEY SOON MET THE SAME FATE.
OKAY, I'M DONE WITH FOOLING AROUND! IT'S TIME TO GET A LITTLE SLEEP!

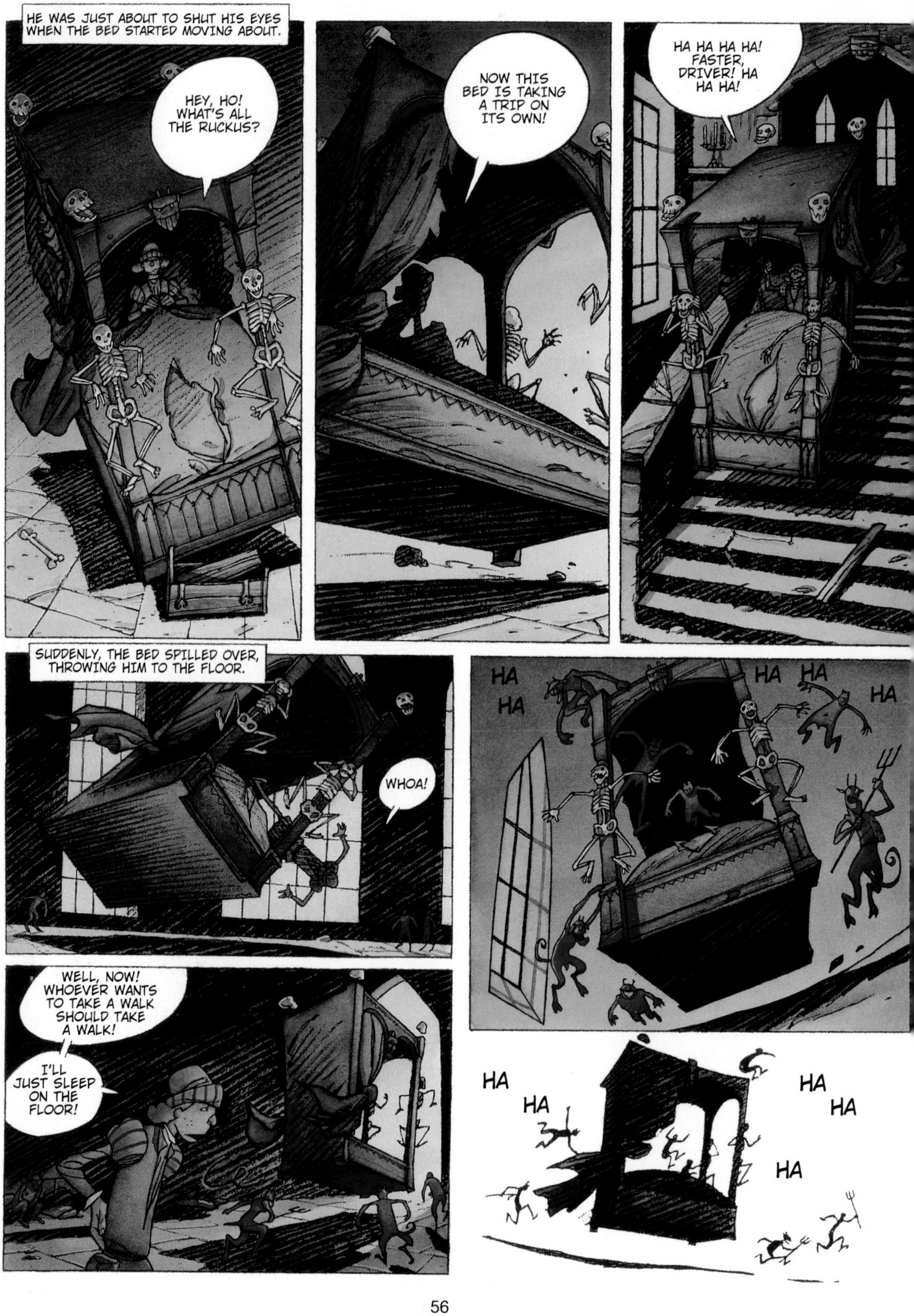
HE WAS JUST ABOUT TO SHUT HIS EYES WHEN THE BED STARTED MOVING ABOUT.
HEY, HO! WHAT'S ALL THE RUCKUS?
NOW THIS BED IS TAKING A TRIP ON ITS OWN!
HA HA HA HA! FASTER, DRIVER! HA HA HA!
SUDDENLY, THE BED SPILLED OVER, THROWING HIM TO THE FLOOR.
WHOA!
HA HA
HA HA HA
WELL, NOW! WHOEVER WANTS TO TAKE A WALK SHOULD TAKE A WALK!
I'LL JUST SLEEP ON THE FLOOR!
HA HA
HA HA
HA

AT DAWN, THE KING CAME TO THE CASTLE.

SEEING THE BOY STRETCHED OUT ON THE FLOOR, THE KING THOUGHT HE WAS DEAD, DEFEATED BY THE GHOSTS.

IT'S TOO BAD, HE SEEMED LIKE SUCH A COURAGEOUS YOUNG MAN...

HEY, NOW! DON'T BURY ME RIGHT AWAY!

?

?

?

HE'S ALIVE!

HALLELUJAH!

AWK!

HOW DID IT GO?

FINE MOSTLY... THAT'S ALREADY ONE NIGHT DOWN.

BUT I'M DISAPPOINTED. I STILL HAVEN'T LEARNED TO SHUDDER!

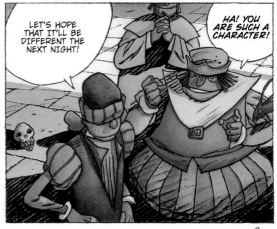

LET'S HOPE THAT IT'LL BE DIFFERENT THE NEXT NIGHT!

HA! YOU ARE SUCH A CHARACTER!

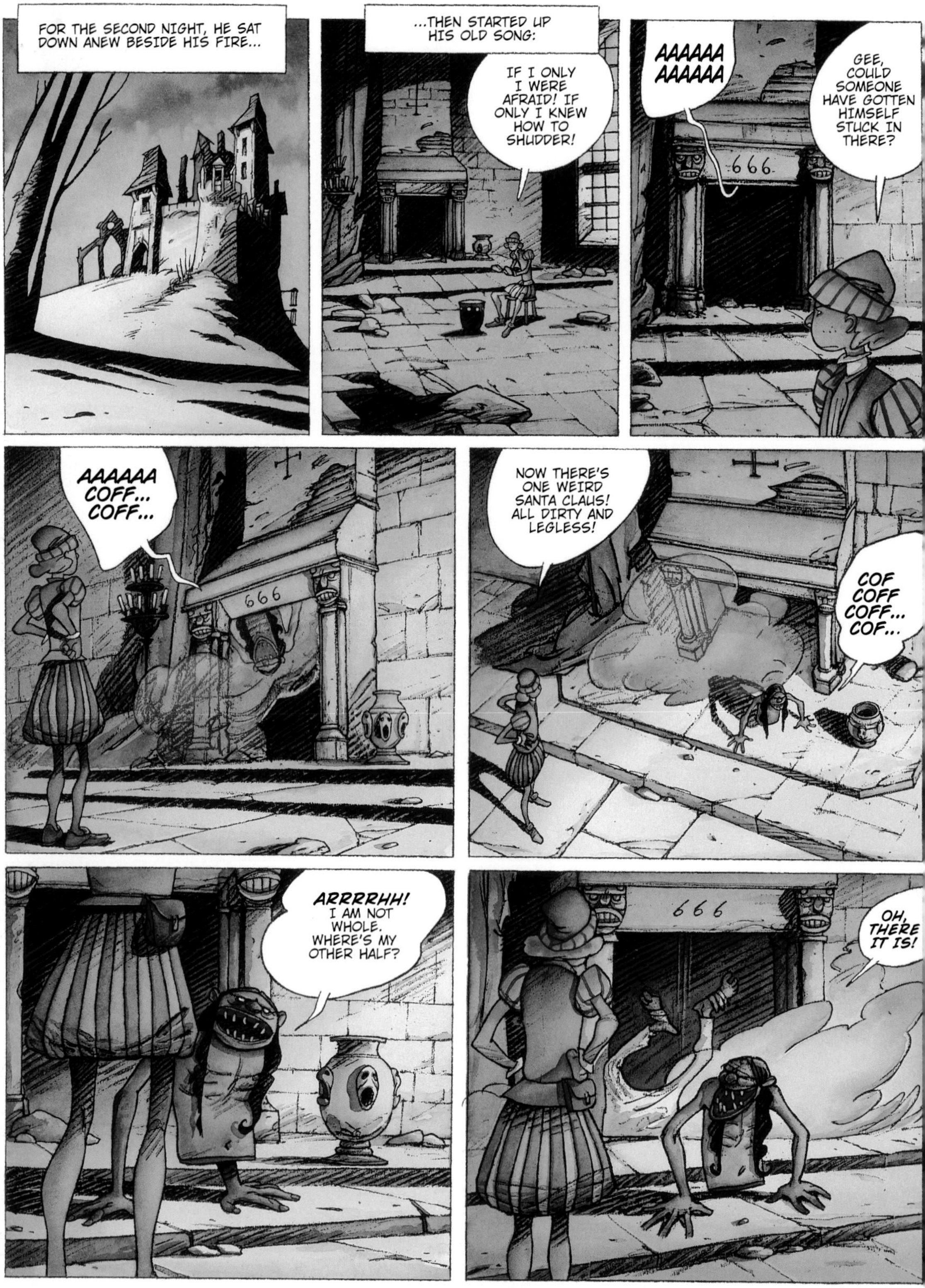

FOR THE SECOND NIGHT, HE SAT DOWN ANEW BESIDE HIS FIRE...
...THEN STARTED UP HIS OLD SONG:
IF I ONLY I WERE AFRAID! IF ONLY I KNEW HOW TO SHUDDER!
AAAAAA AAAAAA
GEE, COULD SOMEONE HAVE GOTTEN HIMSELF STUCK IN THERE?
666
AAAAAA COFF... COFF...
666
NOW THERE'S ONE WEIRD SANTA CLAUS! ALL DIRTY AND LEGLESS!
COF COFF COFF... COF...
ARRRRHH! I AM NOT WHOLE. WHERE'S MY OTHER HALF?
666
OH, THERE IT IS!

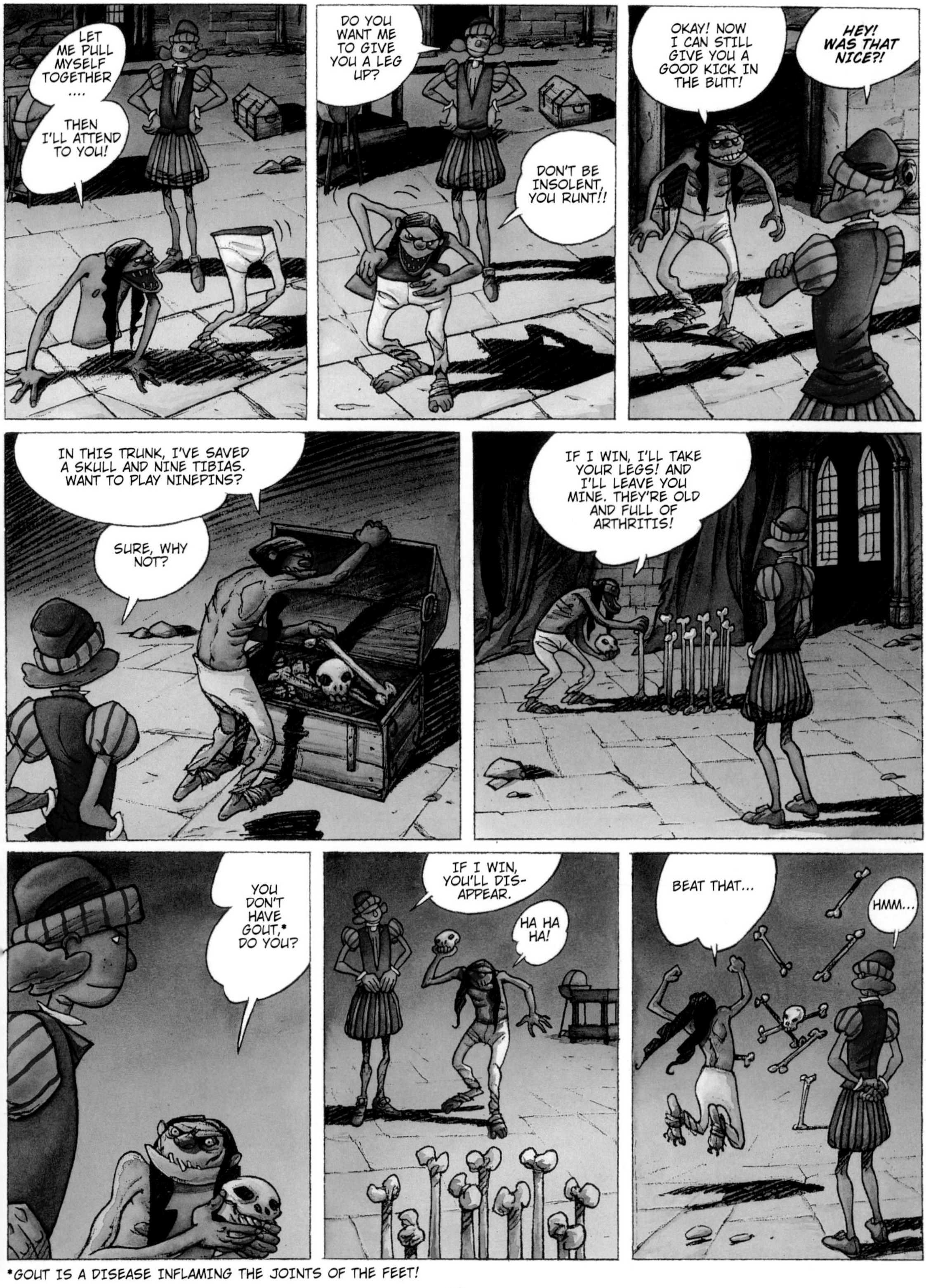
LET ME PULL MYSELF TOGETHER ....
THEN I'LL ATTEND TO YOU!
DO YOU WANT ME TO GIVE YOU A LEG UP?
DON'T BE INSOLENT, YOU RUNT!!
OKAY! NOW I CAN STILL GIVE YOU A GOOD KICK IN THE BUTT!
HEY! WAS THAT NICE?!
IN THIS TRUNK, I'VE SAVED A SKULL AND NINE TIBIAS. WANT TO PLAY NINEPINS?
SURE, WHY NOT?
IF I WIN, I'LL TAKE YOUR LEGS! AND I'LL LEAVE YOU MINE. THEY'RE OLD AND FULL OF ARTHRITIS!
YOU DON'T HAVE GOUT,* DO YOU?
IF I WIN, YOU'LL DIS-APPEAR.
HA HA HA!
BEAT THAT...
HMM...

*GOUT IS A DISEASE INFLAMING THE JOINTS OF THE FEET!

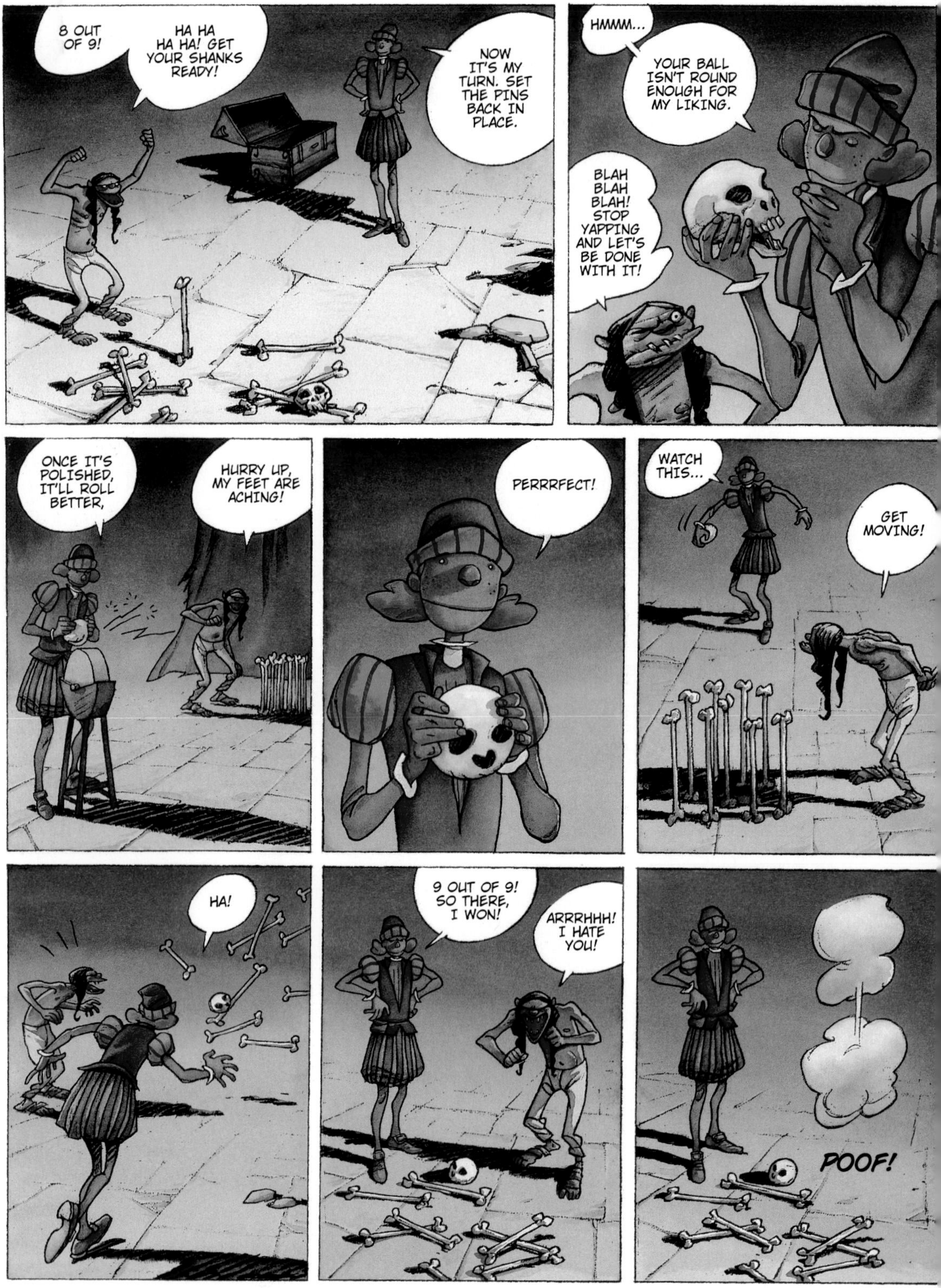
8 OUT OF 9!
HA HA HA HA! GET YOUR SHANKS READY!
NOW IT'S MY TURN. SET THE PINS BACK IN PLACE.
HMMM...
YOUR BALL ISN'T ROUND ENOUGH FOR MY LIKING.
BLAH BLAH BLAH! STOP YAPPING AND LET'S BE DONE WITH IT!
ONCE IT'S POLISHED, IT'LL ROLL BETTER,
HURRY UP, MY FEET ARE ACHING!
PERRRFECT!
WATCH THIS...
GET MOVING!
HA!
9 OUT OF 9! SO THERE, I WON!
ARRRHHH! I HATE YOU!
POOF!

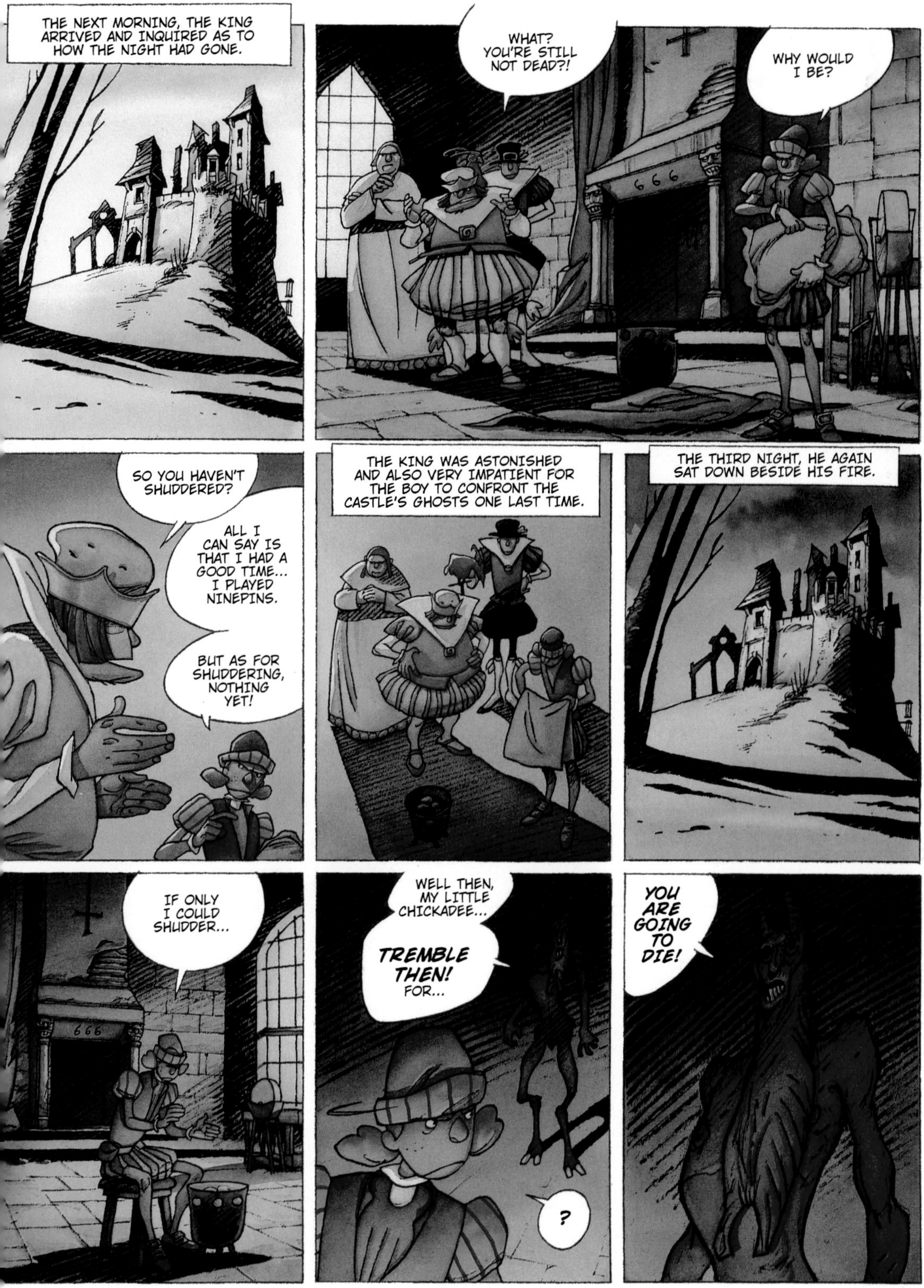
THE NEXT MORNING, THE KING ARRIVED AND INQUIRED AS TO HOW THE NIGHT HAD GONE.
WHAT? YOU'RE STILL NOT DEAD?!
WHY WOULD I BE?
SO YOU HAVEN'T SHUDDERED?
ALL I CAN SAY IS THAT I HAD A GOOD TIME... I PLAYED NINEPINS.
BUT AS FOR SHUDDERING, NOTHING YET!
THE KING WAS ASTONISHED AND ALSO VERY IMPATIENT FOR THE BOY TO CONFRONT THE CASTLE'S GHOSTS ONE LAST TIME.
THE THIRD NIGHT, HE AGAIN SAT DOWN BESIDE HIS FIRE.
IF ONLY I COULD SHUDDER...
666
WELL THEN, MY LITTLE CHICKADEE...
TREMBLE THEN! FOR...
?
YOU ARE GOING TO DIE!

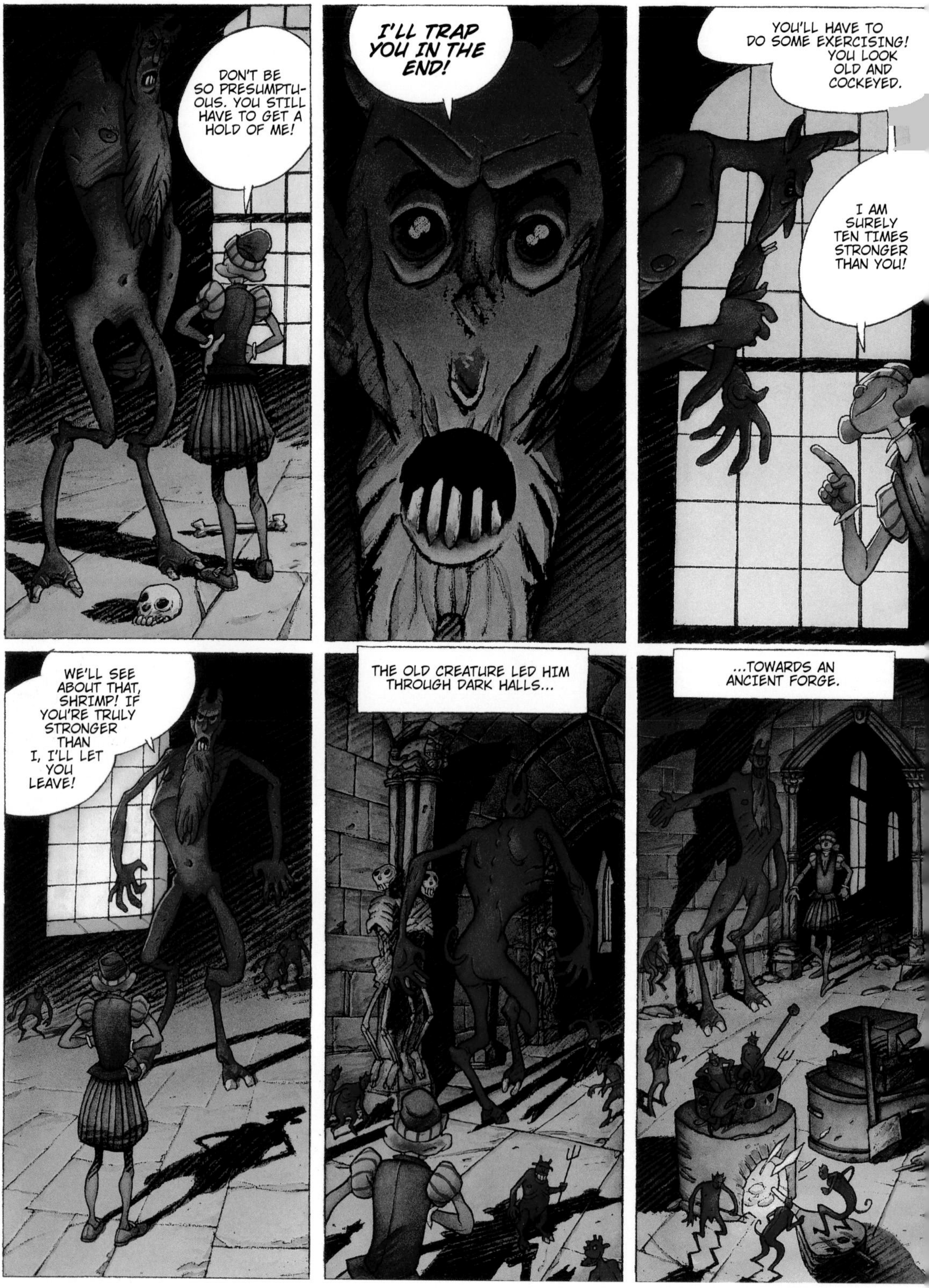
DON'T BE SO PRESUMPTU-OUS. YOU STILL HAVE TO GET A HOLD OF ME!
I'LL TRAP YOU IN THE END!
YOU'LL HAVE TO DO SOME EXERCISING! YOU LOOK OLD AND COCKEYED.
I AM SURELY TEN TIMES STRONGER THAN YOU!
WE'LL SEE ABOUT THAT, SHRIMP! IF YOU'RE TRULY STRONGER THAN I, I'LL LET YOU LEAVE!
THE OLD CREATURE LED HIM THROUGH DARK HALLS...
...TOWARDS AN ANCIENT FORGE.

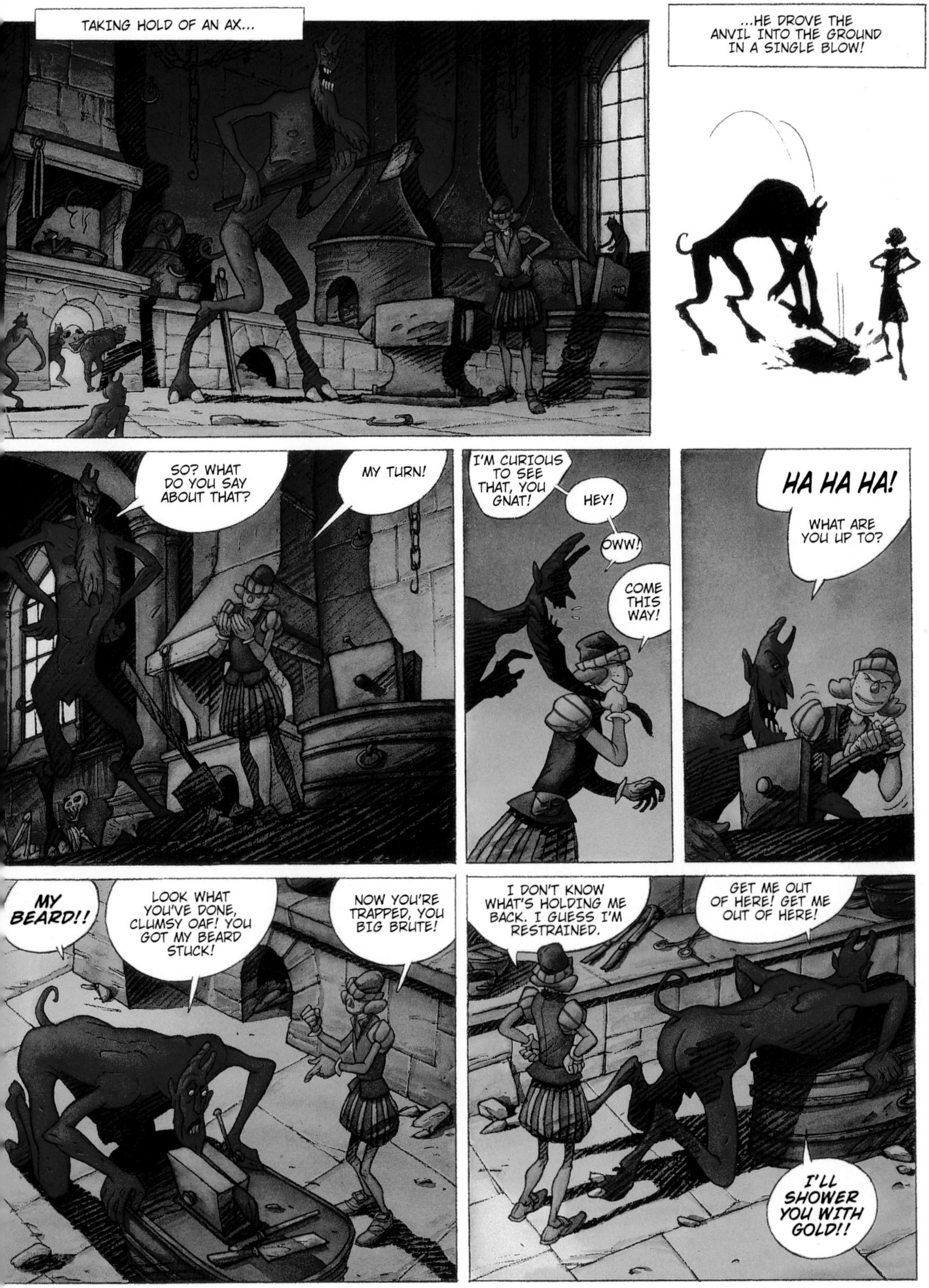
TAKING HOLD OF AN AX...
...HE DROVE THE ANVIL INTO THE GROUND IN A SINGLE BLOW!
SO? WHAT DO YOU SAY ABOUT THAT?
MY TURN!
I'M CURIOUS TO SEE THAT, YOU GNAT!
HEY!
OWW!
COME THIS WAY!
HA HA HA!
WHAT ARE YOU UP TO?
MY BEARD!!
LOOK WHAT YOU'VE DONE, CLUMSY OAF! YOU GOT MY BEARD STUCK!
NOW YOU'RE TRAPPED, YOU BIG BRUTE!
I DON'T KNOW WHAT'S HOLDING ME BACK. I GUESS I'M RESTRAINED.
GET ME OUT OF HERE! GET ME OUT OF HERE!
I'LL SHOWER YOU WITH GOLD!!

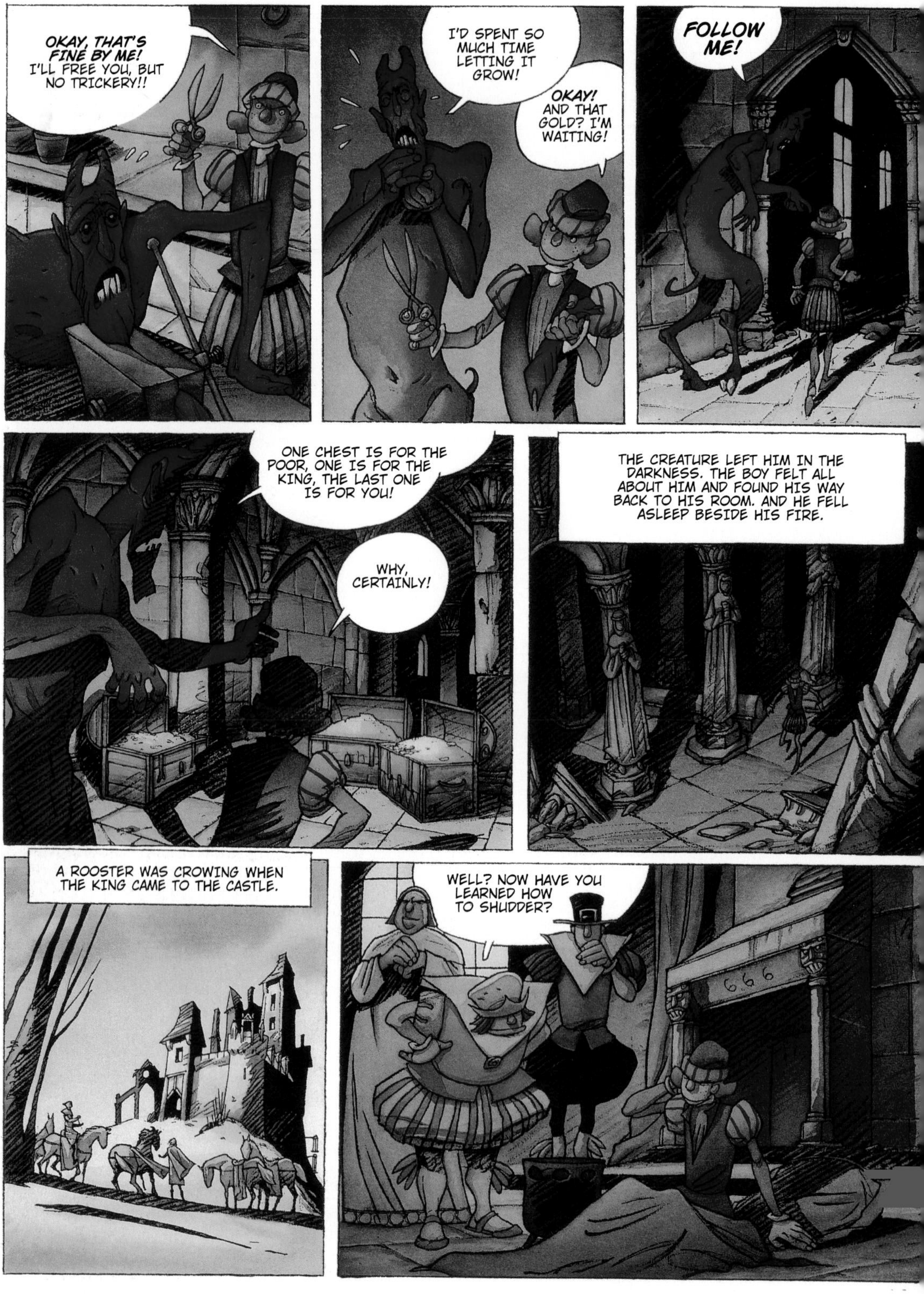
OKAY, THAT'S FINE BY ME! I'LL FREE YOU, BUT NO TRICKERY!!
I'D SPENT SO MUCH TIME LETTING IT GROW!
OKAY! AND THAT GOLD? I'M WAITING!
FOLLOW ME!
ONE CHEST IS FOR THE POOR, ONE IS FOR THE KING, THE LAST ONE IS FOR YOU!
WHY, CERTAINLY!
THE CREATURE LEFT HIM IN THE DARKNESS. THE BOY FELT ALL ABOUT HIM AND FOUND HIS WAY BACK TO HIS ROOM. AND HE FELL ASLEEP BESIDE HIS FIRE.
A ROOSTER WAS CROWING WHEN THE KING CAME TO THE CASTLE.
WELL? NOW HAVE YOU LEARNED HOW TO SHUDDER?
666

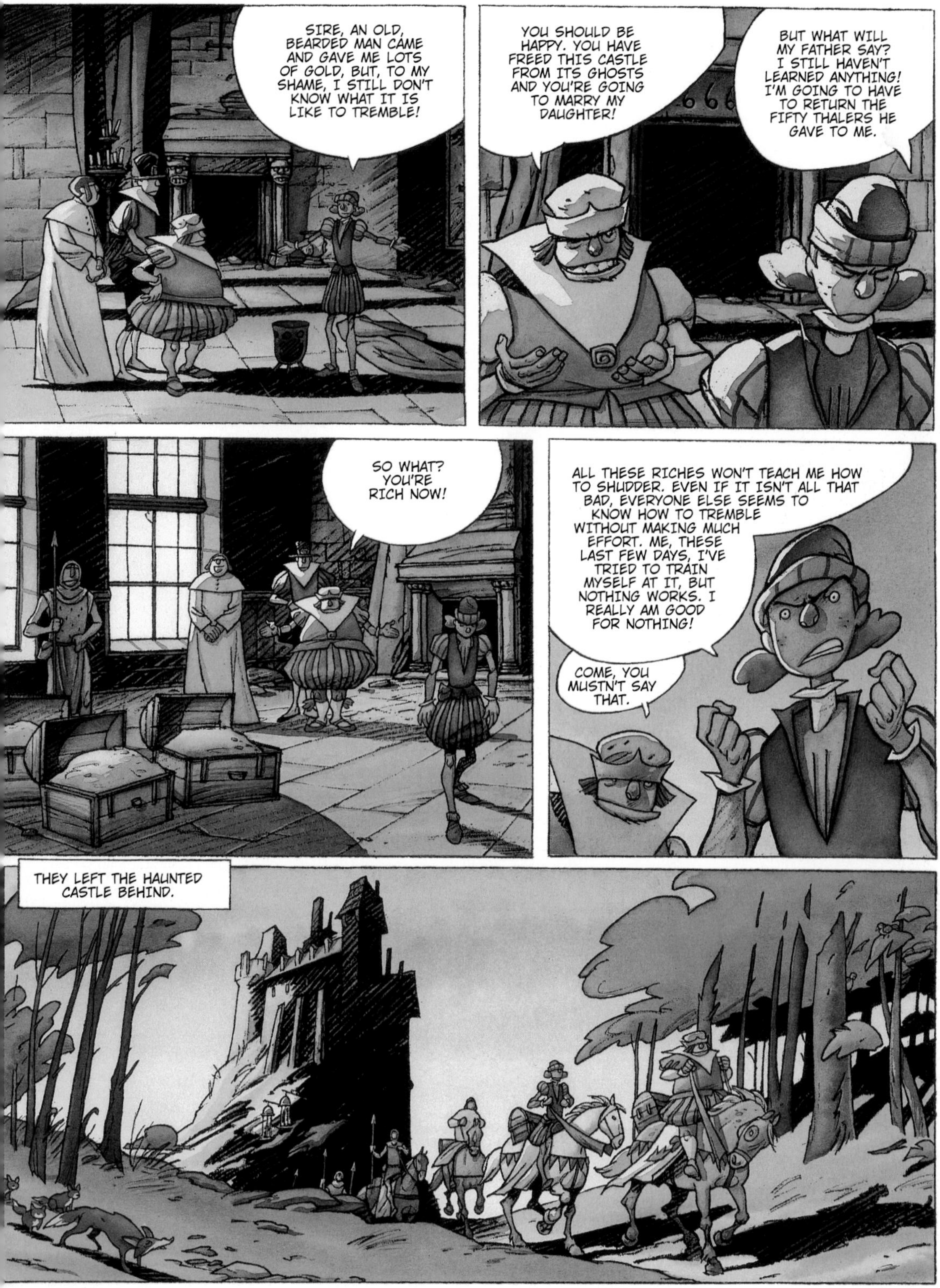
SIRE, AN OLD, BEARDED MAN CAME AND GAVE ME LOTS OF GOLD, BUT, TO MY SHAME, I STILL DON'T KNOW WHAT IT IS LIKE TO TREMBLE!
YOU SHOULD BE HAPPY. YOU HAVE FREED THIS CASTLE FROM ITS GHOSTS AND YOU'RE GOING TO MARRY MY DAUGHTER!
BUT WHAT WILL MY FATHER SAY? I STILL HAVEN'T LEARNED ANYTHING! I'M GOING TO HAVE TO RETURN THE FIFTY THALERS HE GAVE TO ME.
SO WHAT? YOU'RE RICH NOW!
ALL THESE RICHES WON'T TEACH ME HOW TO SHUDDER. EVEN IF IT ISN'T ALL THAT BAD, EVERYONE ELSE SEEMS TO KNOW HOW TO TREMBLE WITHOUT MAKING MUCH EFFORT. ME, THESE LAST FEW DAYS, I'VE TRIED TO TRAIN MYSELF AT IT, BUT NOTHING WORKS. I REALLY AM GOOD FOR NOTHING!
COME, YOU MUSTN'T SAY THAT.
THEY LEFT THE HAUNTED CASTLE BEHIND.

SOON, BELLS WERE RINGING, AND THE WEDDING WAS CELEBRATED.

BUT THE YOUNG KING, ALTHOUGH HE LOVED HIS WIFE AND WAS AS HAPPY AS ONE COULD BE, STILL DRONED ON:

AH! IF ONLY I COULD TREMBLE! IF ONLY I KNEW HOW TO SHUDDER!

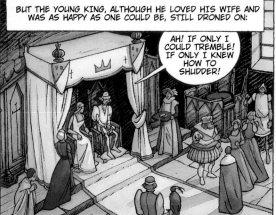

...WHICH ENDED UP EXASPERATING HER MAJESTY.

JUST WAIT, MY QUEEN, I KNOW A GOOD WAY TO GIVE HIM A JOLT!!

THEY WENT INTO THE GARDEN WHERE A SMALL STREAM FLOWED AND THEY FILLED A BUCKET WITH ELECTRIC EELS.

YEEOW!

WE'LL GET A LAUGH WITH THIS!!

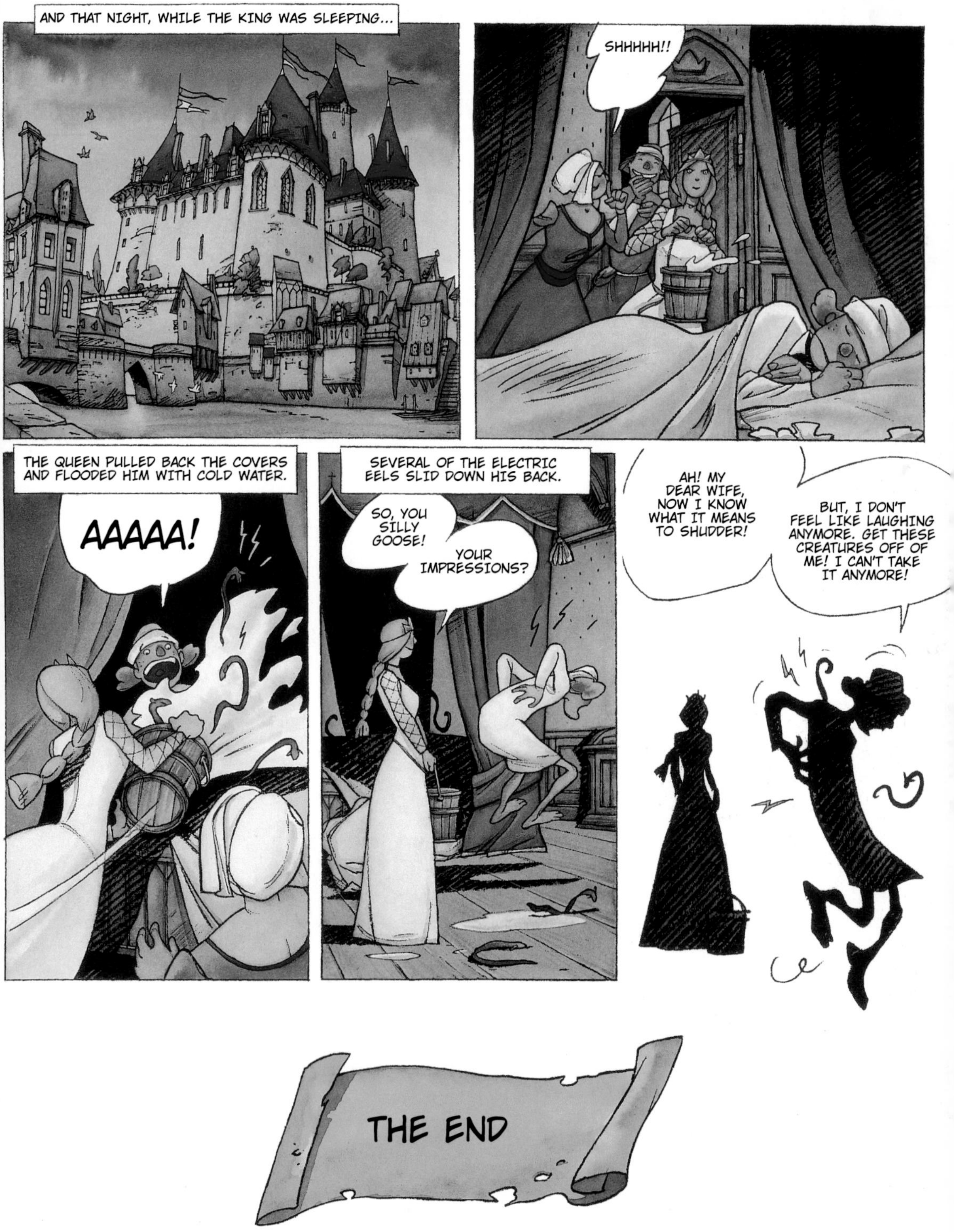
AND THAT NIGHT, WHILE THE KING WAS SLEEPING...
SHHHHH!!
THE QUEEN PULLED BACK THE COVERS AND FLOODED HIM WITH COLD WATER.
AAAAA!
SEVERAL OF THE ELECTRIC EELS SLID DOWN HIS BACK.
SO, YOU SILLY GOOSE!
YOUR IMPRESSIONS?
AH! MY DEAR WIFE, NOW I KNOW WHAT IT MEANS TO SHUDDER!
BUT, I DON'T FEEL LIKE LAUGHING ANYMORE. GET THESE CREATURES OFF OF ME! I CAN'T TAKE IT ANYMORE!
THE END

THE DEVIL
AND THE
THREE GOLDEN HAIRS

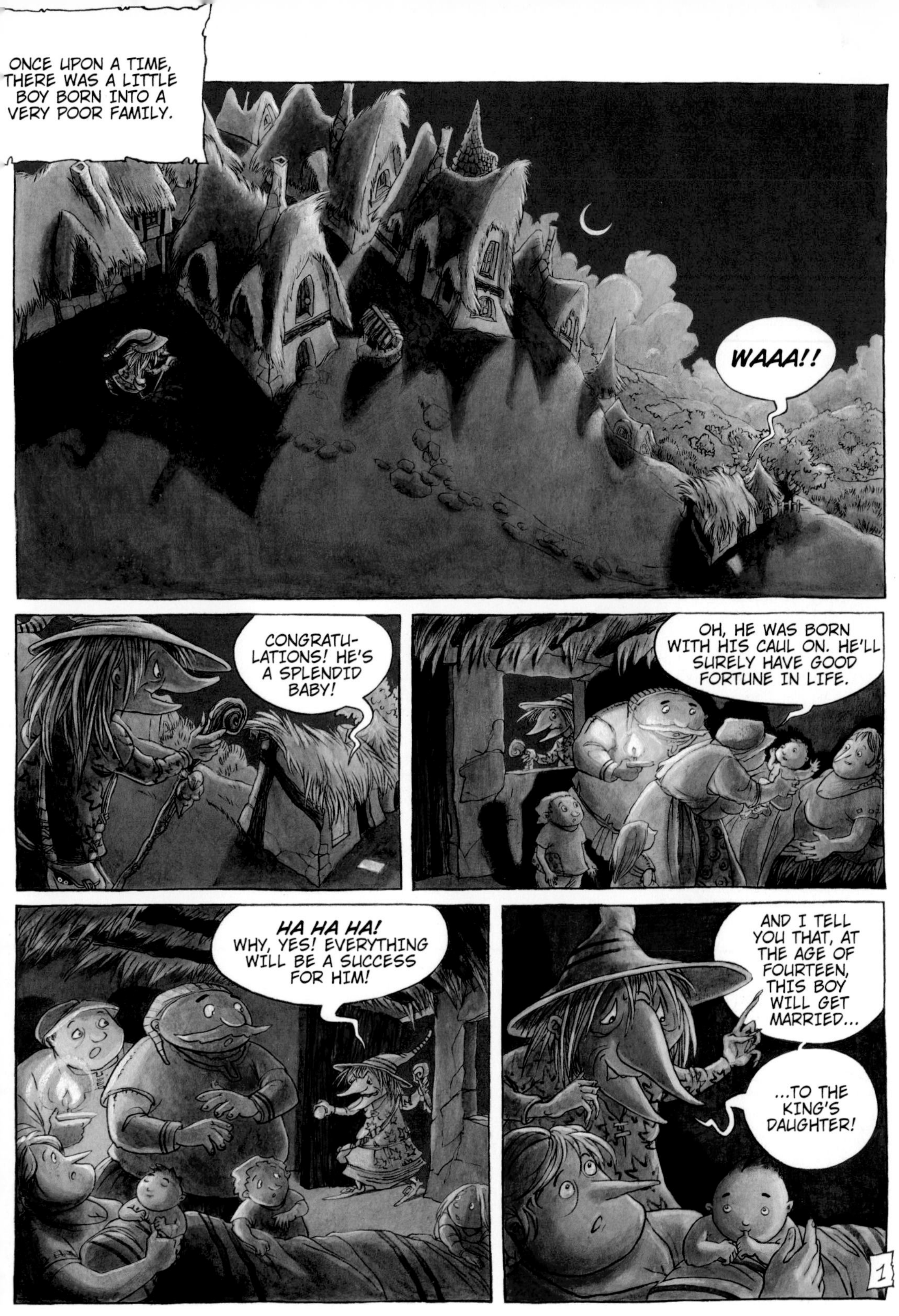

ONCE UPON A TIME, THERE WAS A LITTLE BOY BORN INTO A VERY POOR FAMILY.
WAAA!!
CONGRATU-LATIONS! HE'S A SPLENDID BABY!
OH, HE WAS BORN WITH HIS CAUL ON. HE'LL SURELY HAVE GOOD FORTUNE IN LIFE.
HA HA HA! WHY, YES! EVERYTHING WILL BE A SUCCESS FOR HIM!
AND I TELL YOU THAT, AT THE AGE OF FOURTEEN, THIS BOY WILL GET MARRIED...
...TO THE KING'S DAUGHTER!
1

SHORTLY THEREAFTER, THE KING CAME TO THE VILLAGE UNANNOUNCED, AND NOBODY RECOGNIZED HIM...

GREETINGS, GOOD PEOPLE. WHAT'S NEW HERE?

YOU HAVEN'T HEARD? IT'S A CHILD OF GOOD FORTUNE.

YES! HE WAS A BABY BORN WITH HIS CAUL ON! AND HE WAS BORN INTO THE POOREST FAMILY IN THE VILLAGE!

AND THAT'S NOT ALL. IT WAS PREDICTED THAT AT THE AGE OF FOURTEEN, HE'LL TAKE THE KING'S DAUGHTER AS HIS WIFE!

WHAT?

WHAT IMPUDENCE!

BAHH! IF THAT'S TRUE, THAT'S JUST TOO MUCH!

NO WAY WILL SOME LOUT MARRY MY DAUGHTER!

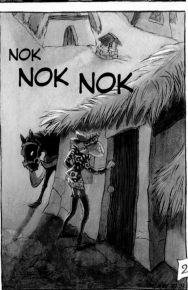

NOK

NOK NOK

2

70

YES?

HELLO, GOOD FELLOW! I'VE HEARD THE HAPPY NEWS!

OH! THE MARVELOUS LITTLE BOY! I WASN'T DECEIVED! PROVIDENCE HAS TOUCHED YOUR LIVES!

WHAT A HORRIBLE, LITTLE TOAD!

COOCHIE COOCHIE COO!

YOU POOR SAD PEOPLE...

HOW LUCKY YOU ARE THAT I CAME ALONG. I CAN TAKE CARE OF YOUR CHILD.

...BUT...UH...THAT'S NOT WHAT WE WANT.

COME NOW! YOU MUST NOT BE SO SELFISH!

THINK OF THE BOY. I DON'T WANT HIM TO SUFFER!

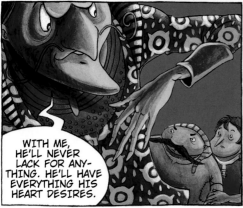

WITH ME, HE'LL NEVER LACK FOR ANYTHING. HE'LL HAVE EVERYTHING HIS HEART DESIRES.

HE'LL BE IN THE BEST OF HANDS.

AND LOOK WHAT I'M OFFERING YOU IN EXCHANGE!

3

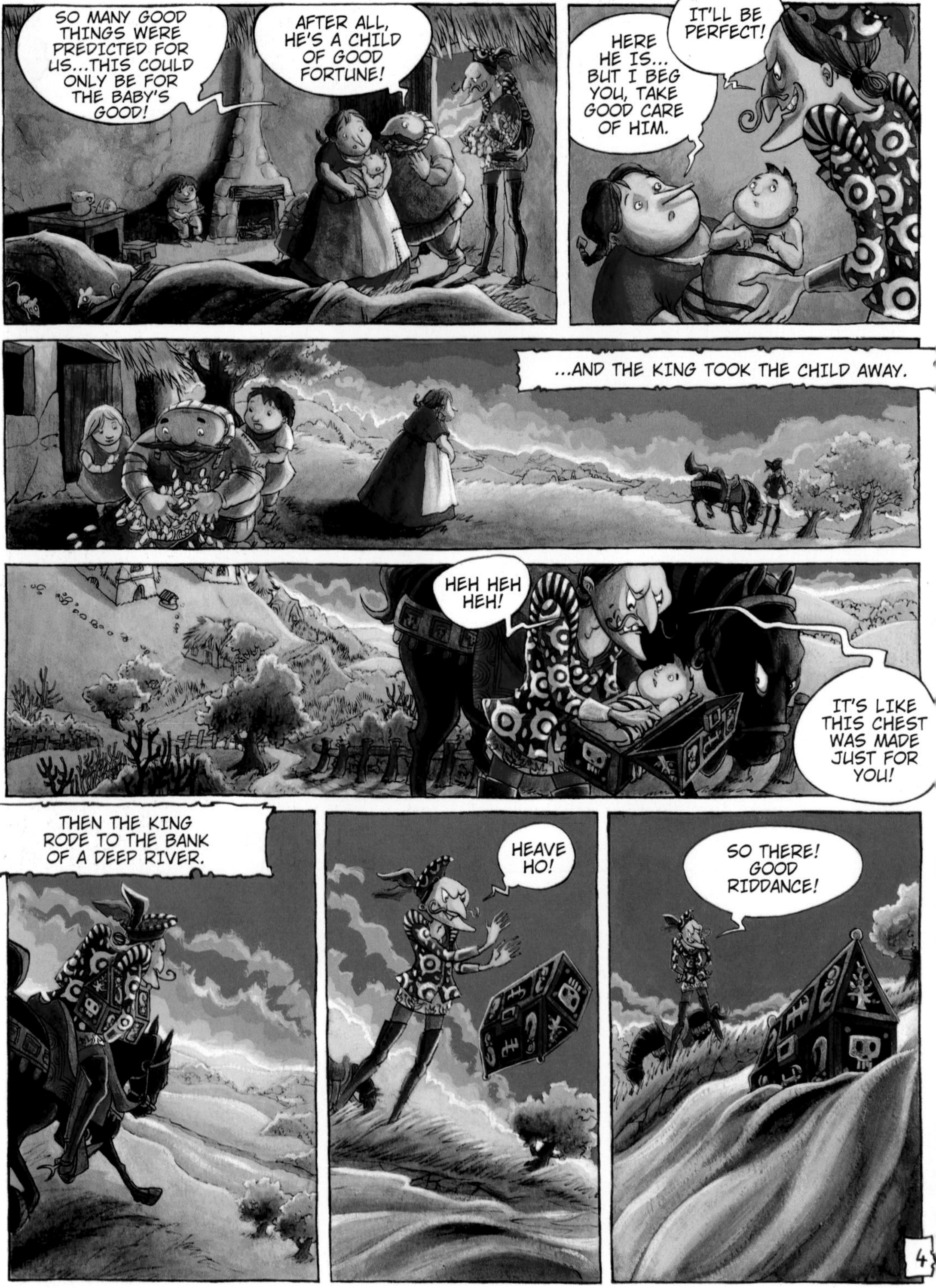
SO MANY GOOD THINGS WERE PREDICTED FOR US...THIS COULD ONLY BE FOR THE BABY'S GOOD!
AFTER ALL, HE'S A CHILD OF GOOD FORTUNE!
HERE HE IS... BUT I BEG YOU, TAKE GOOD CARE OF HIM.
IT'LL BE PERFECT!
...AND THE KING TOOK THE CHILD AWAY.
HEH HEH HEH!
IT'S LIKE THIS CHEST WAS MADE JUST FOR YOU!
THEN THE KING RODE TO THE BANK OF A DEEP RIVER.
HEAVE HO!
SO THERE! GOOD RIDDANCE!
4

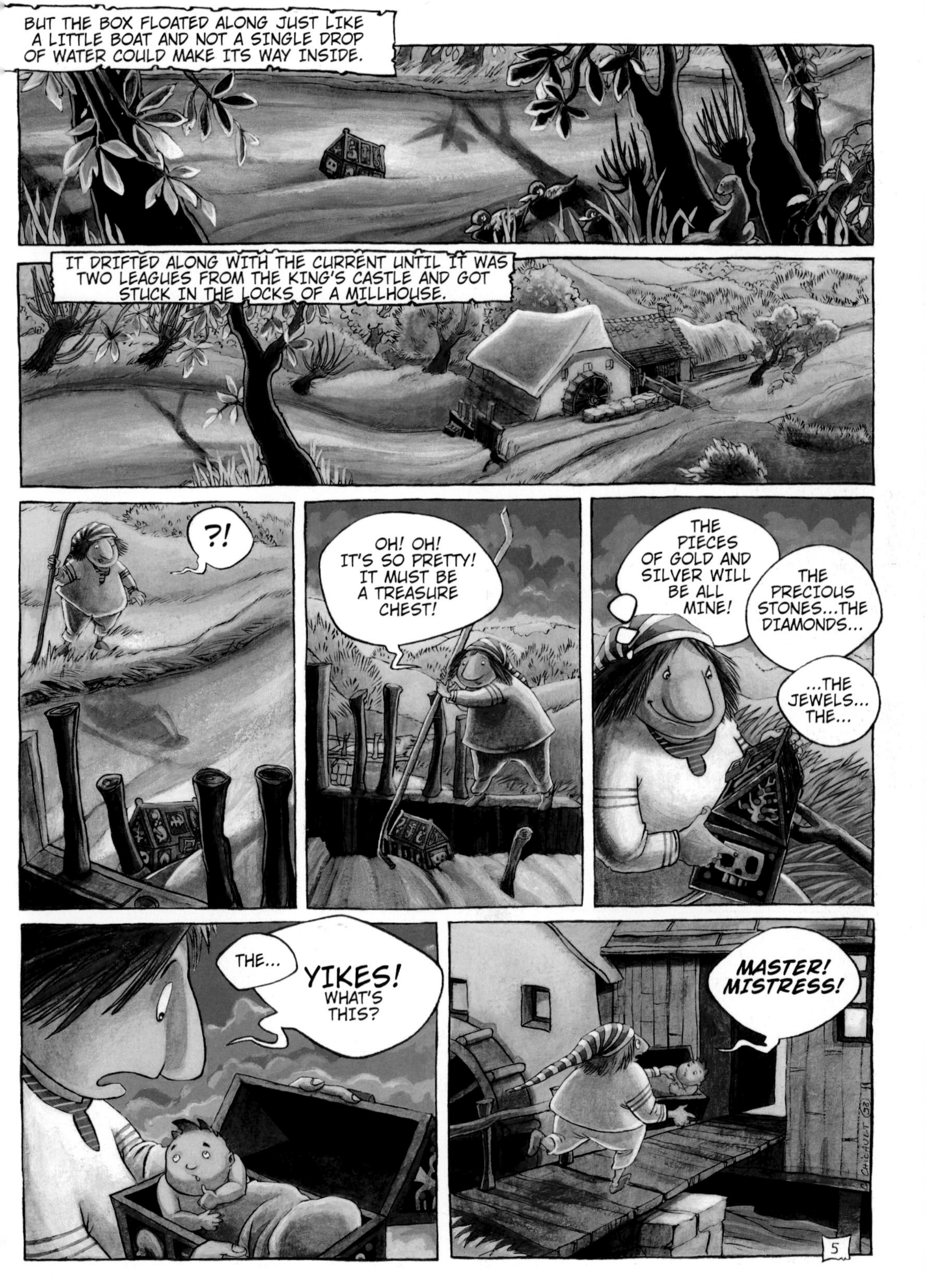
BUT THE BOX FLOATED ALONG JUST LIKE A LITTLE BOAT AND NOT A SINGLE DROP OF WATER COULD MAKE ITS WAY INSIDE.
IT DRIFTED ALONG WITH THE CURRENT UNTIL IT WAS TWO LEAGUES FROM THE KING'S CASTLE AND GOT STUCK IN THE LOCKS OF A MILLHOUSE.
?!
OH! OH! IT'S SO PRETTY! IT MUST BE A TREASURE CHEST!
THE PIECES OF GOLD AND SILVER WILL BE ALL MINE!
THE PRECIOUS STONES...THE DIAMONDS...
...THE JEWELS... THE...
THE...
YIKES! WHAT'S THIS?
MASTER! MISTRESS!
5

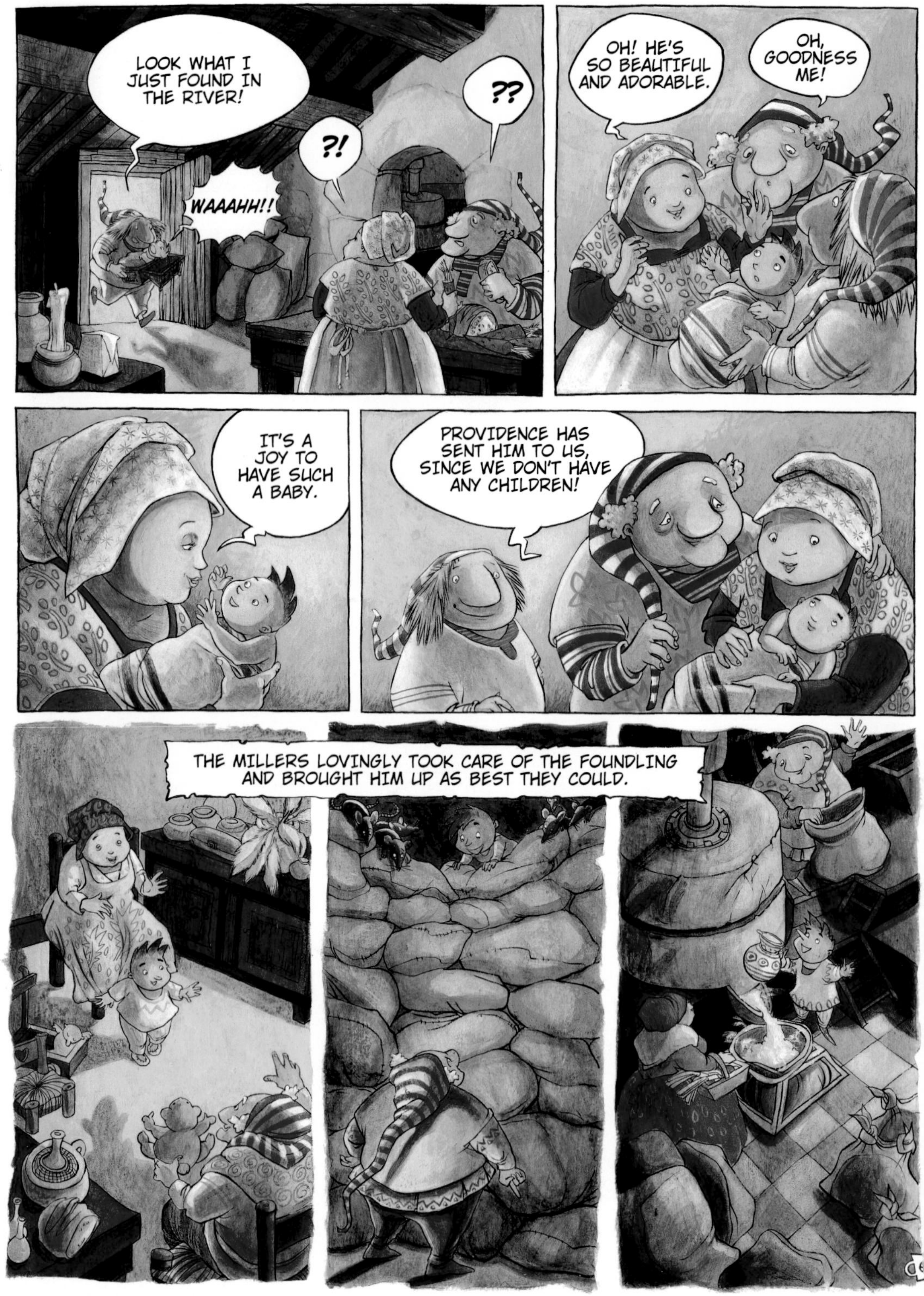
LOOK WHAT I JUST FOUND IN THE RIVER!
WAAAHH!!
?!
??
OH! HE'S SO BEAUTIFUL AND ADORABLE.
OH, GOODNESS ME!
IT'S A JOY TO HAVE SUCH A BABY.
PROVIDENCE HAS SENT HIM TO US, SINCE WE DON'T HAVE ANY CHILDREN!
THE MILLERS LOVINGLY TOOK CARE OF THE FOUNDLING AND BROUGHT HIM UP AS BEST THEY COULD.

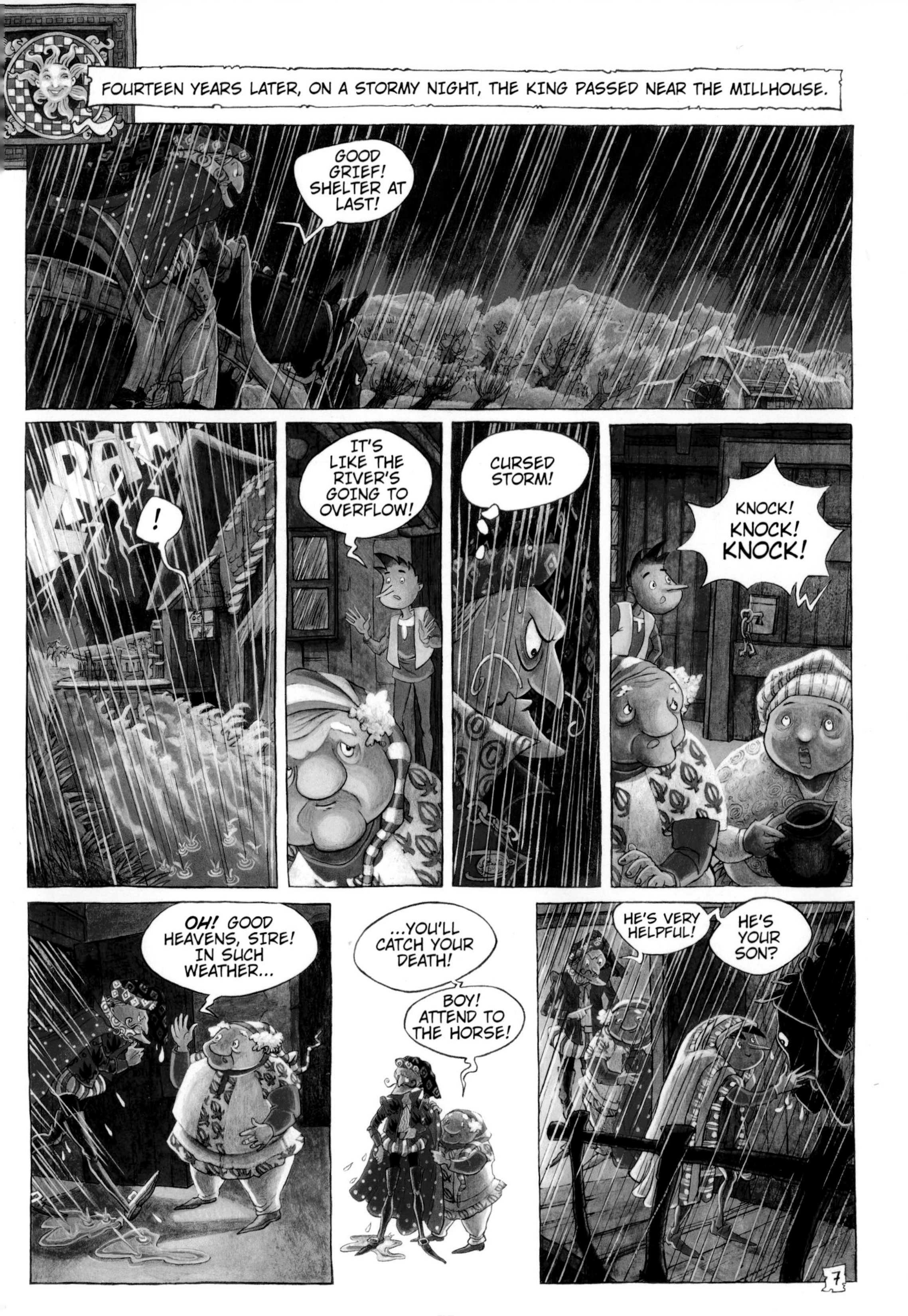
FOURTEEN YEARS LATER, ON A STORMY NIGHT, THE KING PASSED NEAR THE MILLHOUSE.
GOOD GRIEF! SHELTER AT LAST!
!
IT'S LIKE THE RIVER'S GOING TO OVERFLOW!
CURSED STORM!
KNOCK! KNOCK! KNOCK!
OH! GOOD HEAVENS, SIRE! IN SUCH WEATHER...
...YOU'LL CATCH YOUR DEATH!
BOY! ATTEND TO THE HORSE!
HE'S VERY HELPFUL!
HE'S YOUR SON?
7

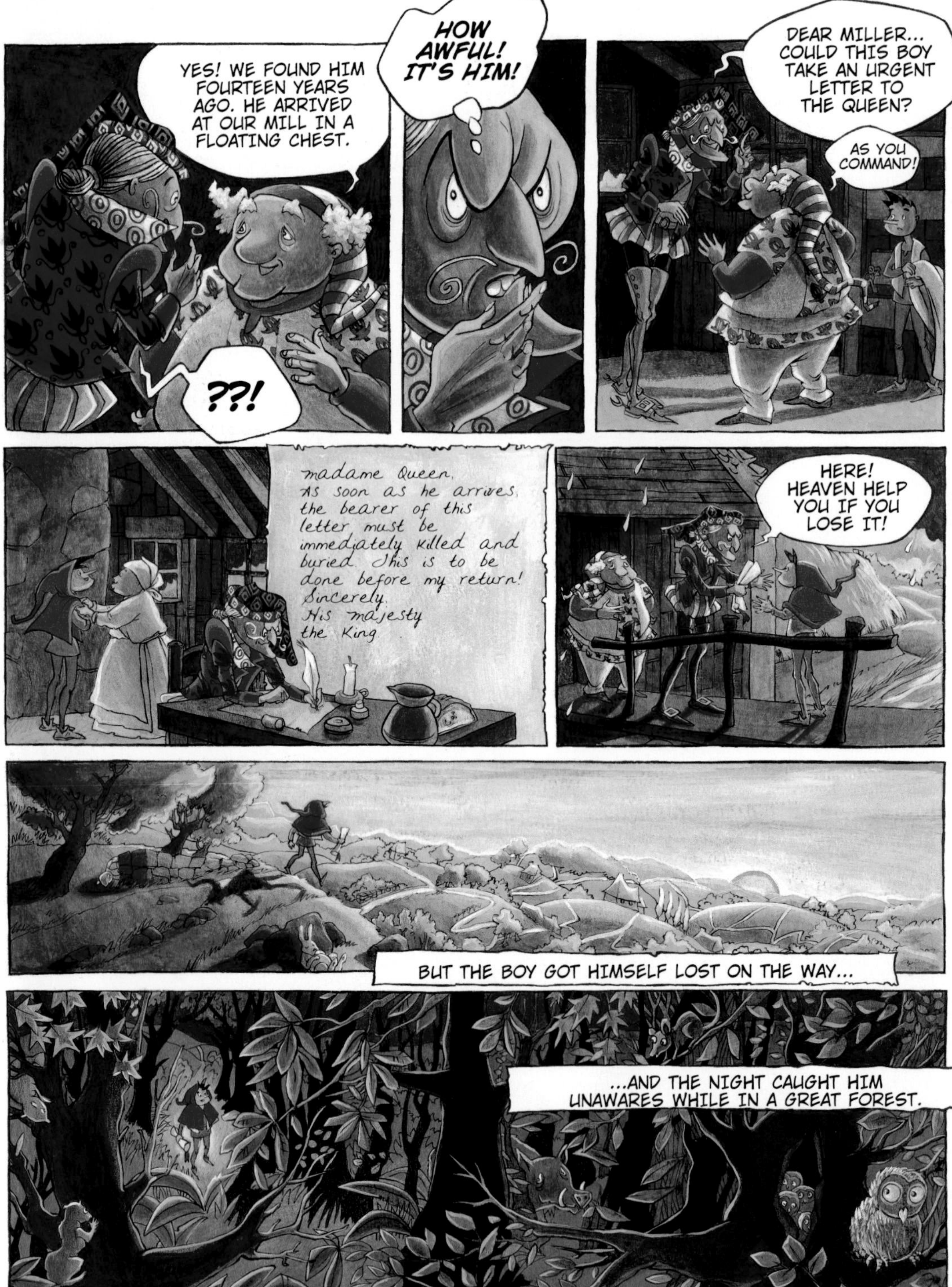
YES! WE FOUND HIM FOURTEEN YEARS AGO. HE ARRIVED AT OUR MILL IN A FLOATING CHEST.
??!
HOW AWFUL! IT'S HIM!
DEAR MILLER... COULD THIS BOY TAKE AN URGENT LETTER TO THE QUEEN?
AS YOU COMMAND!
Madame Queen,
As soon as he arrives, the bearer of this letter must be immediately killed and buried. This is to be done before my return!
Sincerely,
His majesty the King.
HERE! HEAVEN HELP YOU IF YOU LOSE IT!
BUT THE BOY GOT HIMSELF LOST ON THE WAY...
...AND THE NIGHT CAUGHT HIM UNAWARES WHILE IN A GREAT FOREST.
8

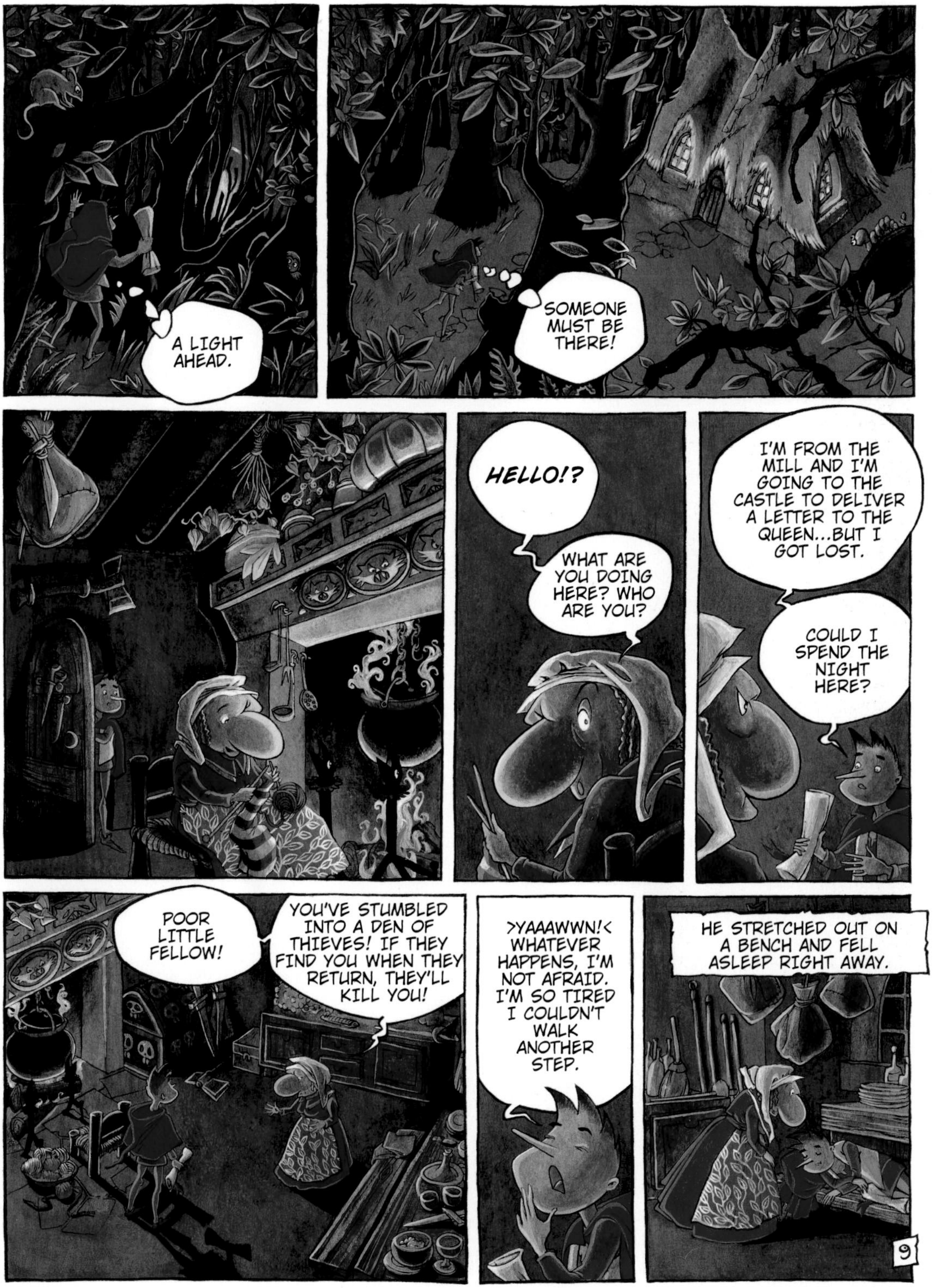
A LIGHT AHEAD.
SOMEONE MUST BE THERE!
HELLO!?
WHAT ARE YOU DOING HERE? WHO ARE YOU?
I'M FROM THE MILL AND I'M GOING TO THE CASTLE TO DELIVER A LETTER TO THE QUEEN...BUT I GOT LOST.
COULD I SPEND THE NIGHT HERE?
POOR LITTLE FELLOW!
YOU'VE STUMBLED INTO A DEN OF THIEVES! IF THEY FIND YOU WHEN THEY RETURN, THEY'LL KILL YOU!
>YAAAWWN!< WHATEVER HAPPENS, I'M NOT AFRAID. I'M SO TIRED I COULDN'T WALK ANOTHER STEP.
HE STRETCHED OUT ON A BENCH AND FELL ASLEEP RIGHT AWAY.
9

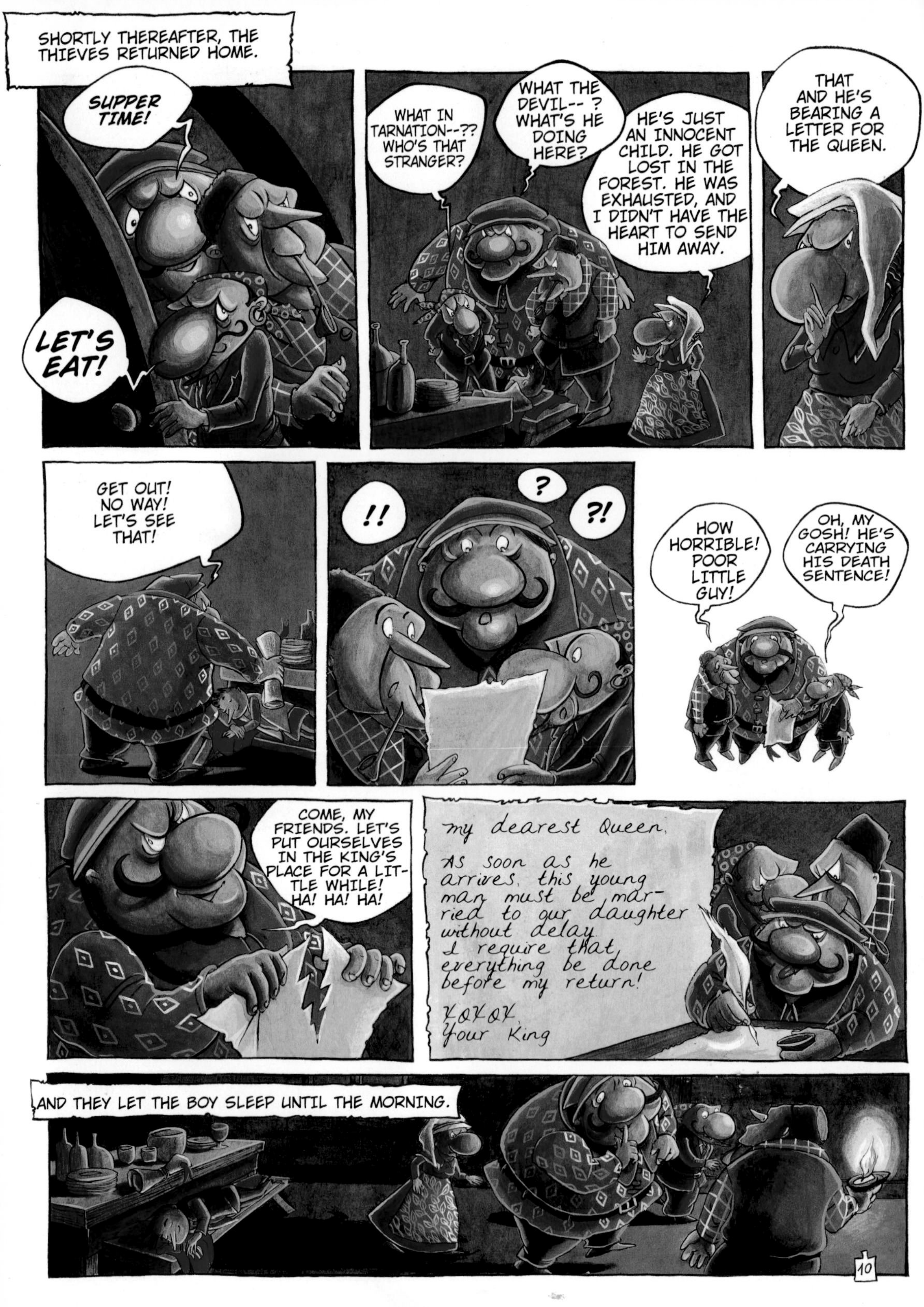
SHORTLY THEREAFTER, THE THIEVES RETURNED HOME.
SUPPER TIME!
LET'S EAT!
WHAT IN TARNATION--?? WHO'S THAT STRANGER?
WHAT THE DEVIL-- ? WHAT'S HE DOING HERE?
HE'S JUST AN INNOCENT CHILD. HE GOT LOST IN THE FOREST. HE WAS EXHAUSTED, AND I DIDN'T HAVE THE HEART TO SEND HIM AWAY.
THAT AND HE'S BEARING A LETTER FOR THE QUEEN.
GET OUT! NO WAY! LET'S SEE THAT!
!!
?
?!
HOW HORRIBLE! POOR LITTLE GUY!
OH, MY GOSH! HE'S CARRYING HIS DEATH SENTENCE!
COME, MY FRIENDS. LET'S PUT OURSELVES IN THE KING'S PLACE FOR A LITTLE WHILE! HA! HA! HA!
My dearest Queen,
As soon as he arrives, this young man must be married to our daughter without delay.
I require that everything be done before my return!
XOXOX,
Your King
AND THEY LET THE BOY SLEEP UNTIL THE MORNING.
10

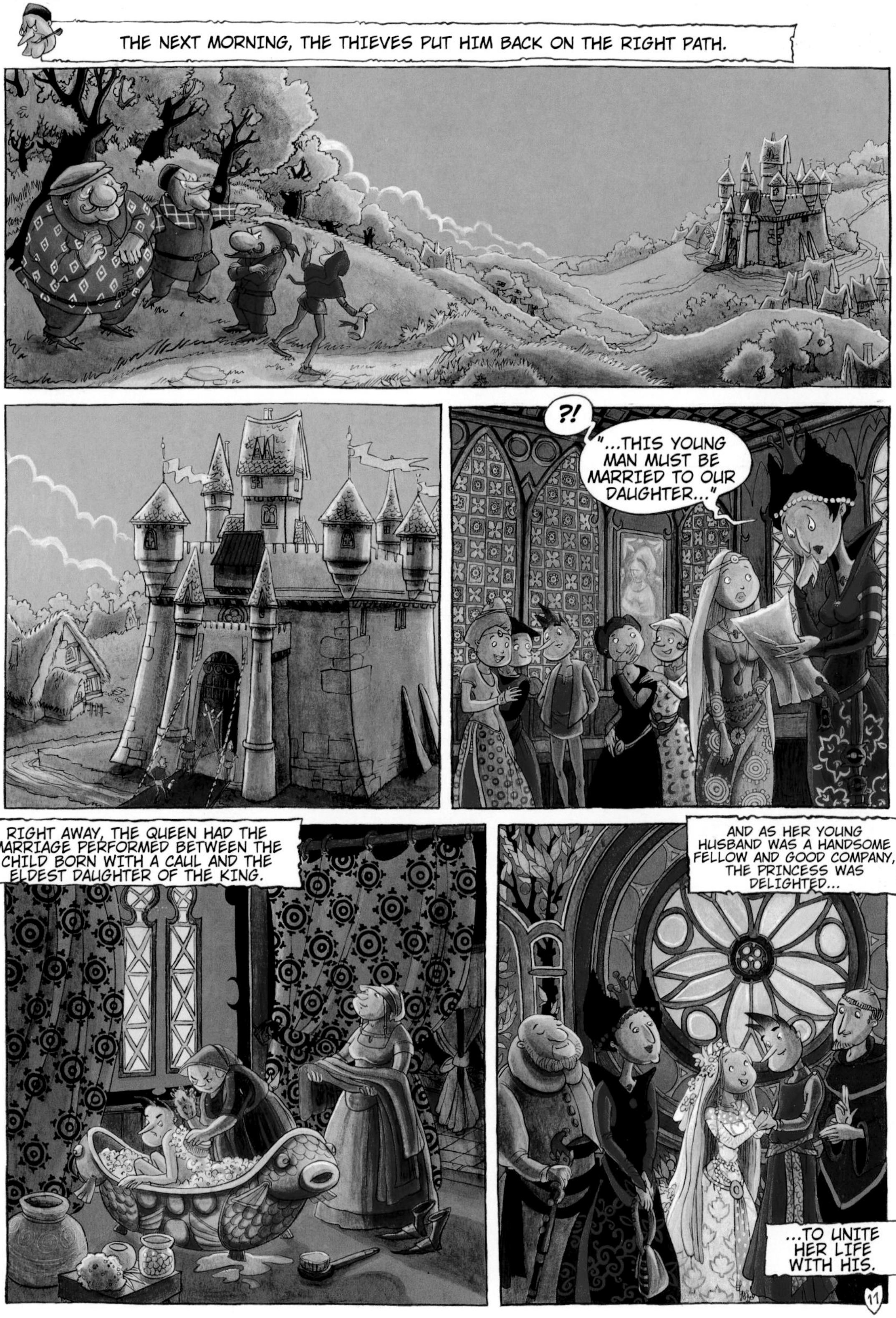
THE NEXT MORNING, THE THIEVES PUT HIM BACK ON THE RIGHT PATH.
?!
"...THIS YOUNG MAN MUST BE MARRIED TO OUR DAUGHTER..."
RIGHT AWAY, THE QUEEN HAD THE MARRIAGE PERFORMED BETWEEN THE CHILD BORN WITH A CAUL AND THE ELDEST DAUGHTER OF THE KING.
AND AS HER YOUNG HUSBAND WAS A HANDSOME FELLOW AND GOOD COMPANY, THE PRINCESS WAS DELIGHTED...
...TO UNITE HER LIFE WITH HIS.
11

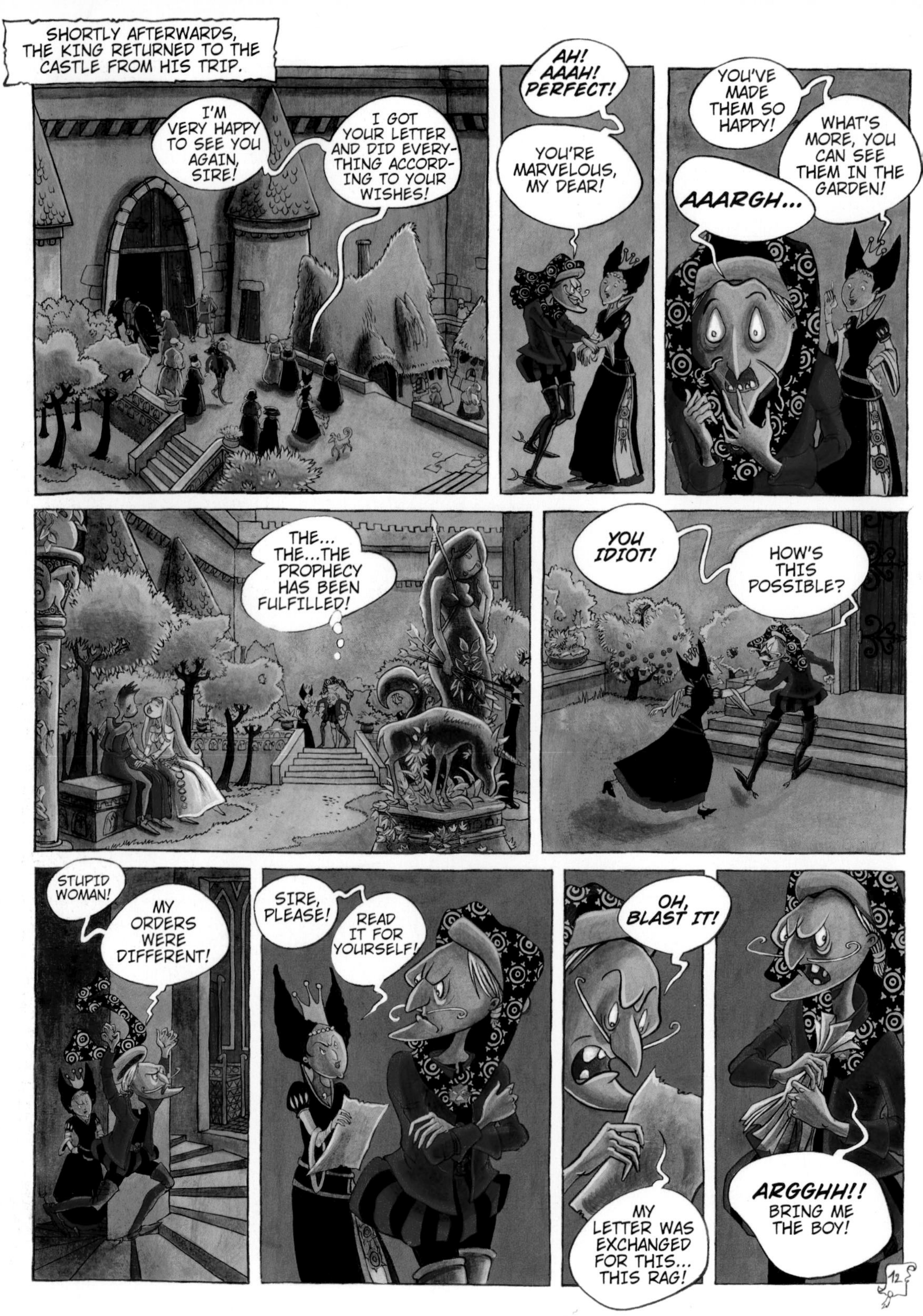
SHORTLY AFTERWARDS, THE KING RETURNED TO THE CASTLE FROM HIS TRIP.
I'M VERY HAPPY TO SEE YOU AGAIN, SIRE!
I GOT YOUR LETTER AND DID EVERY-THING ACCORD-ING TO YOUR WISHES!
AH! AAAH! PERFECT!
YOU'RE MARVELOUS, MY DEAR!
YOU'VE MADE THEM SO HAPPY!
WHAT'S MORE, YOU CAN SEE THEM IN THE GARDEN!
AAARGH...
THE... THE...THE PROPHECY HAS BEEN FULFILLED!
YOU IDIOT!
HOW'S THIS POSSIBLE?
STUPID WOMAN!
MY ORDERS WERE DIFFERENT!
SIRE, PLEASE!
READ IT FOR YOURSELF!
OH, BLAST IT!
MY LETTER WAS EXCHANGED FOR THIS... THIS RAG!
ARGGHH!! BRING ME THE BOY!
12

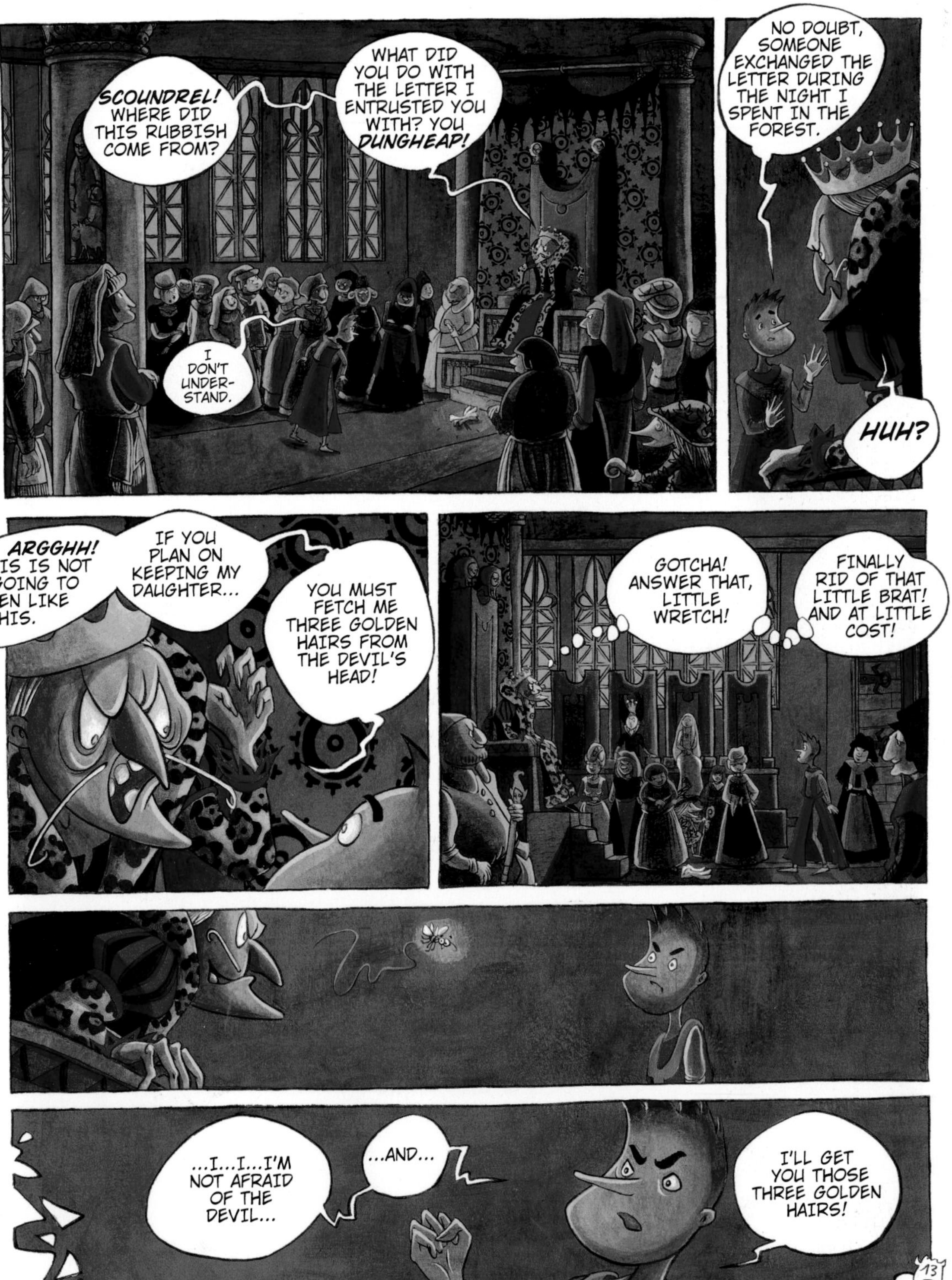
SCOUNDREL! WHERE DID THIS RUBBISH COME FROM?
WHAT DID YOU DO WITH THE LETTER I ENTRUSTED YOU WITH? YOU DUNGHEAP!
I DON'T UNDER-STAND.
NO DOUBT, SOMEONE EXCHANGED THE LETTER DURING THE NIGHT I SPENT IN THE FOREST.
HUH?
ARGGHH! THIS IS NOT GOING TO PPEN LIKE THIS.
IF YOU PLAN ON KEEPING MY DAUGHTER...
YOU MUST FETCH ME THREE GOLDEN HAIRS FROM THE DEVIL'S HEAD!
GOTCHA! ANSWER THAT, LITTLE WRETCH!
FINALLY RID OF THAT LITTLE BRAT! AND AT LITTLE COST!
...I...I...I'M NOT AFRAID OF THE DEVIL...
...AND...
I'LL GET YOU THOSE THREE GOLDEN HAIRS!
13

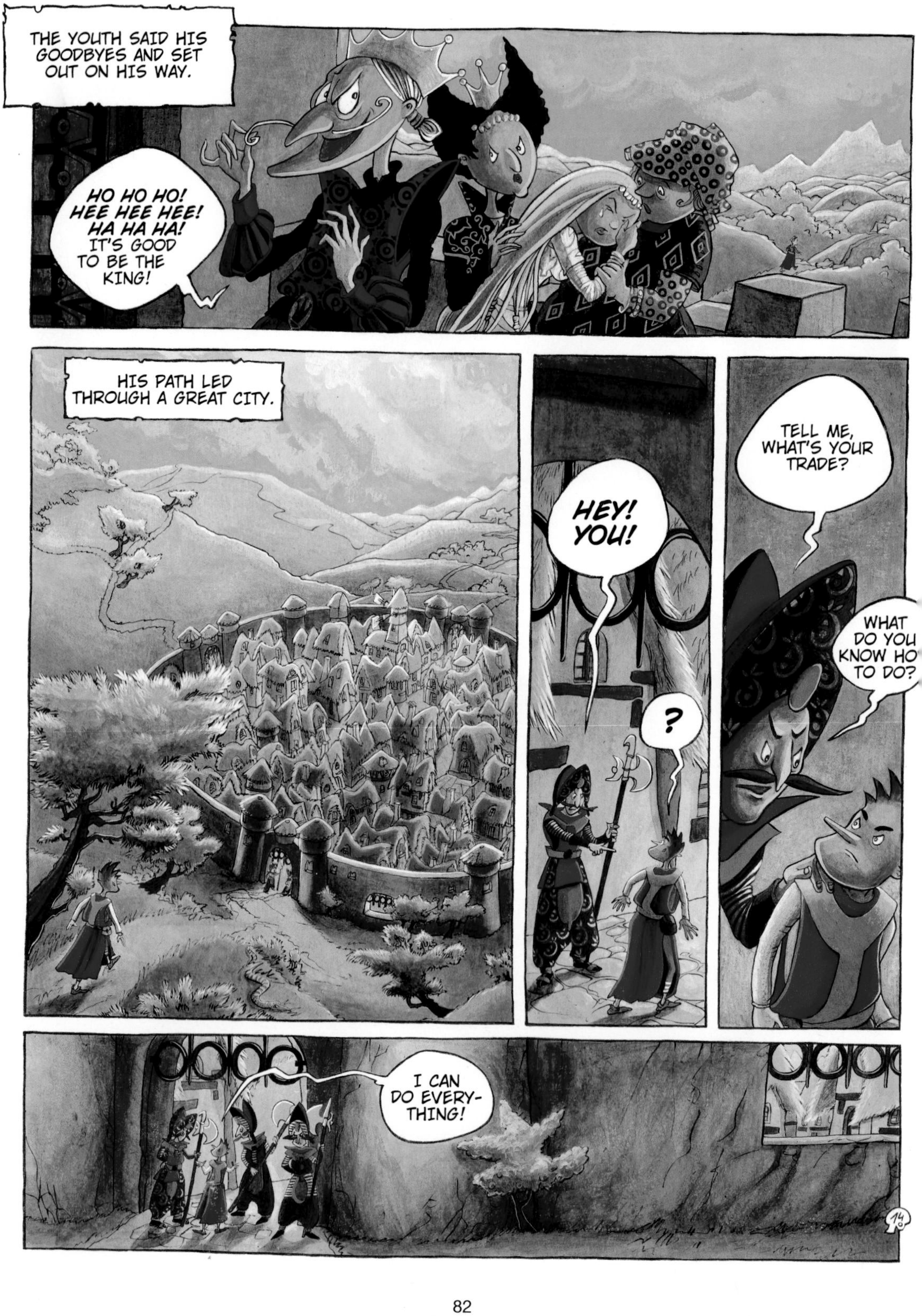
THE YOUTH SAID HIS GOODBYES AND SET OUT ON HIS WAY.
HO HO HO! HEE HEE HEE! HA HA HA! IT'S GOOD TO BE THE KING!
HIS PATH LED THROUGH A GREAT CITY.
HEY! YOU!
?
TELL ME, WHAT'S YOUR TRADE?
WHAT DO YOU KNOW HO TO DO?
I CAN DO EVERY-THING!
14

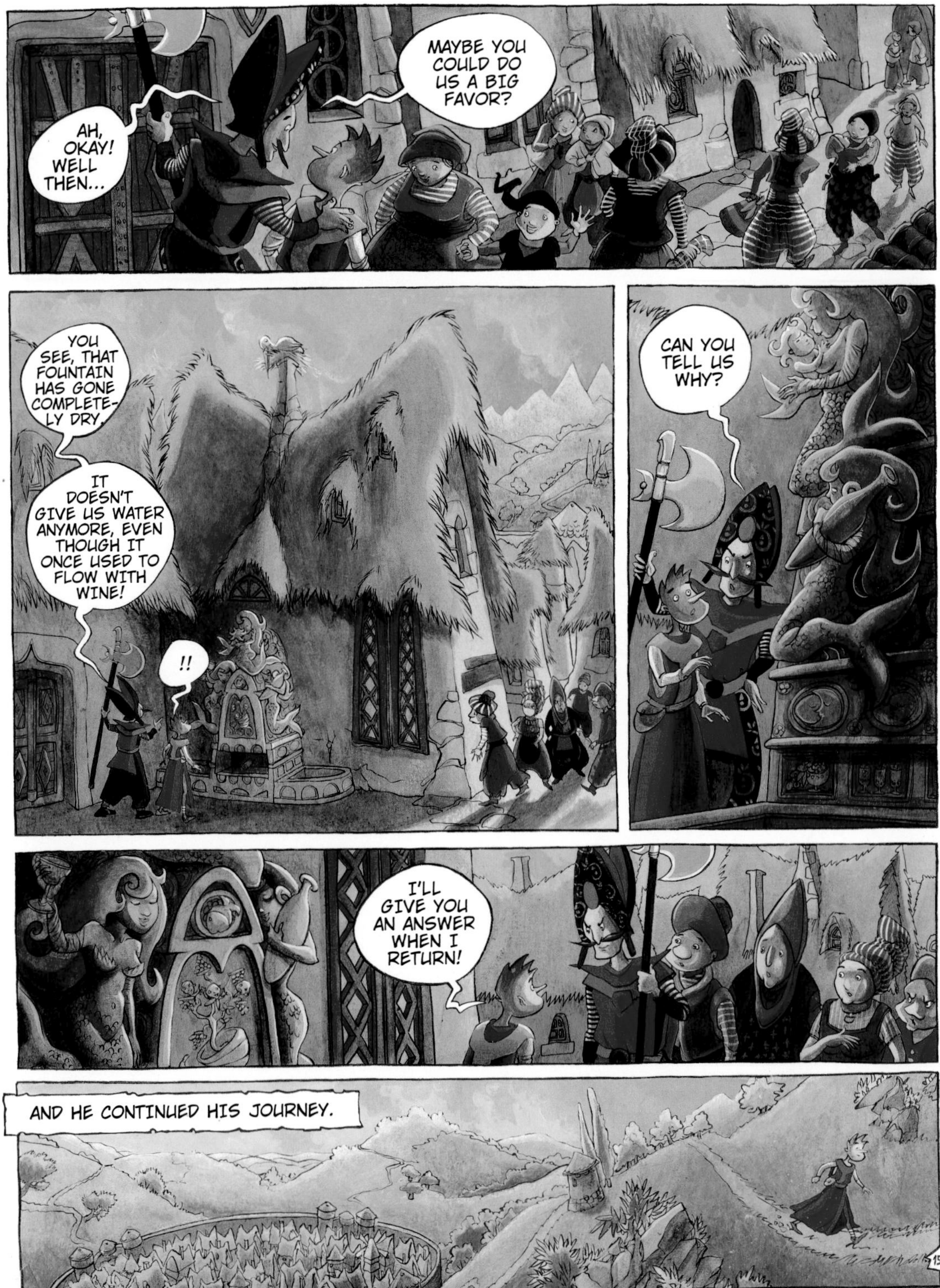
AH, OKAY! WELL THEN...
MAYBE YOU COULD DO US A BIG FAVOR?
YOU SEE, THAT FOUNTAIN HAS GONE COMPLETELY DRY.
IT DOESN'T GIVE US WATER ANYMORE, EVEN THOUGH IT ONCE USED TO FLOW WITH WINE!
!!
CAN YOU TELL US WHY?
I'LL GIVE YOU AN ANSWER WHEN I RETURN!
AND HE CONTINUED HIS JOURNEY.
15

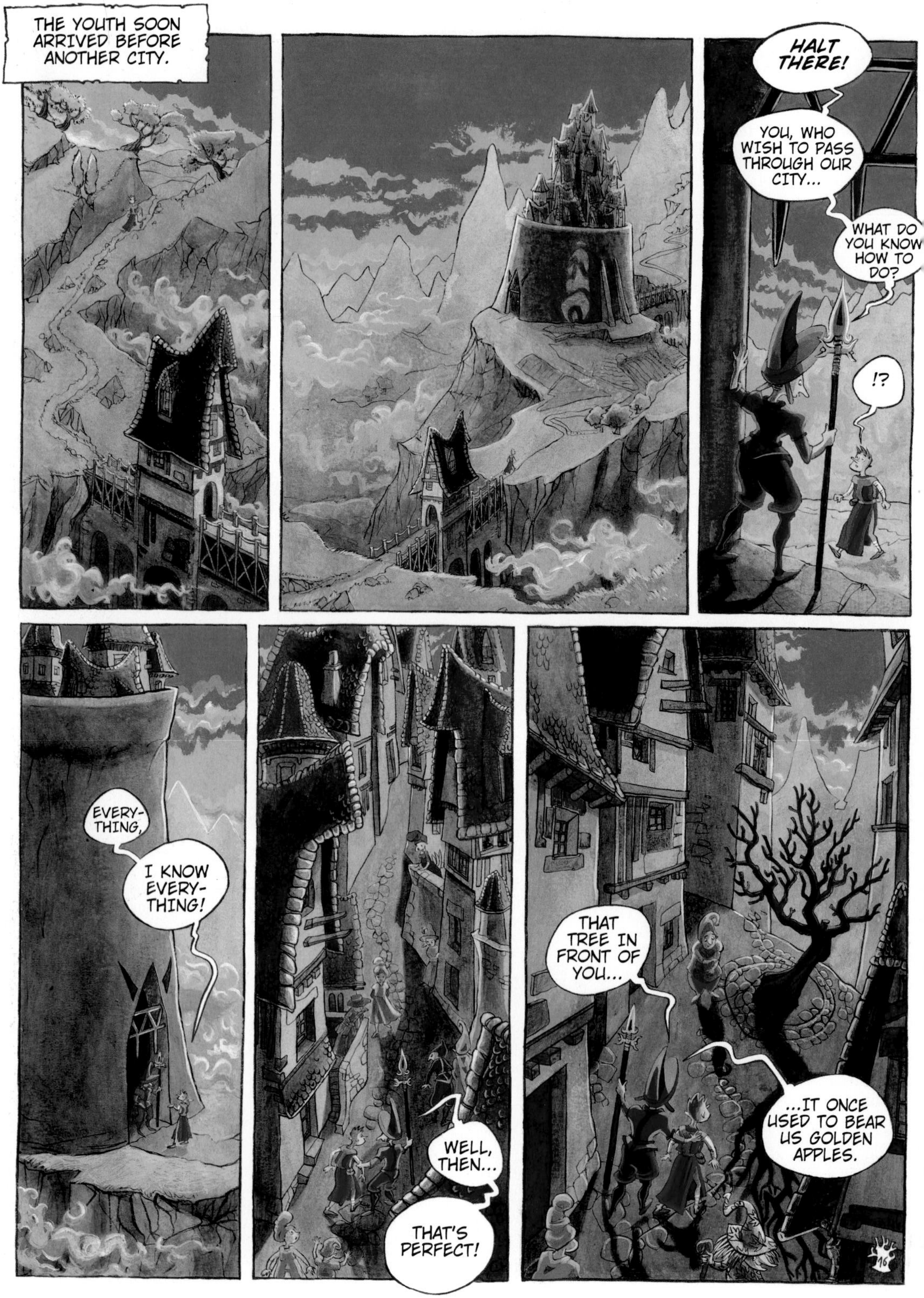
THE YOUTH SOON ARRIVED BEFORE ANOTHER CITY.
HALT THERE!
YOU, WHO WISH TO PASS THROUGH OUR CITY...
WHAT DO YOU KNOW HOW TO DO?
!?
EVERY- THING,
I KNOW EVERY- THING!
WELL, THEN...
THAT'S PERFECT!
THAT TREE IN FRONT OF YOU...
...IT ONCE USED TO BEAR US GOLDEN APPLES.
16

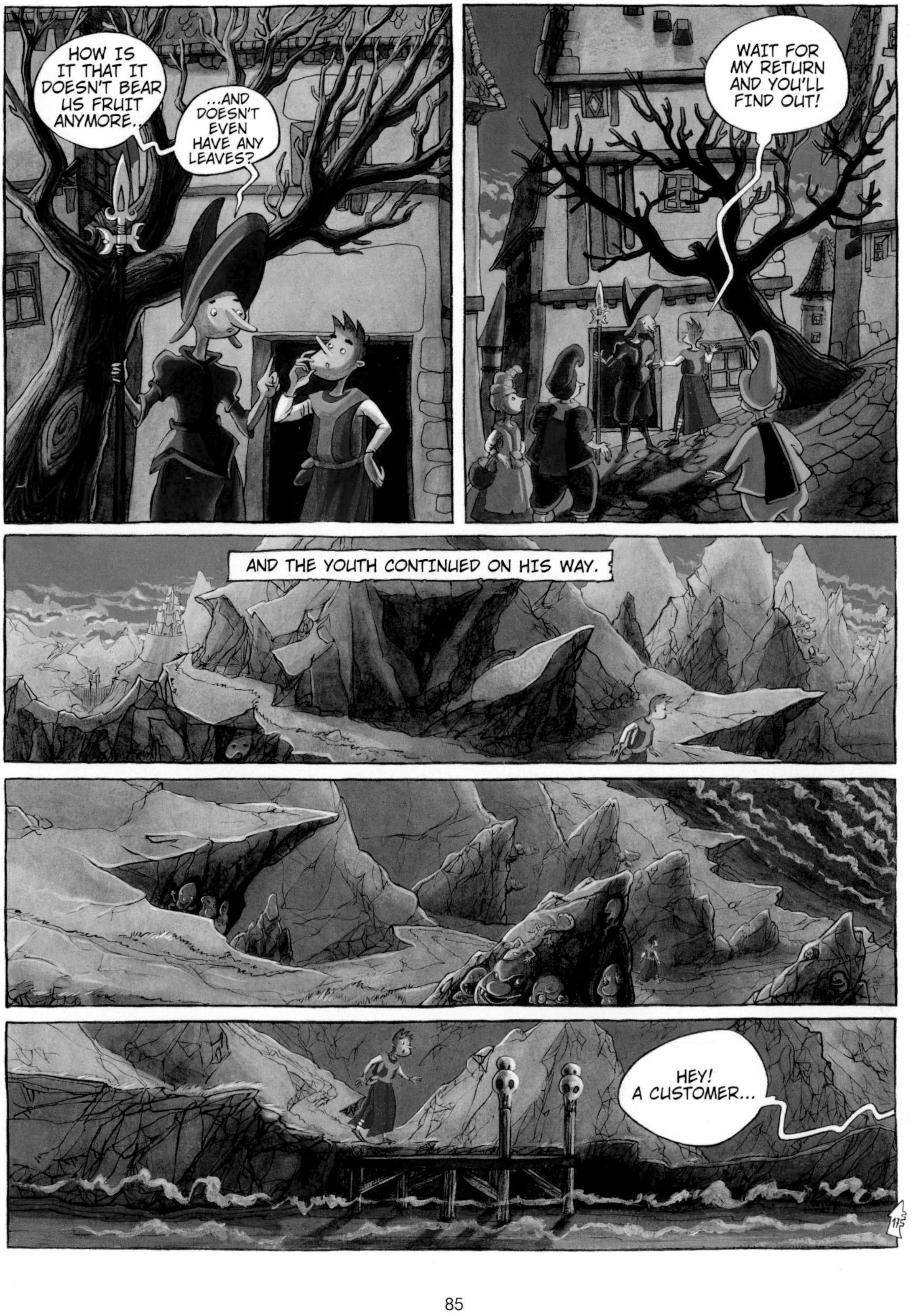
HOW IS IT THAT IT DOESN'T BEAR US FRUIT ANYMORE...
...AND DOESN'T EVEN HAVE ANY LEAVES?
WAIT FOR MY RETURN AND YOU'LL FIND OUT!
AND THE YOUTH CONTINUED ON HIS WAY.
HEY! A CUSTOMER...

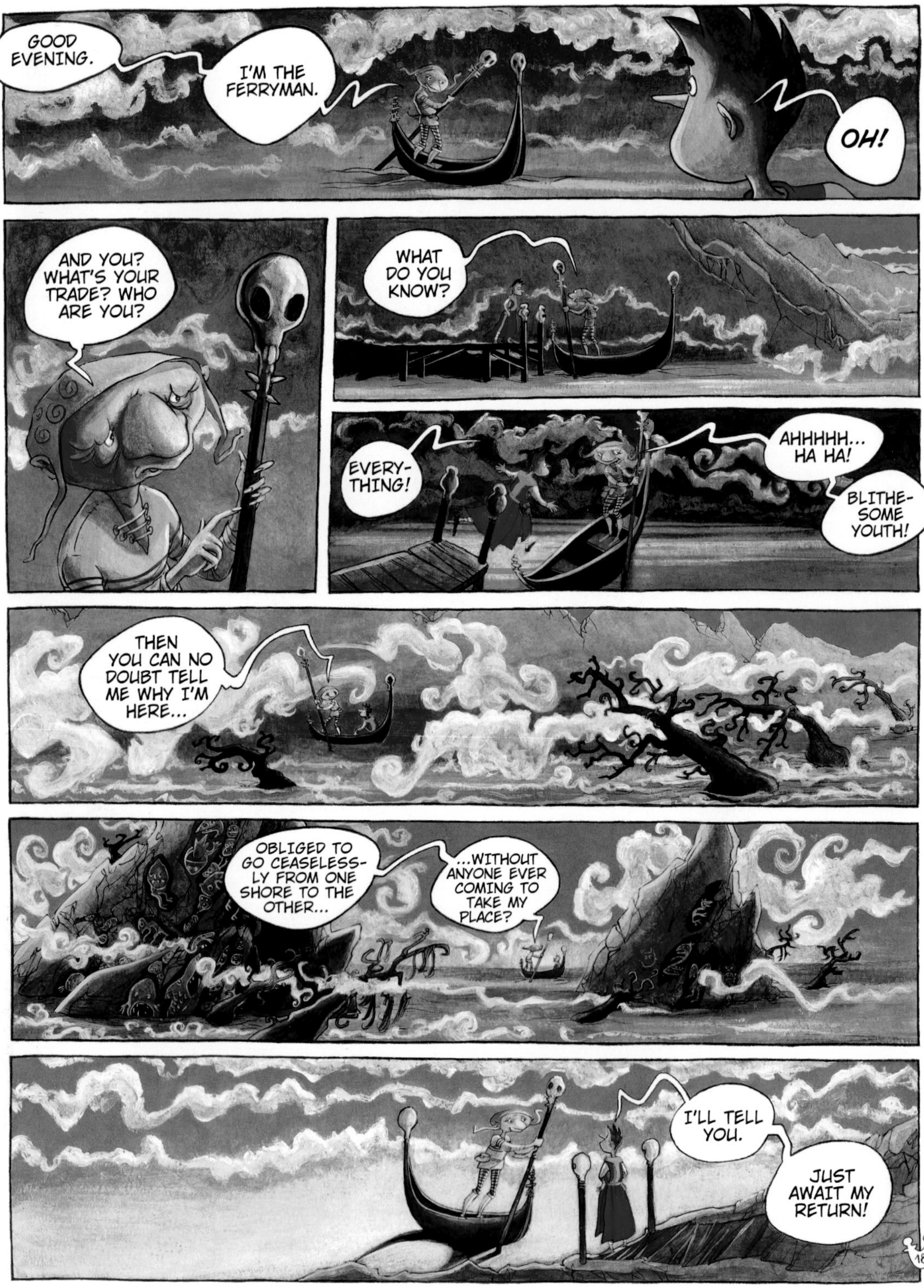
GOOD EVENING.
I'M THE FERRYMAN.
OH!
AND YOU? WHAT'S YOUR TRADE? WHO ARE YOU?
WHAT DO YOU KNOW?
EVERY-THING!
AHHHHH... HA HA!
BLITHE-SOME YOUTH!
THEN YOU CAN NO DOUBT TELL ME WHY I'M HERE...
OBLIGED TO GO CEASELESS-LY FROM ONE SHORE TO THE OTHER...
...WITHOUT ANYONE EVER COMING TO TAKE MY PLACE?
I'LL TELL YOU.
JUST AWAIT MY RETURN!
18

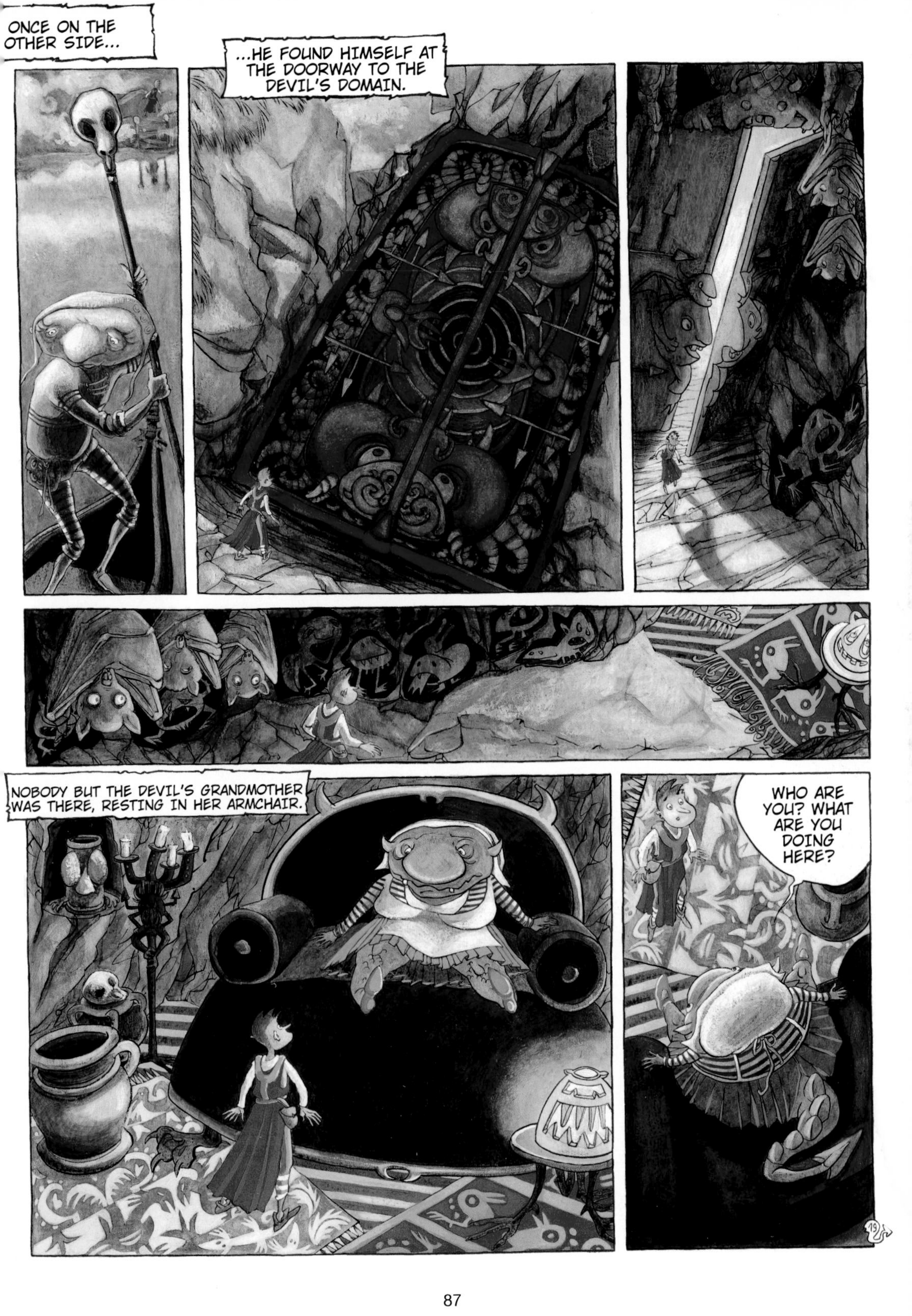
ONCE ON THE OTHER SIDE...
...HE FOUND HIMSELF AT THE DOORWAY TO THE DEVIL'S DOMAIN.
NOBODY BUT THE DEVIL'S GRANDMOTHER WAS THERE, RESTING IN HER ARMCHAIR.
WHO ARE YOU? WHAT ARE YOU DOING HERE?
19

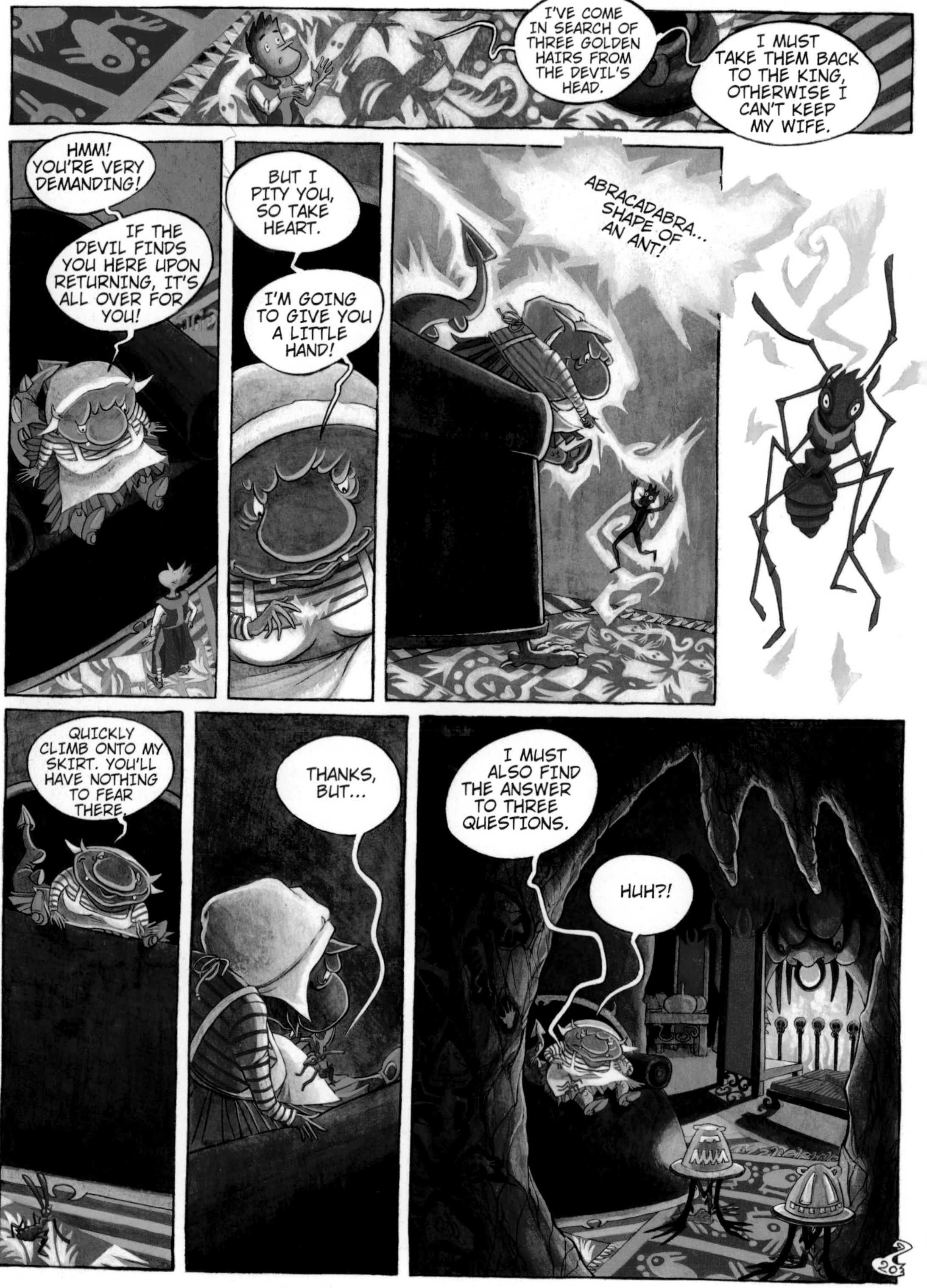
I'VE COME IN SEARCH OF THREE GOLDEN HAIRS FROM THE DEVIL'S HEAD.
I MUST TAKE THEM BACK TO THE KING, OTHERWISE I CAN'T KEEP MY WIFE.
HMM! YOU'RE VERY DEMANDING!
IF THE DEVIL FINDS YOU HERE UPON RETURNING, IT'S ALL OVER FOR YOU!
BUT I PITY YOU, SO TAKE HEART.
I'M GOING TO GIVE YOU A LITTLE HAND!
ABRACADABRA... SHAPE OF AN ANT!
QUICKLY CLIMB ONTO MY SKIRT. YOU'LL HAVE NOTHING TO FEAR THERE.
THANKS, BUT...
I MUST ALSO FIND THE ANSWER TO THREE QUESTIONS.
HUH?!

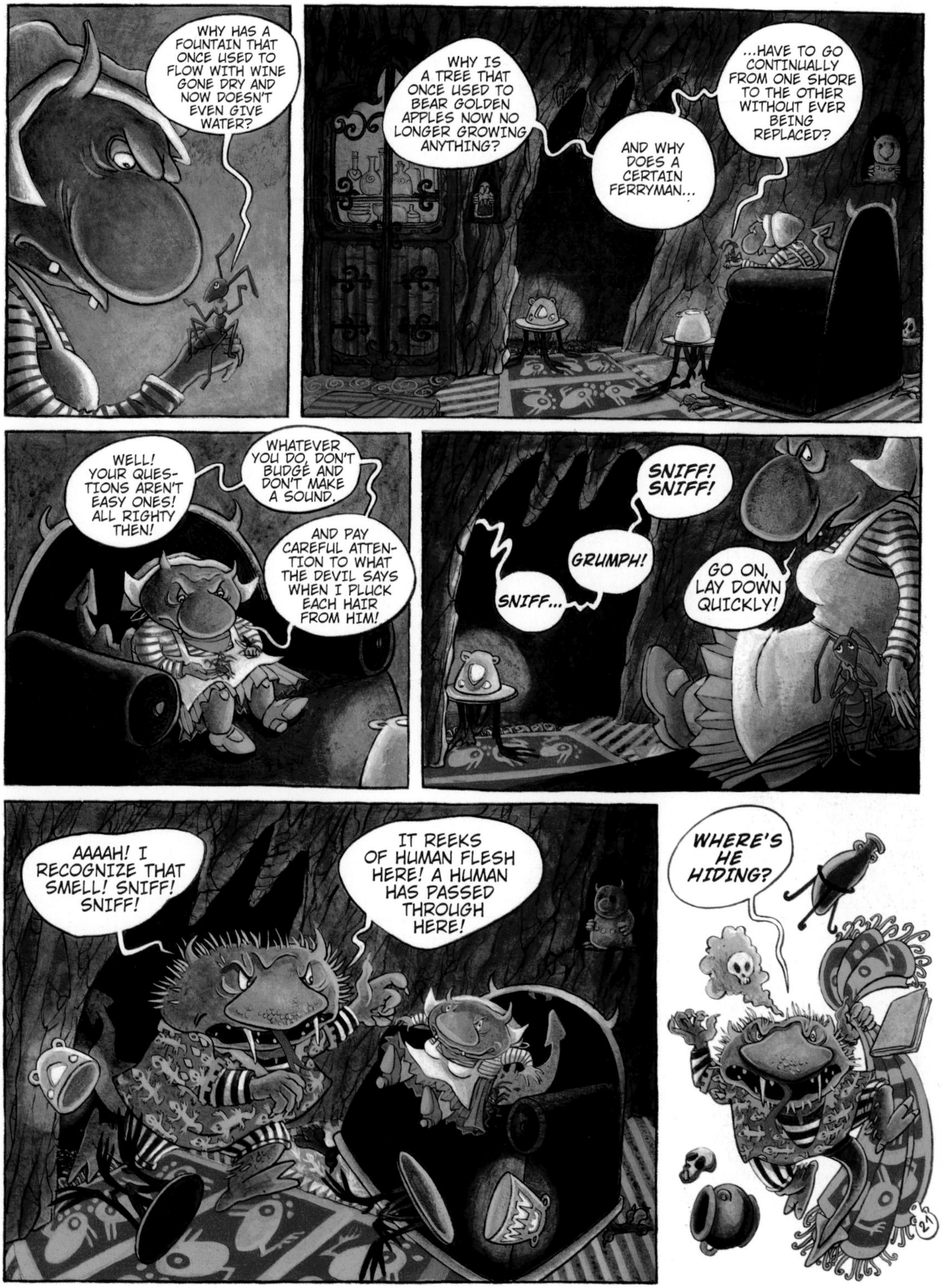
WHY HAS A FOUNTAIN THAT ONCE USED TO FLOW WITH WINE GONE DRY AND NOW DOESN'T EVEN GIVE WATER?
WHY IS A TREE THAT ONCE USED TO BEAR GOLDEN APPLES NOW NO LONGER GROWING ANYTHING?
AND WHY DOES A CERTAIN FERRYMAN...
...HAVE TO GO CONTINUALLY FROM ONE SHORE TO THE OTHER WITHOUT EVER BEING REPLACED?
WELL! YOUR QUESTIONS AREN'T EASY ONES! ALL RIGHTY THEN!
WHATEVER YOU DO, DON'T BUDGE AND DON'T MAKE A SOUND.
AND PAY CAREFUL ATTENTION TO WHAT THE DEVIL SAYS WHEN I PLUCK EACH HAIR FROM HIM!
SNIFF! SNIFF!
GRUMPH!
SNIFF...
GO ON, LAY DOWN QUICKLY!
AAAAH! I RECOGNIZE THAT SMELL! SNIFF! SNIFF!
IT REEKS OF HUMAN FLESH HERE! A HUMAN HAS PASSED THROUGH HERE!
WHERE'S HE HIDING?
21

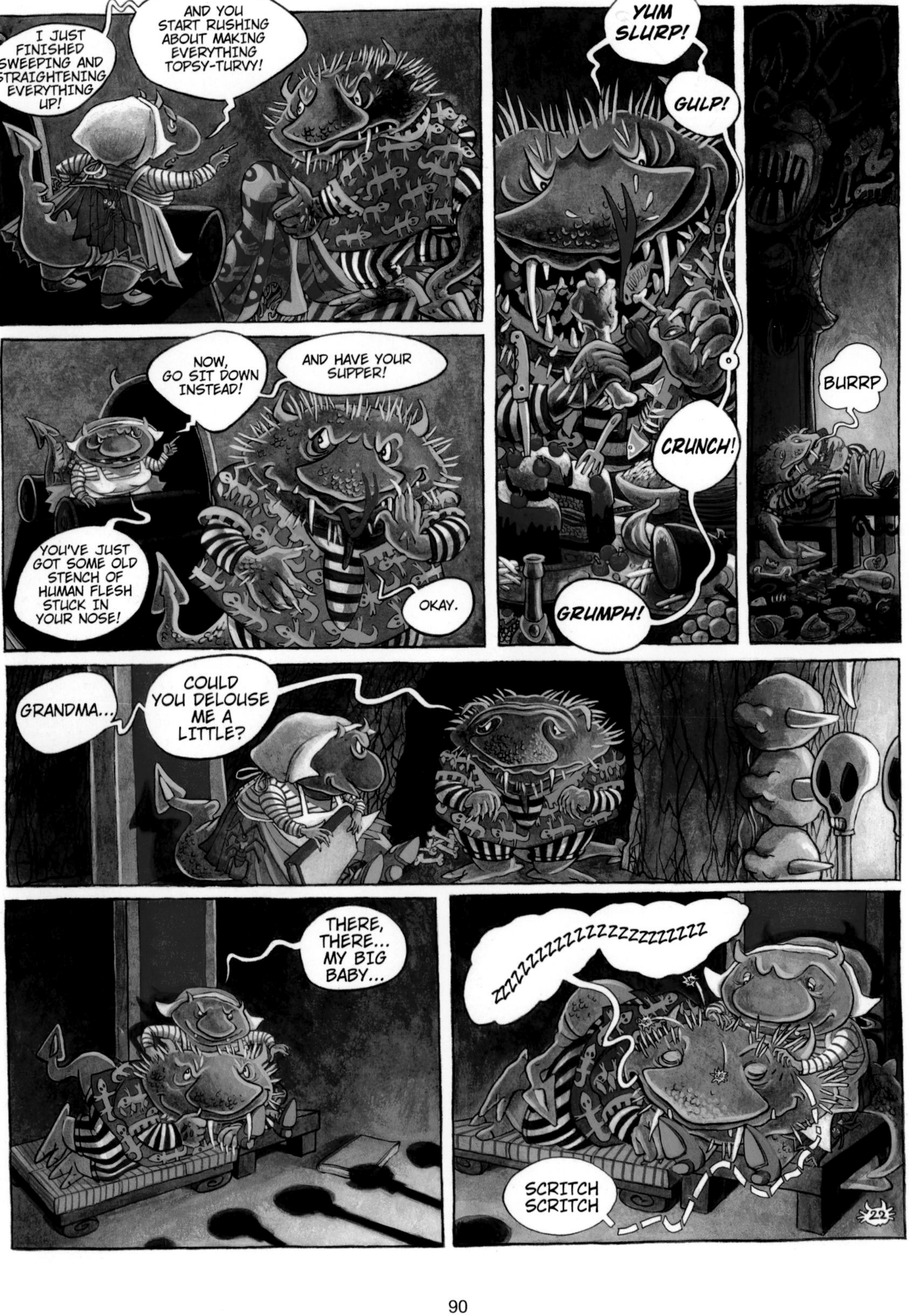

I JUST FINISHED SWEEPING AND STRAIGHTENING EVERYTHING UP!
AND YOU START RUSHING ABOUT MAKING EVERYTHING TOPSY-TURVY!
NOW, GO SIT DOWN INSTEAD!
AND HAVE YOUR SUPPER!
YOU'VE JUST GOT SOME OLD STENCH OF HUMAN FLESH STUCK IN YOUR NOSE!
OKAY.
YUM SLURP!
GULP!
CRUNCH!
GRUMPH!
BURRP
GRANDMA...
COULD YOU DELOUSE ME A LITTLE?
THERE, THERE... MY BIG BABY...
ZZZZZZZZZZZZZZZZZZZZZZZ
SCRITCH SCRITCH
22

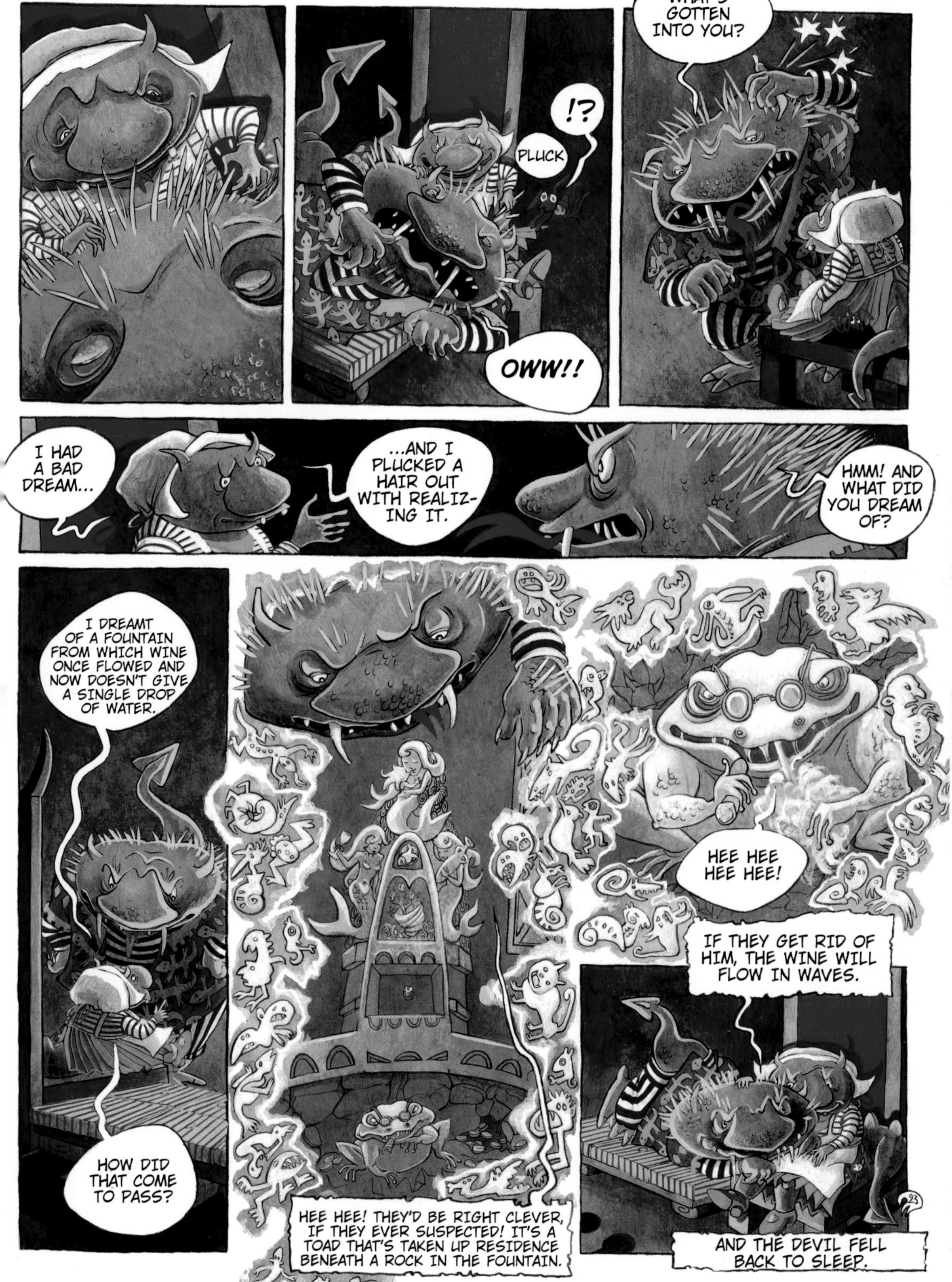
PLUCK
!?
OWW!!
WHAT'S GOTTEN INTO YOU?
I HAD A BAD DREAM...
...AND I PLUCKED A HAIR OUT WITH REALIZING IT.
HMM! AND WHAT DID YOU DREAM OF?
I DREAMT OF A FOUNTAIN FROM WHICH WINE ONCE FLOWED AND NOW DOESN'T GIVE A SINGLE DROP OF WATER.
HOW DID THAT COME TO PASS?
HEE HEE! THEY'D BE RIGHT CLEVER, IF THEY EVER SUSPECTED! IT'S A TOAD THAT'S TAKEN UP RESIDENCE BENEATH A ROCK IN THE FOUNTAIN.
HEE HEE HEE HEE!
IF THEY GET RID OF HIM, THE WINE WILL FLOW IN WAVES.
AND THE DEVIL FELL BACK TO SLEEP.
23

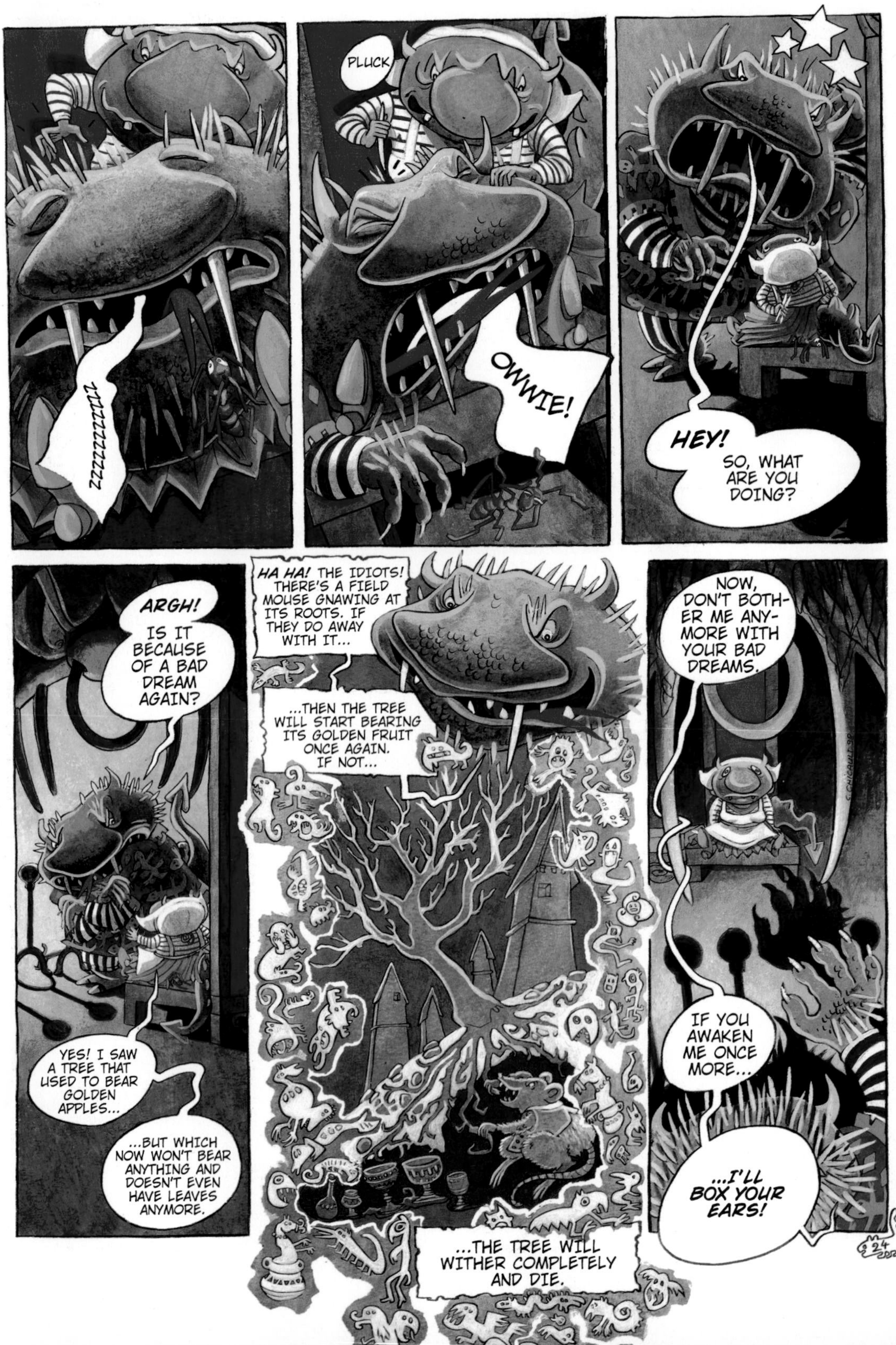
ZZZZZZZZZZZ
PLUCK
OWWIE!
HEY! SO, WHAT ARE YOU DOING?
ARGH! IS IT BECAUSE OF A BAD DREAM AGAIN?
YES! I SAW A TREE THAT USED TO BEAR GOLDEN APPLES...
...BUT WHICH NOW WON'T BEAR ANYTHING AND DOESN'T EVEN HAVE LEAVES ANYMORE.
HA HA! THE IDIOTS! THERE'S A FIELD MOUSE GNAWING AT ITS ROOTS. IF THEY DO AWAY WITH IT...
...THEN THE TREE WILL START BEARING ITS GOLDEN FRUIT ONCE AGAIN. IF NOT...
...THE TREE WILL WITHER COMPLETELY AND DIE.
NOW, DON'T BOTHER ME ANYMORE WITH YOUR BAD DREAMS.
IF YOU AWAKEN ME ONCE MORE...
...I'LL BOX YOUR EARS!
24

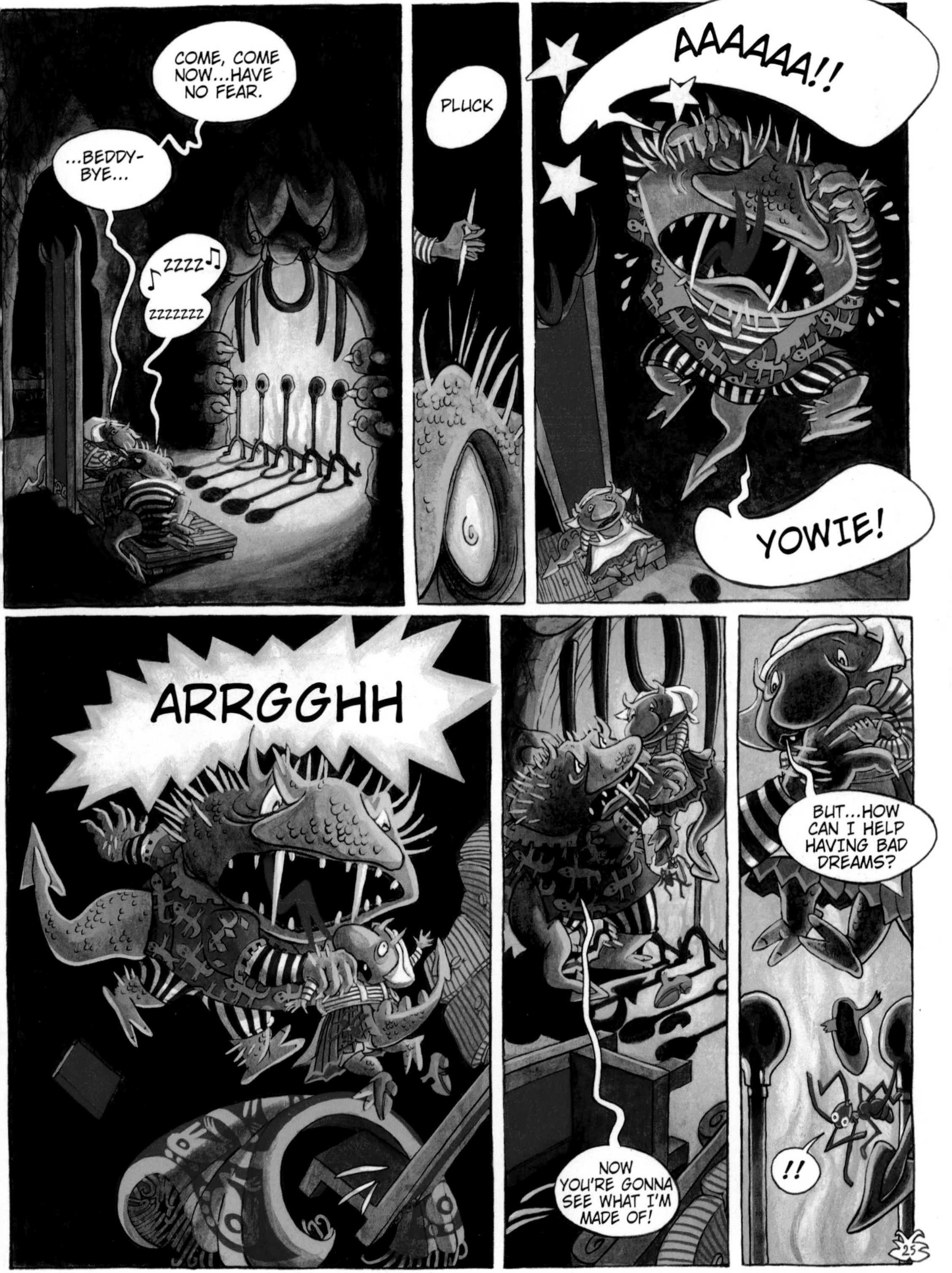
COME, COME NOW...HAVE NO FEAR.
...BEDDY-BYE...
ZZZZ
ZZZZZZZ
PLUCK
AAAAAA!!
YOWIE!
ARRGGHH
NOW YOU'RE GONNA SEE WHAT I'M MADE OF!
BUT...HOW CAN I HELP HAVING BAD DREAMS?
!!
25

ARRGH! WHAT DID YOU DREAM NOW?

I SAW A FERRYMAN GOING CEASE-LESSLY.

...FROM ONE SHORE TO THE OTHER WITHOUT EVER BEING REPLACED.

!

HA HA HA! THE OLD IMBECILE!

PLOP!

PLIF!

IF SOMEONE WERE TO COME ALONG WANTING TO GET TO THE OTHER SIDE, HE ONLY HAS TO PUT HIS POLE IN THE OTHER ONE'S HANDS. THEN HE'LL BE FREE.

IT'S THE OTHER GUY WHO'LL HAVE TO TAKE HIS TURN BEING THE FERRYMAN.

FINALLY, THEY LET THE DEVIL GET HIS NIGHT'S SLEEP.

ZZZZZZZZZZZZZZZZZZZZZZZZZZZZZZZZZZZZZZZZZZZZZ

AT DAY-BREAK...

...THE DEVIL LEFT AGAIN TO DO HIS WORK...

SO, THERE YOU GO, LITTLE ONE.

94

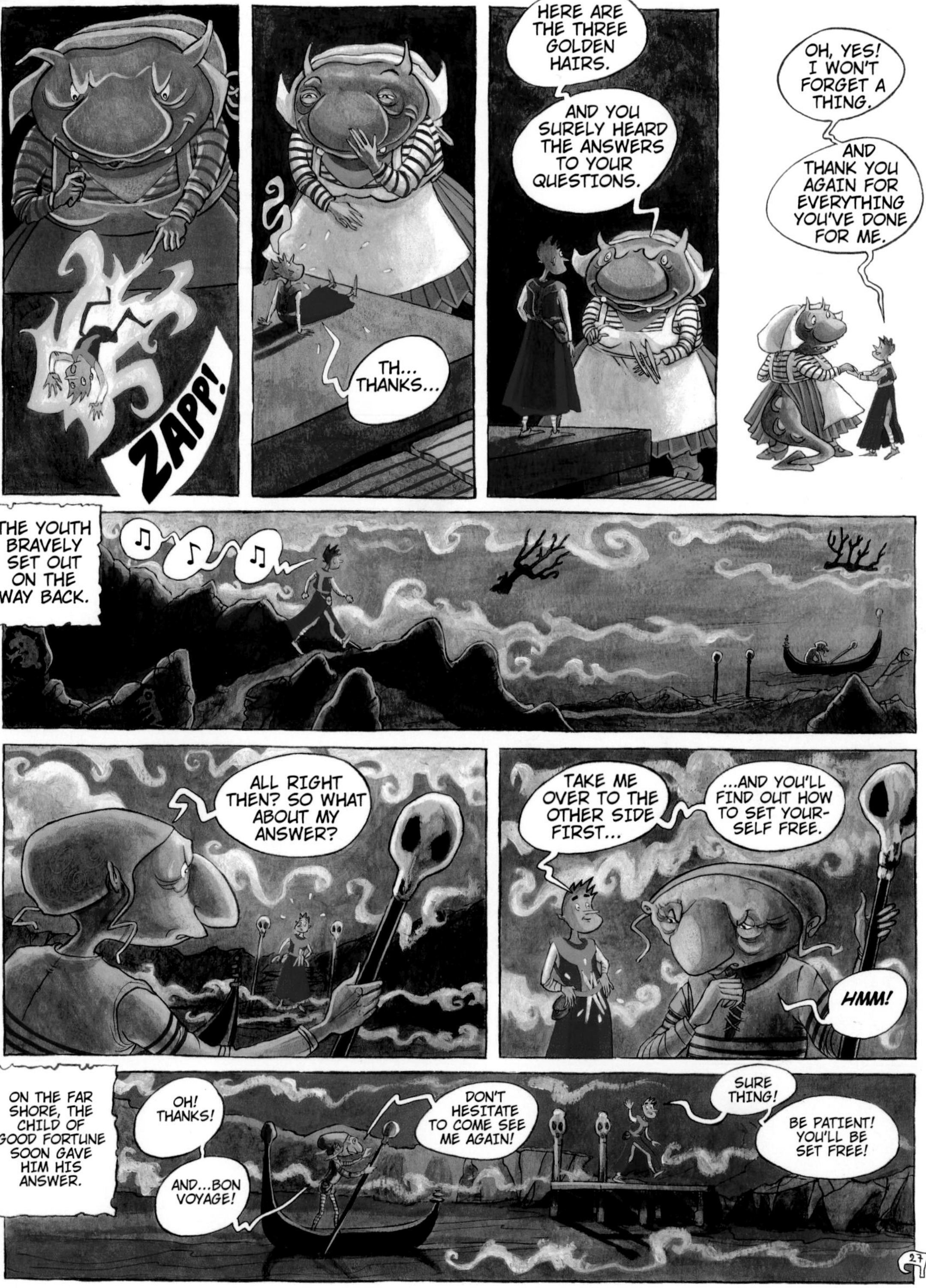
ZAPP!
TH... THANKS...
HERE ARE THE THREE GOLDEN HAIRS.
AND YOU SURELY HEARD THE ANSWERS TO YOUR QUESTIONS.
OH, YES! I WON'T FORGET A THING.
AND THANK YOU AGAIN FOR EVERYTHING YOU'VE DONE FOR ME.
THE YOUTH BRAVELY SET OUT ON THE WAY BACK.
♫ ♪ ♫
ALL RIGHT THEN? SO WHAT ABOUT MY ANSWER?
TAKE ME OVER TO THE OTHER SIDE FIRST...
...AND YOU'LL FIND OUT HOW TO SET YOURSELF FREE.
HMM!
ON THE FAR SHORE, THE CHILD OF GOOD FORTUNE SOON GAVE HIM HIS ANSWER.
OH! THANKS!
AND...BON VOYAGE!
DON'T HESITATE TO COME SEE ME AGAIN!
SURE THING!
BE PATIENT! YOU'LL BE SET FREE!
27

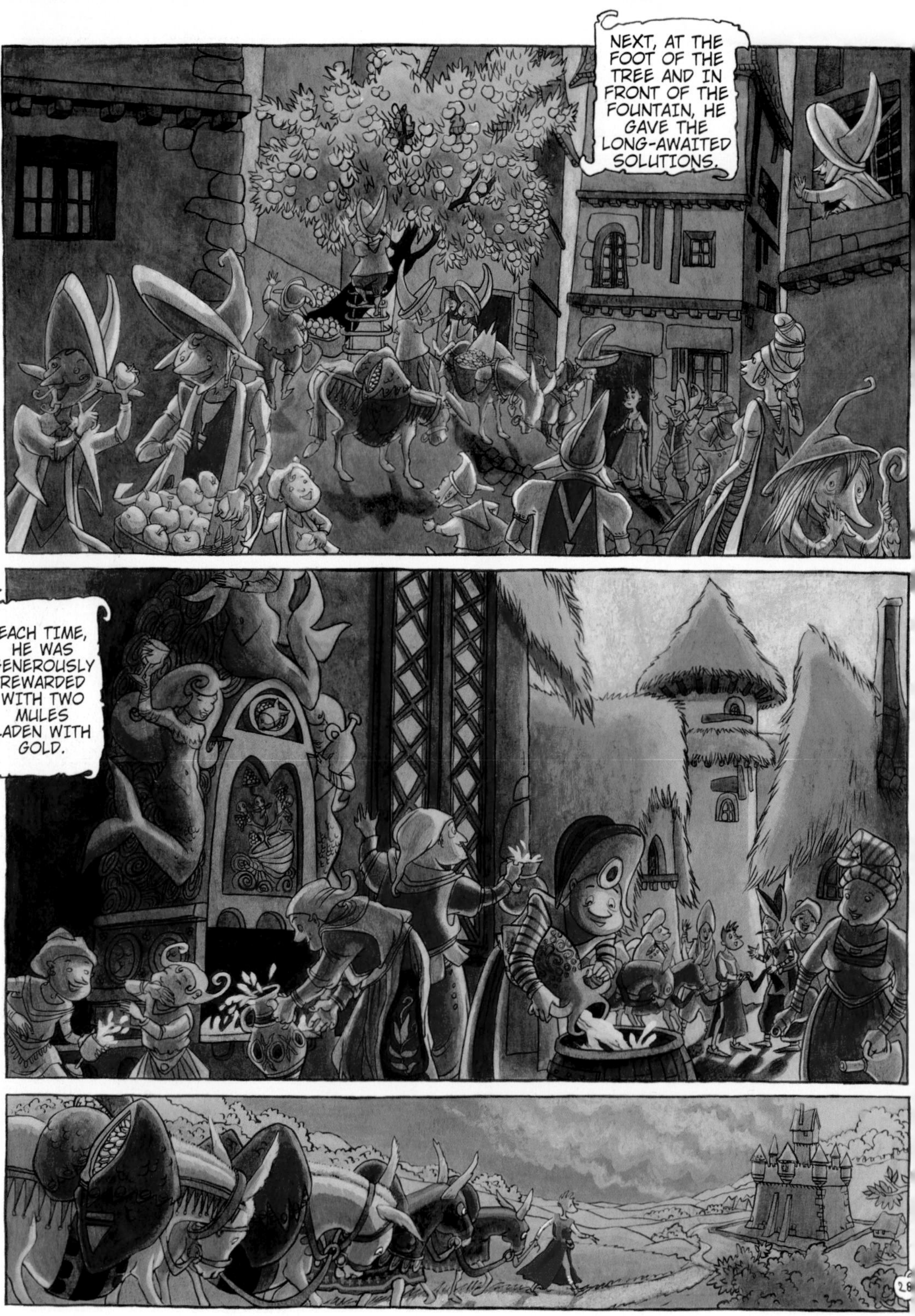
NEXT, AT THE FOOT OF THE TREE AND IN FRONT OF THE FOUNTAIN, HE GAVE THE LONG-AWAITED SOLUTIONS.
EACH TIME, HE WAS GENEROUSLY REWARDED WITH TWO MULES LADEN WITH GOLD.

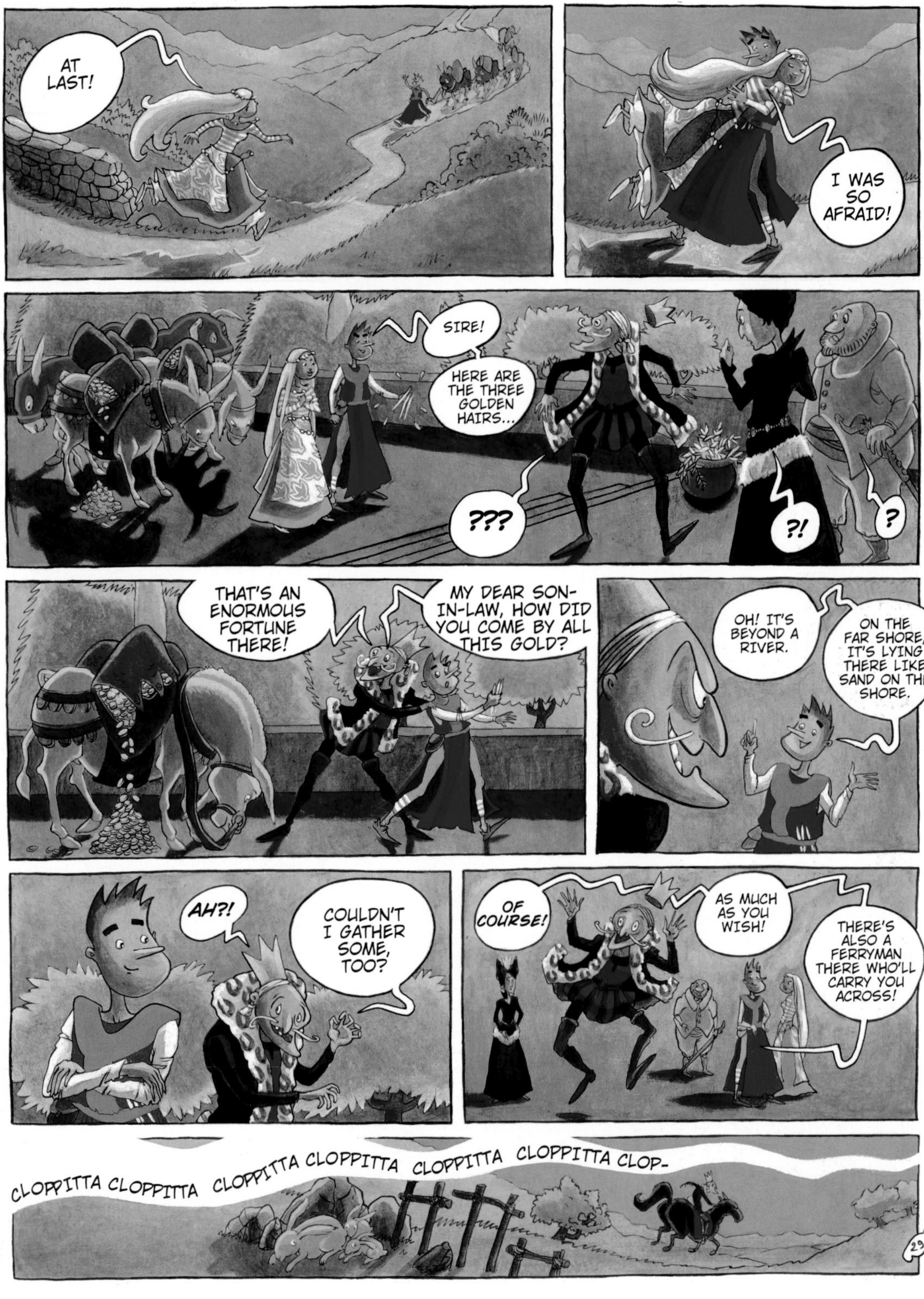
AT LAST!
I WAS SO AFRAID!
SIRE!
HERE ARE THE THREE GOLDEN HAIRS...
???
?!
?
THAT'S AN ENORMOUS FORTUNE THERE!
MY DEAR SON-IN-LAW, HOW DID YOU COME BY ALL THIS GOLD?
OH! IT'S BEYOND A RIVER.
ON THE FAR SHORE, IT'S LYING THERE LIKE SAND ON THE SHORE.
AH?!
COULDN'T I GATHER SOME, TOO?
OF COURSE!
AS MUCH AS YOU WISH!
THERE'S ALSO A FERRYMAN THERE WHO'LL CARRY YOU ACROSS!
CLOPPITTA CLOPPITTA CLOPPITTA CLOPPITTA CLOPPITTA CLOPPITTA CLOP-
29

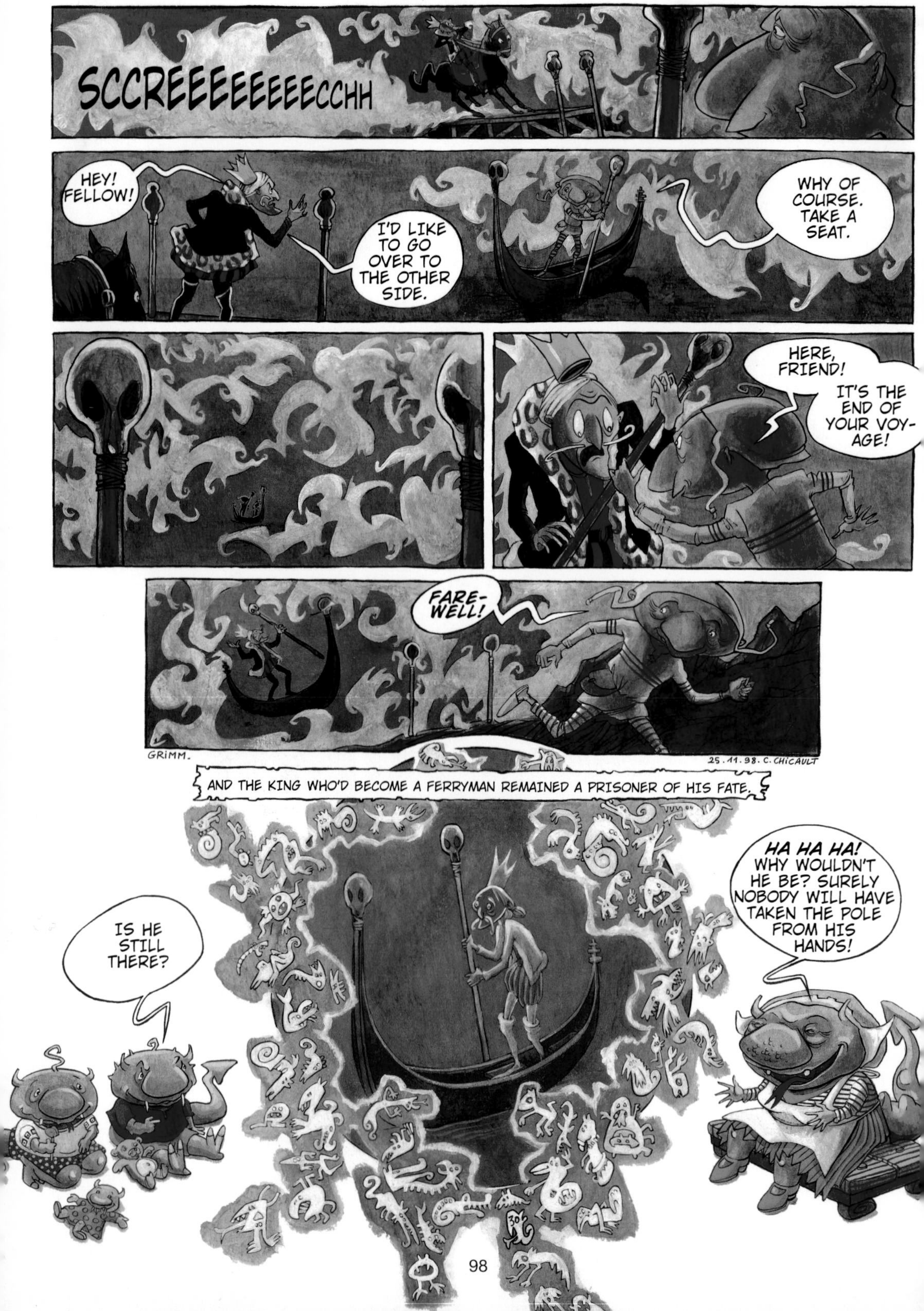
SCCREEEEEEEEECCHH
HEY! FELLOW!
I'D LIKE TO GO OVER TO THE OTHER SIDE.
WHY OF COURSE. TAKE A SEAT.
HERE, FRIEND!
IT'S THE END OF YOUR VOY-AGE!
FARE-WELL!
GRIMM.
25.11.98. C. CHICAULT
AND THE KING WHO'D BECOME A FERRYMAN REMAINED A PRISONER OF HIS FATE.
IS HE STILL THERE?
HA HA HA! WHY WOULDN'T HE BE? SURELY NOBODY WILL HAVE TAKEN THE POLE FROM HIS HANDS!

THE VALIANT LITTLE TAILOR

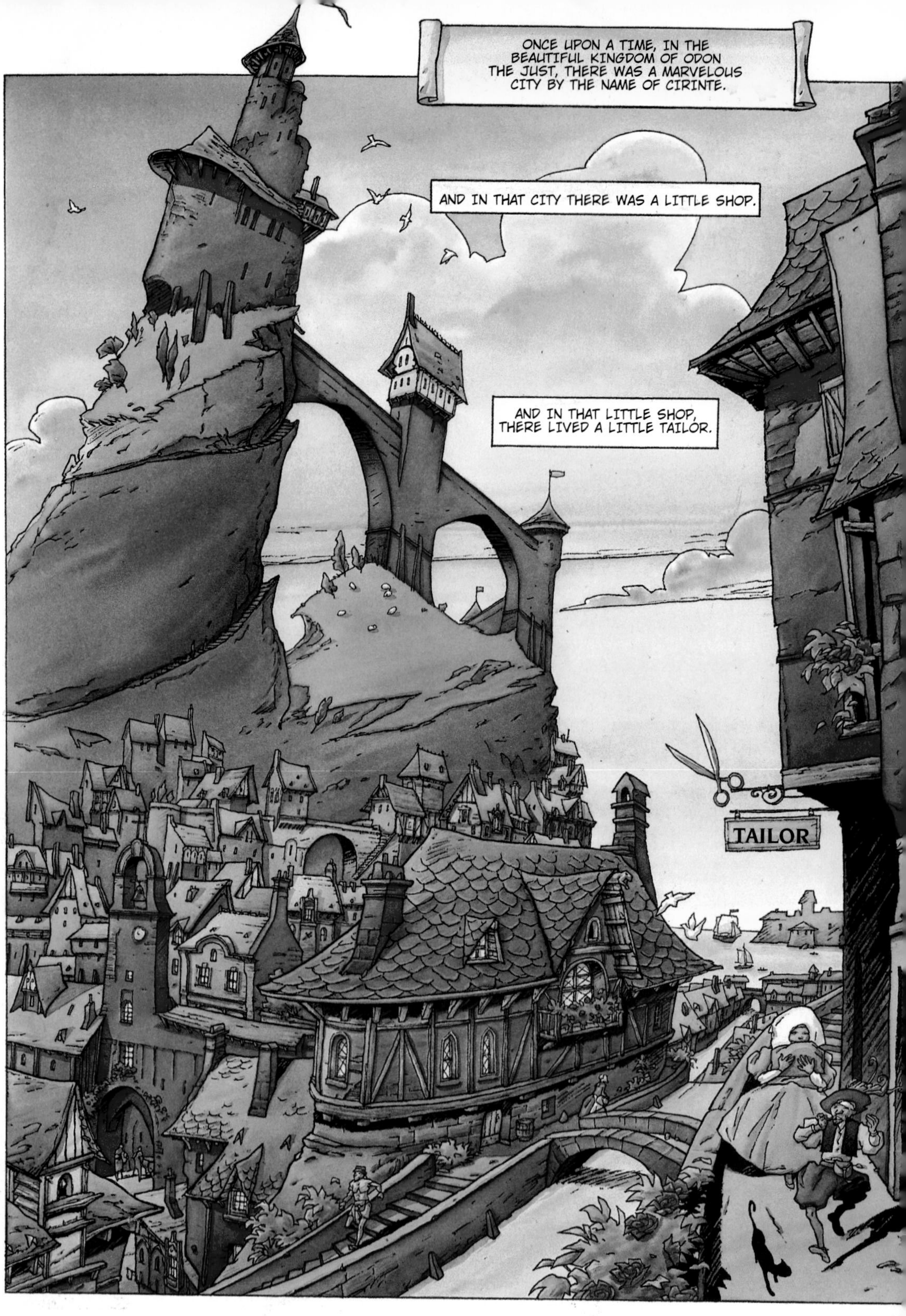

ONCE UPON A TIME, IN THE BEAUTIFUL KINGDOM OF ODON THE JUST, THERE WAS A MARVELOUS CITY BY THE NAME OF CIRINTE.
AND IN THAT CITY THERE WAS A LITTLE SHOP.
AND IN THAT LITTLE SHOP, THERE LIVED A LITTLE TAILOR.
TAILOR

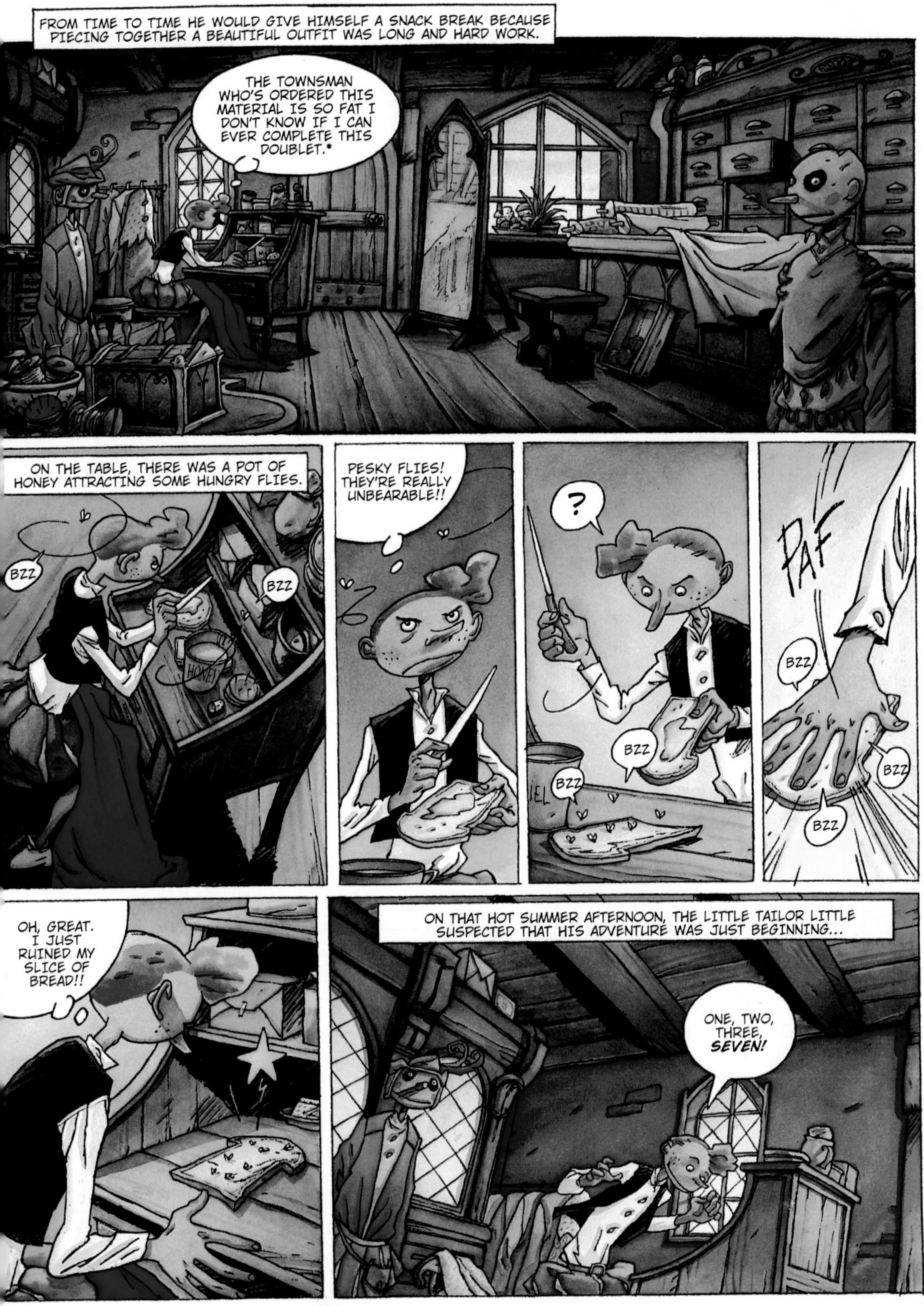
FROM TIME TO TIME HE WOULD GIVE HIMSELF A SNACK BREAK BECAUSE PIECING TOGETHER A BEAUTIFUL OUTFIT WAS LONG AND HARD WORK.
THE TOWNSMAN WHO'S ORDERED THIS MATERIAL IS SO FAT I DON'T KNOW IF I CAN EVER COMPLETE THIS DOUBLET.*
ON THE TABLE, THERE WAS A POT OF HONEY ATTRACTING SOME HUNGRY FLIES.
BZZ
BZZ
HONEY
PESKY FLIES! THEY'RE REALLY UNBEARABLE!!
?
BZZ
BZZ
PAF
BZZ
BZZ
BZZ
OH, GREAT. I JUST RUINED MY SLICE OF BREAD!!
ON THAT HOT SUMMER AFTERNOON, THE LITTLE TAILOR LITTLE SUSPECTED THAT HIS ADVENTURE WAS JUST BEGINNING...
ONE, TWO, THREE, **SEVEN!**

*AN ARTICLE OF CLOTHING WORN DURING THE MIDDLE AGES.

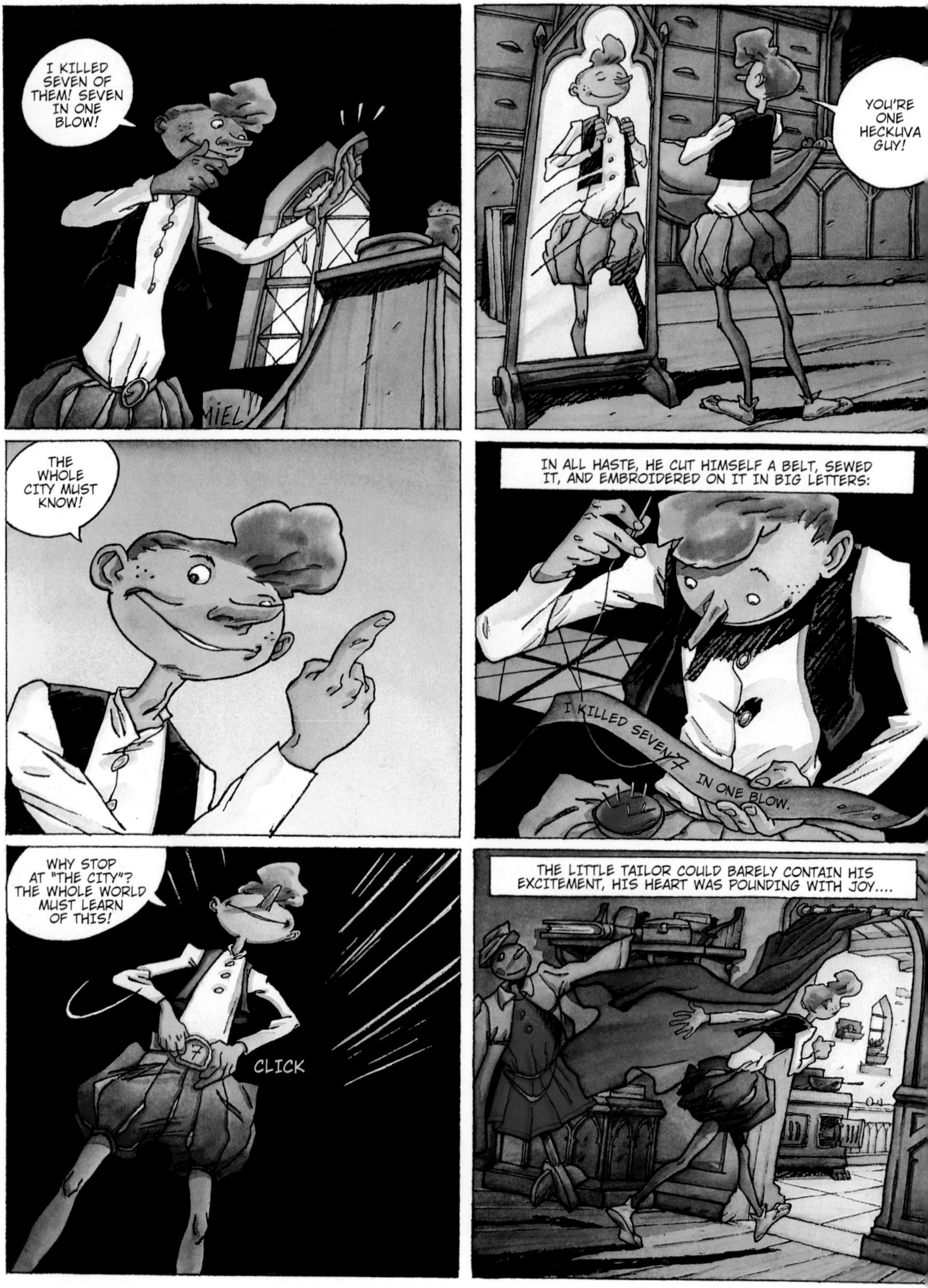
I KILLED SEVEN OF THEM! SEVEN IN ONE BLOW!
MIEL
YOU'RE ONE HECKUVA GUY!
THE WHOLE CITY MUST KNOW!
IN ALL HASTE, HE CUT HIMSELF A BELT, SEWED IT, AND EMBROIDERED ON IT IN BIG LETTERS:
I KILLED SEVEN 7 IN ONE BLOW.
WHY STOP AT "THE CITY"? THE WHOLE WORLD MUST LEARN OF THIS!
7
CLICK
THE LITTLE TAILOR COULD BARELY CONTAIN HIS EXCITEMENT, HIS HEART WAS POUNDING WITH JOY....

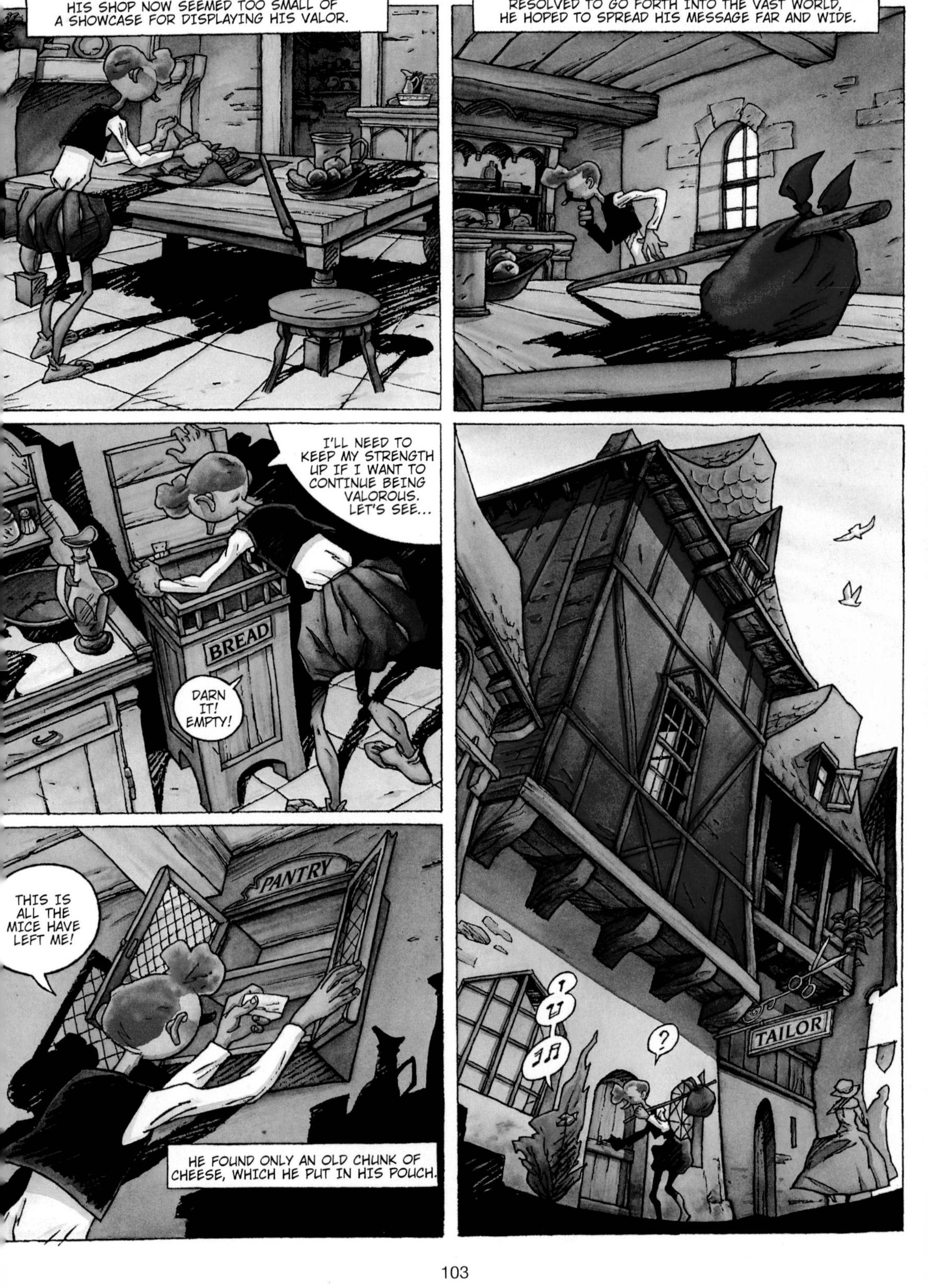
HIS SHOP NOW SEEMED TOO SMALL OF A SHOWCASE FOR DISPLAYING HIS VALOR.
RESOLVED TO GO FORTH INTO THE VAST WORLD, HE HOPED TO SPREAD HIS MESSAGE FAR AND WIDE.
I'LL NEED TO KEEP MY STRENGTH UP IF I WANT TO CONTINUE BEING VALOROUS. LET'S SEE...
BREAD
DARN IT! EMPTY!
PANTRY
THIS IS ALL THE MICE HAVE LEFT ME!
HE FOUND ONLY AN OLD CHUNK OF CHEESE, WHICH HE PUT IN HIS POUCH.
?
TAILOR

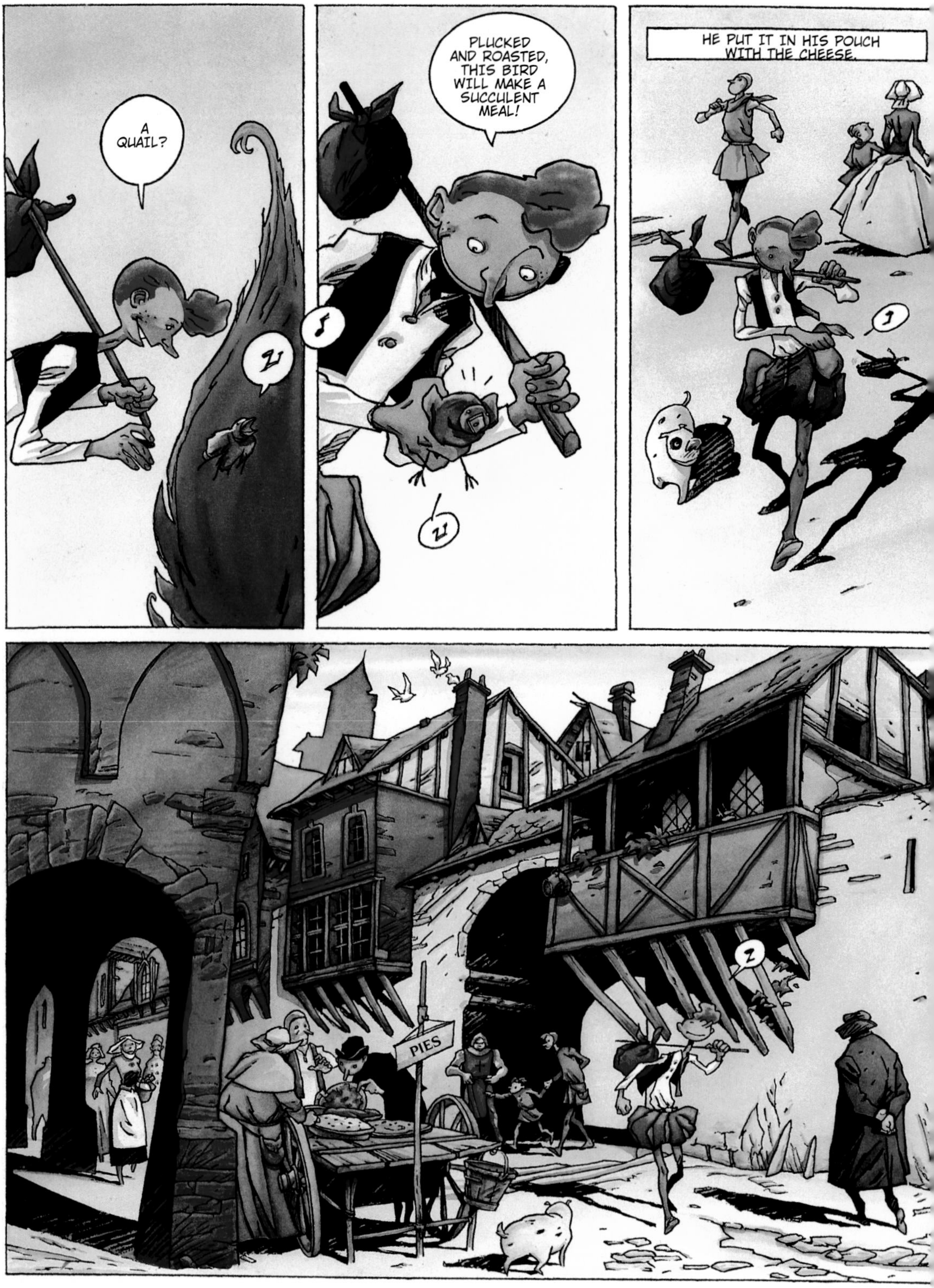
A QUAIL?
PLUCKED AND ROASTED, THIS BIRD WILL MAKE A SUCCULENT MEAL!
HE PUT IT IN HIS POUCH WITH THE CHEESE.
PIES

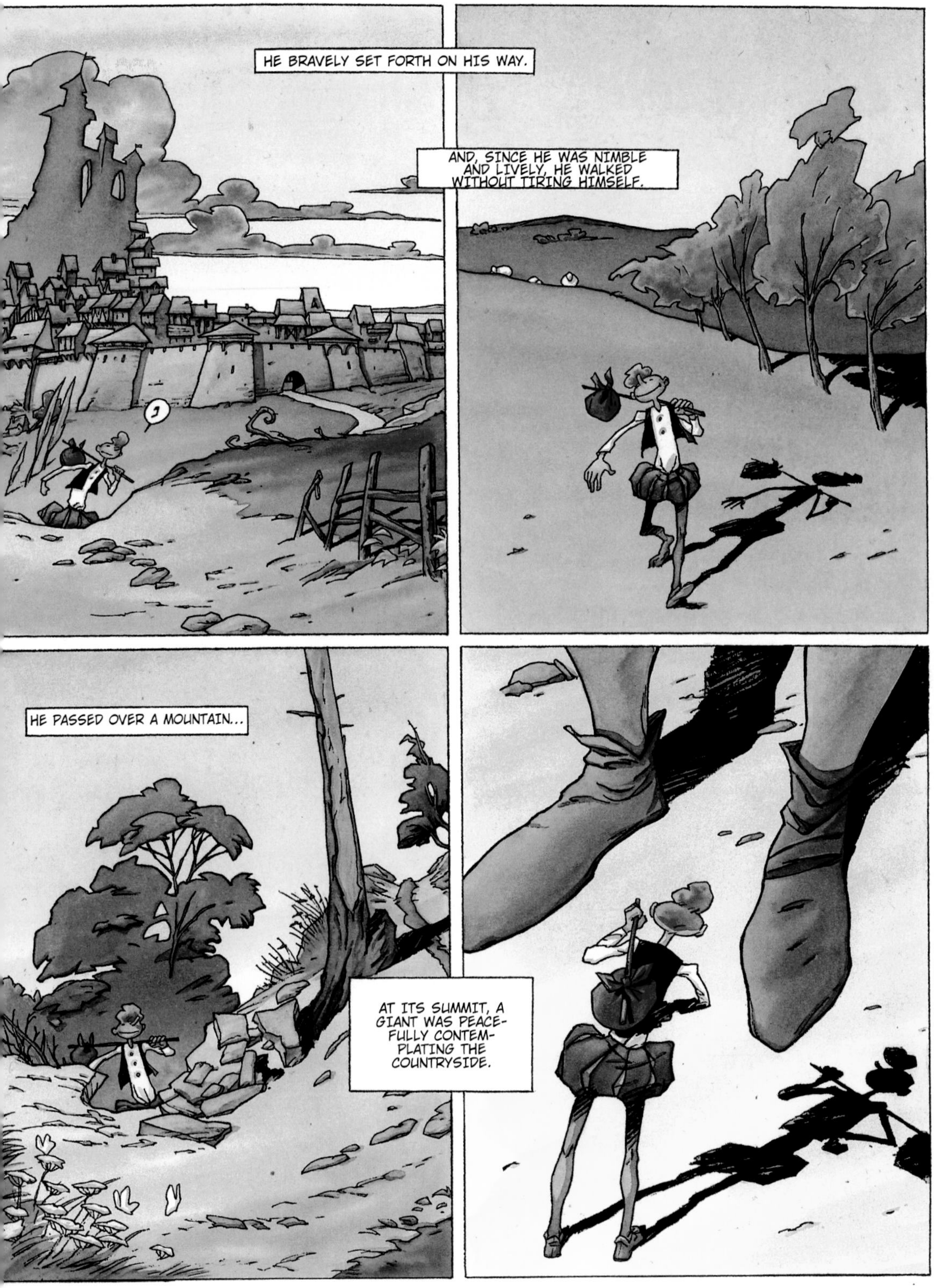
HE BRAVELY SET FORTH ON HIS WAY.
AND, SINCE HE WAS NIMBLE AND LIVELY, HE WALKED WITHOUT TIRING HIMSELF.
HE PASSED OVER A MOUNTAIN...
AT ITS SUMMIT, A GIANT WAS PEACEFULLY CONTEMPLATING THE COUNTRYSIDE.

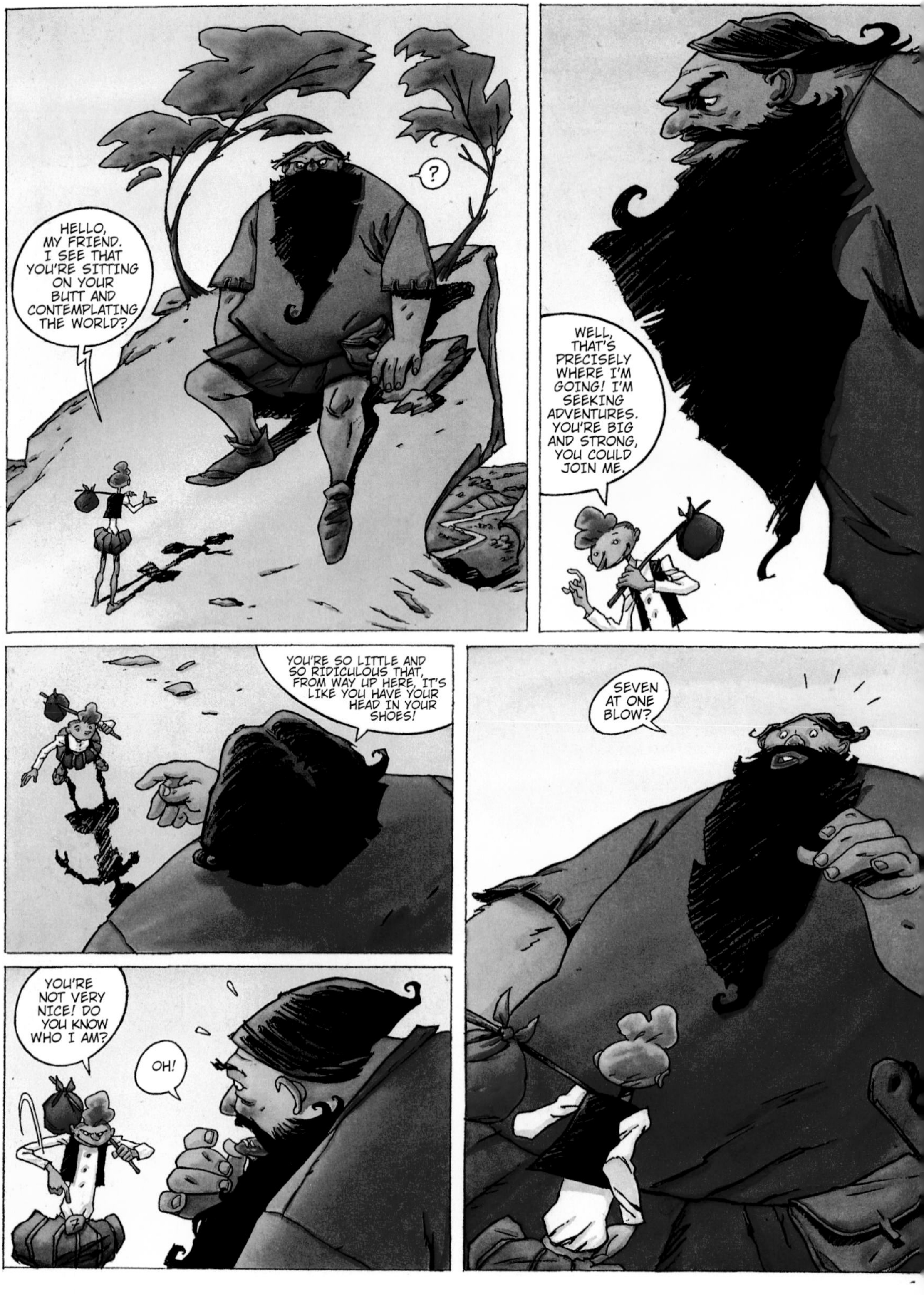
?
HELLO, MY FRIEND. I SEE THAT YOU'RE SITTING ON YOUR BUTT AND CONTEMPLATING THE WORLD?
WELL, THAT'S PRECISELY WHERE I'M GOING! I'M SEEKING ADVENTURES. YOU'RE BIG AND STRONG, YOU COULD JOIN ME.
YOU'RE SO LITTLE AND SO RIDICULOUS THAT, FROM WAY UP HERE, IT'S LIKE YOU HAVE YOUR HEAD IN YOUR SHOES!
YOU'RE NOT VERY NICE! DO YOU KNOW WHO I AM?
OH!
SEVEN AT ONE BLOW?

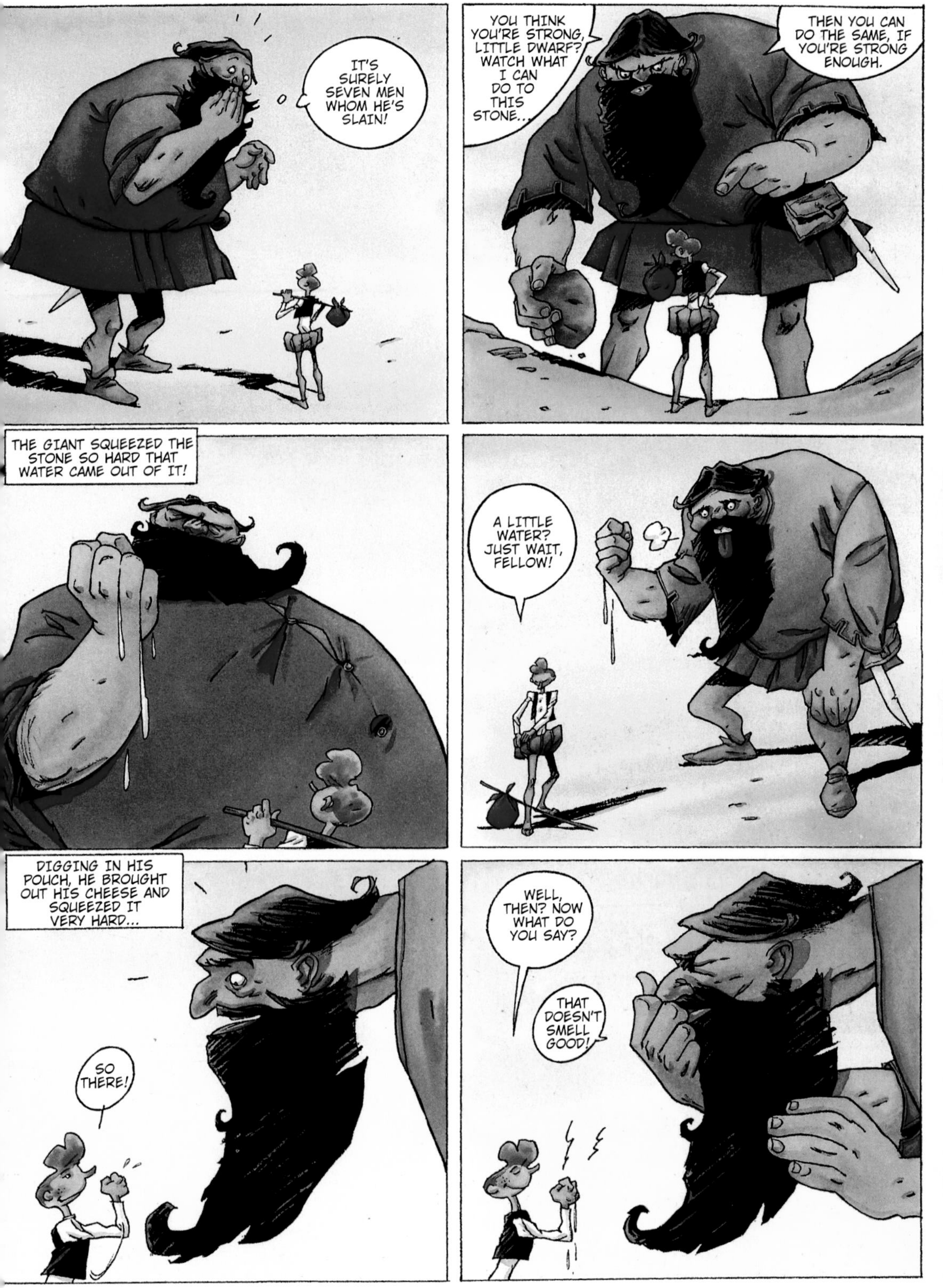
IT'S SURELY SEVEN MEN WHOM HE'S SLAIN!
YOU THINK YOU'RE STRONG, LITTLE DWARF? WATCH WHAT I CAN DO TO THIS STONE...
THEN YOU CAN DO THE SAME, IF YOU'RE STRONG ENOUGH.
THE GIANT SQUEEZED THE STONE SO HARD THAT WATER CAME OUT OF IT!
A LITTLE WATER? JUST WAIT, FELLOW!
DIGGING IN HIS POUCH, HE BROUGHT OUT HIS CHEESE AND SQUEEZED IT VERY HARD...
SO THERE!
WELL, THEN? NOW WHAT DO YOU SAY?
THAT DOESN'T SMELL GOOD!

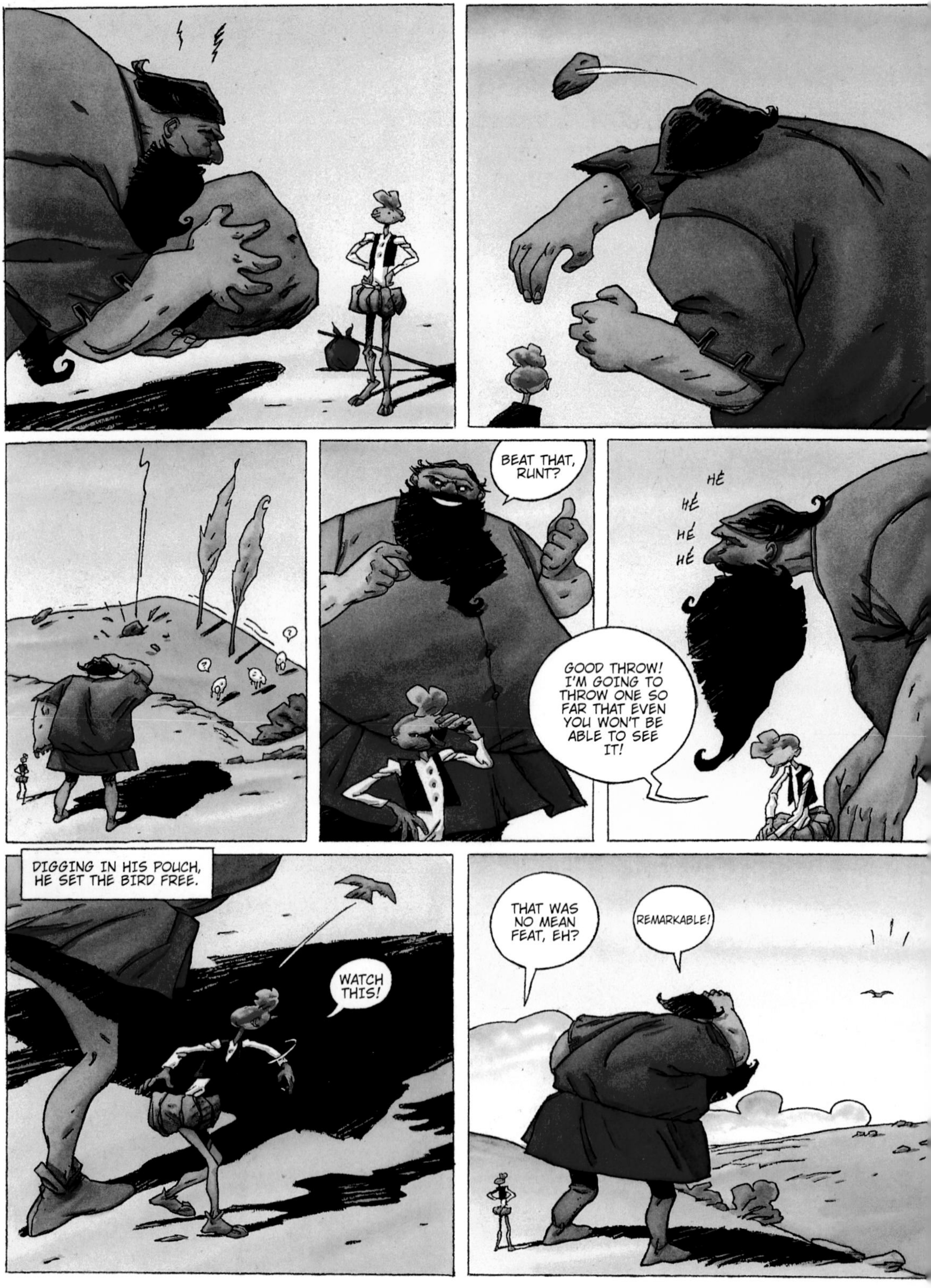
BEAT THAT, RUNT?
HÉ
HÉ
HÉ
HÉ
GOOD THROW! I'M GOING TO THROW ONE SO FAR THAT EVEN YOU WON'T BE ABLE TO SEE IT!
DIGGING IN HIS POUCH, HE SET THE BIRD FREE.
WATCH THIS!
THAT WAS NO MEAN FEAT, EH?
REMARKABLE!

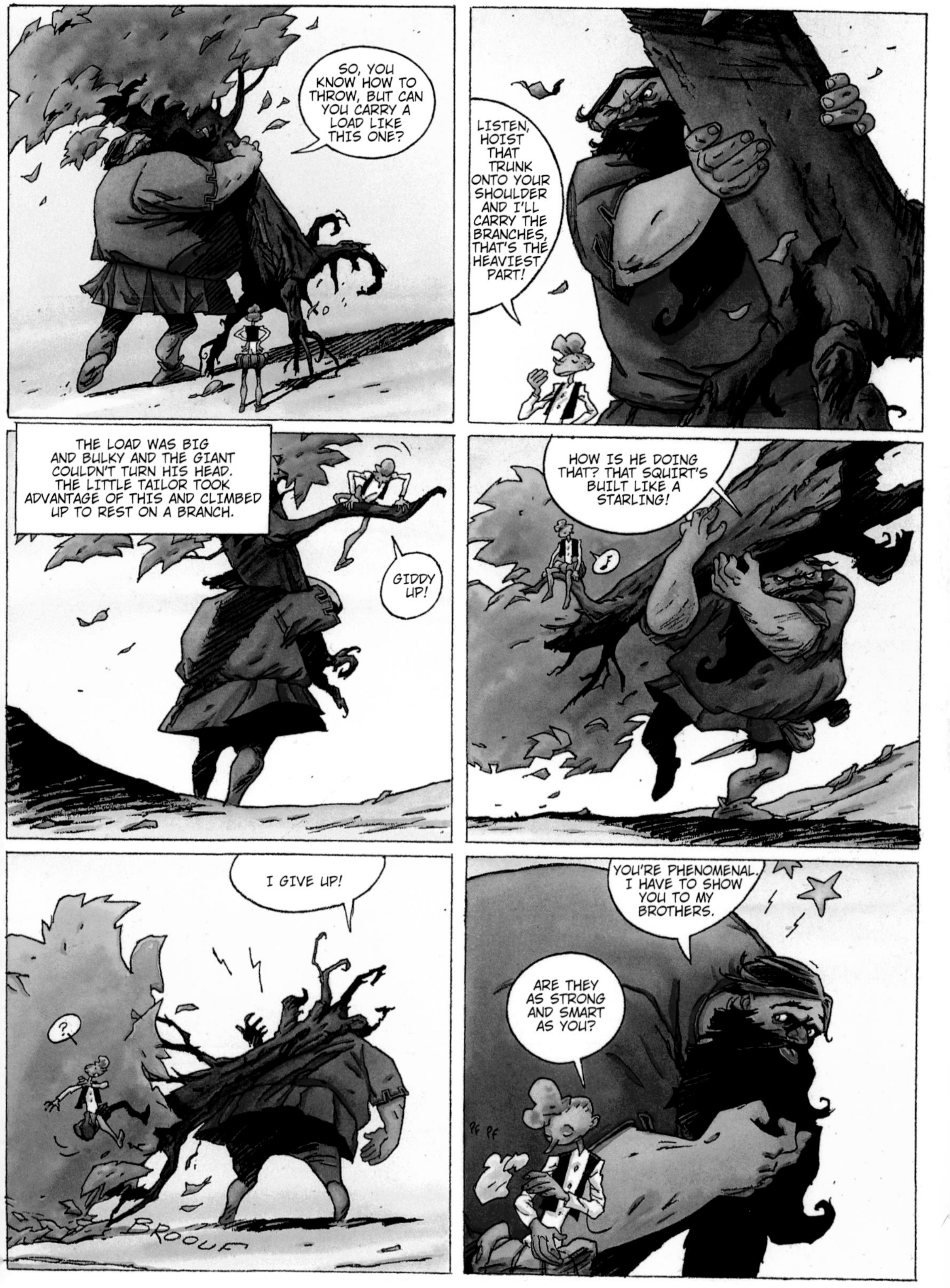
SO, YOU KNOW HOW TO THROW, BUT CAN YOU CARRY A LOAD LIKE THIS ONE?
LISTEN, HOIST THAT TRUNK ONTO YOUR SHOULDER AND I'LL CARRY THE BRANCHES, THAT'S THE HEAVIEST PART!
THE LOAD WAS BIG AND BULKY AND THE GIANT COULDN'T TURN HIS HEAD. THE LITTLE TAILOR TOOK ADVANTAGE OF THIS AND CLIMBED UP TO REST ON A BRANCH.
GIDDY UP!
HOW IS HE DOING THAT? THAT SQUIRT'S BUILT LIKE A STARLING!
I GIVE UP!
?
BROOUF
YOU'RE PHENOMENAL. I HAVE TO SHOW YOU TO MY BROTHERS.
ARE THEY AS STRONG AND SMART AS YOU?
PF PF

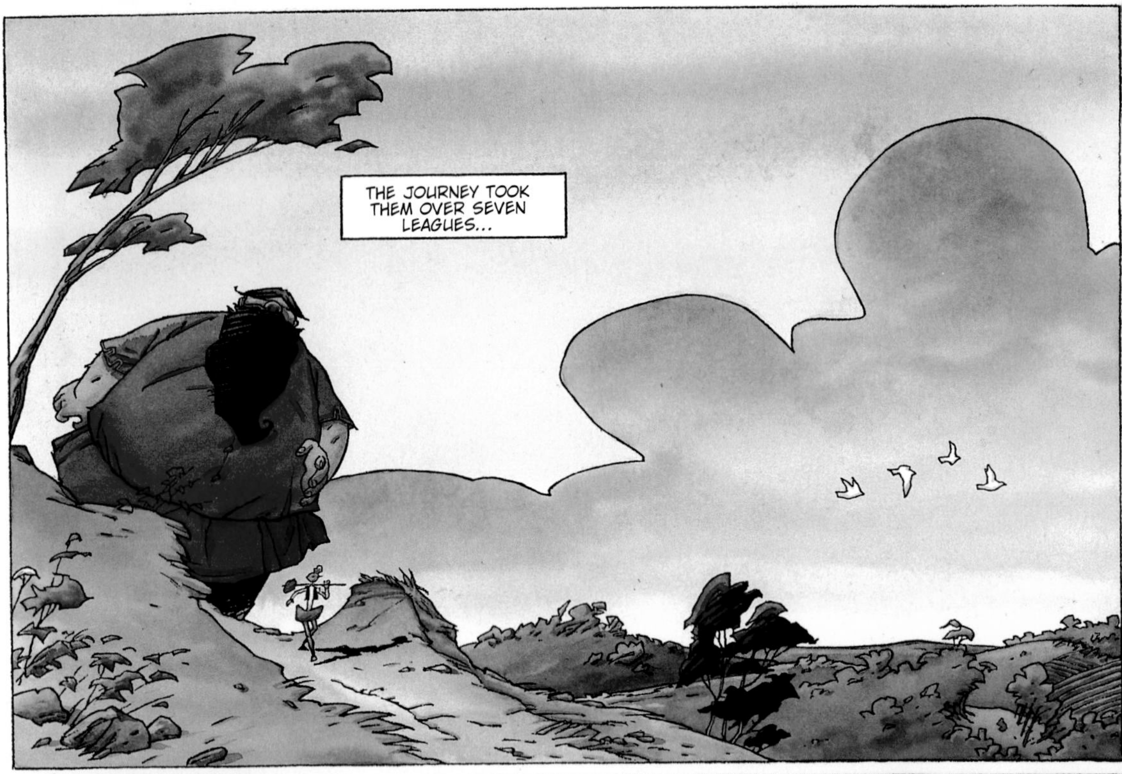
THE JOURNEY TOOK THEM OVER SEVEN LEAGUES...

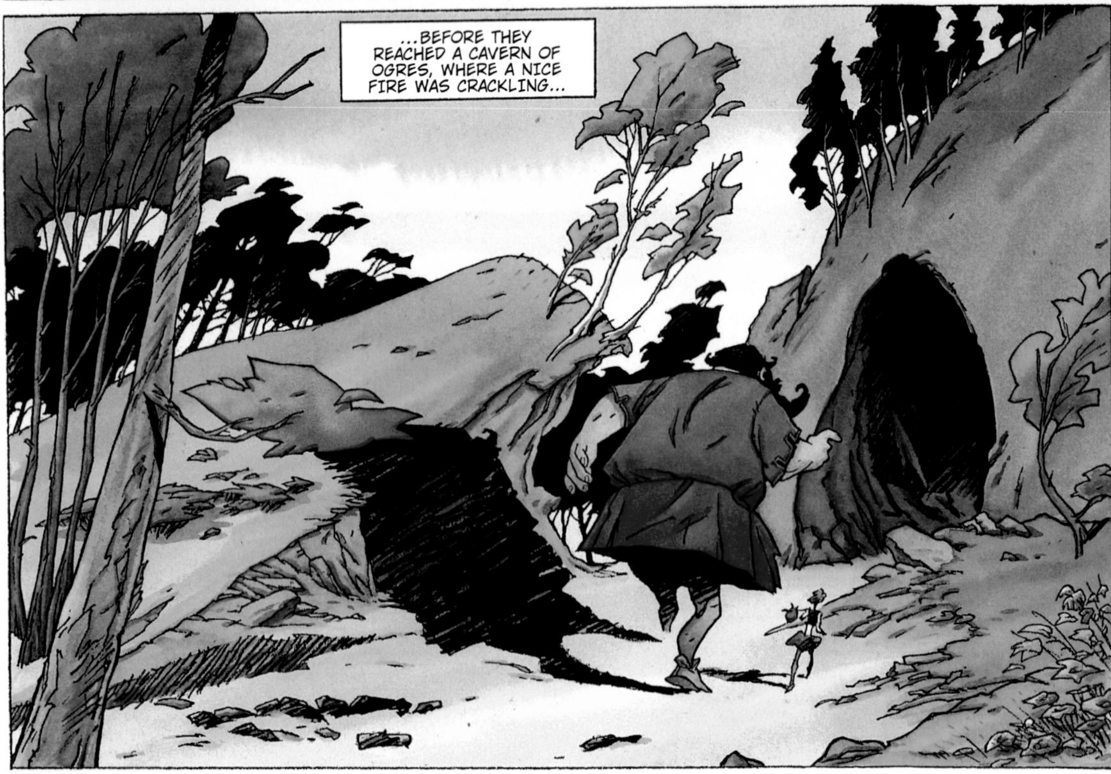
...BEFORE THEY REACHED A CAVERN OF OGRES, WHERE A NICE FIRE WAS CRACKLING...

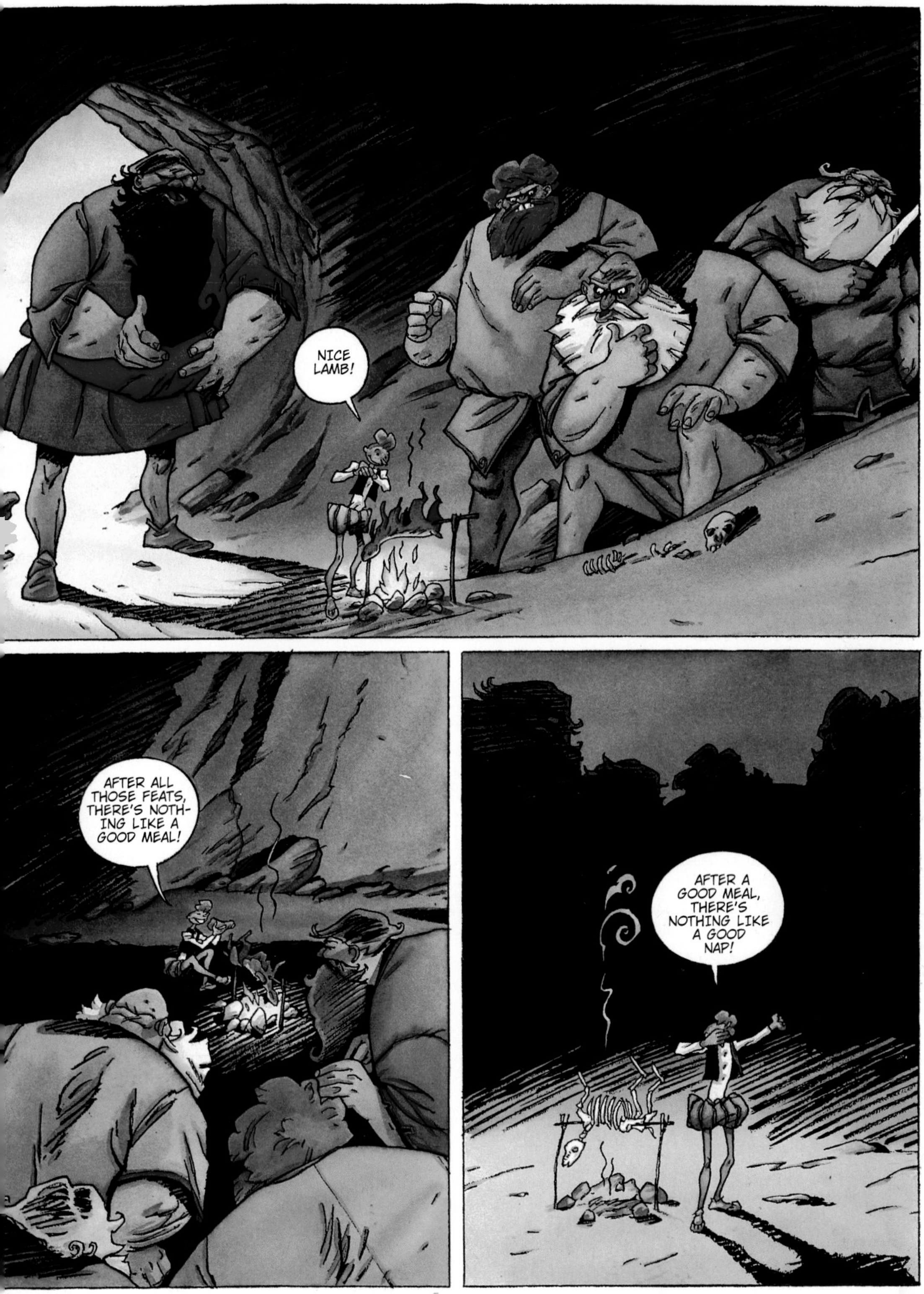
NICE LAMB!
AFTER ALL THOSE FEATS, THERE'S NOTHING LIKE A GOOD MEAL!
AFTER A GOOD MEAL, THERE'S NOTHING LIKE A GOOD NAP!

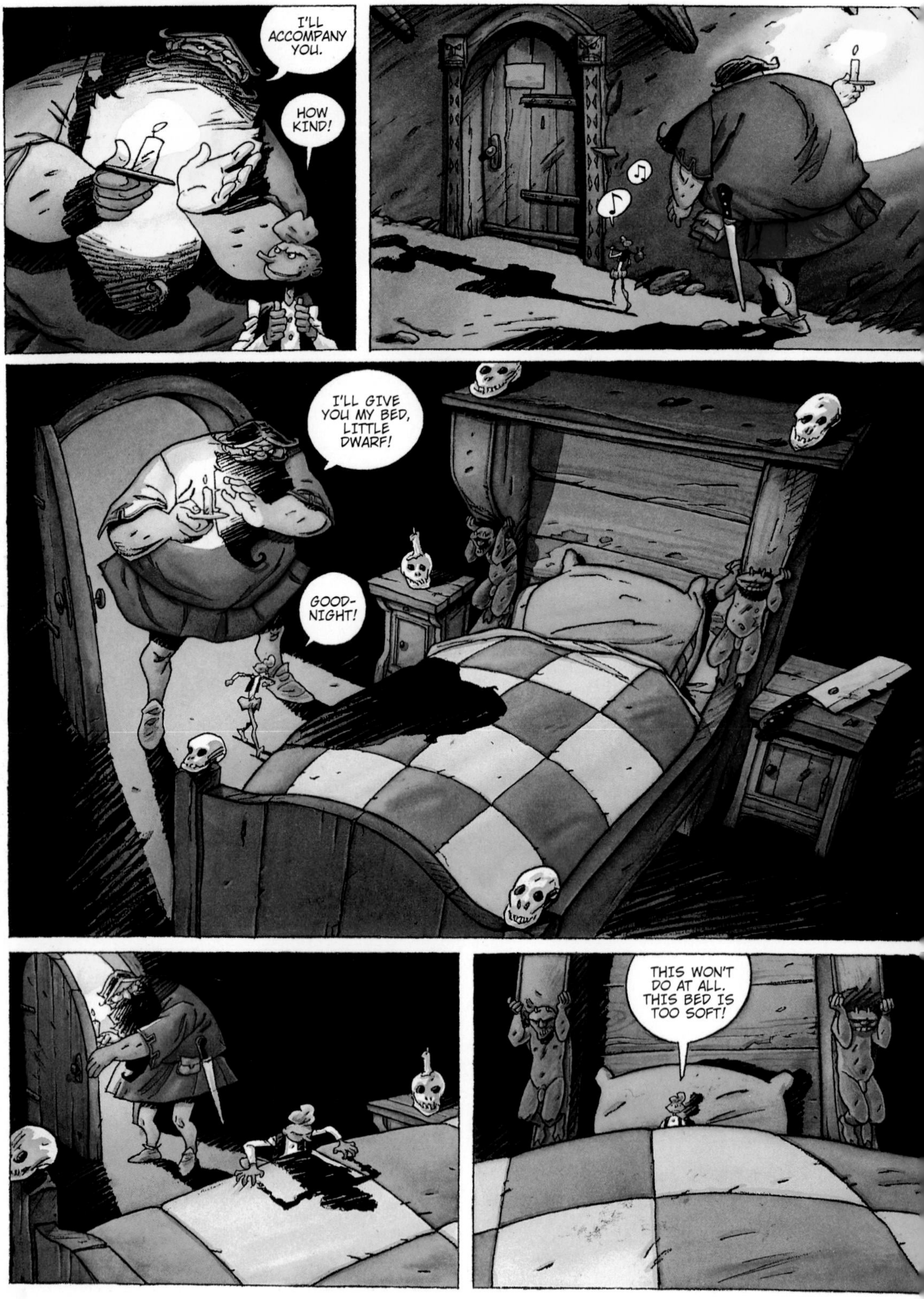
I'LL ACCOMPANY YOU.
HOW KIND!
I'LL GIVE YOU MY BED, LITTLE DWARF!
GOOD-NIGHT!
THIS WON'T DO AT ALL. THIS BED IS TOO SOFT!

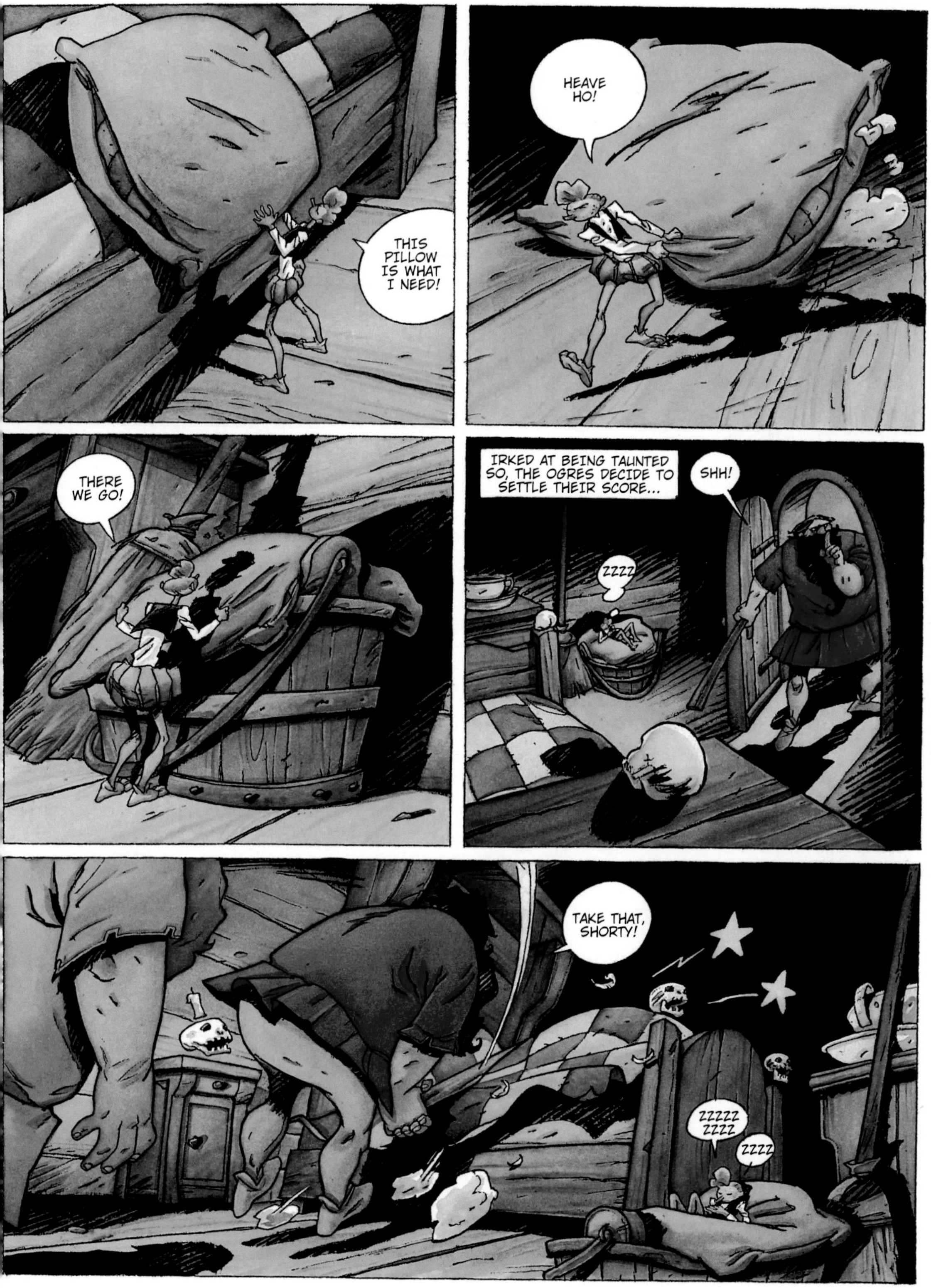
THIS PILLOW IS WHAT I NEED!
HEAVE HO!
THERE WE GO!
IRKED AT BEING TAUNTED SO, THE OGRES DECIDE TO SETTLE THEIR SCORE...
SHH!
ZZZZ
TAKE THAT, SHORTY!
ZZZZZ ZZZZ
ZZZZ

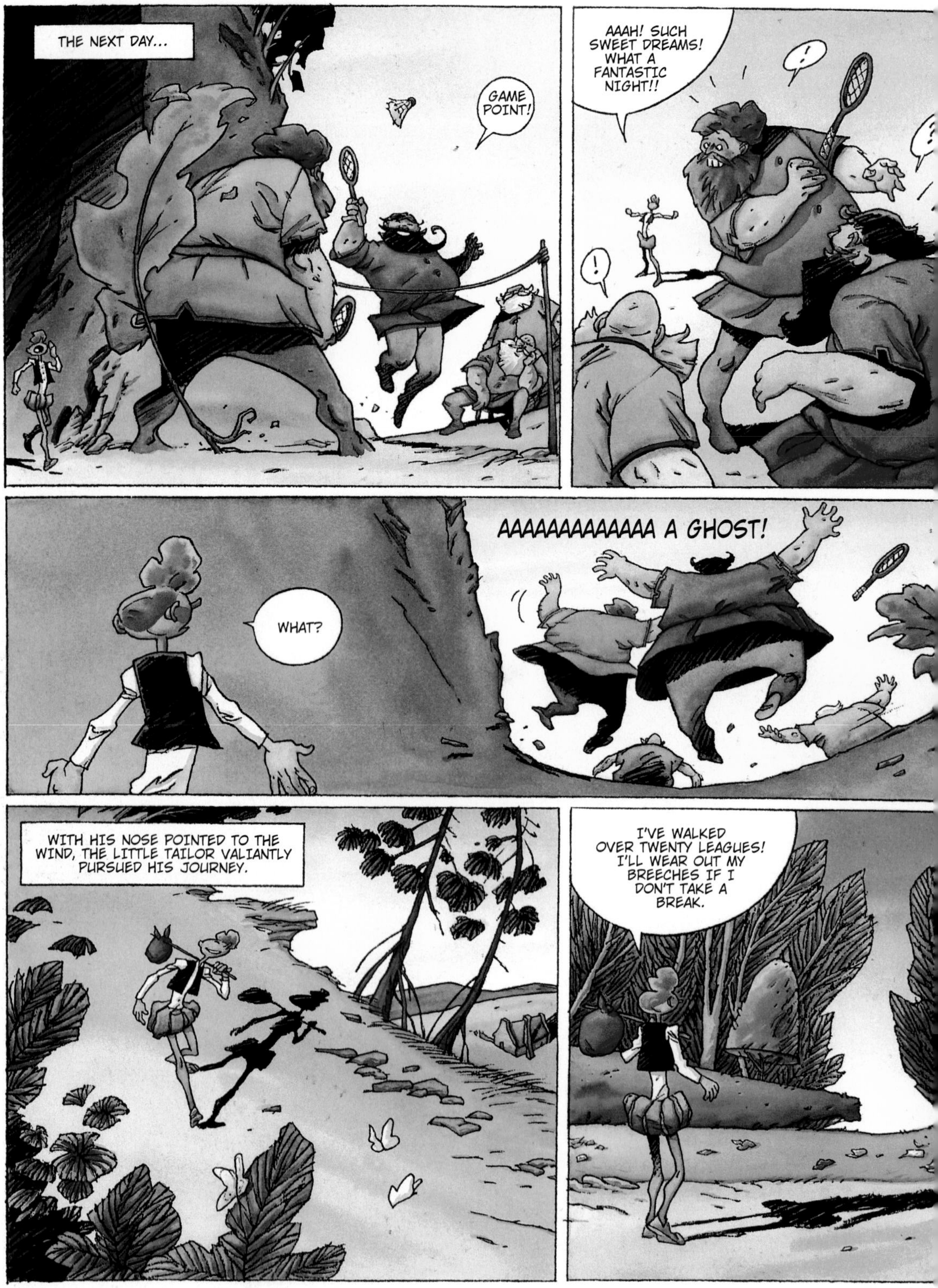
THE NEXT DAY...
GAME POINT!
AAAH! SUCH SWEET DREAMS! WHAT A FANTASTIC NIGHT!!
!
!
!
AAAAAAAAAAAAA A GHOST!
WHAT?
WITH HIS NOSE POINTED TO THE WIND, THE LITTLE TAILOR VALIANTLY PURSUED HIS JOURNEY.
I'VE WALKED OVER TWENTY LEAGUES! I'LL WEAR OUT MY BREECHES IF I DON'T TAKE A BREAK.

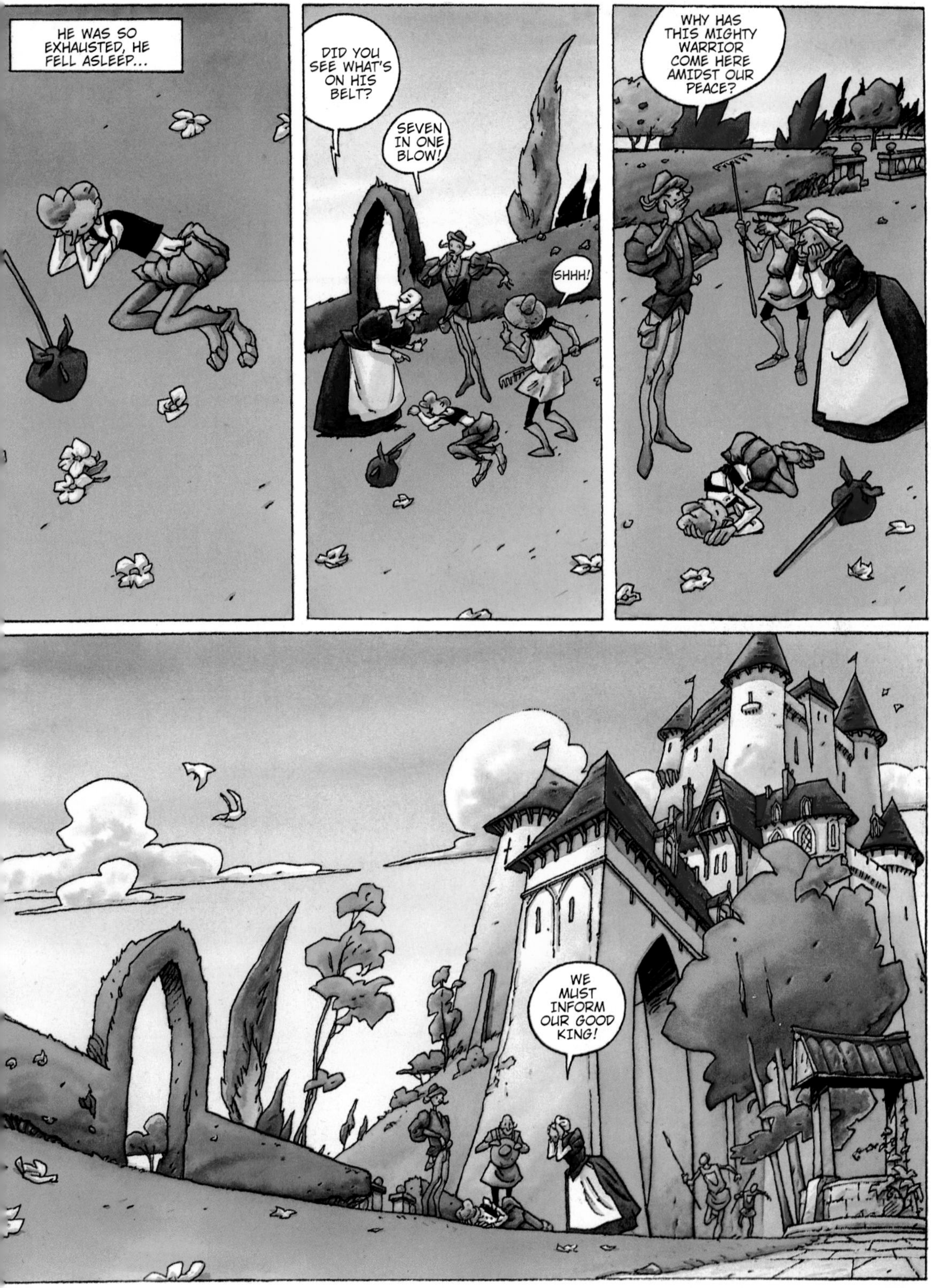
HE WAS SO EXHAUSTED, HE FELL ASLEEP...
DID YOU SEE WHAT'S ON HIS BELT?
SEVEN IN ONE BLOW!
SHHH!
WHY HAS THIS MIGHTY WARRIOR COME HERE AMIDST OUR PEACE?
WE MUST INFORM OUR GOOD KING!

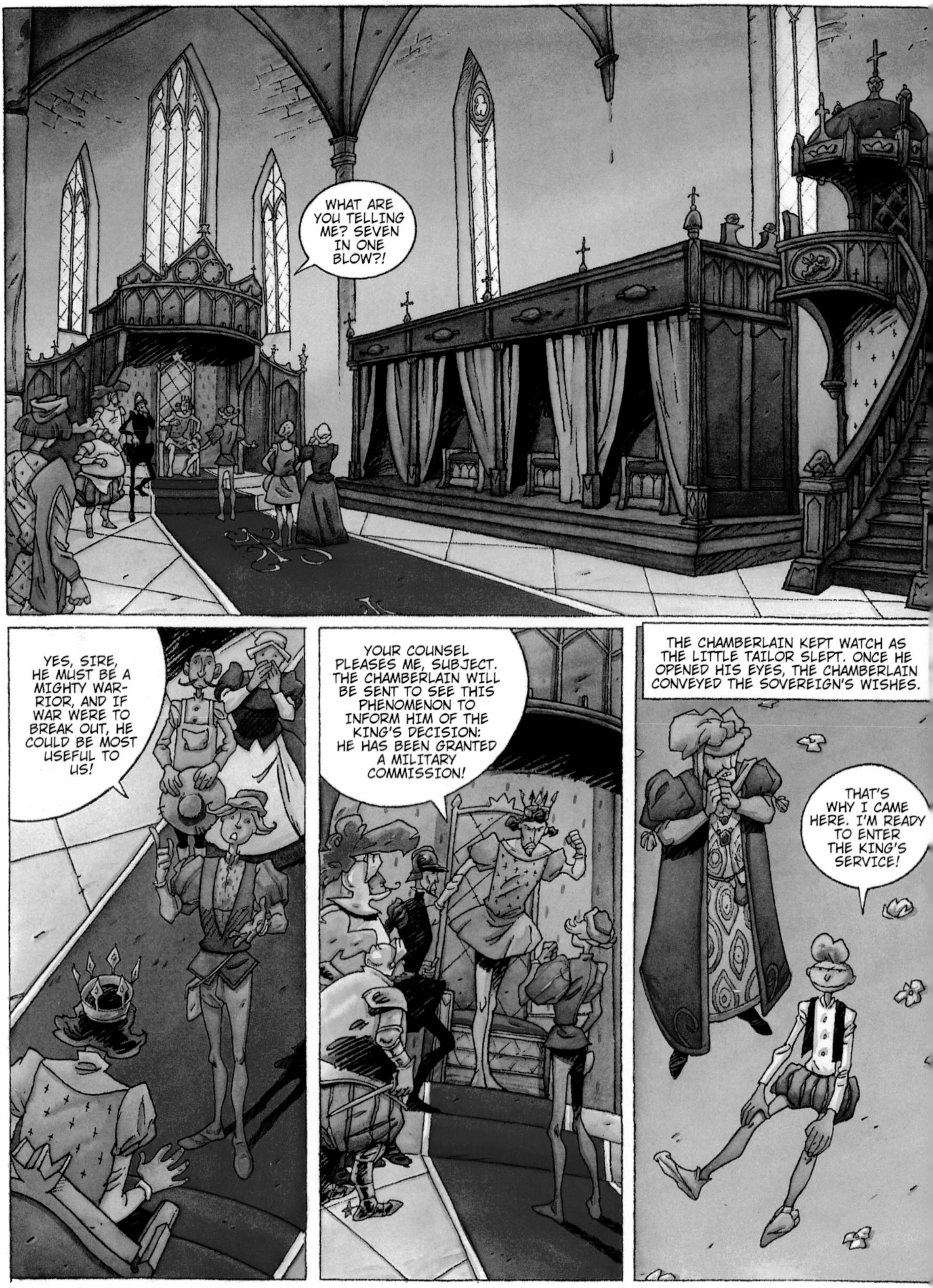
WHAT ARE YOU TELLING ME? SEVEN IN ONE BLOW?!
YES, SIRE, HE MUST BE A MIGHTY WARRIOR, AND IF WAR WERE TO BREAK OUT, HE COULD BE MOST USEFUL TO US!
YOUR COUNSEL PLEASES ME, SUBJECT. THE CHAMBERLAIN WILL BE SENT TO SEE THIS PHENOMENON TO INFORM HIM OF THE KING'S DECISION: HE HAS BEEN GRANTED A MILITARY COMMISSION!
THE CHAMBERLAIN KEPT WATCH AS THE LITTLE TAILOR SLEPT. ONCE HE OPENED HIS EYES, THE CHAMBERLAIN CONVEYED THE SOVEREIGN'S WISHES.
THAT'S WHY I CAME HERE. I'M READY TO ENTER THE KING'S SERVICE!

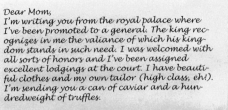

Dear Mom,
I'm writing you from the royal palace where I've been promoted to a general. The king recognizes in me the valiance of which his kingdom stands in such need. I was welcomed with all sorts of honors and I've been assigned excellent lodgings at the court. I have beautiful clothes and my own tailor (high class, eh!). I'm sending you a can of caviar and a hundredweight of truffles.

Your son, of whom you can be very proud

BUT THE OFFICERS WERE JEALOUS OF HIM AND WISHED HE WAS THOUSANDS OF MILES AWAY.

WHATEVER WOULD BECOME OF US IF WE WERE TO HAVE SOME QUARREL WITH HIM?

HE'D SLAY US! SEVEN IN EACH BLOW!

LIKE FLIES!

IT'D BE A CLEVER ONE WHO ESCAPED HIM!

SO, MY MEN AT ARMS, WHAT NEW RUCKUS IS THIS?

SIRE, WE CANNOT REMAIN WITH A MAN WHO KILLS SEVEN IN A SINGLE BLOW!

WE MUST SURRENDER OUR COAT-OF-ARMS AND LEAVE YOU!

HOW I WISH I'D NEVER MET THAT MAN AND WOULD GLADLY BE RID OF HIM, BUT IF I DISMISS HIM, HE'LL KILL ME, TAKE MY THRONE AND MY KINGDOM!

BUT I HAVE AN IDEA!

BLAH BLAH BLAH BLAH BL BL BLAH BLAH BLAH BLAH

EXCELLENT! I ALWAYS KNEW YOU WERE A GREAT STRATEGIST!

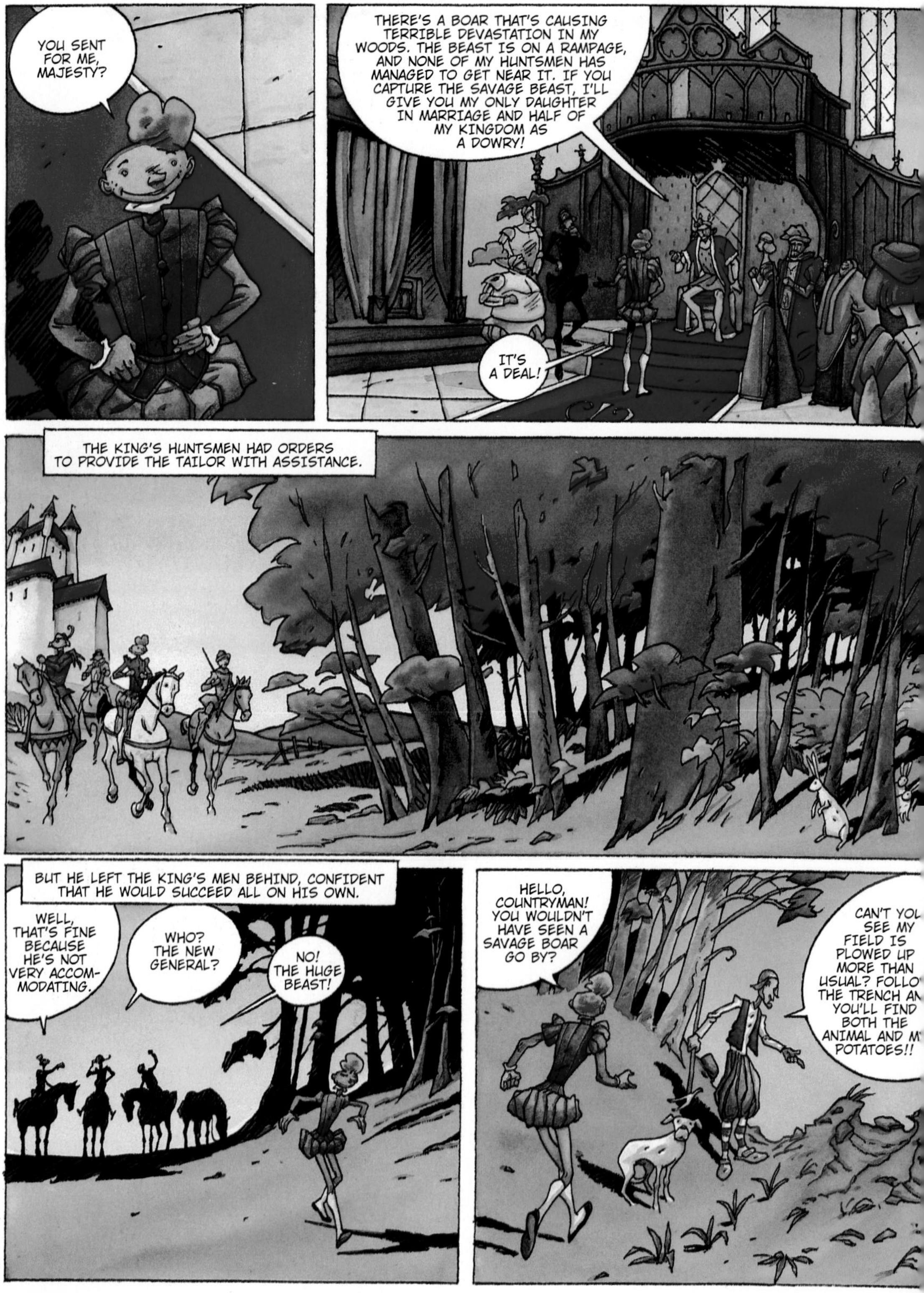
YOU SENT FOR ME, MAJESTY?
THERE'S A BOAR THAT'S CAUSING TERRIBLE DEVASTATION IN MY WOODS. THE BEAST IS ON A RAMPAGE, AND NONE OF MY HUNTSMEN HAS MANAGED TO GET NEAR IT. IF YOU CAPTURE THE SAVAGE BEAST, I'LL GIVE YOU MY ONLY DAUGHTER IN MARRIAGE AND HALF OF MY KINGDOM AS A DOWRY!
IT'S A DEAL!
THE KING'S HUNTSMEN HAD ORDERS TO PROVIDE THE TAILOR WITH ASSISTANCE.
BUT HE LEFT THE KING'S MEN BEHIND, CONFIDENT THAT HE WOULD SUCCEED ALL ON HIS OWN.
WELL, THAT'S FINE BECAUSE HE'S NOT VERY ACCOM-MODATING.
WHO? THE NEW GENERAL?
NO! THE HUGE BEAST!
HELLO, COUNTRYMAN! YOU WOULDN'T HAVE SEEN A SAVAGE BOAR GO BY?
CAN'T YOU SEE MY FIELD IS PLOWED UP MORE THAN USUAL? FOLLO THE TRENCH AN YOU'LL FIND BOTH THE ANIMAL AND M POTATOES!!

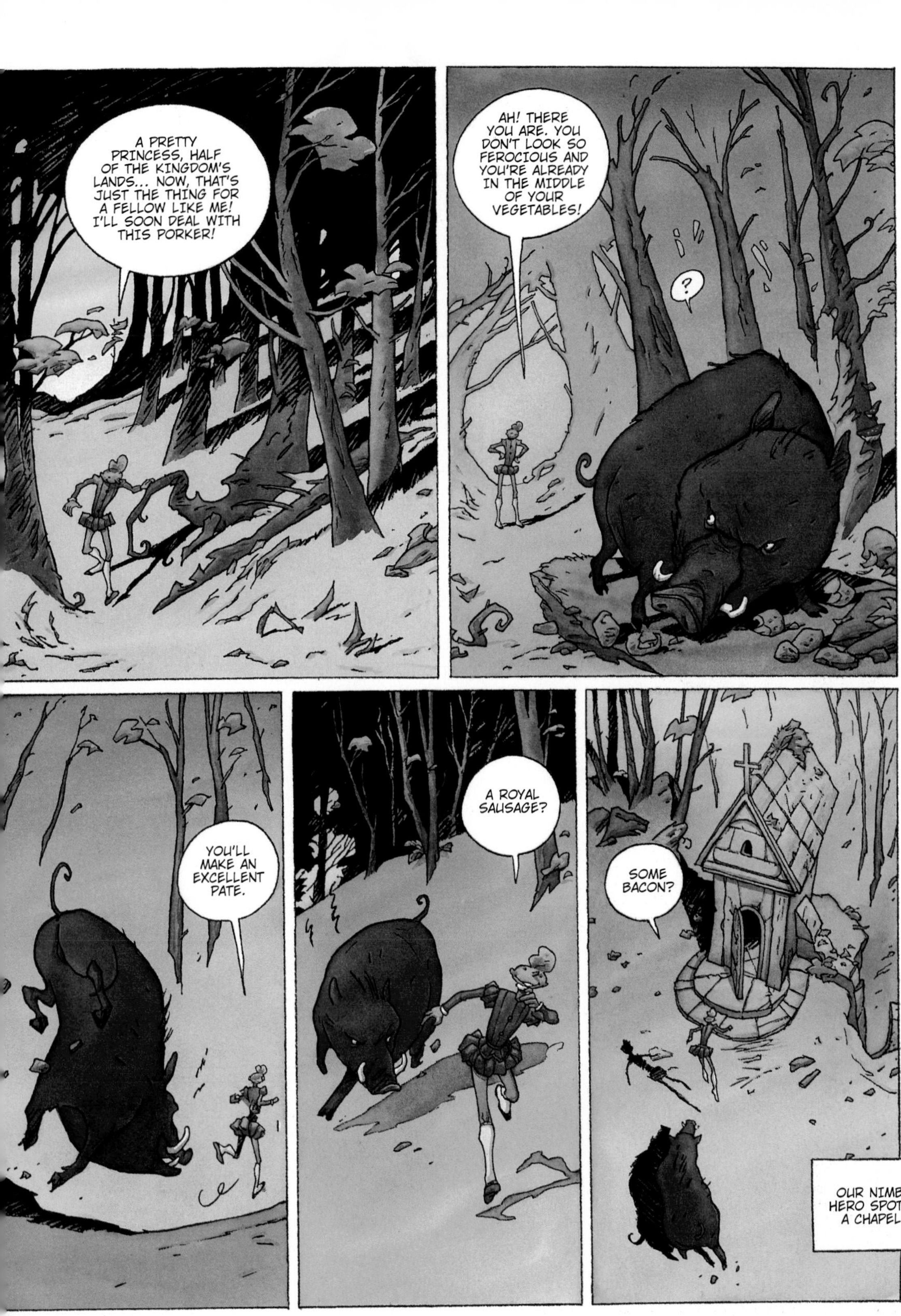
A PRETTY PRINCESS, HALF OF THE KINGDOM'S LANDS... NOW, THAT'S JUST THE THING FOR A FELLOW LIKE ME! I'LL SOON DEAL WITH THIS PORKER!
AH! THERE YOU ARE. YOU DON'T LOOK SO FEROCIOUS AND YOU'RE ALREADY IN THE MIDDLE OF YOUR VEGETABLES!
?
YOU'LL MAKE AN EXCELLENT PATE.
A ROYAL SAUSAGE?
SOME BACON?
OUR NIMBLE HERO SPOTTED A CHAPEL...

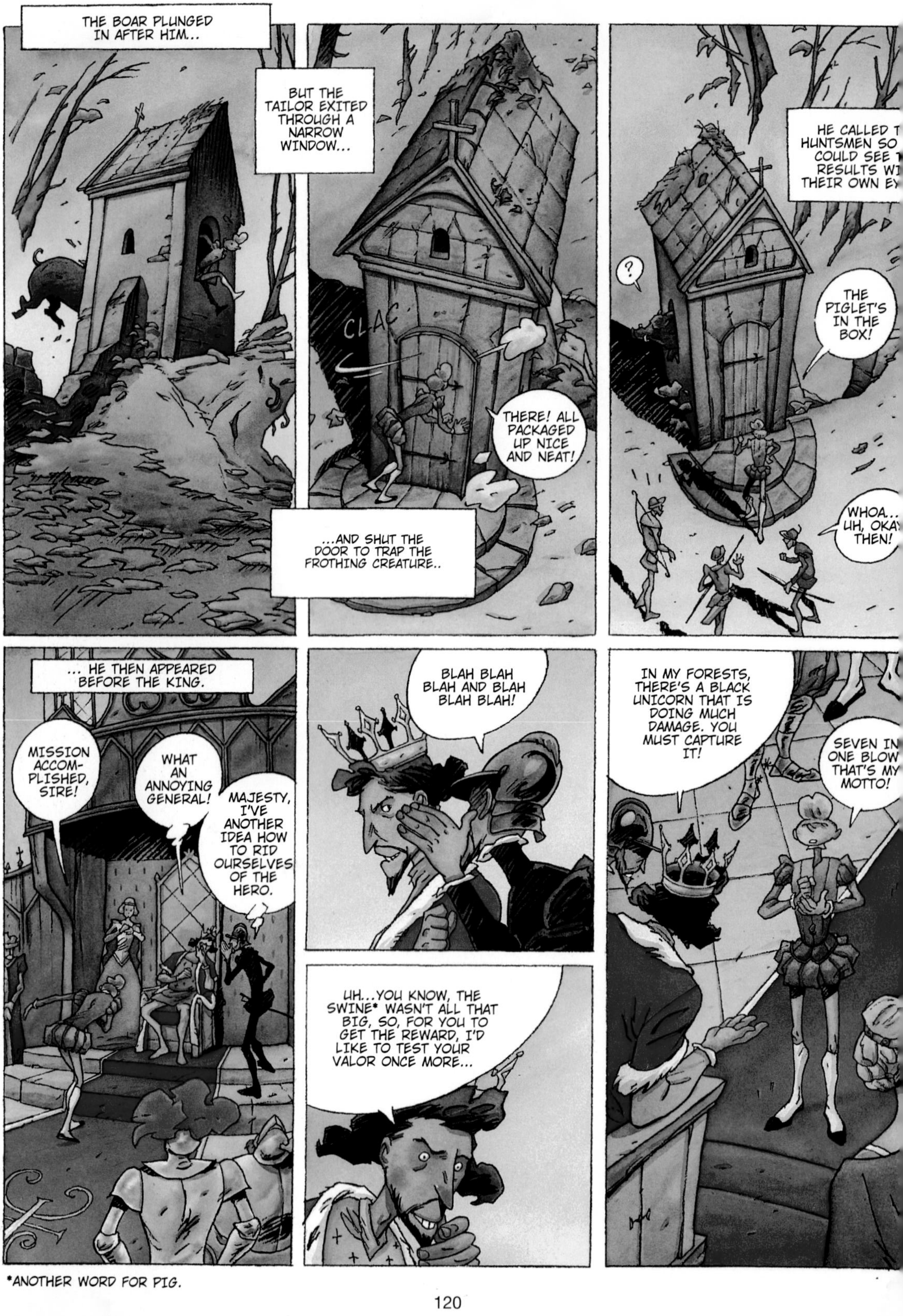
THE BOAR PLUNGED IN AFTER HIM...
BUT THE TAILOR EXITED THROUGH A NARROW WINDOW...
CLAC
THERE! ALL PACKAGED UP NICE AND NEAT!
...AND SHUT THE DOOR TO TRAP THE FROTHING CREATURE..
HE CALLED T HUNTSMEN SO COULD SEE T RESULTS WI THEIR OWN EY
?
THE PIGLET'S IN THE BOX!
WHOA... UH, OKA THEN!
... HE THEN APPEARED BEFORE THE KING.
MISSION ACCOMPLISHED, SIRE!
WHAT AN ANNOYING GENERAL!
MAJESTY, I'VE ANOTHER IDEA HOW TO RID OURSELVES OF THE HERO.
BLAH BLAH BLAH AND BLAH BLAH BLAH!
UH...YOU KNOW, THE SWINE* WASN'T ALL THAT BIG, SO, FOR YOU TO GET THE REWARD, I'D LIKE TO TEST YOUR VALOR ONCE MORE...
IN MY FORESTS, THERE'S A BLACK UNICORN THAT IS DOING MUCH DAMAGE. YOU MUST CAPTURE IT!
SEVEN IN ONE BLOW THAT'S MY MOTTO!

*ANOTHER WORD FOR PIG.

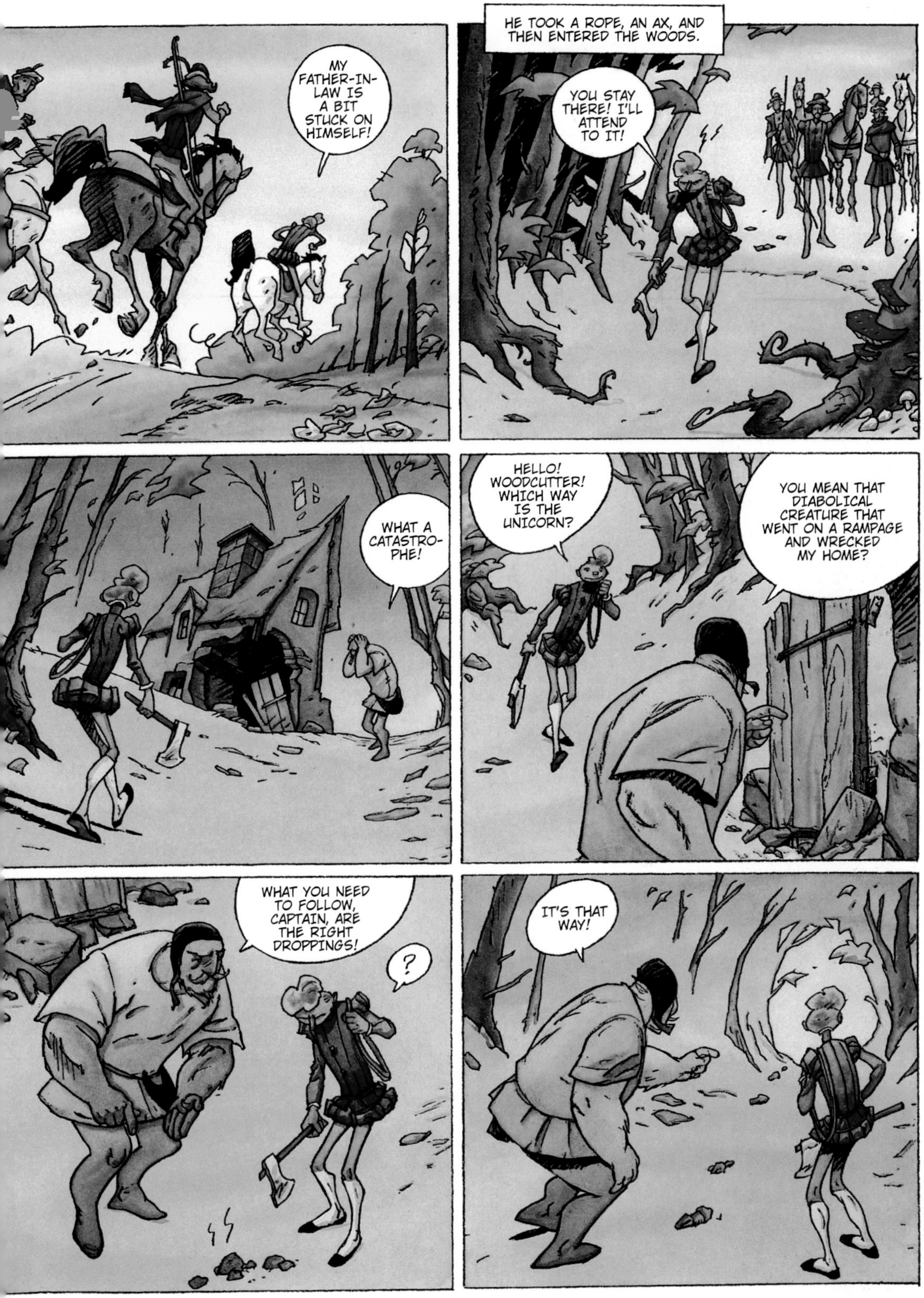
MY FATHER-IN-LAW IS A BIT STUCK ON HIMSELF!
HE TOOK A ROPE, AN AX, AND THEN ENTERED THE WOODS.
YOU STAY THERE! I'LL ATTEND TO IT!
WHAT A CATASTROPHE!
HELLO! WOODCUTTER! WHICH WAY IS THE UNICORN?
YOU MEAN THAT DIABOLICAL CREATURE THAT WENT ON A RAMPAGE AND WRECKED MY HOME?
WHAT YOU NEED TO FOLLOW, CAPTAIN, ARE THE RIGHT DROPPINGS!
?
IT'S THAT WAY!

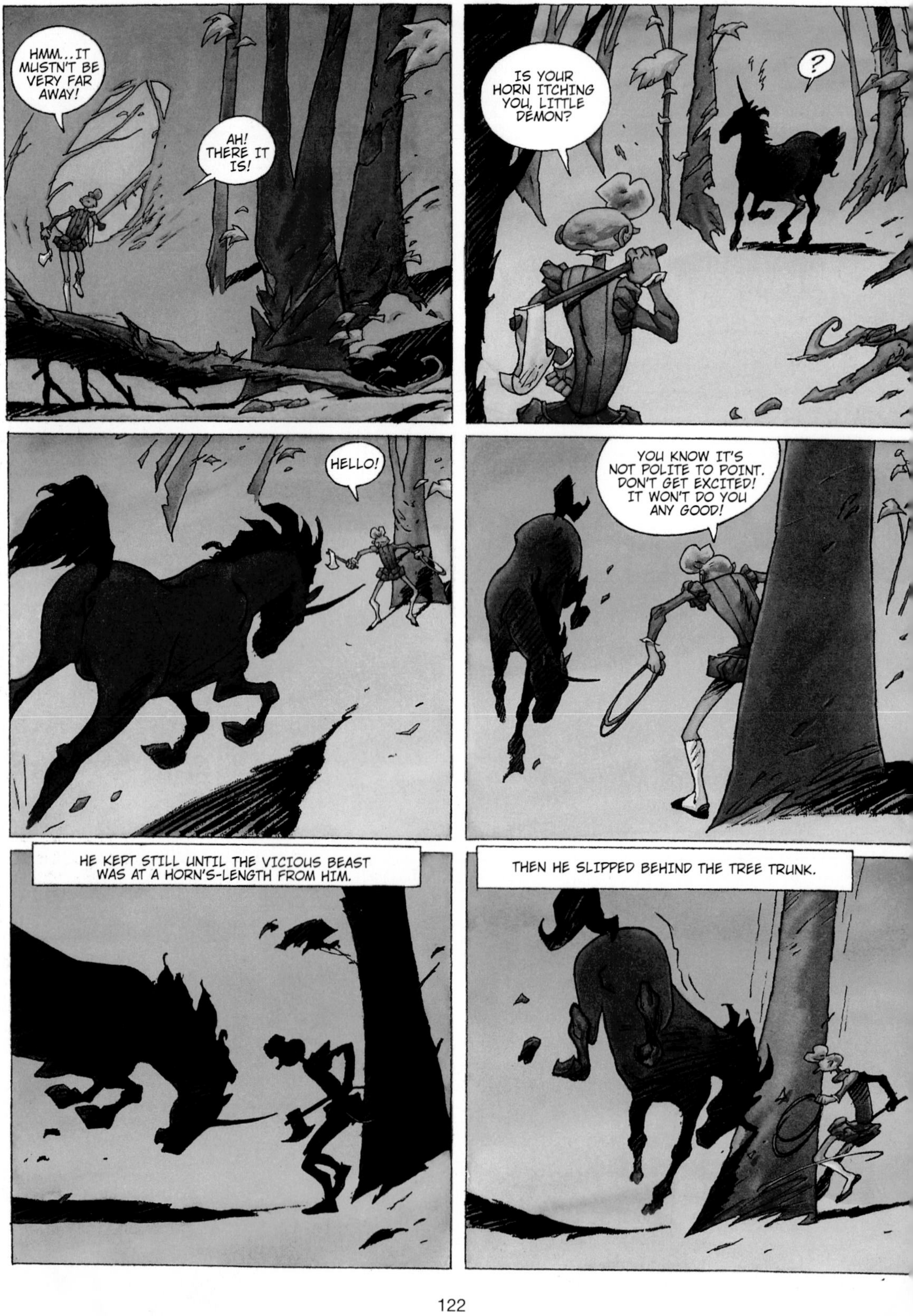
HMM...IT MUSTN'T BE VERY FAR AWAY!
AH! THERE IT IS!
IS YOUR HORN ITCHING YOU, LITTLE DEMON?
?
HELLO!
YOU KNOW IT'S NOT POLITE TO POINT. DON'T GET EXCITED! IT WON'T DO YOU ANY GOOD!
HE KEPT STILL UNTIL THE VICIOUS BEAST WAS AT A HORN'S-LENGTH FROM HIM.
THEN HE SLIPPED BEHIND THE TREE TRUNK.

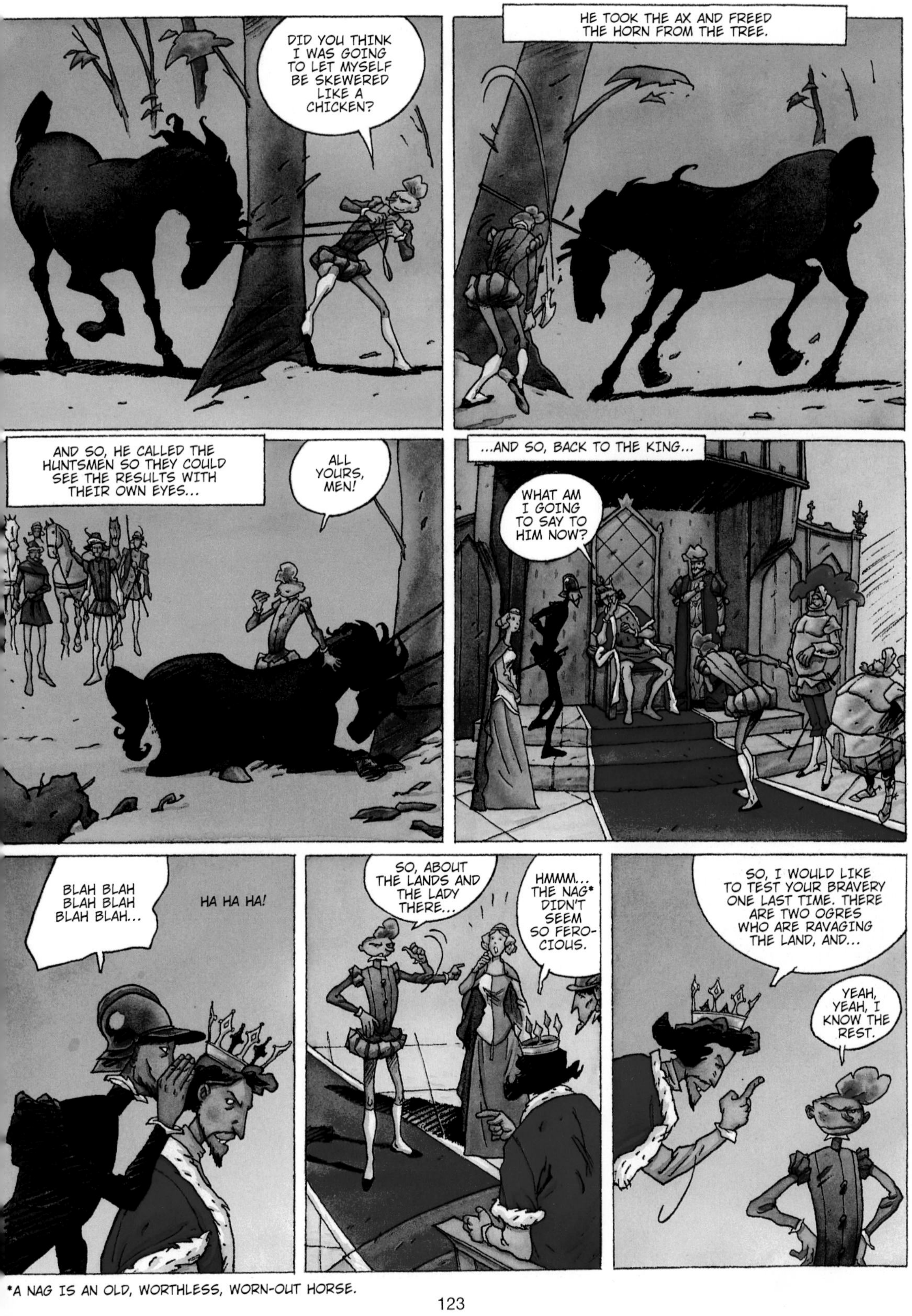
DID YOU THINK I WAS GOING TO LET MYSELF BE SKEWERED LIKE A CHICKEN?
HE TOOK THE AX AND FREED THE HORN FROM THE TREE.
AND SO, HE CALLED THE HUNTSMEN SO THEY COULD SEE THE RESULTS WITH THEIR OWN EYES...
ALL YOURS, MEN!
...AND SO, BACK TO THE KING...
WHAT AM I GOING TO SAY TO HIM NOW?
BLAH BLAH BLAH BLAH BLAH BLAH...
HA HA HA!
SO, ABOUT THE LANDS AND THE LADY THERE...
HMMM... THE NAG* DIDN'T SEEM SO FERO- CIOUS.
SO, I WOULD LIKE TO TEST YOUR BRAVERY ONE LAST TIME. THERE ARE TWO OGRES WHO ARE RAVAGING THE LAND, AND...
YEAH, YEAH, I KNOW THE REST.

*A NAG IS AN OLD, WORTHLESS, WORN-OUT HORSE.

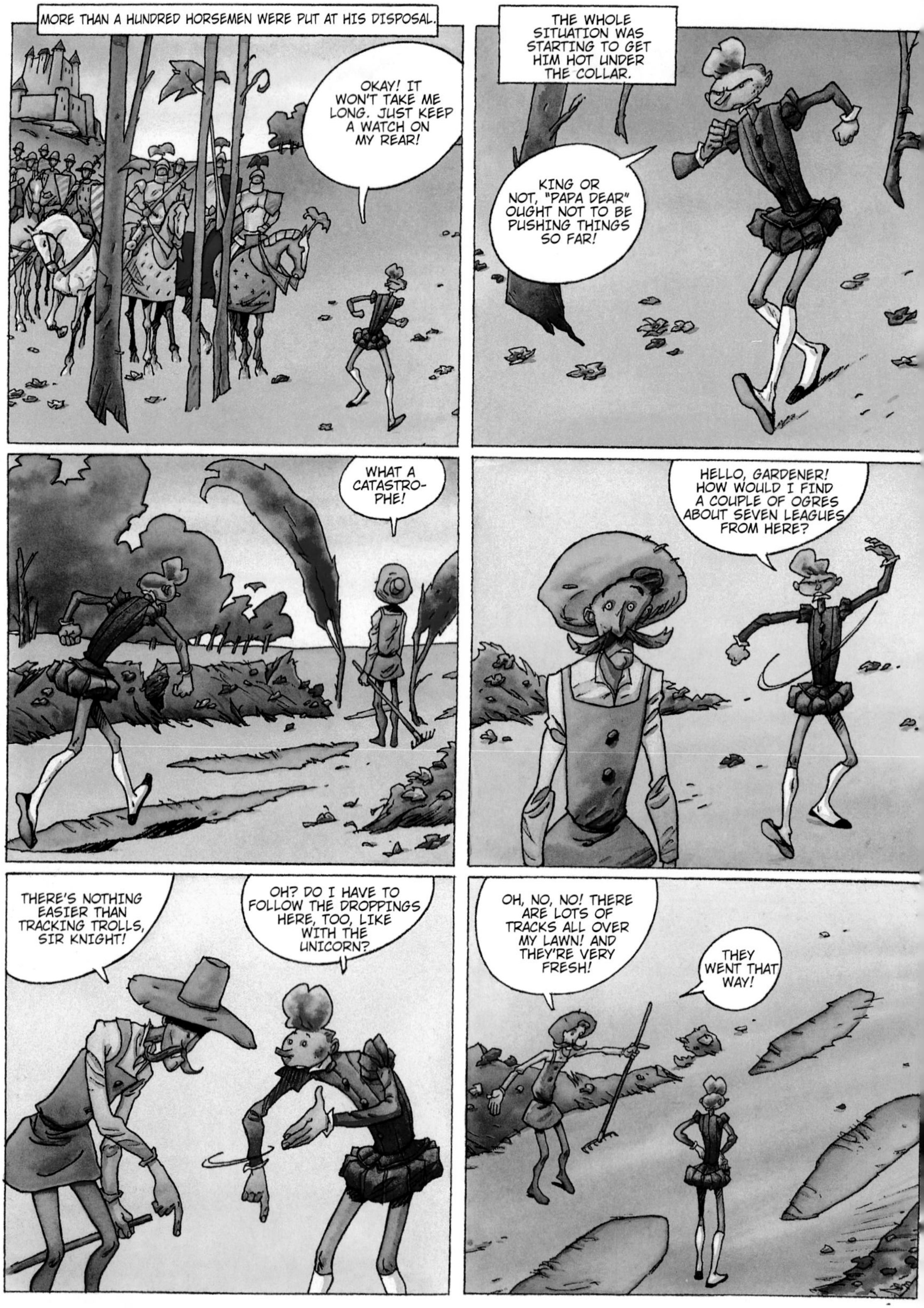

MORE THAN A HUNDRED HORSEMEN WERE PUT AT HIS DISPOSAL.
OKAY! IT WON'T TAKE ME LONG. JUST KEEP A WATCH ON MY REAR!
THE WHOLE SITUATION WAS STARTING TO GET HIM HOT UNDER THE COLLAR.
KING OR NOT, "PAPA DEAR" OUGHT NOT TO BE PUSHING THINGS SO FAR!
WHAT A CATASTRO-PHE!
HELLO, GARDENER! HOW WOULD I FIND A COUPLE OF OGRES ABOUT SEVEN LEAGUES FROM HERE?
THERE'S NOTHING EASIER THAN TRACKING TROLLS, SIR KNIGHT!
OH? DO I HAVE TO FOLLOW THE DROPPINGS HERE, TOO, LIKE WITH THE UNICORN?
OH, NO, NO! THERE ARE LOTS OF TRACKS ALL OVER MY LAWN! AND THEY'RE VERY FRESH!
THEY WENT THAT WAY!

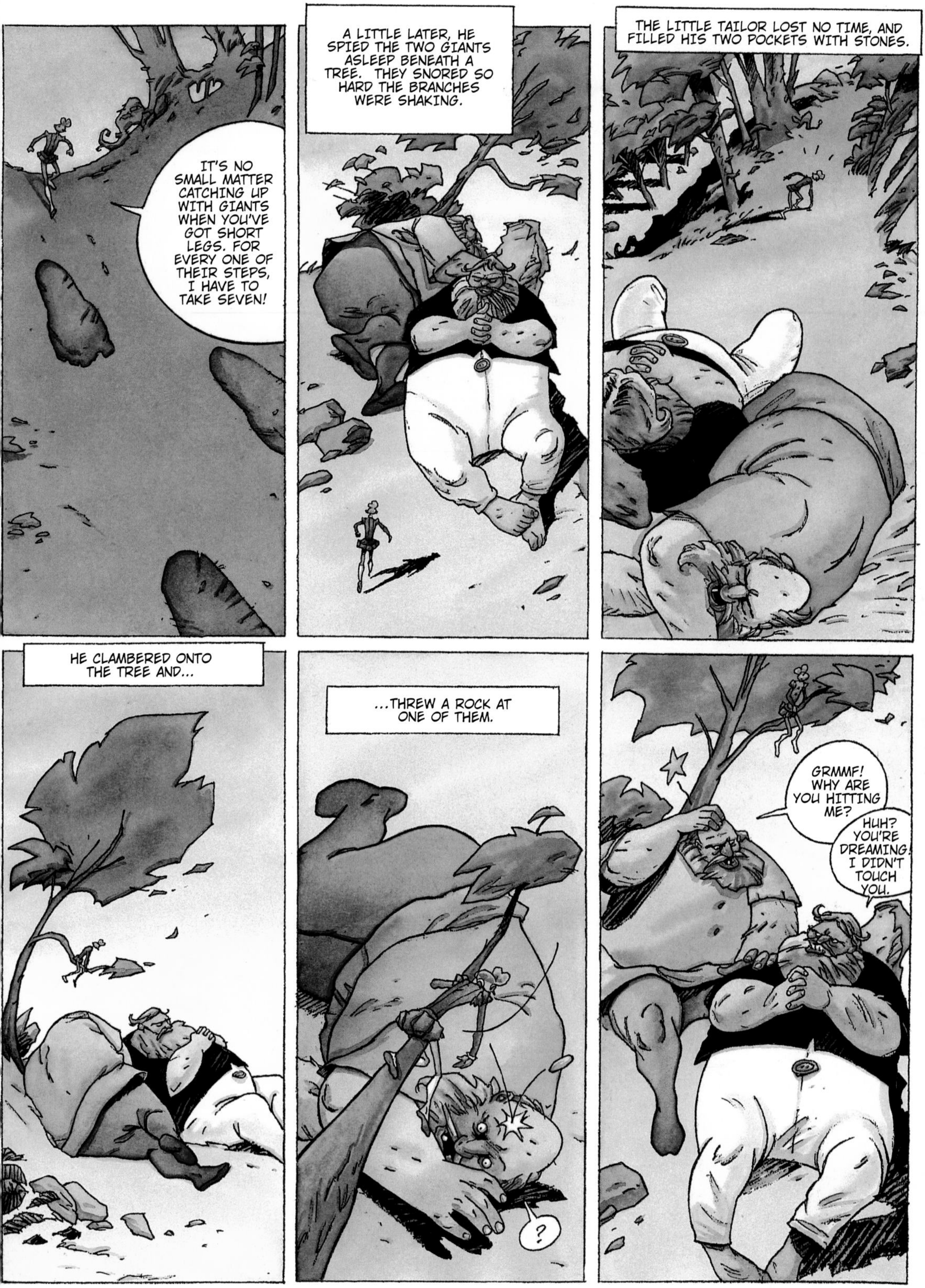
IT'S NO SMALL MATTER CATCHING UP WITH GIANTS WHEN YOU'VE GOT SHORT LEGS. FOR EVERY ONE OF THEIR STEPS, I HAVE TO TAKE SEVEN!
A LITTLE LATER, HE SPIED THE TWO GIANTS ASLEEP BENEATH A TREE. THEY SNORED SO HARD THE BRANCHES WERE SHAKING.
THE LITTLE TAILOR LOST NO TIME, AND FILLED HIS TWO POCKETS WITH STONES.
HE CLAMBERED ONTO THE TREE AND...
...THREW A ROCK AT ONE OF THEM.
?
GRMMF! WHY ARE YOU HITTING ME?
HUH? YOU'RE DREAMING! I DIDN'T TOUCH YOU.

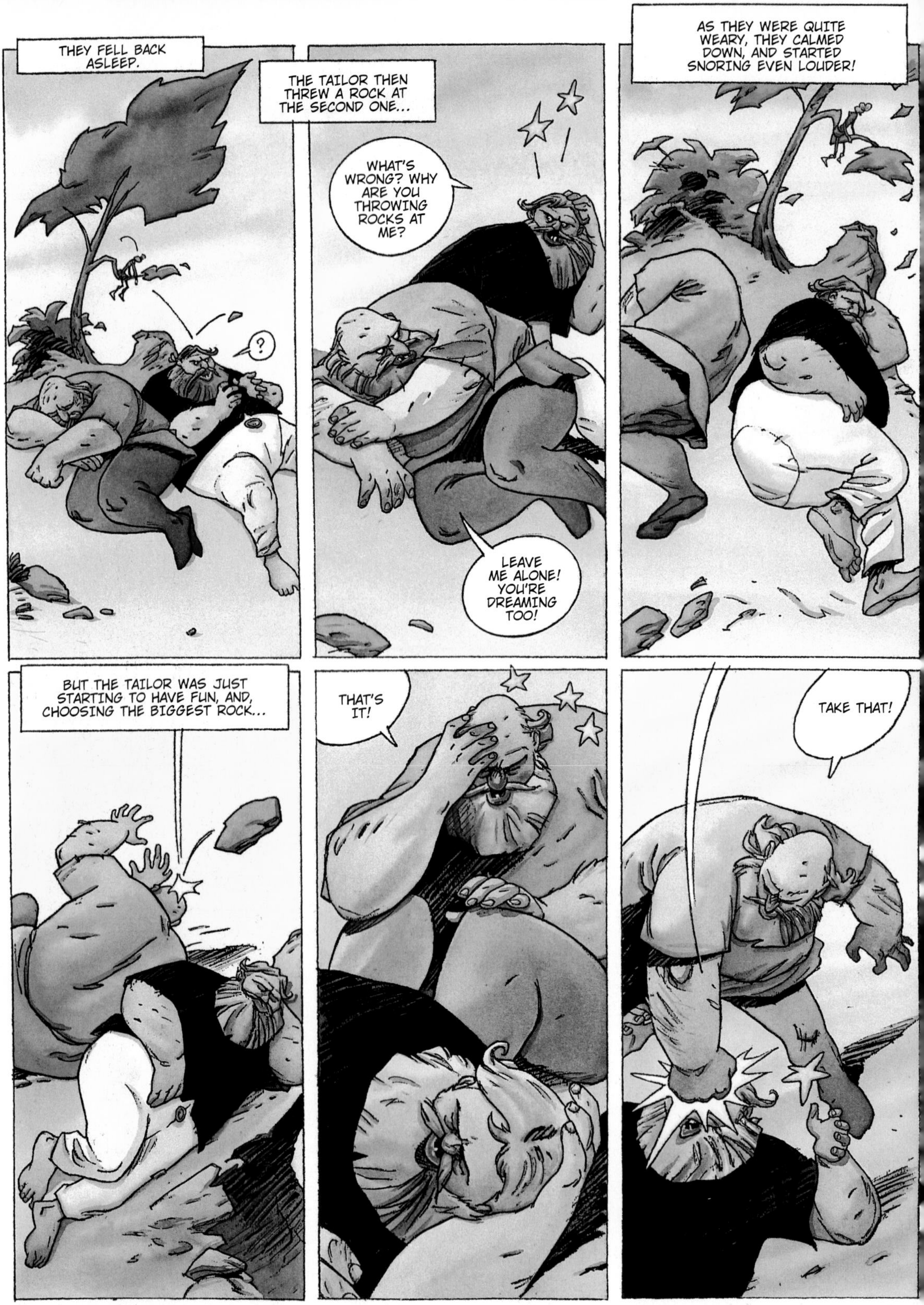

THEY FELL BACK ASLEEP.
?
THE TAILOR THEN THREW A ROCK AT THE SECOND ONE...
WHAT'S WRONG? WHY ARE YOU THROWING ROCKS AT ME?
LEAVE ME ALONE! YOU'RE DREAMING TOO!
AS THEY WERE QUITE WEARY, THEY CALMED DOWN, AND STARTED SNORING EVEN LOUDER!
BUT THE TAILOR WAS JUST STARTING TO HAVE FUN, AND, CHOOSING THE BIGGEST ROCK...
THAT'S IT!
TAKE THAT!

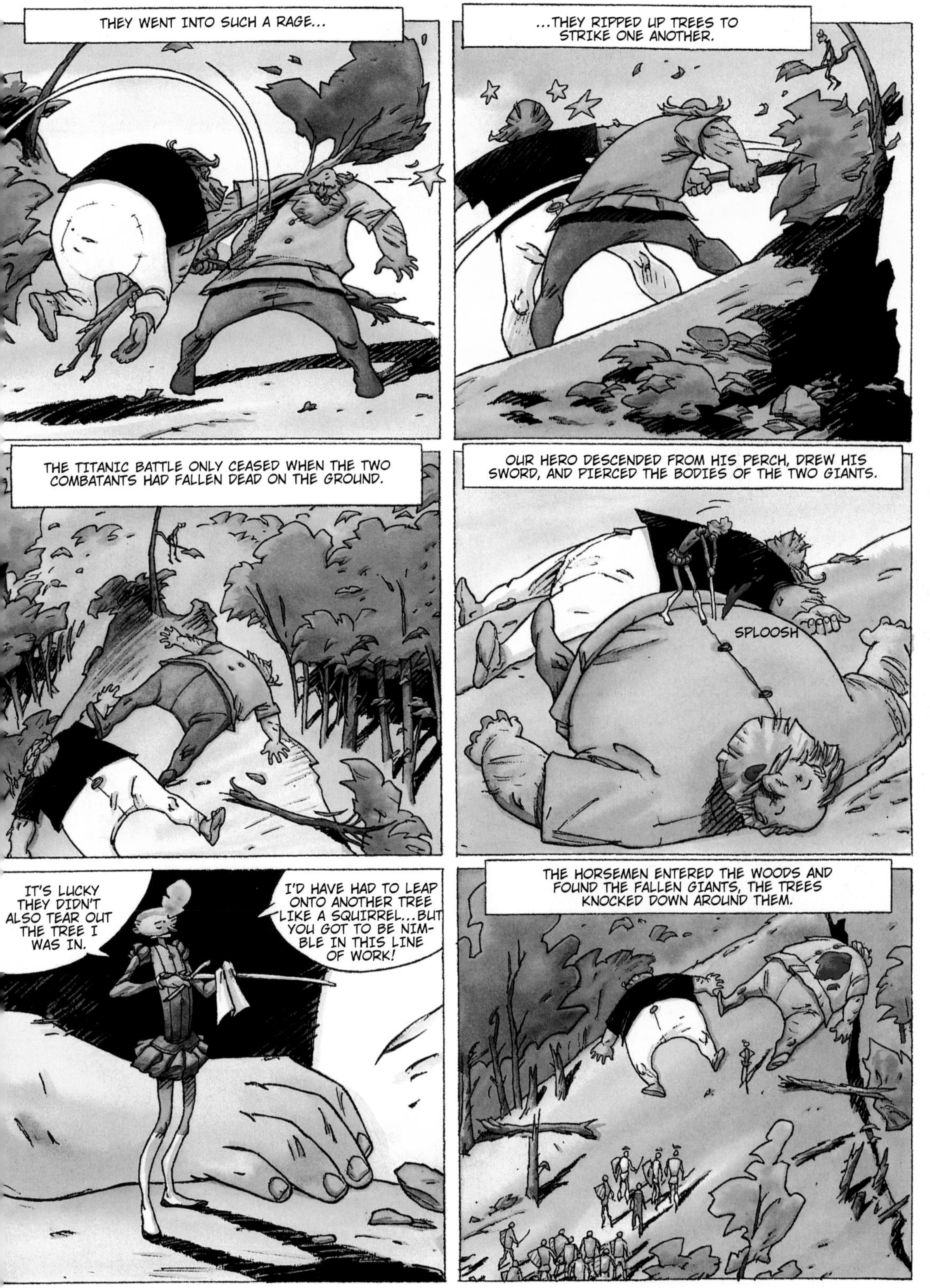
THEY WENT INTO SUCH A RAGE...
...THEY RIPPED UP TREES TO STRIKE ONE ANOTHER.
THE TITANIC BATTLE ONLY CEASED WHEN THE TWO COMBATANTS HAD FALLEN DEAD ON THE GROUND.
OUR HERO DESCENDED FROM HIS PERCH, DREW HIS SWORD, AND PIERCED THE BODIES OF THE TWO GIANTS.
SPLOOSH
IT'S LUCKY THEY DIDN'T ALSO TEAR OUT THE TREE I WAS IN.
I'D HAVE HAD TO LEAP ONTO ANOTHER TREE LIKE A SQUIRREL...BUT YOU GOT TO BE NIMBLE IN THIS LINE OF WORK!
THE HORSEMEN ENTERED THE WOODS AND FOUND THE FALLEN GIANTS, THE TREES KNOCKED DOWN AROUND THEM.

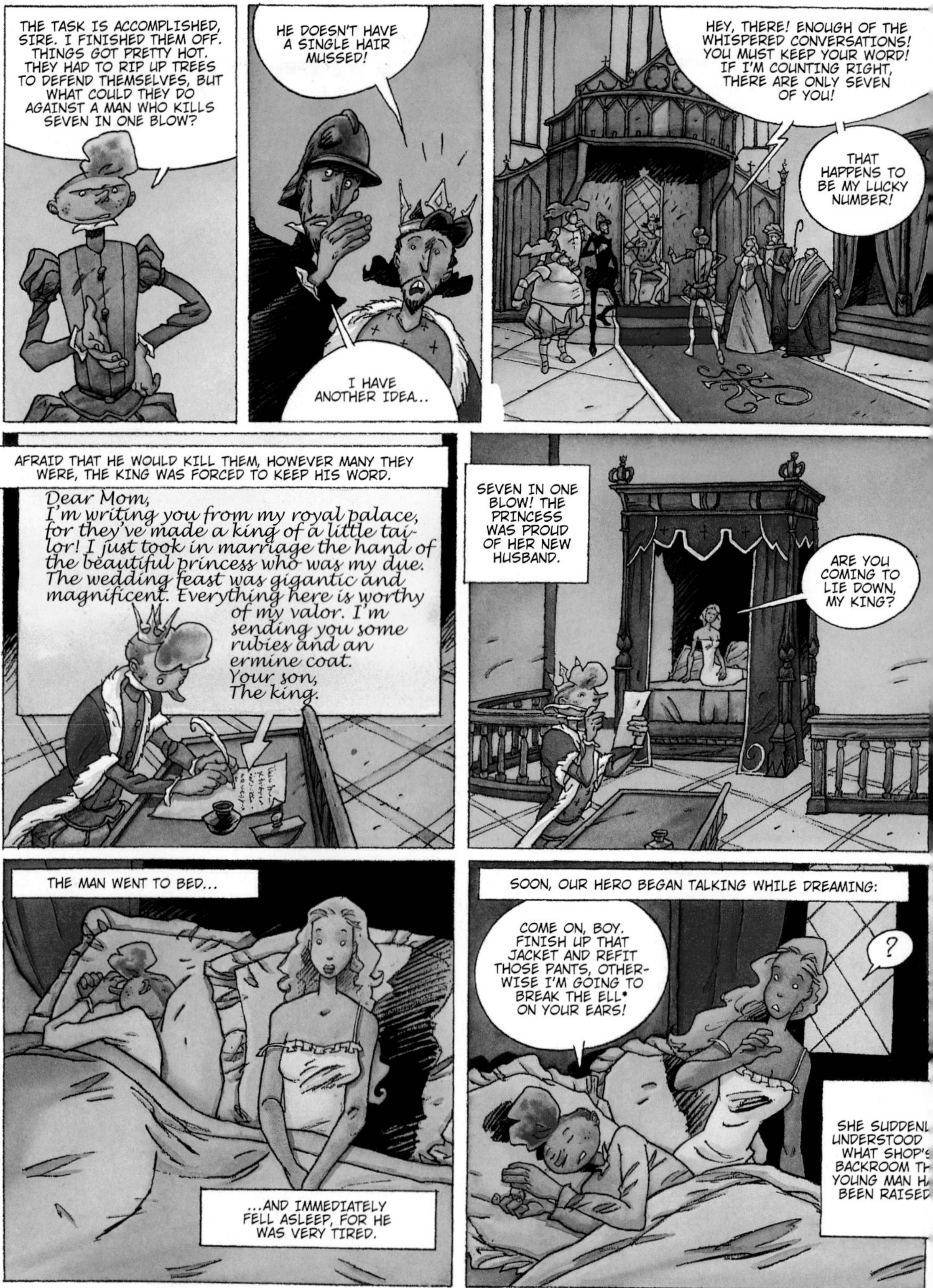
THE TASK IS ACCOMPLISHED, SIRE. I FINISHED THEM OFF. THINGS GOT PRETTY HOT. THEY HAD TO RIP UP TREES TO DEFEND THEMSELVES, BUT WHAT COULD THEY DO AGAINST A MAN WHO KILLS SEVEN IN ONE BLOW?
HE DOESN'T HAVE A SINGLE HAIR MUSSED!
I HAVE ANOTHER IDEA...
HEY, THERE! ENOUGH OF THE WHISPERED CONVERSATIONS! YOU MUST KEEP YOUR WORD! IF I'M COUNTING RIGHT, THERE ARE ONLY SEVEN OF YOU!
THAT HAPPENS TO BE MY LUCKY NUMBER!
AFRAID THAT HE WOULD KILL THEM, HOWEVER MANY THEY WERE, THE KING WAS FORCED TO KEEP HIS WORD.
Dear Mom, I'm writing you from my royal palace, for they've made a king of a little tailor! I just took in marriage the hand of the beautiful princess who was my due. The wedding feast was gigantic and magnificent. Everything here is worthy of my valor. I'm sending you some rubies and an ermine coat. Your son, The king.
SEVEN IN ONE BLOW! THE PRINCESS WAS PROUD OF HER NEW HUSBAND.
ARE YOU COMING TO LIE DOWN, MY KING?
THE MAN WENT TO BED...
...AND IMMEDIATELY FELL ASLEEP, FOR HE WAS VERY TIRED.
SOON, OUR HERO BEGAN TALKING WHILE DREAMING:
COME ON, BOY. FINISH UP THAT JACKET AND REFIT THOSE PANTS, OTHERWISE I'M GOING TO BREAK THE ELL* ON YOUR EARS!
?
SHE SUDDENL UNDERSTOOD WHAT SHOP'S BACKROOM TH YOUNG MAN H BEEN RAISED

* ELL: AN OLD MEASUREMENT OF LENGTH

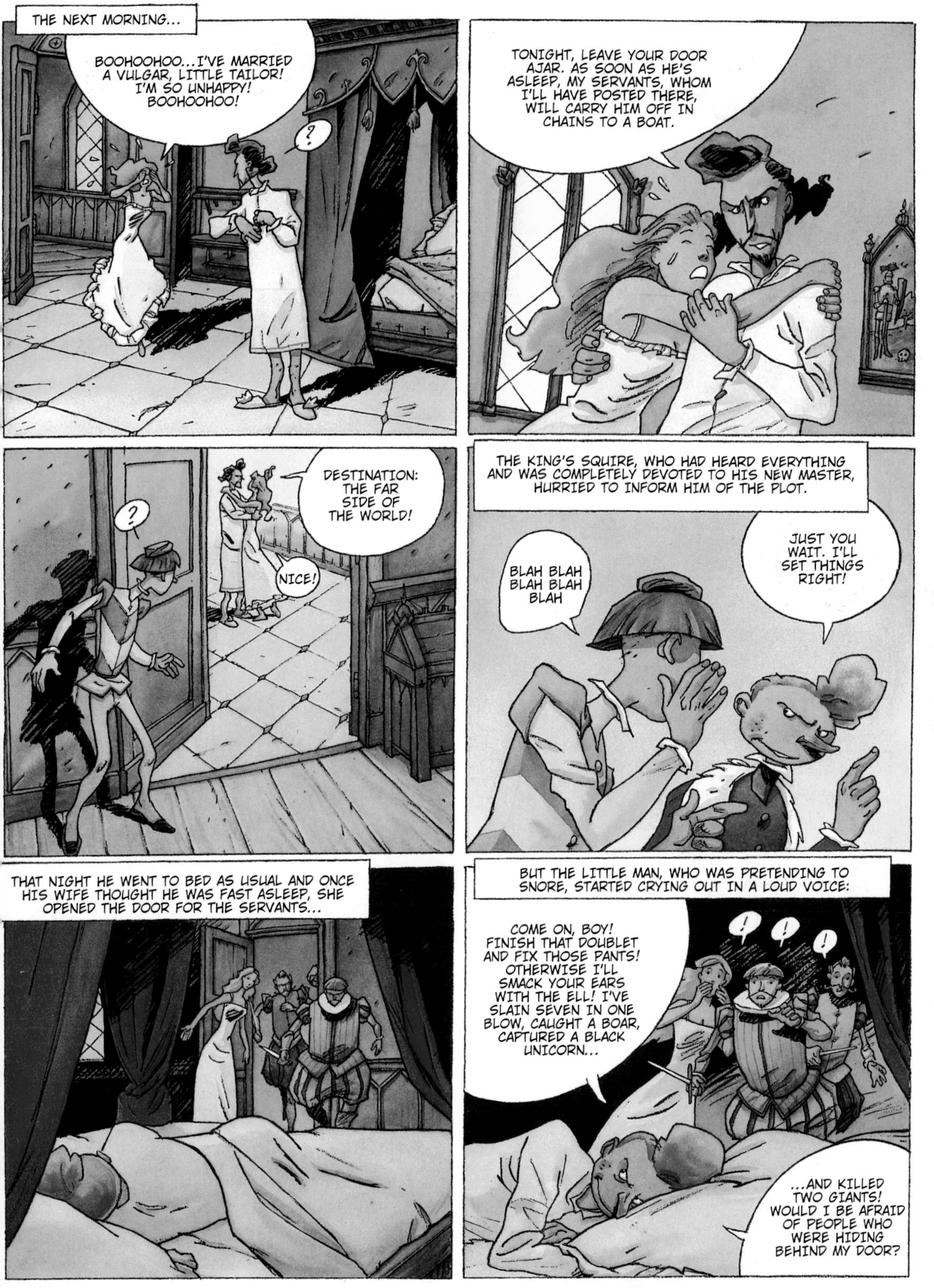
THE NEXT MORNING...
BOOHOOHOO...I'VE MARRIED A VULGAR, LITTLE TAILOR! I'M SO UNHAPPY! BOOHOOHOO!
?
TONIGHT, LEAVE YOUR DOOR AJAR. AS SOON AS HE'S ASLEEP, MY SERVANTS, WHOM I'LL HAVE POSTED THERE, WILL CARRY HIM OFF IN CHAINS TO A BOAT.
?
DESTINATION: THE FAR SIDE OF THE WORLD!
NICE!
THE KING'S SQUIRE, WHO HAD HEARD EVERYTHING AND WAS COMPLETELY DEVOTED TO HIS NEW MASTER, HURRIED TO INFORM HIM OF THE PLOT.
BLAH BLAH BLAH BLAH BLAH
JUST YOU WAIT. I'LL SET THINGS RIGHT!
THAT NIGHT HE WENT TO BED AS USUAL AND ONCE HIS WIFE THOUGHT HE WAS FAST ASLEEP, SHE OPENED THE DOOR FOR THE SERVANTS...
BUT THE LITTLE MAN, WHO WAS PRETENDING TO SNORE, STARTED CRYING OUT IN A LOUD VOICE:
COME ON, BOY! FINISH THAT DOUBLET AND FIX THOSE PANTS! OTHERWISE I'LL SMACK YOUR EARS WITH THE ELL! I'VE SLAIN SEVEN IN ONE BLOW, CAUGHT A BOAR, CAPTURED A BLACK UNICORN...
! ! !
...AND KILLED TWO GIANTS! WOULD I BE AFRAID OF PEOPLE WHO WERE HIDING BEHIND MY DOOR?

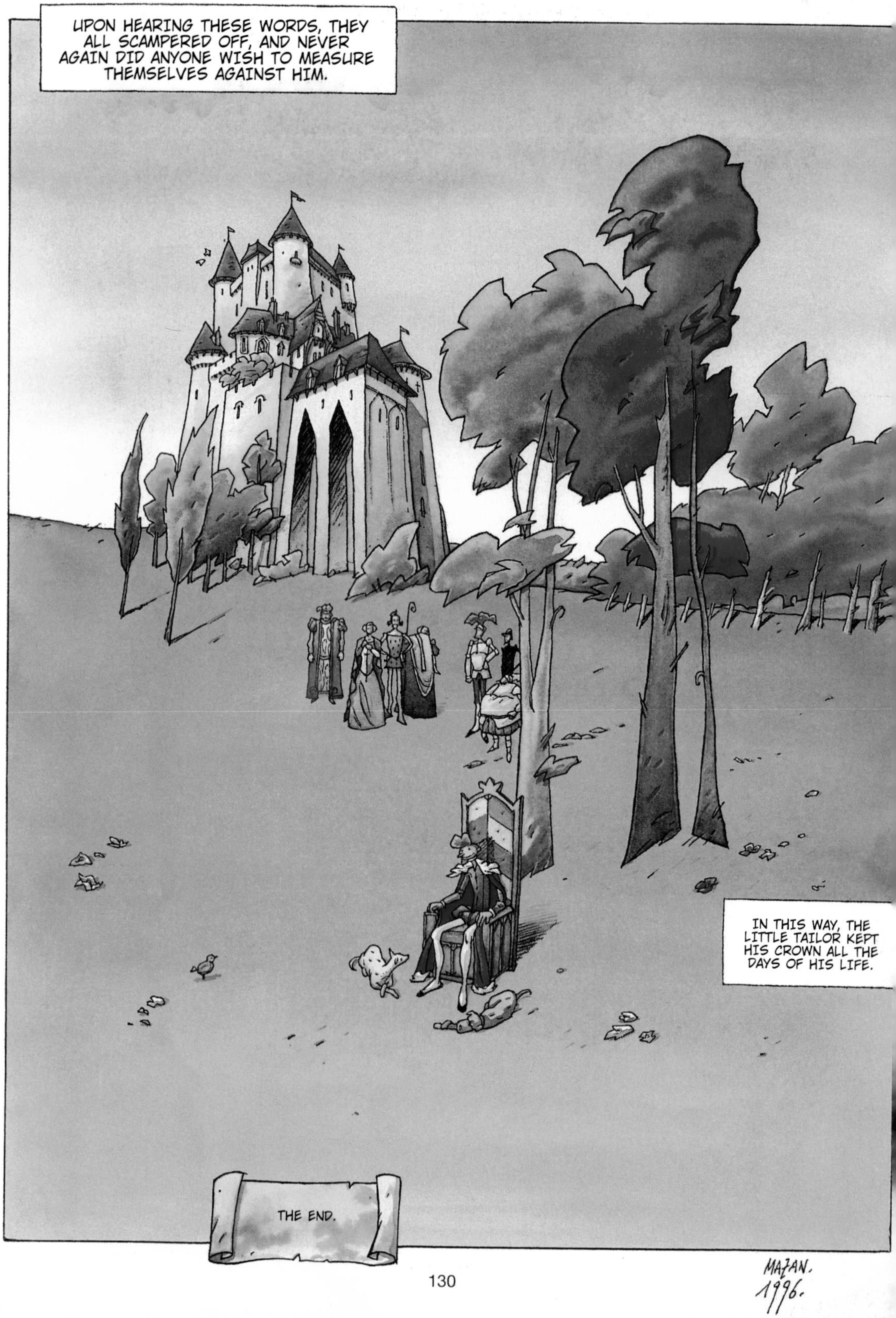
UPON HEARING THESE WORDS, THEY ALL SCAMPERED OFF, AND NEVER AGAIN DID ANYONE WISH TO MEASURE THEMSELVES AGAINST HIM.
IN THIS WAY, THE LITTLE TAILOR KEPT HIS CROWN ALL THE DAYS OF HIS LIFE.
THE END.
MAZAN. 1996.

WATCH OUT FOR
PAPERCUTZ ™

Welcome to the second volume of CLASSICS ILLUSTRATED DELUXE. I'm Jim Salicrup, Papercutz Editor-in-Chief, and proud to be associated with such a legendary comicbook series. If you're unfamiliar with Papercutz, let me quickly say that we're the graphic novel publishers of such titles as NANCY DREW, THE HARDY BOYS, TALES FROM THE CRYPT, and now, CLASSICS ILLUSTRATED and CLASSICS ILLUSTRATED DELUXE. In the backpages of our titles, we usually run a section, aptly named "the Papercutz Backpages," which is devoted to letting you know all that's happening at Papercutz. You can also check us out at www.papercutz.com for even more information and previews of upcoming Papercuts graphic novels. But this time around, the big news is CLASSICS ILLUSTRATED!

We'll fill you in on why that's such an awesome big deal in the following pages, but right now I need a moment to take it all in. You see, even though I've been in the world of comics for thirty-five years, I'm still very much the same comicbook fan I was when I was a kid! And if my partner, Papercutz Publisher, Terry Nantier, were to magically go back in time, and tell 13 year-old Jim Salicrup that he was going to one day be the editor of NANCY DREW, THE HARDY BOYS, TALES FROM THE CRYPT, and CLASSICS ILLUSTRATED, he'd think Terry was out of his mind!

Let's get real. Back then I'd see CLASSICS ILLUSTRATED comics in their own display rack, apart from all the other comicbooks, at my favorite soda shoppe in the Bronx. Each issue featured a comics adaptation of a classic novel-that's why they called it CLASSICS ILLUSTRATED. But unlike other comicbooks, these were bigger, containing 48 pages per book; cost a quarter, more than twice as much as a regular 12 cent comic; and stayed on sale forever, as opposed to the other comics which were gone in a month. Clearly, these comics were something special.

Bah, I can take a gazillion moments, but this is still way too humungous an event for my puny brain to fully absorb, so I'm going to give up trying and accept that we here at Papercutz must be doing something right to be entrusted with Comicdom's crown jewels! So no more looking back--time to focus on the future. That means doing everything we can to make sure these titles live up to their proud heritage, while gaining a whole new generation of fans.

As usual, you can contact me at salicrup@papercutz.com or Jim Salicrup, PAPERCUTZ, 40 Exchange Place, Ste. 1308, New York, NY 10005 and let us know how we're doing. After all, we want you to be as excited about Papercutz as we are!

Thanks, *Jim*

Caricature drawn by Steve Brodner at the MoCCA Art Fest.

EDITOR-IN-CHIEF

CLASSICS Illustrated

Featuring Stories by the World's Greatest Authors

Returns in two new series from Papercutz!

The original, best-selling series of comics adaptations of the world's greatest literature, CLASSICS ILLUSTRATED, returns in two new formats--the original, featuring abridged adaptations of classic novels, and CLASSICS ILLUSTRATED DELUXE, featuring longer, more expansive adaptations-from graphic novel publisher Papercutz. "We're very proud to say that Papercutz has received such an enthusiastic reception from librarians and school teachers for its NANCY DREW and HARDY BOYS graphic novels as well as THE LIFE OF POPE JOHN PAUL II...*IN COMICS!*, that it only seemed logical for us to bring back the original CLASSICS ILLUSTRATED comicbook series beloved by parents, educators, and librarians," explained Papercutz Publisher, Terry Nantier. "We can't thank the enlightened librarians and teachers who have supported Papercutz enough. And we're thrilled that they're so excited about CLASSICS ILLUSTRATED."

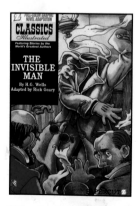  

Titles include The Invisible Man, Tales from the Brothers Grimm, Robinson Crusoe, and (opposite) The Wind In The Willows.

FULL-COLOR GRAPHIC NOVEL ADAPTATION

CLASSICS *Illustrated*

Deluxe

THE WIND IN THE WILLOWS

By Kenneth Grahame

Adapted by
Michel Plessix

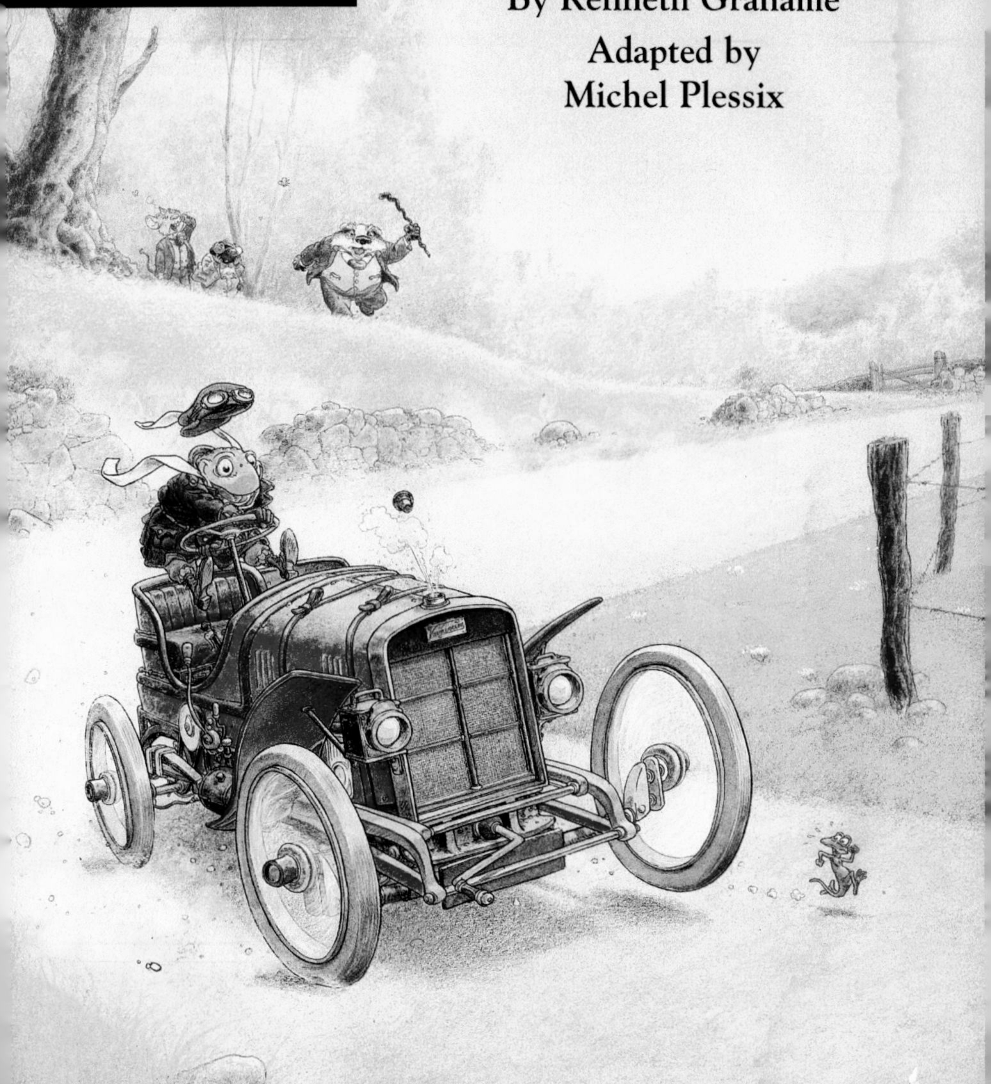

PAPERCUTZ

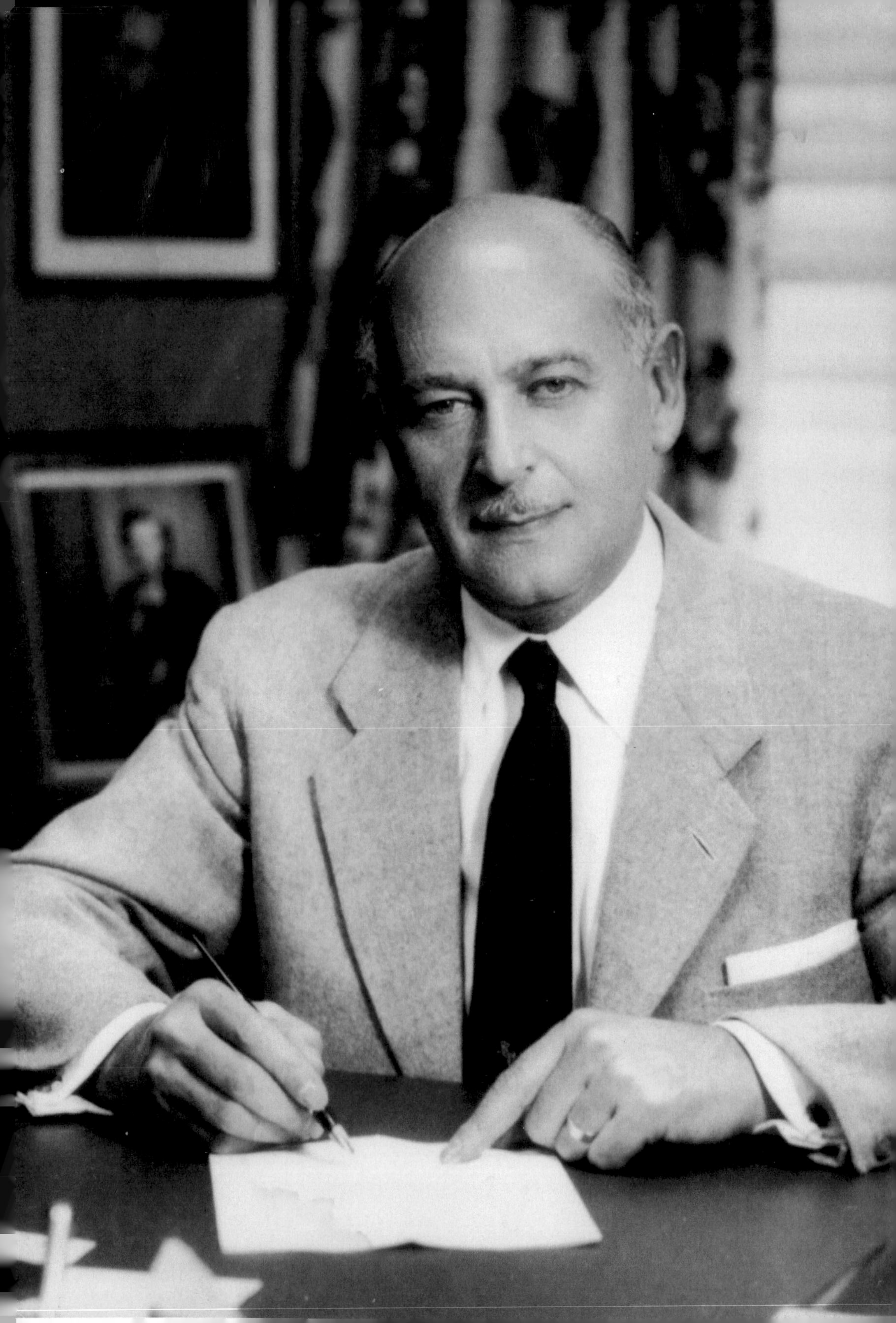

A Short History of CLASSICS ILLUSTRATED...

William B. Jones Jr. is the author of Classics Illustrated: A Cultural History, which offers a comprehensive overview of the original comicbook series and the writers, artists, editors, and publishers behind-the-scenes. With Mr. Jones Jr.'s kind permission, here's a very short overview of the history of CLASSICS ILLUSTRATED from his 2005 essay on Albert Kanter.

CLASSICS ILLUSTRATED was the brainchild of Albert Lewis Kanter, a visionary publisher, who deserves to be ranked among the great teachers of the 20th century. From 1941 to 1971, he introduced young readers to the realms of literature, history, folklore, mythology, and science in such comicbook juvenile series as CLASSICS ILLUSTRATED, CLASSICS ILLUSTRATED JUNIOR, CLASSICS ILLUSTRATED SPECIAL SERIES, and THE WORLD AROUND US.

Born in Baronovitch, Russia on April 11, 1897, Albert Kanter immigrated with his family to the United States in 1904. They settled in Nashua, New Hampshire. A constant reader, Kanter continued to educate himself after leaving high school at the age of sixteen. He worked as a traveling salesman for

Photo of Albert Kanter courtesy of Hal Kanter.

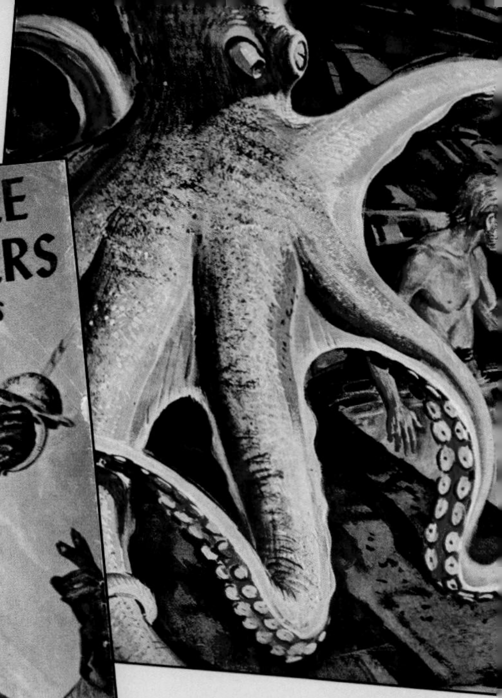

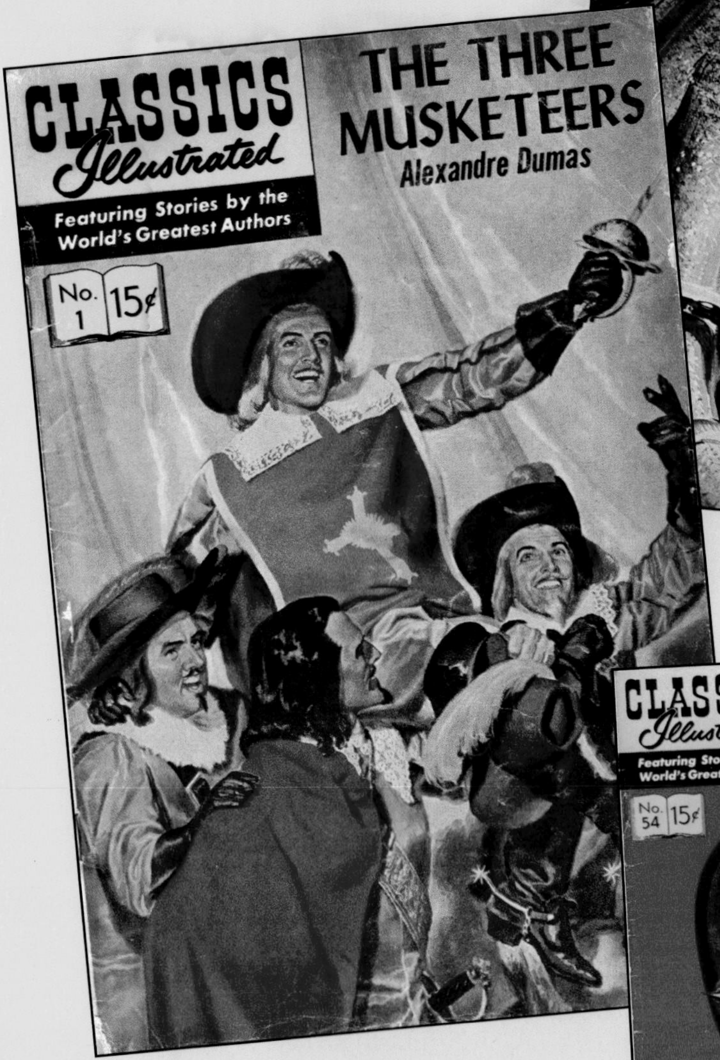
CLASSICS Illustrated
Featuring Stories by the World's Greatest Authors
No. 1 15¢
THE THREE MUSKETEERS
Alexandre Dumas

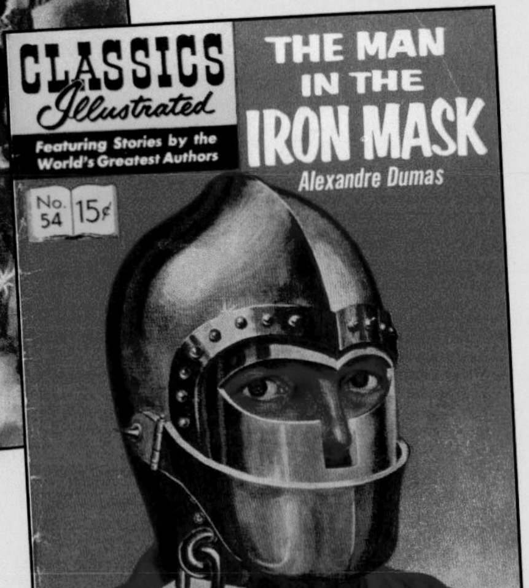
CLASSICS Illustrated
Featuring Stories by the World's Greatest Authors
No. 54 15¢
THE MAN IN THE IRON MASK
Alexandre Dumas

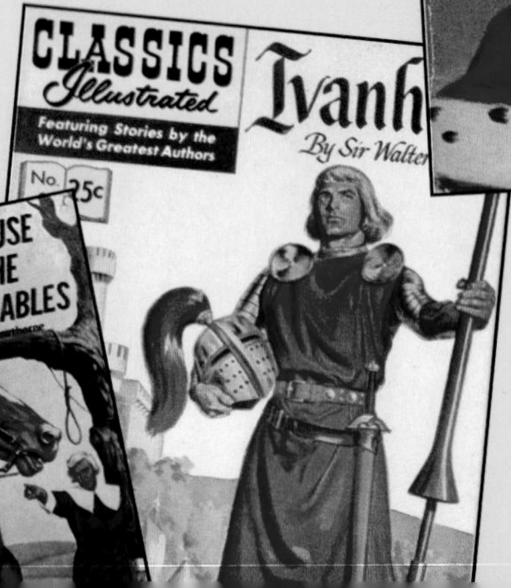
CLASSICS Illustrated
Featuring Stories by the World's Greatest Authors
No. 25¢
Ivanh
By Sir Walter

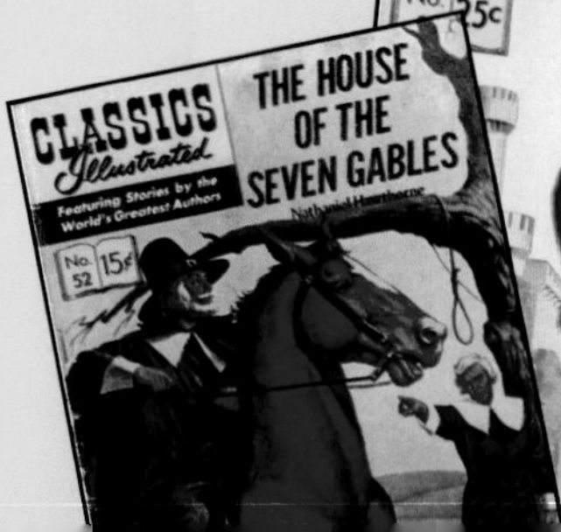
CLASSICS Illustrated
Featuring Stories by the World's Greatest Authors
No. 52 15¢
THE HOUSE OF THE SEVEN GABLES

several years. In 1917, he married Rose Ehrenrich, and the couple lived in Savannah, Georgia, where they had three children, Henry (Hal), William, and Saralea.

They spent several years in Miami, Florida but when the Great Depression ended his real estate venture there, Kanter moved his family to New York. He was employed by the Colonial Press and later the Elliot Publishing Company. During this period, Kanter also designed a popular appointment diary for doctors and dentists and created a toy telegraph and a crystal radio set.

During the late 1930s and early 1940s, millions of youngsters thrilled to the exploits of the new comicbook superheroes. In 1940, Elliot Publishing Company began issuing repackaged pairs of remaindered comics, which sparked a concept in Kanter's mind about a different kind of comicbook. Kanter believed that he could use the same medium to introduce young readers to the world of great literature.

With the backing of two business partners, Kanter launched CLAS-SIC COMICS in October 1941 with issue No. 1, a comics-style adaptation of *The Three Musketeers*. From the beginning, the series stood apart from other comicbook lines. Each issue was devoted to a different literary work such as *Ivanhoe, Moby Dick*, and *A Tale of Two Cities*, and featured a biography of the author and educational fillers. No outside advertising appeared on the covers or pages. And instead of disappearing after a month on the newsstand, titles were reprinted on a regular basis and listed by number in each issue.

When the new publication outgrew the space it shared with Elliot in 1942, Kanter moved the operation and, under the Gilberton Company corporate name, CLASSIC COMICS entered a period of growing readership and increasing recognition as an educational tool. Kanter worked tirelessly to promote his product and protect its image. In 1947, a "newer, truer" name was given to the monthly series – CLASSICS ILLUSTRATED.

Soon, Kanter's comicbook adaptations of works by Shakespeare, Stevenson, Twain, Verne, and other authors, were being used in schools and endorsed by educators. The series was translated and distributed in numerous foreign countries (including Canada, Great Britain, the Netherlands, Greece, Brazil, Mexico, and Australia) and the genial publisher was hailed abroad as "Papa Klassiker." By the beginning of the 1960s, CLASSICS ILLUSTRATED was the largest

I'M AFRAID THERE'S NO FOOD FOR THE YOUNG MAN YOU SPOKE OF. I CAME UPON HIM JUST NOW... I THOUGHT HE WAS YOU!
WHERE, BOY, WHERE?!
ON A HILL YONDER, BUT HE RAN OFF.
HE TOOK THE FILE, AND I LEFT HIM MUTTERING, AS HE SET TO WORK ON THE LEG-IRON
CURSE THE RAT... I'LL GET HIM... I'LL PULL HIM DOWN LIKE A BLOODHOUND!

CLASSICS ILLUSTRATED was re-launched in 1990 in graphic novel/book form by the Berkley Publishing Group and First Publishing, Inc. featuring all-new adaptations by such top graphic novelists as Rick Geary, Bill Sienkiewicz, Kyle Baker, Gahan Wilson, and others. "First had the right idea, they just came out about 15 years too soon. Now bookstores are ready for graphic novels such as these," Jim explains. Many of these excellent adaptations have been acquired by Papercutz and will make up the new series of CLASSICS ILLUSTRATED titles.

The first volume of the new CLASSICS ILLUSTRATED series presents graphic novelist Rick Geary's adaptation of "Great Expectations" by Charles Dickens, the bittersweet tale of one boy's adolescence, and of the choices he makes to shape his destiny. Into an engrossing mystery, Dickens weaves a heartfelt inquiry into morals and virtues-as the orphan Pip, the convict Magwitch, the beautiful Estella, the bitter Miss Havisham, the goodhearted Biddy, the kind Joe and other memorable characters entwine in a battle of human nature. Rick Geary's delightful illustrations capture the newfound awe and frustrations of young Pip as he comes of age, and begins to understand the opportunities that life presents.

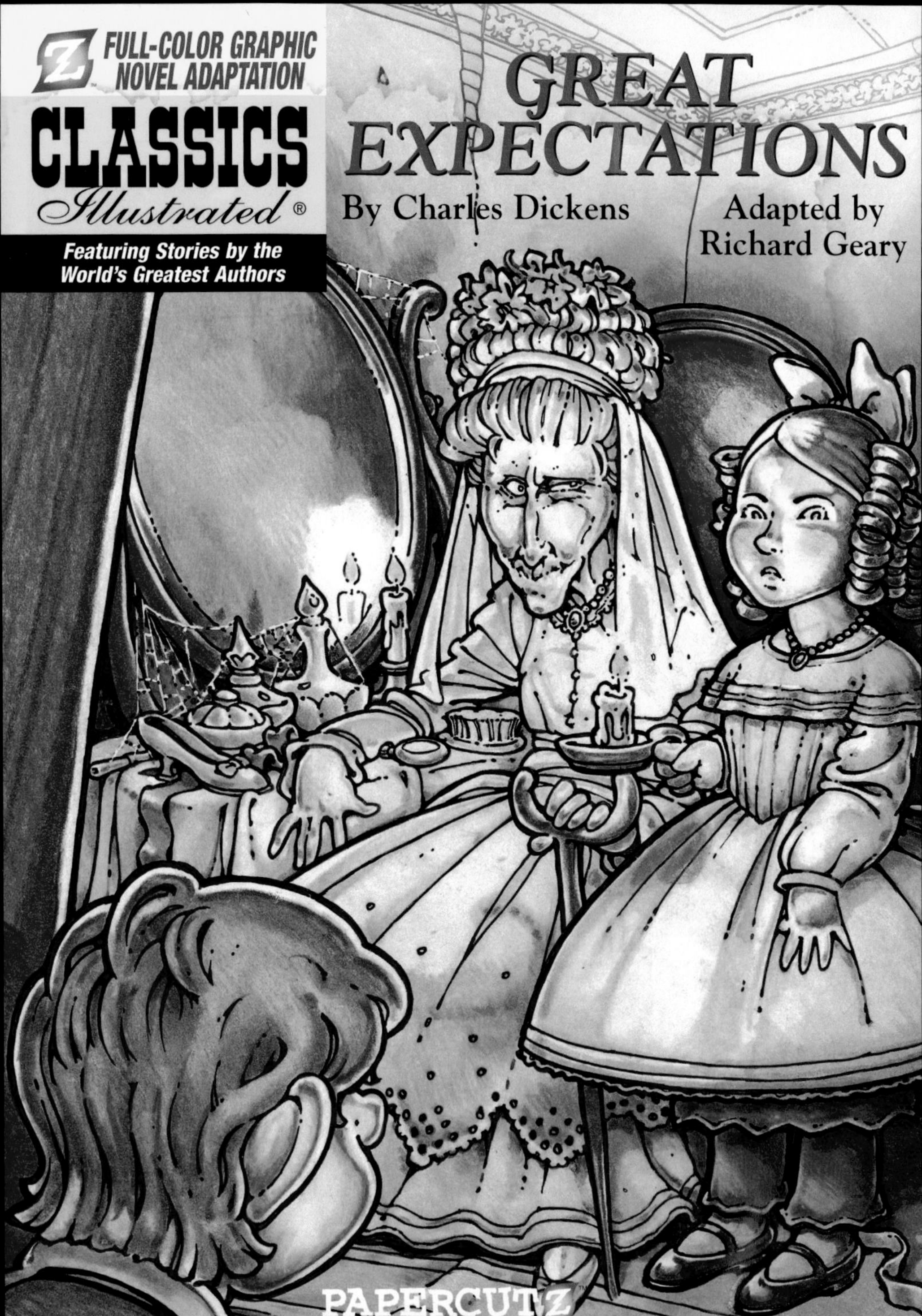
FULL-COLOR GRAPHIC NOVEL ADAPTATION
CLASSICS Illustrated®
Featuring Stories by the World's Greatest Authors
GREAT EXPECTATIONS
By Charles Dickens
Adapted by Richard Geary
PAPERCUTZ